Love, Lies, and

WHISKEY

The Whiskeys

Special Edition

MELISSA FOSTER

Cover Design: Elizabeth Mackey Designs
Cover Jewelry: Artist and Designer Andrey "Anund" Kuznetsov

WORLD LITERARY PRESS
PRINTED IN THE UNITED STATES OF AMERICA

A Note to Readers

I love a second-chance romance. When I first met Doc Whiskey, he was still struggling with a heartbreak he'd endured years ago with his first love, Juliette Adkin, and I couldn't wait to give him his happily ever after. While I wrote the previous books in this series, Juliette was whispering in my ear, and I knew I was on the right path. I never expected how much more they'd have to overcome until I wrote their story. Their heartache runs deep and deals with emotional abuse and a life-changing medical diagnosis, but as always, you'll get a happily ever after that's worth the struggle. I hope you adore their story as much as I do.

If this is your first introduction to my writing, all of my books are written to stand alone and may also be enjoyed as part of the larger series, so dive in and enjoy the ride. The Whiskeys are just one of the many series in my Love in Bloom big-family romance collection. Characters from each series make appearances in future books, so you never miss an engagement, wedding, or birth. A complete list of all series titles is included at the end of this book, along with previews of upcoming publications.

Be sure to check out my online bookstore for discounted pre-orders, early releases, exclusive discounts on bundles in all formats, and more. Ebooks can be read on the e-reader of your choice, and audiobooks can be listened to on the free and easy-to-use BookFunnel app. Shop.MelissaFoster.com

The best way to keep up to date with new releases and sales is to sign up for my newsletter and join my Facebook Fan Club, where I chat with readers often.

www.MelissaFoster.com/Newsletter

www.Facebook.com/groups/MelissaFosterFans

Doc & Juliette

Lucas

Playlist

"What If I Never Get Over You" by Lady A
"Ready to Be Loved" by St. Lundi
"Hurricane" by Luke Combs
"Love Story" by Taylor Swift
"Mercy" by Brett Young
"Every Little Thing" by Carly Pearce
"Are You Gonna Kiss Me or Not" by Thompson Square
"Rest in Pieces" by Saliva
"Need You Now" by Lady A
"All I Forgot" by Ashley Cooke, Joe Jonas
"I Hope You're Happy Now" by Carly Pearce, Lee Brice
"Say Something" by A Great Big World with Christina Aguilera
"Mess It Up" by Gracie Abrams
"Lost Without You" by Freya Ridings
"Basket Case" by Sara Bareilles
"Made Up Story" by Andi
"Giving You Up" by Kameron Marlowe
"Beautiful Things" by Benson Boone
"Wish You the Best" by Lewis Capaldi
"Die from a Broken Heart" by Maddie & Tae
"Love Me Like the First Time" by Rachel Grae
"Someone You Loved" by Lewis Capaldi
"Hello Darlin" by Ryan McMullan
"It's Always Been You" by Caleb Hearn

"Water Under the Bridge" by Adele
"Walked Through Hell" by Anson Seabra
"Versions of Forever" by Matt Hansen
"Back to You" by Selena Gomez
"This Town" by Niall Horan
"I Guess I'm in Love" by Clinton Kane
"Home" by Good Neighbours
"Closer" by Nine Inch Nails
"Something to Someone" by Dermot Kennedy
"Hurtless" by Dean Lewis
"Breakeven" by The Script
"Wanna Be That Song" by Brett Eldredge
"It Is What It Is" by Jenna Raine
"Feels Like" by Gracie Abrams
"Lost in You" by Three Days Grace
"Can't Tame Her" by Zara Larsson
"Roses" by Jenna Raine
"I Choose You" by Forest Blakk
"Hard for Me" by Michele Morrone
"Don't Forget Me" by Dermot Kennedy
"Beautiful Crazy" by Luke Combs
"Giants" by Dermot Kennedy
"Fever Dream" by Jillian Rossi
"miss me (when you're gone)" by Will Linley
"Rome" by Dermot Kennedy
"Moments We Live For" by In Paradise
"Long Story Short" by Forest Blakk
"Hopeless Romantics" by James TW
"Blossom" by Dermot Kennedy
"Iris" by Grace Davies
"Lucky Stars" by Lucy Spraggan

Chapter One

THE RUMBLE AND roar of Seeley "Doc" Whiskey's motorcycle was drowned out by the cheering crowd as he and a convoy of the other members of the Dark Knights motorcycle club drove into the parking lot of Hope Valley Hospital. They were on their annual Reindeer Ride, a fundraiser that benefited the hospital. Doc's grandfather was the original founder of the club, and his father, Tiny Whiskey, had founded the Hope Valley chapter. He and Doc's mother, Wynnie, a psychologist on their second-chance ranch, were leading the pack on Tiny's motorcycle, dressed up as Santa and Mrs. Claus, which was fitting since his father was six foot four, with a pendulous belly, long gray hair, and an equally long beard, and his mother, with her blond shag and kind eyes, always had a warm smile at the ready.

Doc waved to the crowd that had gathered to greet them by the front doors, taking in the wide-eyed pediatric patients watching from wheelchairs and the safety of their parents' arms. Excitement radiated around the kids as they pointed to the decorated motorcycles, festively dressed bikers, and the massive high-sided trailer decked out in holiday colors and overflowing

1

with sacks of presents. Doc's heart always took a hit at events like these, knowing some of the kids they'd be giving presents to wouldn't make it to see the holidays.

That was a harsh reality to face on the heels of such an exciting morning for their family. Sasha, one of his two younger sisters, had gotten engaged to Ezra Moore, a single father to five-year-old Gus, a fellow Dark Knight, and a therapist at their ranch.

The convoy circled the lot before parking in the area that had been cordoned off for the club. Doc climbed off his bike and pulled off his helmet, the necklace of colorful lights and bells his youngest sister, Birdie, had made for him jingling with his movements. He pushed a hand through his thick brown hair, watching as the wives, girlfriends, and children of the Dark Knights climbed off the backs of bikes and out of trucks and cars dressed as elves, flocking together as dozens of the toughest and best men Doc knew, wearing Santa hats, colorful shirts beneath black leather cuts, or full-on holiday costumes, headed for the gift trailer.

Doc locked his helmet on the bike and put on a Santa hat, heading over to join them.

His younger brothers, Cowboy and Dare, fell into step beside him, donning their own Santa hats and necklaces. They'd all inherited their father's height and broad stature, but Cowboy was the largest, with bulbous muscles and sheer breadth few could match, born from working the ranch. With the exception of Birdie, who lived in a neighboring town and co-owned a chocolate shop, they all lived and worked at Redemption Ranch, where they rescued horses and gave troubled souls the therapy and support they needed to find their path in life.

"God, I love making kids smile." Dare's dark eyes sparked

with excitement. A daredevil to his core, and a hell of a therapist, he had tattoos from his neck to his ankles and wrists and a heart that had only ever loved his childhood best friend and now wife, Billie.

Cowboy arched a wheat-colored brow. "Does that mean you and Billie are going to start a family soon?"

"Lord, help us all," Doc teased as they joined the other guys and hoisted sacks of presents over their shoulders.

"Don't worry, Doc. We're having too much fun practicing to tie ourselves down yet." Dare eyed their sacks of presents and snickered. "My sack's bigger than yours."

"That's not what she said," Cowboy said.

"She said mine's bigger," Ezra called out as he walked by with Taz and Hyde, two ranch hands dressed as reindeer, who called out in unison, "Mine too!" their laughter trailing behind them.

Doc flashed an arrogant grin to his brothers. "You boys may have big sacks, but I got the massive candy cane that all the ladies want a piece of."

"Shit. You wish," Cowboy said as Gus ran up to them, dressed as an adorable elf, his mop of dark hair flopping over his eyes.

"Guys! Did you see me riding in Daddy's sidecar? Now I'm a biker like you!" Gus spun around and hollered, "Tiny! Wynnie! Did you see me?" and ran toward them.

Doc and his brothers laughed as Ezra chased after him.

"Gotta love that kid," Cowboy said, his eyes locked on his fiancée, Sully, heading their way with Billie. "I hope we have a dozen exactly like him."

"You planning on saying *I do* first?" Doc asked.

"Hell yes," Cowboy said. "Sully's been through enough. I

told you my girl's going to live out a picture-perfect fairy tale, and I meant it." Sully had been kidnapped as a child and brought up in a cult, which she'd managed to escape last year. She'd always been strong. She'd had to be to survive what she'd been through. But with the help of therapy and Cowboy's love, she'd gone from a willowy and weary girl to a stronger, confident young woman.

Doc clapped a hand on his shoulder. "Well, she's got Prince Charming to carry her off into the sunset."

"As opposed to my wife, who's got a wicked beast who wants to keep her chained up in my love dungeon," Dare said, and they all laughed.

They were raised to be good, fiercely loyal, protective men, but unlike Doc, Cowboy truly *was* every bit a Prince Charming and had been his whole life, always trying to do the right thing, and though Dare had gotten lost for a few years, coming together with Billie had healed him, and she adored her wicked beast.

Billie strutted over in black leather shorts and a red-and-white tank top that had DARE'S NAUGHTY ELF across the chest, with Sully trailing behind her in a sweetly sexy festive elf outfit. It wasn't only Sully who had come a long way. Billie had been every bit the daredevil that Dare was before their other childhood friend, Eddie, was killed during a dare gone wrong. Billie had checked out of the best parts of life, and it had taken Dare years to get her back. Coming together had healed her, too.

Billie tossed her long dark hair over her shoulder and planted a hand on her hip. "What're you fools laughing at?" She was as brazen as Sully was sweet.

"I was telling them how I'd like to keep you chained to my bed," Dare said.

"Promises, promises," Billie said with a hefty dose of sass.

"*God*, I love my badass bride." Dare tugged her into a kiss.

"Today is exciting, in a bittersweet kind of way," Sully said, clutching a drawing pad to her chest, her eyes glittering and her golden-brown hair falling in natural waves just past her shoulders. "My heart breaks for the sick children and their families, but I'm really happy we get to make them smile. I have lots of drawings to give out, and I hope they love the books we sent over." Sully had found a niche illustrating children's books, many of which she and Cowboy had donated for the event. "Are you ready, Callahan?"

She was the only person who called Cowboy by his given name, and every time she said it, Cowboy's serious demeanor softened a tad.

"Always, baby." Cowboy leaned in and kissed her.

Doc watched his brothers mooning over their women as they walked away. There was a time when Doc had thought he had what his brothers had recently found—the friendship and trust of the only woman he'd ever wanted to spend his life with.

He'd been nineteen and had just come home from his freshman year at college. He was thrilled to be back on the ranch, prospecting the club, and working with the horses, when Governor Adkin's security team had swept through the property. The following week, the governor's sixteen-year-old daughter had come to intern with them.

Doc's mind reeled back to the first time he'd seen her. He was grooming a horse beside the barn when his mother's voice had cut through his thoughts.

"Seeley, honey, are you here?"

"Be right there." He set down the brush, and as he rounded the corner of the barn, a brown-haired beauty standing with his mother stopped him in his tracks. She was gazing out at the pasture, wearing a sleeveless sky-blue top that accentuated her curves, a frilly white skirt that showed off her long legs, and expensive Western boots. His cowboy hat shielded his eyes from the sun, but as she tucked her hair behind her ear, wispy strands blew across her face, and there was no shielding his heart from the biggest, bluest eyes he'd ever seen. They'd seemed to reach into his soul, stealing the breath right out of his lungs.

"Seeley," his mother said, jerking him from his trance. "This is Juliette, Governor Adkin's daughter. She's interning with us for the summer and hopes to become a veterinary technician one day. You two will be working closely together. I thought you could show her the ropes."

Was this some sort of test? If ever there was a girl he should stay away from, it was Juliette. The governor's daughter? He cleared his throat in an effort to knock the fog from his brain.

Juliette lowered her eyes briefly, a knowing smile tugging at her lips.

Oh, you think this is funny, darlin'? Two can play at this game. He nodded in greeting and held out his hand. "Ready to get those hands dirty, Juliette?"

Her eyes flicked to his again, landing with the impact of a torch, spreading heat through his chest like wildfire. He was pretty sure the whole damn ranch could feel the sparks as a coy smile bloomed across her face and she shook his hand. "It's nice to meet you, Seeley. I don't usually have to get my hands dirty, but now I'm looking forward to it."

That was the moment he knew he was well and truly fucked.

He wasn't wrong.

They'd burned so hot, it had taken less than a week to shred his control, and from that moment on, they couldn't keep their hands off each other.

He closed his eyes, warding off the memory and was assaulted by another. He and Juliette were skinny-dipping in the lake one evening. As they broke the surface, she grabbed his necklace, pulling him into a kiss. He could still feel her cool, wet lips and slick, supple body against his as her voice whispered through his mind. *It's you and me forever, Seeley Whiskey. I'll never let you go.* Her words had cut straight to his heart. There didn't seem to be a bigger way to show her what he felt than taking off the necklace he'd made with his grandfather when he was just a boy and had worn every day since and slipping it over her head, vowing, *You and me forever, darlin'.*

Just as the memory cut him to his core, another scene pummeled him. Tiny and Cowboy holding him back as he fought to get to Juliette, who was kicking and screaming as her father dragged her toward a black SUV. Two hulking bodyguards stood between them and Doc as her father seethed, *If you ever come near my daughter again, I'll expose you as the predator you are and shut down this damn ranch so fast you won't know what hit you.* Doc could still feel his heart being ripped from his chest as he'd shouted, *Don't do this! I love your daughter!* His throat constricted as Juliette's frantic voice pierced through the pain. *I love you, Seeley! I'm sorry!*

"Ho, ho, ho!" Tiny called out, his deep voice jerking Doc back to the present.

Doc gritted his teeth against how wrong he'd been for believing Juliette's lies and risking everything to get her back in his arms only to have the dagger pushed deeper into his heart. He'd never been dumb enough to make that fucking mistake again.

He shoved that torture down deep, as he'd done a million times before, and headed for the hospital entrance, determined to give the children the greatest day of their lives.

Chapter Two

AFTER TWO HOURS of giving out presents, telling silly jokes to see kids smile, and receiving more hugs and heart-warming giggles than any guy deserves, Doc walked into the last pediatric patients' room on the oncology floor with two presents left to give.

He nodded in greeting to two sets of parents standing dutifully by their little girls' beds and said, "Ho, ho, ho, and a merry summer holiday to you."

The girls giggled. They couldn't be more than five or six years old. The dark-skinned girl turned wide, excited eyes up to him. "You don't look like Santa." Her voice was soft, like Sully's, and she wore a pink cap with purple polka dots on it.

"I *don't?*" Doc made a dramatic show of looking himself over, patting his stomach, and touching his scruffy chin. He gasped. "Someone stole my belly *and* my beard!"

The girls laughed.

"You're funny," the paler girl said from the other bed as she pushed her orange-framed glasses, which matched her orange cap, to the bridge of her nose.

"Thank you, but I was being serious. I had a big ol' belly

and beard when I woke up this morning." More giggles rang out, and he turned to the first girl. "What's your name?"

"Kyra." She beamed.

"Kyra, did you see who stole my belly and beard?"

She giggled up a storm and pointed at the other girl. "Susie took them!"

Kyra's mother shook her head, smiling.

Susie howled with laughter as Doc marched over to her. Feigning his most serious expression, he said, "I'm going to need my beard and belly back."

"I don't *have* them!" she said between laughs.

"You don't?" He scratched his head and wrinkled his brow, looking around the room. Spotting a teddy bear, he went over to it and said, "Did you take my beard and belly?" He put the bear's mouth to his ear, pretending to listen. *"Uh-huh. I see. Thank you."* He put the bear down and dramatically wiped his brow. "Whew. That's a relief."

"What did he say?" Kyra asked.

"He said I don't need the belly *or* the beard to give you gifts!"

The girls exchanged giddy glances.

"Let's see what we have in here." He reached into the sack and pulled out the last two gift-wrapped boxes.

"I hope it's not socks," Susie said.

"*Susie*," her father gently chided.

"That's all right. I don't much like socks, either," Doc said.

"I like fuzzy socks," Kyra exclaimed.

Doc shook the gifts, knowing they weren't socks, and said, "I wonder what they are." He handed each girl a box, and they tore them open, gasping with delight as they pulled out their stuffed toys.

"A Squishmallow unicorn!" Susie exclaimed, hugging hers.

"I got a Squishmallow kitty!" Kyra waved at Susie.

"Thank you!" the girls said in unison, and then they chattered with each other about their gifts.

Doc soaked in their joy. "Happy holidays, sweet girls."

"Happy holidays!" they said, and started playing with their toys together, a sight that warmed his heart.

"Thank you," the parents said in unison.

Doc gave another nod, wishing he had something comforting to give them, too, but he knew seeing their daughters' smiles could only be outdone by handing them a cure. If only he could do that. When he walked out of their room, he threw a silent prayer up to the powers that be for the girls and their families, just as he'd been doing all day.

"There you are!" Birdie hurried purposefully toward him looking like some kind of vampish elf in an off-the-shoulder red minidress with white and green hearts trailing above a white fur-trimmed hem, elbow-length, red-green-and-white-striped fingerless gloves, and red platform boots. Striped suspenders were attached to a thick green belt circling her tiny waist, and a headband with two stuffed candy canes sticking up like ears trapped her wild dark hair.

"I just finished." Doc took off his Santa hat. "I'm heading out."

"Not that way, you're not." She grabbed his arm, dragging him in the opposite direction.

"The elevator is the other way."

"We're taking a different one. Unless you want to see Mandy, who's chatting up another nurse by those elevators."

"Shit." Mandy was a nurse he'd gone out with for much longer than he'd intended, and even though he'd been honest from the start about not looking for more than occasional company, she'd had a hard time letting go. "Thanks for helping me dodge *that* bullet."

They turned down one hall, then another, and came to a set of elevators. Birdie pushed the button. "If you're going to keep doing this extended-stay-motel dating thing, I suggest you do it outside of Hope Valley."

He ground his back teeth against the phrase his brothers had coined about his dating life, because his relationships never lasted longer than two or three months. They weren't wrong, but hearing his little sister say it annoyed the crap out of him.

"Where did you hear that extended-stay shit?"

She rolled her eyes. "First of all, *everyone* is aware of your MO, and God only knows why women still find you mysterious and sexy." She opened her mouth and pretended to put her finger in it and gag.

He scowled.

"Second of all, I heard it from *Dare*."

"Dare needs to learn to keep his mouth shut, and the women I date know damn well I'm not going to catch feelings for them."

"*That's* the problem. They think they can change you. *Girls.*" The word dripped with sarcasm.

"You're a female, Birdie."

"Not a silly one who would waste her time trying to change some stupid man. If a guy says he's not going to catch feelings, I drop him like a hot potato. Unless I'm in it for a night of *fun*, of course. Then…"

He crossed his arms, glowering, drumming his fingers against his muscle to keep from giving her hell.

"Don't look at me like that, doing your finger thing." She

pushed the button again, and the elevator doors opened. As they stepped inside, she said, "Listen, you and I can join forces and be each other's wingmen. Let's hit the Roadhouse tonight. Two lone wolves on the prowl."

Had she lost her fucking mind? "Lone means one, not two, and you damn well better not be *on the prowl*."

She lifted her chin, amusement dancing in her eyes. "Guess I'll be *prowling* alone."

"Over my dead body."

"*Well*, I did just listen to a true crime podcast and learn how to poison someone using eye drops."

"You're a scary little bird."

She grinned. "I told you I could take care of myself."

As they stepped out of the elevator, she said, "The exit is to the right."

He turned to follow her as a woman came around the corner. She looked up, and his chest seized at the hauntingly beautiful blue eyes staring back at him. They both froze.

"*Doc*, what're you doing?" Birdie complained.

Birdie's voice was white noise to the hurt and anger brewing inside him as he gritted out, "*Juliette*."

"Seeley?" tumbled from her lips full of confusion, and the to-go cup she was holding crashed to the floor, sending liquid splashing all over their legs as a teenage boy came around the corner.

"*Mom*," the kid exclaimed. "What happened?" When Juliette didn't respond, he grabbed her arm. "Mom!"

She blinked repeatedly and choked out, "Nothing, honey. It's okay. I'll get it." But she stood stock-still.

"*Juliette?* That's Juliette? Ohmygod!" Birdie said with shock, then lowered her voice. "Doc, it's Juliette!"

"I'm aware," he bit out, and ground his back teeth against the barbed wire twisting around his heart. She'd been gone for years. What the fuck was she doing there?

"It's…been a long time," Juliette said a little shakily.

Glowering, Doc said, "Not nearly long enough," and headed for the exit.

JULIETTE COULDN'T BREATHE. Heartache and anger clawed at her as raw and painful as they had more than a decade ago. Birdie was looking at her like she didn't know what to do, and Lucas—*Oh God, Lucas*—looked horrified *and* angry. She'd known when she'd inherited her maternal grandmother's property and moved to Weston, Colorado, there was a chance she'd run into Seeley, but living in a different town had kept her safe the last few months. They were only in Hope Valley for one of Lucas's bull-riding competitions. When he'd been thrown off a bull, she'd taken him to the closest hospital to be evaluated for a concussion. Seeley hadn't even crossed her mind.

Now it took all of her focus to drag air into her lungs.

"Okay, *um*. Nice to see you. *Or not*. I don't know," Birdie said apologetically. "Have a better day." She hurried after her brother.

"*Mom*, what's going on?" Lucas snapped. "Who are those people?"

She met her son's worried gaze and felt her heart shredding all over again. His eyes were as blue as hers, but the shape and keenness were *all* Seeley's, just like his sharp nose, thick brown hair that refused to be tamed, and the stubbornness that had taken root during puberty. At fifteen, Lucas was practically bursting with it.

She forced her voice to work. "I knew them a long time ago."

"I should've said something to that guy. I shouldn't have let him get away with talking to you like that. He was a dick."

His words pierced her heart. "He's..." She stopped herself from refuting him, because Seeley *had* acted like a dick. Long ago *and* just then. Her anger rose to the surface.

Who the hell does Seeley think he is acting so scorned?

She kept that anger to herself because the mother in her felt a responsibility not to demean her son's biological father, and despite everything, the stupid teenage girl in her had never lost her love for the nineteen-year-old boy who had stolen her heart in less than a week—and had crushed it a few months later.

"I'm sorry you had to see that," she finally managed. "He and I have some history together. It's complicated." She bent down to pick up the coffee cup she'd dropped, trying to regain her composure. "Can you please grab some paper towels from the men's room so I can clean up this mess?"

As he disappeared into the men's room, she exhaled, took a deep breath, and blew it out slowly, trying to get her bearings, but her mind refused to comply. It sent her reeling back to the heartbreaking summer when she'd fallen desperately in love with Seeley Whiskey and her father had torn them apart. She'd been sure Seeley would find a way for them to be together. How many times had he said she was his *ride or die*? His *forever girl*? She'd believed him and had clung to that promise right up until she'd gotten his letter saying he'd moved on and she should, too.

She'd never been able to reconcile the intensely loyal teenager she'd fallen in love with, with the cold one who had turned his back on them. But she couldn't let herself fall into that abyss right now. Lucas needed her to be strong, and after what she'd seen of Seeley, she needed to keep Lucas safe from the truth so he didn't get hurt. He'd already lost the only father he'd ever known. The last thing he needed was to feel unwanted by his biological father.

Lucas came out of the men's room, his eyes still shadowed with worry, and handed her a handful of paper towels.

"Thanks, honey." Her son had his moments when he drove her batty, but he really was the greatest kid. It had been the two of them against the world since he was four years old. Lucas was kind, thoughtful, and emotionally strong. Sometimes she worried he was *too* strong and would get himself in trouble, like the way he wanted to confront Seeley.

"That guy had on a biker vest," he said as she cleaned up the spilled coffee. "Were you some kind of biker chick before you and Dad got together?"

Her chest constricted. She'd been so busy trying to remember how to breathe, she hadn't even registered what Seeley was wearing. "No. But Seeley had a motorcycle." She'd never forget how it felt to ride on the back of that bike, wrapped around Seeley's warm, strong body, the engine vibrating beneath her. She'd felt free and so damn in love, the entire world seemed brighter. Her throat thickened with the memory. She choked it down and pushed to her feet, looking for a trash can.

"Here. Give them to me." Lucas took the wet paper towels and went into the men's room.

When he returned, they headed for the exit. "How's your noggin?"

Lucas was into barrel racing, bull riding, calf roping, and

half a dozen other things. She'd fought him on bull riding at first, but he'd been adamant, and she couldn't help but think some passions were innate, since Seeley had been the reigning champ of those sports when she'd known him.

"I'm *fine*. When you said there's *history* between you two, did you mean you were hooking up or had a relationship?"

"*Lucas*," she warned.

"What? I'm not judging you. Just tell me what you meant."

"I meant I'm not having this conversation with my fifteen-year-old son."

"Why? I know all about hooking up."

She gave him a stern look. "You'd better not know about hooking up."

"Whatever." He flashed a crooked grin.

She fished in her bag for her sunglasses and keys as they stepped outside.

"Holy shit."

"Language, Luca—" She looked up, taking in a crowd of bikers wearing black leather cuts with Dark Knights patches on them, throwing her right back in time again, to the months she'd lived and interned on the ranch, working side by side with Seeley during the day, eating meals with his family and the rest of the people who lived and worked there, hanging out around bonfires, going to events the Dark Knights hosted, and secretly falling into Seeley's arms every chance she got.

"That guy must be part of this gang. Do you think he's dangerous?"

Only to my heart.

She hated the truth in that thought, but here she stood, scanning the crowd for Seeley.

He was nowhere in sight, but her gaze trailed over his

brothers, Cowboy and Dare, who had always been funny and warm and protective of her, like Seeley. Cowboy was massive now, and he had a beard, and Dare was covered in tattoos, but they were still unmistakable, as was his sister Sasha. She was beautiful, and she was holding a little boy. Juliette's chest tightened. That's how she'd once imagined her own future, holding Seeley's child, surrounded by people who loved them and cared about helping others more than wealth or politics or their public images.

There was movement in the crowd, and Juliette spotted Seeley's parents. Her breath caught. They'd barely changed. Tiny was a rough-looking mountainous man, covered in tattoos with an untamed beard and long hair, both of which had turned gray. Wynnie was a little thicker around the middle than she used to be, but weren't they all? She still wore her blond hair in a short shag, and as she leaned in to kiss Tiny, it was apparent their love hadn't dwindled.

Longing sank into Juliette's bones. Tiny and Wynnie used to say that anyone who stayed at the ranch became family, and that's how they had always treated her that summer. She hadn't only fallen for Seeley. She'd fallen for all of them.

Wynnie must have sensed her staring, because she looked over, sending Juliette's heart racing. After the way her father had treated the Whiskeys and the horrible threats he'd made, she didn't know what Seeley's family thought of her. Wynnie's brows knitted, and she took a step in their direction.

Juliette couldn't deal with another confrontation. Especially in front of Lucas. She put on her sunglasses and turned away. Drawing upon all the courage and calmness she could muster, she draped an arm around Lucas, placing her hand on his shoulder, because at five seven to his five ten, putting her arm *over* his shoulder was no longer an option, and started walking toward their car.

"No, I don't think he's dangerous," she said, hoping she didn't sound as rattled as she felt. The weight of Wynnie's stare drilled into her like a laser. "It's been quite a day. Know what we need?"

"A few shots of tequila?" he suggested hopefully.

"After the day we've had, that's tempting."

"*That's* what I'm talking about." He rubbed his hands together. "My first tequila shots."

She gave him a wry smile. "I said *tempting*. It's not going to happen."

"Come *on*, Mom. I've had a tough day, too," he urged with the cheeky grin he used whenever he tried to rile her up. "I lost my competition, and hit my head, *and* I had to witness that douchebag being mean to you."

"Can you *please* stop calling him names?" She unlocked the doors to her truck.

"But he was a douche."

She sighed. "Lucas, *please*? Let's just go get burgers and fries and forget this ever happened. I'll even let you drive." He'd gotten his learner's permit a few weeks ago.

"Fine, but if I ever see him again, I'm going to give him a piece of my mind."

"You'll have to get in line behind me."

Chapter Three

WIND WHIPPED AGAINST Doc's skin as he sped down the dark road on his motorcycle. He'd been riding full throttle for hours, trying to outrun the pain that had been clawing its way up from the dredges of his soul since he'd left the hospital. But for the second time in his life, wind therapy wasn't doing a damn thing to take the edge off his shitty mood. According to his family, it had taken him months to get out from under his anger and pain after that fateful summer, but he knew the truth. It had taken a hell of a lot longer than that. He'd just learned to hide it better.

Why the fuck was Juliette back in Hope Valley?

He chewed on that as he drove toward the ranch. With any luck, his family would still be at the rally. He'd hauled ass away from the hospital before Birdie had a chance to spout off to everyone about what had gone down. He hated that his little sister had witnessed that shit. Not because she would tell everyone, although he knew she would, but because if anyone ever treated her that way, he'd fucking knock their teeth out.

As he turned into the ranch, the tightness in his chest didn't ease like it usually did when he drove beneath the wooden beam with an iron RR on top—the first R, backward.

The ranch spanned a few hundred acres and had been in his family for decades. Doc had grown up there and had never wanted to work or live anywhere else. They'd saved too many horses to count and helped hundreds of people of all ages who were previously incarcerated, in recovery, or just having a rough time finding their footing, giving them support and a sense of family they so desperately needed. But after what happened with Juliette, every fucking inch of that property reminded Doc of her. It was that family—found and biological—and his passion for the ranch's mission, that kept him there.

He drove past the rehabilitation and well-animal barns, the riding arenas and pastures, and the road that led to the therapeutic offices and turned off the main road, navigating the narrow lanes that led to his house. Doc liked his privacy and lived in a three-bedroom log home off the beaten path, away from the cabins that housed live-in clients and staff and out of sight from his family's homes.

As he drove down his driveway, his brothers' and father's motorcycles came into view. He parked beside them, his muscles tensing as he climbed off his bike. His three dogs barreled off the porch—Pickles, a husky/shepherd mix, Mighty, a black Lab, and Sadie, an Irish setter—followed by his father, Cowboy, and Dare.

Seeley was *not* in the mood for an inquisition.

He pulled off his helmet and loved up his dogs, eyeing the others. "Did someone die?"

"You tell us," his father said gruffly.

Doc gritted his teeth. His father was one of the toughest men he knew. Like each of his sons, if the situation called for it, he'd morph from the loyalest, fairest man in the room to the deadliest. He managed the family the same way he managed the ranch, with high expectations, strict rules, and enough rope to let them hang themselves. But he was always there to cut them down before it turned fatal, because beneath that gruff exterior was a warm, loving heart.

The dogs vied for more of his attention, their tails wagging, their noses pushing into Doc's hands. Doc snapped his fingers, commanding, *"Enough."* Sadie plunked down her butt, while Mighty and Pickles bounded off to play.

"Birdie told us what went down with Juliette. Are you okay?" Dare asked. He was always trying to get them to talk shit out.

Fuck no. "I'm fine." He turned on his father, who made it his business to know every single fucking thing that went on in and around their town that could possibly affect their family, the residents of Hope Valley, or the club. "Did you know she was in town?"

"Hal mentioned it a few weeks ago," his father said. Hal Braden was one of his father's oldest friends. He owned a ranch two towns away in Weston, Colorado.

Anger drew Doc's shoulders back, his voice rising. "A few *weeks* ago, and you didn't think you should tell me?" Sadie popped up on all fours, watching them.

"It's not my job to manage your personal life. But what if I had told you?" His father stepped closer, his dark eyes challenging. "You'd've been a fucking mess, and it wouldn't have changed a damn thing about today."

"You don't know that," Doc fumed, his chest puffing out.

Cowboy stepped between them. "Whoa, Doc. He's right. The mention of her name has always set you off."

"There's no shame in that, bro," Dare added too damn

supportively. "I don't know all of what went down back then, but I know enough. The way her father treated you would piss anyone off."

Doc clenched his teeth, his fingers curling tighter around his helmet.

His father put a hand on Cowboy's shoulder. "Move aside, son." Cowboy stepped out from between them, and his father said, "She inherited her grandmother Hazel's estate. She's living in Weston with her boy and working for Jade." Jade Braden was one of Hal's daughters-in-law.

She's back for good? Hazel is dead? The world spun, conflicting emotions pummeling him. He was furious that Juliette was back, but he was also gutted for her. She had been closer to her grandmother, who had bred horses for a living, than she was to her own mother. He hadn't seen Hazel since that long-ago summer, but they'd spent so much time with her, she'd left a mark on his heart, too.

"Do you want to talk about it?" Dare asked.

"I've got nothing to say." Doc plowed past them, heading for the porch.

Cowboy grabbed his arm. "You shouldn't be alone."

Locked in a stare down with Cowboy, he yanked his arm free. "If you stick around, I'll be giving our old man a different answer to his initial question."

"A'right, boys, clear outta here," his father ordered.

"I don't think we should leave," Dare said.

"Then stop thinking and get your ass on that bike," his father said, climbing onto his own motorcycle.

Cowboy gritted out a curse, but he and Dare reluctantly got on their bikes. As they drove away, Doc headed up the porch steps with Sadie in tow.

"*Seeley John*," his father said sharply.

Doc's gut roiled. He steeled himself, readying to be chewed out, which he probably deserved for being a prick. He turned, lifting his chin. "Yeah?"

His father's eyes narrowed, studying him the way he'd done Doc's whole life. Like he could see right through the bullshit, through the fucking lead walls Doc had erected around himself, to the very root of his pain.

Doc swallowed hard, knowing his father was one of only two people who actually *could* read him that accurately.

His father took a deep breath, blowing it out as he nodded, as if he understood every damn thing going on inside Doc's head and heart. But how could he, when Doc didn't even get it?

"You do what you have to tonight, son, but you do it knowing we love you, and we're here for you. The whole damn brotherhood is here for you. I had to put my foot down to keep Ezra, Rebel, Hyde, and Taz from showing up here." His cousin Rebel and their ranch hands Hyde and Taz were all Dark Knights. "But if that burden gets too heavy, you make a call. Ya hear?"

Doc gave a curt nod, his throat thickening.

As he and Sadie headed inside, his father's engine roared to life, fading as he drove away. Doc put his helmet and keys on the table by the door and went directly to his bar. Sadie stuck to him like glue as he grabbed a bottle of whiskey, opening it on his way out the back door.

He took a swig as he sank into a chair on the deck overlooking the creek, relishing the burn as it slid down his throat.

Mighty and Pickles bounded onto the deck.

Doc petted them absently, taking another long pull of whiskey. He looked up at the sky. "What the fuck are you doing?"

He wasn't a religious man, and he didn't know if he was talking to the universe or to himself. But it didn't matter. Nobody answered him.

Tipping the bottle again, he welcomed the warmth spreading through his chest. He couldn't remember the last time he drank himself stupid, but tonight he was determined to speed through stupid and crash into numbness. He swallowed another mouthful and leaned forward, resting his elbows on his knees, gripping the neck of the bottle.

He closed his eyes, trying to focus on the sounds of the creek and crickets and the rustling of leaves, rather than the ghosts of his past rattling the chains he'd used to keep them at bay and hissing in his ears. But his futile attempts were squashed as memories slammed into him.

He was back at college in Fort Collins, unable to concentrate on anything other than seeing Juliette and convincing her father he was making a horrible mistake. It had been two weeks of unanswered calls and texts, and fighting with everyone. He'd begged his father to get the club involved, to shove the governor's threats down his fucking throat. But the governor was a powerful man with a history of ruining anyone who stood in his way, and Tiny wasn't willing to risk everyone's future or the future of the ranch. Most importantly, Tiny had said he wasn't willing to risk Seeley's reputation. That it wouldn't matter if the governor was lying or not. Those were the types of accusations that followed a man like a shadow.

But Seeley hadn't been raised to back down, and he'd had enough. He'd climbed onto his motorcycle and driven to the governor's home in Boulder, mentally rehearsing what he'd say the whole way there.

He drove past the massive brick Colonial twice, noting the same two burly bodyguards flanking the front door that had shown up the day her father had taken her away from the ranch. They were dressed in dark suits, but there was no mistaking their military-type stances. They were ready for battle. So was he. He parked around the corner, his heart thundering as he climbed off his bike, and with his head held high, he went to speak his mind and get the girl he loved with everything he had.

As he approached the front door, the larger of the two body-guards, a bald man with cold eyes, stepped off the porch, blocking his way.

Seeley stood his ground. "I'm here to speak with Governor Ad-kin."

"I'm sorry, Mr. Whiskey. You're not welcome here."

"I'm not leaving until I speak to the governor."

"That's not going to happen."

"My ass it's not." Seeley tried to walk around him, but the man moved with him, and the other bodyguard descended the steps. *Fuck this.* Seeley looked up at the house and shouted, "Hey, Governor! You want to threaten my family? Get out here and face me like a man!"

The bodyguards grabbed his arms, trying to drag him off the property, but he fought back, shouting, hoping causing a scene would be enough to bring the governor outside. "Come on, you coward! Fight your own battles! I love your daughter, and I will make her mine!"

The front door opened, and Governor Adkin stepped outside. "Let him go."

Seeley tore his arms free and barreled up the walkway, but before he could get a word out, the governor's voice cut through the air.

"I actually feel bad for you, Seeley. You think you're something *special to Juliette." With a sinister grin, he shook his head. "My daughter is an expert manipulator. The tears you saw, the proclamations of her love? They were all for show. She could never be serious with a boy like you."*

"You're lying," Seeley bit out. "She doesn't have a manipulative bone in her body." He stepped toward the prick, but the bodyguards moved between them.

"She really did a job on you," the governor said. "That's a shame. You seem like a fairly smart kid. Open your eyes, Seeley. You were her summer fling. Her last hurrah. She's already back together with Josh, so do yourself a favor and find a girl who's more your kind, and don't ever come around here again. This was your one free pass. Next time your family will pay the price."

Seeley saw red. "Juliette is my fucking kind, you lying bastard! Get her out here!" He plowed forward, but the bodyguards grabbed him again. "Let go, you motherfuckers! Juliette! Juliette, come out!"

"Get him out of here," the governor directed over Seeley's shouts and curses. "And make sure he understands my message."

Seeley struggled as the men dragged him around to the back of the house and fought for all he was worth as they carried out the governor's demands.

Doc sat back, taking another swig of whiskey. They'd dropped him, bloody and bruised, in the grass by his bike. He'd been too full of rage to feel the physical blows, but despite not believing what the governor had said, the emotional strikes were torture. Right there and then, lying in the grass, Doc had vowed to save Juliette from that monster's wrath.

He'd never told a soul what went down that day. He didn't want to see the disappointment in his parents' eyes. He'd gone back to school and had told his buddies he'd gotten into a scuffle. He tried to keep his vow to Juliette but made a point of staying away from the governor's house, afraid of his parents having to deal with the repercussions of his actions. For weeks he'd gone by Juliette's private school and all of her favorite hangouts, but he'd never once seen her coming or going.

Two months later Cowboy had sent him a link to Juliette's engagement announcement to Josh Fucking Chambers, putting the nail in that coffin.

Chapter Four

"I'M JUST GOING to listen to your heart," Juliette said to the three-month-old colt she was examining. She'd taken a part-time veterinary position working for Jade Braden, a well-established veterinarian in Weston, so she'd have time for Lucas while they settled into their new home and town. Lucas had signed on with a bull-riding coach when they'd first moved, and he'd started his sophomore year of high school last week. He hadn't been thrilled about moving, but he'd connected with a group of friends and was finding his way.

She pressed the stethoscope against the colt's rib cage and closed her eyes, listening to the steady *lub-dub* of its heartbeat. Pleased with what she heard, she pulled the earpieces out and petted him. "You're a sturdy little guy."

As she continued the exam, she was reminded of a palomino colt the Whiskeys had rescued and allowed her to name the summer she'd interned there. The neglected colt had a white face, white legs from the knee down, and a blond mane and tail. He'd been far too thin, and she'd chosen the name Romeo, which was what she'd secretly called Seeley. She and Seeley had spent weeks taking care of him and nurturing him, hoping to give him all the love he'd missed out on. Memories of that summer were a constant struggle, even after all these years. Those memories had *almost* kept her from pursuing her dreams of working in veterinary medicine. But she'd vowed not to let Seeley take that from her, too.

Juliette's mind tiptoed back to that fateful summer again, when she'd willingly and wantingly given him her virginity and her heart.

She'd always stayed with her grandmother for a few weeks during the summers to help her with her horses. Staying with her grandmother had offered distance from her overbearing father, as they lived in different towns, but it didn't offer freedom. Her father had still kept a tight rein on her. That summer she'd needed veterinary experience to put on college applications, and her father had agreed she could intern at the ranch.

Much to her father's dismay, the week before leaving for her internship she'd ended her relationship with Josh Chambers, her boyfriend of two years and the son of her father's attorney. She had loved Josh only as a trusted friend, while he'd been in love with her. He was devastated by the breakup, but she was excited to finally get out from under her father's thumb and to learn from the ranch's vet. Her grandmother had taught her to ride horses when she was a little girl, and she'd wanted to be a veterinary technician for as long as she could remember. She wasn't expecting to meet a guy there, much less a guy who was in college and made her body come alive from the very first time she saw him.

Her friends at school were a year older and more experienced than she was, as she'd skipped a grade. They'd talked about feeling sparks and getting hot and bothered with certain boys, but she'd never felt anything like the gust of prickling-hot wind that had engulfed her when Seeley had come around the side of the barn her first day on the ranch. He was tall, tanned, and broad-shouldered, with piercing dark eyes that made her pulse race and a chiseled, scruffy jaw. He didn't just walk, like the boys she knew. He *strode*, rugged and powerful, thick legs eating up the space between them, until their eyes had locked like metal to magnet, and he'd stopped cold. She hadn't been sure she'd be able to find her voice when Wynnie introduced them, but Seeley had made a playful comment, and for the first time in her life, she'd felt like she was being seen as something more than her father's daughter, and she'd flirted right back. The sizzle and burn that had chased up her arm when they shook hands should have warned her away, but it only made him more intriguing.

She tried to push those memories away now, focusing on the colt, but laughter drew her attention as the farm owner's twentysomething grandson and his girlfriend walked by holding hands, sending her mind reeling back to the steamy afternoon when she and Seeley had shared their first kiss.

They'd been working together every day for nearly a week, getting to know each other and sharing secret glances and playful flirtations that kept her in a heightened state of hopeful anticipation from the moment they saw each other at breakfast until she fell into bed at night, shamelessly fantasizing about all the things she wanted to do with him. Things she'd heard all about from her friends but had never done, or wanted to do, with Josh.

But every time she and Seeley got close enough that she thought he'd kiss her, he'd clench his jaw, his entire body tensing up, and he'd put distance between them.

He was making her crazy, playing some kind of emotional tug-

of-war, like she was forbidden fruit.

That sunny afternoon, she'd had enough of being treated like she was only the governor's daughter. She and Seeley were rinsing off the horses they'd taken on a muddy trail ride with Cowboy, Dare, and two kids her age who were going through the ranch's program for troubled teens. She and Seeley were the last two down at the barn.

"Damn, it's hot out here." Seeley took off his cowboy hat and hung it on the handle of a pitchfork that was leaning against the side of the barn.

It was all she could do to watch him as he took off his shirt and used it to wipe his face, his body glistening in the sun, muscles flexing as he tossed the shirt aside. She wanted to feel those hot muscles against her. He raked a hand through his wavy brown hair, and she drank him in as he strode back to his horse.

"You gonna share that hose or stare at me all day?"

Embarrassed that he'd caught her staring, she lifted the hose and sprayed him.

His eyes narrowed. "Oh, you want to play, Peaches?"

He called her Peaches because she always carried a package of peach candies. Little did he know she sucked on them throughout the day in case he kissed her.

"Heck yeah, I want to play." She sprayed him again, laughing.

He ran toward her, and she squealed, sprinting away. She turned to spray him, but he caught her around her waist, tugging her back against his chest, both of them laughing as they wrestled for the hose. He ripped it from her hand, his other arm still belted across her stomach, keeping her pressed to him.

"Seeley, don't!" She grabbed his wrist, pushing away as they cracked up.

He tore his wrist free and turned the hose on her, dousing her with cold water. She shrieked, squirming to get free from his other arm, but he held her too tight, both of them laughing hysterically.

"How do you like that, Peaches?" He sprayed her again.

She shriek-laughed. "Stop! I'm already wet enough!"

His body went rigid against her, and he gritted out, "Jesus Christ."

"What's——" She realized what she'd said and heated from the inside out at the way he'd taken it, her laughter silencing as she realized this was her chance to strip away his restraint. She turned in his arms, their wet bodies pressed together. "What's the matter? Don't you like knowing you get me wet?"

His eyes drilled into hers, a stormy mix of restraint and desire. "Fuck."

"What's wrong?" She pressed her breasts against his bare, muscular chest, grinding her hips against him, and felt him get hard. "Am I too close?"

"Juliette," he warned.

"Don't you like the way I feel?" She gathered all her courage and said, "Because it sure feels like you do."

"You're driving me fucking insane." His voice was rough as gravel, his words dripping with desire. "You know I want to get my hands on you, but I'm trying to do the right thing, and you're making it too damn hard."

"I can feel that." Heart racing, she whispered, "And I like it." She went up on her toes and kissed him!

His arm tightened around her middle, and she thought he'd kiss her back, but he tore his mouth away, his volcanic eyes searching hers for only a second, before he gritted out, "Fuck it," dropped the hose, and crushed his mouth to hers, kissing her harder, his tongue sweeping hungrily over hers. His scruff abraded her skin, setting her entire body aflame. He grabbed her hair, angling her mouth beneath his, taking the kiss deeper. He held her tighter, his erection pressing into her belly. She clung to him, returning his efforts with everything she had, kissing him harder, rubbing against him, and wanting so much more. She'd never been kissed so intensely, had never wanted anyone so badly.

When he tore his mouth away, gritting out a curse, stormy eyes scanning the area around them, she worried he'd never kiss her again. "Don't stop," she pleaded. "I want you to kiss me."

He grabbed her hand, hurrying into the barn, and reclaimed her mouth, thoroughly devouring her. Her knees buckled, and her body begged for more. She knew she'd never be the same again.

The colt bobbed his head, startling her out of the memory.

Her heart raced. *What am I doing?* Seeley hadn't even looked back when he'd stalked off the other day. He hadn't given her a single glance.

It had been three days, and anger still bubbled up inside her.

She shouldn't be surprised by his behavior, considering how fast and easily he'd moved on that summer. She knew her father would have followed through on his threats, and she didn't blame Seeley for not wanting to go to jail, but she'd expected him to at least fight for them after learning she was pregnant. Instead, he'd *finally* answered her letters and had severed all ties.

Over the years she'd come to understand that she was only sixteen, too naive to see past the hearts in her eyes, and she must have romanticized that summer.

But that was a long time ago, and she *was* surprised by the way he treated her last weekend. They weren't kids anymore. Wasn't he even curious about his son?

She stewed on that as she finished examining the colt and reported back to her client. When she pulled out of their driveway, she was still too keyed up about Seeley to run the errands she'd planned to take care of before Lucas got home from school. She couldn't go on like this. She needed to clear the air with Seeley once and for all.

DOC GAVE STORMY, a ten-year-old gelding rescue, some extra love as he finished his afternoon rounds. Stormy came to them with squamous cell carcinoma in his eye that had been unresponsive to conventional treatments. Doc had excised the tumor and performed cryotherapy, and he was glad Stormy was recovering comfortably.

He saw Sasha heading his way. She was an equine rehabilitation therapist, and excellent at her job, but his family had been hovering since Saturday, trying to get him to talk about Juliette, and he was sick of it. Even Birdie had been texting to check up on him. She'd pick a scab until it bled.

He quickly finished writing up his notes, hoping to escape before Sasha reached him, but as he put Stormy's chart in the rack beside the stall, Sasha sidled up to him.

"He looks good, doesn't he?" Sasha said.

"Yeah." He headed out of the barn at a fast clip, waking Mighty, who'd been sleeping in the sun.

Sasha stuck by his side. "Cowboy and Hyde are on their way back with two rescue horses. One is in critical condition."

"I got the text. Hannah is setting up the OR." Hannah was one of their temporary veterinary technicians. Doc had always used temporary on-call assistants and interns from a local service, but the rescue had grown over the last couple of years, and he'd recently started thinking about hiring a permanent employee.

Hurrying to keep up, Sasha said, "*Doc*, can you stop walking for a second?"

Gritting his teeth, he stopped, and Mighty followed suit. "Sure, as long as it's not to talk about Juliette." Why the fuck did it still hurt to say her name? He had a club meeting tonight, and he couldn't fucking wait to get there. Being around the brotherhood, hitting up the Roadhouse bar afterward with the guys, and maybe getting lost in a willing woman was exactly what he needed to take his mind off this bullshit.

Sasha's brow wrinkled. "I know you don't want to talk about her, but if you change your mind, I'm a good listener."

"I won't." He took a step away, but she grabbed his arm. He glowered at her.

"Sorry." She let go of him. "But I'm worried about you, and about her. Birdie said you were brutal to her."

"Look, I know you *think* you know what went down between us, but—"

"No, I *don't*," she snapped. "Nobody talks about it. All I know is that you fell for her, and it ended so badly, Mom and Dad put that no-intracompany-dating policy into place."

"I was a fucking fool, okay? End of story." He headed for his veterinary clinic, but she and Mighty hurried after him.

"What does that mean?"

He turned on her. "It means, unlike *her*, I'm honest with the women I'm with just to get my rocks off."

Sasha's eyes widened. "You mean *she* was using *you*?"

"Let it go," he fumed as a red pickup came over the hill. "Who the hell is that?"

"I don't know."

"Mighty, *sit*." The dog sat. "*Stay.*" Doc took a few steps forward, watching the truck slowly approaching. It stopped on the side of the road. The door flung open, and Juliette climbed out. His chest constricted, hurt and anger gnawing at him like a feral beast. "What the fuck does she want?"

Juliette stalked toward him with her chin held high, her brown hair bouncing over the shoulders of a T-shirt that clung to her perfect fucking tits, jeans hugging every goddamn curve.

"That's far enough," he warned when she was about ten feet away. She was his kryptonite. He didn't trust himself to be any closer to her. She'd gotten even more beautiful, which he'd thought impossible, and the blue eyes that had haunted him for a decade and a half still held him captive. He didn't *want* to look at her, much less be close enough to smell or touch her, but he was powerless to look away.

"*Doc*," Sasha chided.

"It's okay, Sasha," Juliette said confidently, her eyes never leaving his. "Hello, Seeley. I'm sure I'm the last person you want to see."

"You're right, so you can go back the way you came."

"Seeley…?" she said a little pleadingly. "We—"

"We *what*, Juliette? Knew each other a lifetime ago?" He scoffed. "I barely remember a second of it, and I have no interest in reliving it. Go back to your family. You have no business here." He stalked toward his office.

Sasha hurried after him, speaking hushed and angry. "*Doc!* Why are you being such a dick?"

"Hey, *Romeo!*" Juliette shouted after him.

He stopped walking, the nickname cutting him to his core. Grinding his teeth and with his hands curled into fists, he fought the urge to turn around because seeing her was too painful.

"It must be nice having a selective memory for all these years," she shouted over the sound of an approaching truck. "While I've been raising our son!"

The earth tilted beneath his feet. He was vaguely aware of Sasha saying, "Ohmygod, *Doc*. You have a son?" as he tried to process what Juliette had said. Was that kid at the hospital *his* son? He'd been so shocked to see Juliette, he'd barely noticed the kid.

He turned in disbelief, seeing everything through a haze as Juliette climbed into her vehicle and Cowboy's truck pulled up beside him, towing the horse trailer.

"Let's go, Doc! This horse is critical!" Cowboy shouted, but he sounded far away.

Juliette was leaving, and Doc's mind was stuck in a loop. *I have a son? Was that my kid?* He ran after her truck, shouting, "Was that my son?" but she was already turning onto the main road that led off the ranch.

Chapter Five

DOC SAT BETWEEN Dare and Cowboy in the Dark Knights clubhouse feeling like he was going to climb out of his skin. His leg bounced under the table, his mind still spinning over the bomb Juliette had dropped. He'd had a hell of a time focusing on the horses they'd rescued, and now the one place that usually centered him made him feel like a caged animal.

His father and Manny Mancini, Billie's father and the vice president of the club, sat at the head table going over club business. All eyes were on them, but they were a blur to Doc, his thoughts a painful tangled web of confusion.

Dare nudged him. "You okay?"

"No, he's not okay," Cowboy hissed. "How could he be?"

"We should talk about it before you go see her," Dare whispered.

"No thanks." There was only one person Doc wanted to talk to about this, and she'd have to wait until the fucking meeting was over.

His father shot them a serious stare, causing some of the other guys to look over, too.

Fuck. Doc had told his brothers what had gone down with

Juliette, but his father had no clue Doc's world was unraveling around him. Then again, a fly couldn't take a piss on the ranch without his father knowing about it. Everyone who lived at the ranch had meals together at the main house. Doc had worked through dinner caring for the horses they'd rescued, but there was a good chance Sasha, or someone else who'd seen him running after Juliette's fucking truck, would've said something to his father.

As Tiny went back to discussing their upcoming Ride Clean anti-drug campaign, which they were hosting at the ranch in a few weeks, it was taking everything Doc had to try to hold on to some semblance of control. But the air was too thick, the battlefield in his head too painful. *Fuck it.* He needed answers before he lost his mind.

He pushed to his feet, ignoring the cautionary looks from his brothers, and felt his father's disapproving stare as he strode toward the door. Not only were club meetings mandatory, but it was the ultimate disrespect to leave while the president was speaking.

Doc filled his lungs as he stepped outside, heading for his bike.

The door flew open behind him, and his father strode out. "Son, you'd better stop right there."

He stilled.

His father closed the distance between them. "What the hell is so important that you'd disrespect me like that?"

"Juliette came by the ranch today. Figured someone would've told you."

His father's expression gave away nothing. "I'm asking *you.*"

"She claims we have a son," he bit out. "You know anything about *that?*"

He shook his head. "When we heard she'd had a baby, your mother and I wondered. It was awfully fast, but Juliette had been seeing the boy she married before she came to the ranch. Like everyone else, we assumed it was his."

"Guess we'll see." He straddled his bike, the ache of Juliette's original betrayal slaying him. But this? If it was true, how could she keep him from his own son for all these years? But none of that was his father's fault. "I'm sorry for disrespecting you. I'll take whatever repercussions you want to dole out, but I can't sit in there not knowing if that kid is mine or not."

"We both know family comes first. Just don't make a habit of it."

DOC GROUND HIS back teeth as he climbed the steps to Juliette's grandmother's house, trying to keep his memories from bullying their way in. But he was assaulted by images of kissing Juliette in Hazel's barn and behind the shed, going on trail rides and making love in the fields, having dinners with Hazel, and holding Juliette's hand under the table. He'd held her hand so often, it had felt like an extension of his own.

Fighting against those memories, his heart hammering in his chest, he knocked on the door. He heard Juliette calling out, "I've got it!" and then her face appeared in the sidelight, her big blue eyes filling with concern. *Fuck.*

She opened the door and quickly stepped outside, pulling it closed behind her, looking too damn sexy in cutoffs and a T-shirt. "*Seeley,* what are you doing here?"

"What the hell do you think I'm doing here? You can't drop

a bomb like that and expect me not to want to know the truth. How do you know that kid's mine?"

"How can you even ask me that?" She looked stricken. "You *know* I never slept with anyone else that summer."

"I don't know *what* to believe anymore. I used to think I could trust the things you said, but that was a long time ago, and I learned really quickly how much of a fool I was. But if I was the only guy you slept with, then why didn't you tell me you were pregnant?"

"I *did*," she said sharply.

"What the hell are you talking about? You didn't tell me shit. I called and texted every fucking day. You didn't return a single one."

"My father took away my phone!"

"And there were no other phones in that big fucking house? You couldn't borrow one from a friend or buy a fucking burner phone?" He couldn't stop his voice from escalating. "While you were out rekindling your relationship with Josh, I was trying to *save* us. I went to your house, and I went to your school every damn day looking for you. I waited for you to reach out, and you went radio silent on me. I don't know what kind of game you're playing or why now after all this time."

"I'm *not* playing a game!" she insisted, her eyes tearing up. "I didn't have your cell number memorized. It was in my phone, so I called the ranch, but they said you went back to school, and I didn't want to leave a message because of my father! I was afraid he'd do something to your family. But I wrote you letters!"

"*Bullshit.* I never got any fucking letters. Goddamn it, Juliette. What do you want from me? Why are you doing this?"

"Because Lucas is *your son*, and I can't—"

The front door opened, and Lucas stormed out. "What's going on? Why are you yelling at my mother?"

Fuck.

"Lucas—"

"*No*, Mom. This guy treated you like crap at the hospital. I'm *not* going to let him do that again." Lucas stepped between them, staring Doc down, full of piss and vinegar, not unlike Doc was at that age. "I don't know who you think you are, but that's no way to treat a woman."

The kid—*Lucas*—was tall and lean, on the cusp of broadening shoulders and sharper features. Doc studied his hawklike eyes, straight nose, and wavy brown hair, all so similar to his own, he couldn't fucking believe it.

Lucas crossed his arms, drumming his fingers, his chin lifting in defiance.

Doc's heart nearly stopped, remembering how Juliette used to call *him* an arm drummer. He glanced at her over the boy's shoulder.

As if she'd read his mind, she nodded.

Doc forced himself to take a good, hard look at *her* and saw the truth staring back at him. Battling anger at her betrayal, he tried to quiet the questions in his mind as he returned his attention to Lucas. To his *son*. His heart ached and filled up at once. "I'm sorry. You're right. That's no way to speak to a woman. Juliette, it seems we have a lot to talk about. I'll be around all night. You know where to find me." He looked at Lucas, his throat thickening. "I won't raise my voice at her again. You have my word on that."

"You better not," Lucas warned. "Next time I won't be so nice about it."

"*Lucas*," Juliette chided. "Sorry, Seeley."

"It's okay. I have a feeling he comes by it naturally."

"YOU'RE NOT REALLY going to go see him, are you?" Lucas asked as Seeley drove away on his motorcycle.

Juliette was still stuck on the things Seeley had said. He didn't believe what she'd said back then? He'd never gotten her letters? He'd gone to her house? To her school? None of that made sense. He was so angry, it was hard *not* to want to believe him. But she knew better. She had the letter he'd sent telling her he wanted nothing to do with her or their baby.

So the real question was, what kind of game was *he* playing?

"Yes, I am," she said, and went inside.

Lucas followed her. "Mom."

She needed a second to get her head on straight and went into the kitchen for a glass of water. Because guzzling wine when she was angry wouldn't set a good example for Lucas.

"Why are you going?" he demanded. "Why was he even here? I've never heard the name Seeley in my life, and suddenly he's showing up at our house and yelling at you?"

She took a drink, considering her response. She hadn't been much older than Lucas when she'd fallen in love with Seeley, and this was *not* how she'd envisioned their lives panning out. Sometimes she had to remind herself that Lucas hadn't grown up hearing her argue with Josh, or any other adult for that matter. She'd cut her parents out of their lives so long ago, he'd been too little to remember those arguments. She didn't want him to think it was okay for adults to yell at each other, either, but she'd held on to so many years of hurt and anger, she couldn't have stifled it if she'd tried. It sounded like Seeley couldn't either, but that didn't make him a bad person.

"I told you we have a complicated past. We were important to each other a long time ago, and things didn't end well."

"So? Why bother with him after all this time?"

Because he's your father, and I never stopped loving him. "He lives in Hope Valley, and now that we're living here, there's a chance we'll run into him again. I don't want any bad blood between us. After I grab a sweatshirt and check on the horses, I'm going over to talk to him."

He crossed his arms. "Then I'm going with you."

"*No*, you're not," she said firmly. "You're going to stay here and do your homework, text with your friends, play your games, and not worry about *me*."

"But—"

"Lucas, this is not negotiable. I know you're not used to seeing me argue with anyone, and you've witnessed two uncomfortable interactions with Seeley, but sometimes adults argue, the same way kids do."

"You never argued with Dad," he retorted.

Her heart was breaking. She felt like she'd spent her entire life hiding and lying, and she *had* to stop. "Yes, I did. We argued a lot. We were just careful not to do it around you."

He set his jaw, drumming his fingers, looking so much like a younger Seeley, she felt a pang of longing and pain, underscoring why she needed to get to the bottom of the things Seeley had said.

"Honey, I love that you want to protect me, but that's *not* your job. Your job is to be a teenager, and to focus on school, enjoy your friends, take care of the horses, and try not to give me any more heart attacks when you're bull riding." The doctor had suggested he take a few days off before he got back on a bull, and although Lucas had fought her on it, he'd abided by her rules and would return to practicing next week. "Okay?"

"Whatever," he grumbled.

"Get over here." She tugged him into a hug, and he stood rigid, his arms at his sides. "I'm not letting go until you hug me back."

He huffed and finally hugged her.

She held on a little tighter, hoping she hadn't totally screwed up their lives.

Chapter Six

JULIETTE WAS UPSET with herself for letting her anger get the better of her twice in one day. She gripped the steering wheel tighter as she neared the ranch.

When she'd driven onto the ranch earlier, she'd been nervous about talking to Seeley, and she'd been furious with him when she'd left. This time, as she turned into the ranch, her emotions were all over the place. She was angry that he'd denied writing the letter, thankful that he'd pulled himself together once Lucas had come outside, and confused to no end about what was going on.

She hadn't thought to ask *where* he'd be on the ranch, so she drove to the veterinary clinic, which she'd seen earlier was still located just past the rehab barns. She'd sleuthed Seeley over the years. Not often, but enough to see whether he'd ever married or if he had a family. She'd been happy for him when she first learned he'd followed his dream and was working on the ranch. But that happiness had been squashed seconds later by resentment.

As she wound through the ranch on roads she'd once known by heart, it took her a great deal of effort to stuff that still-present resentment down deep. Especially after he'd basically called her a liar. She drove up to the clinic, and when she saw Seeley's motorcycle parked out front, resentment reared its ugly head again. He'd had everything he ever wanted for all this time, and she'd had it all ripped out from under her. She'd had to fight for her freedom, and every single thing she and Lucas had.

She was so nervous, she felt sick as she parked beside his bike. Leaving the engine running, she rolled down the window and closed her eyes, trying to regain control so she wouldn't fly off the handle. She took one long, deep breath after another, missing her grandmother, wishing she were there to lean on. Grandma Hazel always knew how to talk her off the ledge. She pictured her grandmother's face, dotted with sun spots and mapped with wrinkles. Her grandmother had called them *sun kisses* and *lifelines*. She'd said every time she got to feeling sorry for herself, she'd remember she'd earned every one of those spots and wrinkles.

Juliette conjured her grandmother's loving blue-gray eyes, remembering the day she'd told her about Seeley's letter, and her grandmother's raspy voice whispered through her mind. *That doesn't sound like the boy who looked at you like you were the prettiest filly in the barn. But I've been fooled before.* Juliette had sobbed until she had no tears left to fall. Her grandmother had taken her by the shoulders, holding her teary gaze, and said, *Listen carefully, Juliegirl. Your heart has found its voice, and it will always speak louder than your head. I fear there will be no quieting those screams, so it's up to you to learn to think past them in order to do what's best for your baby.*

The sound of footsteps on gravel startled her, and her eyes flew open as Seeley strode up to her truck. Why did he have to look so damn hot in those low-slung jeans and that black leather cut? He put a hand on the door, his T-shirt straining against his muscles with the movement. His jaw clenched, his dark eyes scrutinizing her in a way that made her heart beat so hard, she was sure he could hear it. "Your boy okay?" he asked.

"*Our* boy" flew angrily out before she could check it. "He's *our* boy, Seeley. Lucas is *our* son."

His eyes narrowed. "Does *he* know that?"

"No."

His jaw ticked. "We can talk at my place. Follow me."

So much for not flying off the handle.

As she followed his motorcycle down the narrow lanes and turned toward the creek, she filled with disbelief. Unless they'd developed more of the property back there, she knew *exactly* where he was going. They used to sneak off to an empty cabin in the woods by the creek. It was where they had first made love. The cabin that he'd claimed, the night before she'd been taken away by her father, would be theirs one day.

She'd never forget that first time. The ranch had kept a tight rein on kids her age, and they all stayed in rooms on the second floor of the main house. The gathering space, kitchen, dining area, and offices were on the first floor. A big, bald man named Dwight had been the cook and resident manager in charge of watching over them. That night she and the two kids they'd gone on a trail ride with had gone to hang out by the horses. A little while later she'd told the other kids she was going for a walk but had really gone to meet Seeley. She hadn't wanted them to know, for fear they'd get in trouble if she and Seeley got caught sneaking out together.

Seeley had been waiting for her at the end of the lane that led to the cabin, and his whole face had lit up when he'd seen her. He'd drawn her into a kiss so deep and powerful, she could still feel it curling her toes. His voice had been gruff but tender. *Are you sure you want to do this?* She hadn't even hesitated to say *yes*, and when he led her into the cabin, there were candles flickering on sheets of metal to protect the scuffed and marred wooden floor, two sleeping bags zipped together, a pillow, and a tin can full of wildflowers he'd picked from beside the creek. He'd been so loving with her, so careful not to hurt her. But their emotions had quickly taken over, just as they had with all the other things they'd done, and there was no holding back.

That cabin had become their love nest, and a few weeks later, he'd carved a heart with their initials in it into the floorboards with his pocketknife and had said it would be theirs one day.

Her throat thickened as she followed his motorcycle around the last turn, and his headlight illuminated a beautiful log home with a deep front porch. She couldn't believe he'd torn their cabin down. Wiped away their memories. Was it that easy for him to forget what they'd had? That easy to obliterate his memories of her and move on?

Of course it was. Otherwise he never would have written that letter.

While she'd been naively giving her heart and soul to him, he'd been merely satiating a physical desire. Anger and hurt prickled her skin as she parked and cut the engine.

She watched him climb off his bike and walk around her truck to help her out. She'd been taking care of herself and Lucas forever. She didn't want to give him the satisfaction of thinking she needed him for *anything*, so she threw open her door.

He stepped back, his brow furrowing as she climbed out.

He reached for the truck door, but she got it first and pushed it shut. Those muscles in his jaw bunched, and she was pretty sure hers were, too. She didn't want to be that angry *or* that petty. She didn't want to feel that much, *period*, but she couldn't help it. Being there was unearthing everything they'd said and done to each other, bringing it all back in painful detail.

An Irish setter stretched at the top of the porch steps as two other dogs bounded around the side of the house, heading straight for Juliette. Seeley whistled and patted his thigh. As if he'd carved a new path for them, the dogs ran around her directly to him.

"I see you're still a dog whisperer. Are they all yours?" Juliette asked.

"Yeah. This is Sadie." He petted the Irish setter's head. "Mighty." He petted the black Lab. "And Pickles." He ruffled the fur of the husky mix.

"Pickles?" she asked with amusement.

"I found him on the side of the road. He was emaciated, and he smelled like pickles." The dogs pushed their noses into him even as he petted them. He snapped his fingers. "Enough." The dogs stepped back. "Go play." They scampered away. "Let's go inside and talk."

She followed him up the porch steps, memories of whispered secrets and their naked bodies entangled in the cabin, deeper in the woods, and in the lake, came at her like a swarm of mosquitoes she couldn't bat away.

He held the door open, and as she stepped inside, she told herself not to look around. For all she knew he had a girlfriend and there would be pictures of them everywhere.

She shouldn't care, but jealousy speared her, and her gaze skated over a rustic yet lavish kitchen to her left with several windows, a large island, and a stone wall behind the cooking area. To their right was a spacious, two-story living room with a dark leather sectional, a stone fireplace with a live-edge mantel covered with framed photos, a bar with the same live-edge design, and an old rocking chair. Two large windows flanked glass patio doors, and the peaked wall above the doors boasted four massive windows. The walls were a mix of wide-planked knotty wood and stone, which might have seemed too dark if not for the plethora of windows and three large skylights. The skylights brought memories of the nights they'd lain in the grass by the creek, wishing on stars, sharing secrets, and making plans for a future they'd never have together. Her heart squeezed with the memories.

"Can I get you something to drink?" Seeley asked, heading for the bar.

"Yes, please." She needed it.

He lifted his chin as if asking what she'd like.

"Whatever you're having is fine."

"I'm having whiskey."

One glass to calm my nerves. "Perfect."

He cocked a brow, amusement dancing in his eyes.

She smiled, having forgotten how much she'd liked his sense of humor, and shook her head. "I meant the *drink*."

He carried the bottle and two glasses into the living room and motioned to the couch.

"I like your home," she said as they sat down. "Do your dogs stay outside?"

"No. They have doggie doors, but they like to patrol the property." He poured them each a drink and handed her a glass. He downed his own, then poured himself another. "Sorry for showing up at your place out of the blue. I didn't mean to cause trouble with Lucas."

"I wasn't exactly discreet when I was here earlier." She felt guilty for what she'd yelled. "I didn't mean to blurt it out the way I did in front of everyone, but you were being such a jerk, I was just…" The hurt came out with a crack in her voice, and she hated that. She took a drink, wincing at the burn as it slid down her throat. "I don't know why you think you have the right to be an asshole toward *me* after how you threw us away back then."

"I never threw us away," he said angrily.

"Seeley, I don't want to play games. You destroyed me that summer, and I *get* it. I was young and naive and you were just doing what nineteen-year-old guys do, but I'm *not* naive anymore. I grew up really fast after that summer, and all I want is to clear the air."

"I *don't* play games," he said through gritted teeth. "I loved you more than I have ever loved anything in my entire life. Everything I said tonight was true. I *went* to your house, I confronted your father, and his bodyguards kicked my ass." He pushed to his feet, pacing.

"*What?* They hurt you? *When* did you go to my house?" she demanded, stepping in front of him.

"I don't *know*. A couple of weeks after you left the ranch. I kept waiting for you to reach out, and I couldn't take it anymore." His words flew fast and angry. "I thought I'd be able to reason with him. I thought if I showed him how much I loved you, he'd come around. But I was a fucking fool to believe you loved me. He told me about you and Josh. He said I was your last hurrah. I was so fucking stupid, I didn't believe him. I spent *weeks* looking for you at your school and at the hangouts you told me about, and then I saw the fucking engagement announcement. So don't you *dare* tell me *I* threw us away, when you were out there fucking around with that guy." He turned away.

"Seeley, *wait!*" She grabbed his arm, spinning him around.

"This isn't getting us anywhere," he snapped. "It's fucking torture. I can't handle any more lies."

"I *never* lied to you! Not then and not now. I begged my father to let me see you. He wouldn't let me out of the fucking house. I never knew you came by." Tears welled in her eyes, the pain hitting anew. "He monitored all the phones. That's why I wrote those letters and gave them to Ana to give to you." Their housekeeper had been the only person in that house she'd trusted.

"Ana? That woman who came to see you at the ranch? She never gave me any fucking letters."

"Stop lying!" She pushed her hand into the back pocket of her shorts and pulled out the letter, thrusting it toward him. "I kept the letter you wrote me, because it broke my fucking heart. I was not *with* Josh back then, either. I didn't even talk to him until after I got your letter, and then he was the only friend my father let me see. But I *never* slept with Josh until *after* Lucas was born!"

"You *married* him." His voice dripped with venom.

"Because I was *sixteen* and had no choice. I found out I was pregnant in late September, right before my birthday, and like an idiot, I told my parents I was pregnant because I thought my mother would stand up for me for once, and my father would give in and let us be together. But you know my mother. She's all about appearances, and it only infuriated my father that I would *let myself* get pregnant by some guy from a biker family. After I got your letter and realized you'd turned your back on me, I had no choice. It was either marry Josh or abort our baby. So stop pretending that *I'm* the one who gave up on us."

Tears streamed down her cheeks, and she shook the letter at him. "You can't lie your way out of this."

DOC SNATCHED THE paper from her, and read it.

Juliette,

I figured if I didn't respond to your letters, you'd stop writing. I guess I was wrong. I don't know if your letter is a desperate attempt to get my attention, or if you're really knocked up. But if you are, I doubt the kid is even mine. I don't know who else you've been with, and I don't really care, but don't drag me into your mess. I've moved on, and you should too.

Seeley

Rage burned through him. "What the hell?" He read it again, studying the handwriting, which was identical to his. "I didn't fucking write this. Where did you get it?"

"That's your handwriting, Seeley." She set her jaw like she had set it as a teenager, her eyes shooting daggers, her voice full of disappointment, hurt, and disbelief.

It was the disbelief that made him even angrier. "*Where* did you get this, Juliette?"

"Ana gave it to me. She got it from her brother. You *know* that. He brought all my letters to you at college, and that was the *only* time you ever wrote back."

"How many times do I have to tell you, I never got *any*

fucking letters? How could you even believe I'd write something like this? I fucking *loved* you. I risked my future and my family's ranch to be with you. I would've burned down the entire fucking *world* for you." He shook the letter, trying to harness his fury. "Whoever wrote this is going to pay."

Her father was going to answer for this, too. For the years the bastard had stolen from him with Juliette and for the years he'd lost with his son. But that would have to wait, because right now the only thing that mattered was the woman standing before him crying—the woman he had never stopped loving—and getting to know the son he'd unknowingly left behind.

"Are you...?" She swallowed hard, swiping at the tears flooding her cheeks. "Are you being honest right now? You really didn't write the letter? Because I don't know what to believe."

He stepped closer, needing her to know, to remember who he was and realize he never could have written that letter. "Did I *ever* give you a reason to believe I'd write something like this?"

"*No*, but—"

"Did I ever lie to you about anything when we were together? Big or small?"

"No," she choked out.

His chest felt like it was cracking open. "Then why would you believe I'd write this garbage? You were *everything* to me. I was a fucking mess after you left, and when you got married?" He slammed his fist against his chest. "You broke my fucking heart."

"I broke my own heart, but it was either marry Josh or lose the only piece of you I had. I cried myself to sleep every night when I was pregnant, but our baby kept me going, and even if I *was* naive and you *were* using me, it didn't change the fact that I loved you."

"*Fuck.*" He hauled her into his arms, holding her tight, struggling against the emotions swamping him. "I never used you. Don't ever say that. None of this makes sense, but I *believe* you, and we're going to get to the bottom of it."

He framed her face in his hands, gazing into her eyes, wishing he could take away the pain he saw there. He wiped her tears with the pads of his thumbs, gritting out, "Do you believe *me* about the letter?"

She nodded. "Yes."

Thank God. He touched his forehead to hers. "All these years, I thought you played me. I'm sorry. I'm so fucking sorry."

"I loved you." She clung to him, tipping her face up, fresh tears hitting his thumbs. "I never stopped loving you."

Her words sent the room spinning. "*Jule*" fell from his lips as he crushed them to hers. Their mouths fused like molten metal, their tongues sweeping deep and greedy in a fierce devouring. Blown away by how right and unfuckingbelievably incredible it felt to kiss her after all these years, he tore his mouth away, needing to know he wasn't imagining it and that she felt it, too. She was clutching his shirt, desire brimming in her eyes. Neither spoke, but in the silence an unstoppable tsunami of want and need brewed. *Holy shit. Nothing has changed.*

Their mouths crashed together, their tongues plunging, possessing, *claiming* more by the second. Their hands were everywhere at once, their desire so powerful, her back hit the wall, but neither broke their connection. He reveled in her hunger for him, in her hauntingly familiar taste and needful touch that had fueled his fantasies and driven him out of his fucking mind for years. He'd been with dozens of women, chasing this high, but none had sparked white-hot passion or unleashed the beast in him the way Juliette always did.

It was like no time had passed and a lifetime had gone by in equal measure, and he couldn't get enough of her soft womanly curves and needy sounds. Desire burned through him as they groped and moaned, their bodies grinding together. He fisted his hands in her hair, growling against her lips, "I fucking missed you."

He took her in another punishingly intense kiss and stripped off her shirt and bra, freeing her full breasts. "*Jesus, Jule.* You're fucking gorgeous." He palmed her breasts and lowered his mouth, teasing one nipple with his tongue as he squeezed the other. She cried out, clinging to him as he sucked her nipple to the roof of his mouth, *hard.* The way she used to like it.

"*Ohgod. Seeley.*"

As he sucked, fondled, and teased, her fingernails dug into his flesh, her moans and pleas fueling his desire. He unbuttoned her shorts and pushed his hand into her panties, sliding through her slickness. "You're so fucking wet for me."

"Only for you," she panted out, breaking the last shred of his control.

He crushed his mouth to hers, feasting as he pushed two fingers inside her tight heat, gritting out a curse when she moaned. He swallowed her moans and mewls as he fucked her with his fingers, her sexy sounds searing through him, making his cock ache to be inside her. He fisted his other hand in her hair, ravenously devouring her, wanting to reclaim every inch of her. "I need my mouth on you."

He tore off her boots, shorts, and panties and buried his face between her legs. She tasted so fucking sweet. "*Seeley,*" she panted out. *"Feels so good."* She'd always said his name when they'd made love, and it still brought a primal pleasure that nothing else had ever come close to. She was his drug, her pleasure, his addiction. Taking her clit between his teeth, he pushed his fingers inside her again, stroking the spot that had her thighs flexing, her breath coming in fast gasps. He licked and sucked, taking his fill, sending her climax crashing over her. *"Seeleyseeleyseeley—"*

He took everything she had to give, soaked in the sounds of pleasure sailing from her lips, even as the last shudder rippled through her. He rose to his feet, taking her in a brutal kiss, needing to be inside her more than he needed his next breath. She was right there with him, tugging open his jeans. He lifted her into his arms, and her legs wound around him as he carried her down the hall and into his bedroom.

He laid her on the bed and stripped off his clothes and boots in three seconds flat.

"I need you," she said breathlessly, reaching for him as he came down over her.

His mouth covered hers, rough and urgent, and he entered her in one hard thrust, pleasure searing through him like fire. She gasped, and he cursed. "Did I hurt you?"

"No. You just feel so good." She pulled his mouth back to hers.

They thrusted and gyrated, feasted and fucked with reckless abandon. She was so damn tight, so insanely perfect and familiar, he felt like he'd been lost, starved, and she was the only person who could satiate him. He felt like he'd *finally* come home. He lifted her ass, angling her hips, taking her deeper, driving, stretching, *claiming* her. "I fucking missed you," he gritted out between feverish kisses.

"*So much,*" she said, clinging to him, her nails digging into his flesh.

Their bodies grew slick with their efforts, the sounds of their lovemaking filling the room. He pushed his arms under her, holding her tighter, thrusting harder. "*Don't stop,*" she pleaded. Didn't she know it would take a fucking act of God to drag him away?

He quickened his efforts, her pussy squeezing him so perfectly, every sensation magnified. Their kisses were more powerful, their touches more intense, and the sounds they made were drenched with dark desires, as if they'd bottled up all their passion for each other during the years they were apart, just waiting for this moment. It took everything he had not to come. He sank his teeth into her neck, and she cried out, her hips bucking and her inner muscles spasming around his cock, sending an earth-shattering release barreling into him. "*Fuuck. Jule—*"

They rode the waves of their pleasure, moaning and thrusting, consumed with passion, with each other's pleasure, which went on longer and was more intense than ever before. Doc had never felt anything like it.

When they finally collapsed to the mattress, breathlessly kissing, their tangled bodies jerking with aftershocks, he held her tighter. After sixteen years of missing her, his sweet, fiery *Jule* was right there in his arms, and he was *never* letting her go.

AS THE WORLD came back into focus, Juliette reveled in the feel of Seeley's big, warm body cocooning her. In his arms had been the only place she'd ever felt truly safe. His body was thicker and stronger now, his scruff more abrasive, his moves more nuanced and powerful. But the way he touched her, the way he felt inside her, while more intense, was as familiar as if he were still a part of her.

He kissed her forehead, those delicious lips curving into a sexy smile. "You okay, darlin'?"

Her heart squeezed at the endearment. "Mm-hm." She'd seen flashes of the tattoos on his chest, shoulders, and upper arms. She wished she'd been there when he'd gotten them and knew the secrets behind each one.

His phone chimed from somewhere on the floor, drawing her from her reverie. His eyes shifted in the direction of the sound. She leaned back, putting space between them. "Do you need to get that?"

"No. Get back here." He pulled her into a kiss.

Why did she have to love that so much? How many times had he done the same thing during that fateful summer? Fighting the end of whatever time they'd stolen together. As if by doing so he could stretch each hour into two.

More chimes rang out in rapid succession, and his muscles tensed, bringing reality, and anxiety, rushing in. She forced herself to push away again. "*What* are we doing? We have so much to talk about, and sex complicates things." Not that she regretted it or could've stopped herself from wanting everything he was willing to give. They were as explosive as they'd always been, but they weren't irresponsible kids anymore. They needed to deal with reality.

"Things are already complicated." He pulled her close again, but she put her hand on his chest, stopping him.

"Seeley, we have a lot to talk about. I came over to clear the air. I didn't expect to need a suit of armor to battle the heat between us." She couldn't suppress her smile. "Not that I'm complaining, but we didn't even use protection."

"*Shit.* I'm sorry. I lost my head. You're not on birth control?"

"No. I can't get pregnant anymore. Josh and I tried, but it never happened."

His brows knitted. "I'm sorry to hear that."

"It's okay. I have Lucas, but *please* tell me I don't have to worry about diseases."

"Jesus, Jule. Do you really think I'd be with you if you did?"

"I'd like to think you wouldn't, but we don't know each other anymore. I don't even know if you're involved with anyone, and those texts sounded important."

"Those texts are probably from my brothers making sure I'm okay because I took off early from a club meeting to see you, and I'm not involved with anyone." His brows slanted. "Oh *fuck*. Are you still married?"

"*No.*" She pushed to her feet, hurt by the question, which made no sense given that she'd asked him a similar one. But her heart was racing, and she wasn't exactly thinking rationally. "Despite what you've thought of me for all these years, I wouldn't have slept with you if I were."

She hurried into the bathroom and shut the door. Leaning her back against it, she closed her eyes. *Breathe. Just breathe.* With everything that was at stake, how could she let herself get carried away like that? She told herself what was done was done. It was just sex. They were adults. They could handle this.

She opened her eyes, taking in the dark wood-and-stone bathroom, which was as ruggedly handsome as the man who had knocked the sense right out of her with a single kiss. She looked in the mirror and winced. Her hair was a mess. Seeley had always loved having his hands in it, but her body had changed so much. She was strong from working with horses, but she was also thicker and softer around the middle, and her breasts were heavier and far from the perky girls she'd had at sixteen.

Chiding herself for worrying about what she looked like, she used the toilet and washed up, trying to figure out how to navigate this. *The same way you've navigated the last decade and a half. Head-on.*

She dried her hands, took a deep breath, and opened the door.

Seeley was standing *right there*, ridiculously handsome in a pair of black boxer briefs, looking at her with an apologetic expression. He handed her one of his T-shirts. As she put it on, he said, "I'm sorry. I shouldn't have gotten carried away."

"It's not your fault. We both got carried away." Feeling awkward, she tried to step around him.

He gently grabbed her hand and drew her into his arms, holding her tight. "I know we need to talk, but give me a second. That was pretty intense."

She closed her eyes, soaking him in, glad she wasn't alone in those feelings.

"Why don't I make a fire and we can sit outside. I think we could both use some air."

"Okay."

"Do you need to check in with Lucas?"

She loved that he considered him. "No. I told him I might be gone for a while, but thanks for thinking of him."

"I have a feeling you two will be all I'm thinking about for a very long time." He released her hand, a tease glimmering in his eyes. "I should make you talk naked, so you can't storm off."

"*You're* the expert at that."

He nodded, his expression serious. "I'm sorry about that, too, darlin'. I won't do that to you again. Let's get dressed." His brows knitted, and he plucked something from her shoulder and held it up. "Sadie's fur. Sorry."

She smiled. "They sleep with you?"

"Every night."

As she headed into the living room to find her clothes, still missing him so much that she ached with it, she wondered if he had any full-body armor she could borrow.

Chapter Seven

JULIETTE'S NERVES WERE working overtime. She was glad Seeley had brought out a glass of wine *and* a glass of water for her. She'd probably need both.

They were sitting in heavy wooden chairs by the firepit. She tried to calm her nerves, taking in the large deck, and the rest of his backyard, which was exactly like she'd imagined it might be. There were no manicured gardens or stone paths, just natural beauty. The spotty grass, rocky terrain, bushes, and trees were left to grow as they wished. Wildflowers added pops of color along the banks of the creek and around rocks and tree trunks. She saw the old wooden bridge they'd used that fateful summer to cross the creek.

She was surprised he hadn't torn that down, too. She couldn't help but wonder if he ever used it anymore, or went to the spots they'd once called their own.

Pushing those thoughts away, she watched Seeley take a drink of his beer. He was wearing a Dark Knights T-shirt, jeans, and black leather boots, looking at her so intently, it made her wonder what he saw.

She fidgeted with the sleeve of her sweatshirt. "Where do we start?"

"I'd like to talk about Lucas," he said evenly. "But first I think I need to understand more about how we got here and what you've been through. You said your father gave you an ultimatum, and your mother didn't help, which must've fucking crushed you. I know you had hoped she'd eventually get out from under your father's thumb."

She'd considered her father a lost cause well before meeting Seeley, but when she was younger, she had held out hope that her mother might open her eyes to her controlling husband and side with her on something. *Anything.* Her grandmother had cautioned her against that misguided hope many times, insisting her mother wasn't under anyone's thumb, but a gold digger who resented her station in life. Once she'd landed Juliette's father, she'd become even more materialistic. As Juliette had witnessed too many times to count, her mother had no issue going along with whatever her father decided for every aspect of their lives in order to keep that gravy train going, even when it meant forsaking her own daughter's future.

"I should have listened to my grandmother. She was right about her." She sipped her wine. "I used to wish my mother was more like yours. Or at least like the person your mom was when I knew her."

"She's still the same loving person you knew. She'll be furious when she hears about all of this."

"I'm embarrassed, and I feel guilty about how my father treated you and your family."

"You were a kid. You had no control, and everyone knows that." He leaned his elbows on his knees. "I carry a lot of guilt for what I put my family through, too." His dark eyes found hers again. "But I have never apologized for how I felt about you, and I never will. There's a difference between regretting something and feeling guilty because of the trouble it caused others."

She felt like she was going to cry. Nobody had ever loved her the way he did, and the vehemence in his voice confirmed everything she'd believed he'd felt when they were together.

"The thing I can't make sense of," he said, "is why Hazel didn't step in to help you. She adored you."

"She offered to take me in, and I wanted to go live with her, but my father threatened to ruin her business. He said he'd make sure she never earned another penny. I couldn't do that to her."

"That fucking cowardly bastard." He picked up a poker and stoked the fire, sending sparks crackling toward the sky. "I should've taken care of him when I had the chance."

"What do you mean, when you had the chance?"

He sat back. "Before the engagement announcement, when I still thought your father had lied to me about you and Josh, I was home for the weekend and got rip-roaring drunk. I grabbed one of our rifles and climbed into a truck to hunt him down."

"*Seeley.* What were you thinking?" She was shocked. Not that he'd want to go after her father, but he'd always been careful about not drinking and driving or doing things that could unnecessarily endanger others. "If you'd managed to do it, you'd be in prison right now, and that's assuming you didn't kill yourself or someone else first by driving drunk."

"That's basically what my old man said when he hauled my ass out of the truck and gave me hell."

"Thank God he did." She hesitated for a minute before adding, "As much as I hate that my father turned you into someone who would even think about doing something like that, when I thought you didn't fight for us, I was devastated. As wrong as it is, I'm kind of glad to hear you were trying to after all."

He shook his head, his lips curving into a slightly sorrowful smile. But it lasted only a few seconds before his expression turned serious again. "I was pretty messed up over losing you." He took a drink and gazed out at the creek.

She studied his profile, seeing so much of Lucas in him, the relief of knowing he hadn't written that letter hit her anew, bringing with it a wave of longing for the time Seeley and Lucas had lost. She had no idea how she was going to manage to break the news to Lucas, but she was getting ahead of herself. There was still a lot to wade through.

He met her gaze. "I don't think I ever got over it."

The honesty in his eyes drew her own confession. "That makes two of us." Their gazes held for so long, the air felt electrically charged. She couldn't afford to let that take hold and glanced at the fire.

"How did your father get Josh to agree to everything?" Seeley asked. "Taking on a wife and someone else's kid is a lot for anyone, and he was, what? Eighteen?"

"It wasn't hard to convince him. He'd loved me since we were kids, and I told you that summer how devastated he was when I broke up with him. I was such a mess when I thought you'd written that letter, Josh would have done anything to make me happier. I feel horrible about roping him into the whole situation, but I think there was more to it. His dad was my father's attorney, and he was as corrupt as my father was. I don't know much about their crooked business dealings, but knowing my father, he probably had something to hold over Josh's father's head."

Seeley's jaw clenched so tight, it had to hurt. "I'm thankful Josh agreed, and you were with someone who loved you. Did you get the wedding you always wanted?"

She shook her head, remembering how she and Seeley had made plans to get through college and vet school and get married on the ranch. She sipped her wine, trying to push away those painful memories. "We had a small ceremony in my parents' backyard shortly after the announcement came out. I got my GED, and my father used his influence to get me into Stanford, where Josh was going to school. He rented us a house and paid for a nanny after Lucas was born so I could continue my education."

"So Lucas thinks Josh is his father?"

She nodded, feeling guilty. "I'm sorry, but after I got that letter, I didn't want him to grow up thinking he was unwanted, so I never told him the truth."

"I understand." Pain shadowed his eyes. "You said you're not married anymore, but is Josh good to you and Lucas?"

"We separated when Lucas was four, and Josh was killed two months later in a hit-and-run accident." It had been years, but it still hurt to think about him being gone.

"*Jesus.* I'm sorry."

"Me too. He was a good father."

"Good. I appreciate that." The tension in his voice was palpable. "Did you love him?"

Not like I love you. "I loved him like a close friend who I'd known forever, and I loved him for saving me from having to give up our baby. But everything changed after Lucas was born."

"When's Lucas's birthday?"

"March thirteenth. He was born three weeks early, which

worked in my father's favor. Since I had broken up with Josh the week before I came to the ranch, nobody questioned the timing."

"*March thirteenth*," he repeated with a small smile.

"And his middle name is John."

Disbelief rose in his eyes, but as quickly as it appeared, it was gone, replaced with gratitude. "Thank you for giving him that piece of me."

Struggling against a rush of emotions, she said, "Even after everything I was tricked into believing, I still couldn't let you go. After he was born, I wanted to reach out to you so badly, to show you the beautiful little boy we made, but that letter..." She paused with the painful memories. "The idea that you might turn me away again was too much to bear."

"That *fucking* letter." He set a serious stare on her. "Is that why things got harder with Josh? Did he know you wanted to reach out to me?"

"No. I never told him, but he knew how much I loved you. He was there when I was crying myself to sleep every night. But Josh loved Lucas, and he loved me. I mean, as much as he could love someone who didn't reciprocate the same kind of love. It was just hard to be parents and keep up with school. We were kids, and there was a lot of pressure. I was happy when I was with Lucas, but I was heartbroken over you, and furious with my parents. Between school, Lucas, and being so unhappy, I had nothing left to give Josh. Toward the end of our relationship, he thought if we had a child together it might help. We tried, but I never got pregnant. Eventually we grew apart. He started partying and staying out later. I didn't blame him. The situation was so unfair."

Seeley turned his chair toward her. "I'm sorry I couldn't

stop that farce from happening. If I had known the truth, I would've been there for you and Lucas every fucking minute of every day." He leaned forward, pulling her to the edge of her chair, and embraced her. "It kills me that you had to go through all of that, thinking the worst about me, and us, and…" He held her tighter. "I'm so damn sorry, darlin'."

"It's not your fault. We were both manipulated. I just never realized how badly."

He drew back, his eyes blazing. "Your father is going to pay for this."

"As much as I want him to, we have to be careful. I've seen what he's capable of."

"He can't hurt us anymore, but I don't want Lucas to think I'm a monster if I go after his grandfather to set things straight."

"My parents haven't been a part of our lives for a long time. When Josh and I first got married, I figured I'd be as ruthless as my parents were and let them pay for college and vet school to ensure Lucas and I had a solid future."

"That was smart. It's amazing you could think straight with all that was going on."

"Thanks." She appreciated that he recognized how difficult it was for her. "But it ended up being too hard to fake for long. I never went to see them and didn't answer their calls. I only came back to Colorado for quick trips to see my grandmother, and I didn't tell my parents because I didn't want to see them or get her in trouble. I missed my grandmother so much, and I hated the threat of my parents making me feel like I couldn't see her."

"I'm sure she missed you, too."

"She did. We talked on the phone a lot. But my parents would show up on my doorstep without notice, and I had no choice but to let them see Lucas. I hated that with a vengeance. Then one day Lucas said he wanted to be like Grandpa Marvin when he grew up, and the thought made me physically ill. I'd had enough. I didn't care if I had to live in a homeless shelter. I needed to protect Lucas and get out of my fake marriage, but to do that, I had to completely cut my parents off. I didn't want to involve my grandmother, but I had just graduated from college and I'd been accepted to vet school. I didn't want to give that up, so I called her and asked if I could borrow whatever money I couldn't get through student loans. She fought me on paying her back, but I needed to feel like I was standing on my own two feet. She helped me pay for a room on a small farm, and for babysitting, both of which she paid directly so there was no way for my father to trace it to my account."

"And your parents let you go without a fight after all that?"

"I wish. There were weeks of ignoring my father's calls and threats to take away Lucas. But I told my parents I'd get a restraining order against them, and you know how they are about their precious public image."

"What a fucking nightmare. What about Josh? Where was he in all that?"

"He was ready for our relationship to end, too, and by then he understood why I needed to sever ties with my parents. But he loved Lucas and continued seeing him. And as I said, two months later, he was killed. We hadn't filed divorce papers, so his insurance money came to me. That was the one piece of advice I was glad my father had given us when Lucas was born. He told us we had to have life insurance, and in the end that was my savior. I paid my grandmother back and was able to pay our way as long as I was frugal."

"Jesus, Jule. That must have been awful for you, and I can

only imagine how devastating it was for Lucas."

"It was awful for both of us. I blamed myself. Josh and I were fighting a lot back then, and he'd gone out partying and was hit when he was crossing a street. If he hadn't married me, he may never have started partying and maybe he'd still be alive."

Seeley took her hand in his. "You can't take on that responsibility. He made a choice to marry you. Nobody said it would be easy."

"I know, but still."

"How did Lucas handle it?"

"He had a hard time letting me out of his sight, which was understandable. The older couple who owned the farm where we lived were wonderful. They referred us to a grief counselor. It took a long time to find our new normal after that, but we made it. Eventually I finished vet school, and thanks to you pushing me that summer to believe in myself, I became a vet instead of a vet tech."

"All I did was point out the obvious. You were always impressive as hell, darlin'. I knew you were strong, but this…" He shook his head. "You've lost your family, your husband, your grandmother, and you believed awful things about me for years. It's hard to believe you're still standing, much less raised our son on your own and managed to make a career for yourself."

"For the longest time, I wondered if the pain of my parents' betrayal, and the pain of yours, would ever go away," she confessed. "But years of therapy helped me accept who my parents are and move past it. The strange thing is, therapy didn't do a damn thing to help me move past my feelings for you."

He leaned forward again, putting his hands on her outer

thighs, bringing their faces closer together. "What we have has always been too big to deny."

Her pulse quickened, his declaration filling the space between them like a living, breathing entity, the truth ensnaring them like a lasso, binding them together. His gaze bored into her, as if he were daring her to refute his claim.

She couldn't refute the obvious.

She wanted to climb into his lap, to be wrapped in the safety of his arms again. Not that she needed protecting. She hadn't needed that in years. It was the comfort of *him* she longed for. That feeling she'd never found in anyone else's arms.

But this wasn't the time to be selfish. The only person that mattered right now was Lucas, and that's what she focused on.

"There's no denying our chemistry." She reached for her wineglass, breaking their connection, and went for levity. "I think I'm going to need a lot more therapy now."

THERE WERE SO many things Doc wanted to know about her and Lucas, but it had been an emotional night, and he didn't want to overwhelm her any more than he already had. So he bit back the questions about *her* that still remained and focused on their son.

"The most important thing is making sure Lucas gets through this without totally screwing him up for the rest of his life. Maybe we should talk to my mother or another therapist about the best way to handle this. I don't want to lie to him. There's been enough deceit already."

"I agree," she said, glad he was putting Lucas, and honesty, first. "But I think I can handle talking to him."

"Do you want me to be there when you do it?"

"*No*," she said quickly. "I don't know how he's going to react, and he's not exactly your biggest fan at the moment."

"Right." He'd cursed himself a hundred times for being an asshole. "I'm going to make that up to both of you. If you change your mind or want to talk to someone about it, let me know."

"I will."

Seeley finished his beer and set the bottle down. "Can you tell me about him? What's he like? What grade is he in? Is he a good kid?"

"He's an amazing kid." Her smile reached her eyes. "He's funny and incredibly smart and compassionate, and he's a *good* person, Seeley. He likes working with his hands and figuring things out. From the time he was little, if something broke, he'd get his plastic tools and try to fix it. And he *loves* horses. He's been riding since he was little, when we moved to the farm, and if he's ever in a bad mood, a few hours with the horses usually perks him up."

"Like a certain girl I used to know."

She smiled.

"What about the move? When did you get here, and how did Lucas handle it? It couldn't have been easy at his age."

"We moved at the beginning of June, right after his school year ended. Leaving his friends was hard on him. He spent so much time in the barn the first few weeks, I was worried he'd start sleeping there. But he settled in. He got his learner's permit this summer, which he's really excited about. I, on the other hand, am terrified every time I take him driving."

"Is he a good driver?"

"Yeah, he's careful. He loves old cars, and he has some respect for vehicles, which is good."

"And school? You said he's smart, but does he like it?"

"As much as teens can like school, I guess. He just started his sophomore year, and he's making friends."

"That's great. The way he stood up to me was admirable. You two must be close."

"We are. I'm lucky we get along so well. Although, teenagerhood has its challenges, and he definitely has a lot of you in him."

Seeley grinned. "Why do you say that?"

"Because you're alike in so many ways. You saw him. He's got your build, your height, your hair and nose. Sometimes the way he smiles or stands catches me off guard, and my thoughts stumble for a minute."

"I noticed he's an arm drummer. Did Josh do that, too?"

"No. That's been Lucas's go-to defensive stance since he was eight or nine. As if that barrier makes him untouchable. The first time he did it, my heart nearly stopped. I thought I was seeing things. But he's like you in other ways, too. He's got your confidence and riding skills, and from the time he was little, nothing was fast or dangerous enough for him. He loves roping cattle, barrel racing, and bull riding. He's good, too."

"Bull riding, huh?" He couldn't stop a prideful grin from breaking free.

"That's why we were at the hospital. He fell off a bull. He was wearing a helmet, and they checked him out at the competition, but he seemed a little off right after, so I took him to the hospital. He was fine. He didn't have a concussion or anything. Let me tell you, there's a huge difference between cheering you on when you were bull riding and watching my son out there. I'm terrified every time he climbs on a bull. Do you still ride?"

"No." He watched the flames flickering in the firepit, rubbing one fist with his other hand, his chest tightening. "I haven't ridden since that summer."

"*Oh*. That's too bad," she said compassionately. "You were good. Why did you stop?"

"It was too hard to focus." He cocked his head, meeting her gaze. "I kept picturing you cheering me on, and I knew I'd end up hurting myself. Better to focus on schoolwork and helping at the ranch when I was home."

"I'm sorry I ruined that for you."

"You didn't, Jule. Your father did." He sat up, holding her gaze. "I know we've got years to catch up on, and we're not the same people we were back then. But I want to be in your and Lucas's life."

"Seeley—"

He held up his hand. "Please let me finish. We obviously still have feelings for each other, and I'd like to see where that takes us as time allows. We have a lot to deal with, and of course Lucas has to come first, and if you don't want to see what's still between us, that's okay. I mean, I'll fucking hate it, but…"

She laughed softly.

He smiled, but he was worried. They had explosive chemistry, but they had something so much bigger and deeper. He hoped to hell she wasn't going to say that having sex had been nothing more than years of repressed desires breaking free and pleaded his case. "You need to know that even if you decide you don't want to pursue anything with me, it's not going to change my wanting to be in Lucas's life. I'm here for him whether or not you want anything more with me. And as the mother of my child and the woman I've never stopped loving, I'll be there to help you from this day forward, even if you don't want there to be an *us*. No hard feelings."

She opened her mouth to speak, but he held up a finger, quickly adding, "But for the record, I think that would be a big mistake on your part. I've got issues, like anyone else, but I'm an honest, loyal man, I'm easy on the eyes, and you know I'm great in bed," he said playfully, earning another smile. "I'm not the cocky, carefree kid I was when you knew me before, and you might not like that about me, and I work a lot." He realized what he'd said. "*Shit.* I'm not doing a very good job of selling myself, am I?"

"Seeley, *stop*," she said with a laugh. "You don't have to sell me on who you are. I'd like to see if there's more to us, too, but Lucas has to come first."

"Of course. I wouldn't expect anything less."

"I know. I should probably go."

He wanted her to stay and talk all night, but he knew better than to put that out there. "I'll walk you to your truck."

As they headed around the side of the house, he put a hand on her lower back and said, "You know, nobody calls me Seeley anymore."

"What do they call you?"

"Doc. It's my road name."

"*Doc.* I like it. It makes sense. Do you want me to call you that?"

"No. I like hearing you call me Seeley far too much." He opened her truck door and then took her hand and pulled her into an embrace, breathing her in. "I can't believe you're back."

She tipped her face up, those baby blues drawing him in.

"Can I kiss you good night?"

"Yes," she whispered.

He touched his lips to hers in a tender kiss, but she rose up onto her toes, and he couldn't resist taking it a little deeper, holding her a little tighter. She moaned, and it took everything he had not to back her up against that truck and kiss her senseless. "I still love kissing you," he said softly.

"*Mm*. Me too."

He kissed her again, slower and more sensually, groaning as he forced himself to break away. "You have to go."

"Yeah." She sank down to her heels and trapped her lower lip between her teeth, looking too damn sexy.

"*Jesus*, Jule. Don't look at me like that," he gritted out. "Get in your truck before I lose my mind."

"Yeah, I'd better go." She climbed into her truck.

"Do you think I could get your phone number?"

She laughed. "Why do I feel sixteen again?"

He put her number in his contacts as she rattled it off, and then he texted her so she'd have his number, too, and pocketed his phone. "When are you thinking about breaking the news to Lucas?"

"As soon as I can, which will probably be tomorrow when he gets home from school."

"I'm here if you need me." He closed her door, fighting the urge to lean in for another kiss as she started the truck. "Thank you for raising our son when it might have been easier to make a different choice."

"There was never a choice to be made. I wanted you, and I wanted him. End of story."

Fuck it. He leaned in, sliding his hand to the nape of her neck, and kissed the hell out of her. When their lips finally parted, she sighed dreamily. "Drive safely, Peaches."

As he stepped back from the window, she whispered, "*Peaches.*"

He stood there, watching her drive away until he could no longer see or hear her truck. Then he went back to sit by the fire. When enough time had passed that he was pretty sure she was off the road and home safely, he took out his phone, thumbing out, *That wasn't the end of our story, darlin'. We're just getting started*, and sent the text.

Chapter Eight

JULIETTE'S PHONE VIBRATED in her pocket as she finished washing the mixing bowl she'd used to make cookies. She set it in the dish drainer and took out her phone. Her pulse quickened at the sight of Seeley's name on the text bubble. She hadn't responded to his text last night. Her emotions had been reeling when she'd gotten home, and when she'd read it—*That wasn't the end of our story, darlin'. We're just getting started*—she'd wanted to grab ahold of it like a brass ring. But she couldn't, because as good as it felt, she was too scared that their new beginning might mean an end to the safety and security that Lucas counted on. His world was about to change, and she had no idea what that would mean for any of them.

She'd been surprised when Seeley had texted this morning. But he hadn't pushed for more. He'd said he appreciated their talk last night, and if she changed her mind and wanted him to be there when she told Lucas, to let him know. She wanted to do it alone, but it felt really good knowing she didn't *have to* handle something alone after all these years of feeling like the entire world rested on her shoulders.

She swiped the screen to read the new text.

Seeley: *YGT. TNYCD!* He'd added a flexed biceps emoji, a thumbs-up emoji, and a heart.

Memories of their youthful coded messages brought a smile. They'd had to text in code because her father had monitored her phone, and she never knew how much he could see. That's why they'd never taken pictures using her phone, either. It seemed like he had spies everywhere, and nothing was off-limits or too far-reaching for him. She knew the *YGT* meant *You've got this*, but it took her a few minutes to puzzle out the rest of the message. *There's nothing you can't do!*

Seeley's support brought a rush of emotions. For all these years, she'd been a pillar of strength, making decisions for her and Lucas and never second-guessing or regretting them or allowing herself to lean on anyone. But she never realized how alone she'd felt until now. Not that she was looking for an easier road or for anyone to take over. It had been a long time since someone cared enough about her to cheer her on.

The oven timer chimed, drawing her from her thoughts.

She pulled a tray of Lucas's favorite mint chocolate chip cookies out of the oven and glanced out the window toward the barn. Lucas had gone straight there when he'd gotten off the school bus, like he did most days. She should be thankful that he took his chores seriously and always made time for their horses, Warrior and Maxine, before doing anything else. But she couldn't help missing the days when he'd run off the bus and into her arms as if he'd waited all day to see her.

She wasn't selfish like her own parents, needing control. She'd worked hard to help Lucas become independent, teaching him to believe in himself and to think outside the box when problems arose. She'd never take that away from him just to appease her own maternal longing.

She spotted him coming out of the barn. His hair was a tousled mess, his backpack slung over his shoulder, and he was thumbing something into his phone as he made his way toward the house. He wore a crooked grin that she knew would melt hearts one day, if it wasn't already. He stopped walking, laughed at something on his phone, and took a selfie. He went back to texting and headed up the hill.

Guess you are already melting hearts.

She wished she could freeze time so he could continue loving life, safe from the deception and heartache her family had caused. But as hard as this was going to be, she knew it was the right thing to do.

She tossed the oven mitt onto the counter and poured herself a glass of water. She was reaching for a plate when Lucas came through the kitchen door, his eyes still trained on his phone. She watched his brows knit as he sniffed the air.

"You made cookies?" He pocketed his phone and dropped his backpack.

"Mint chocolate chip." She transferred several to a plate and set it on the table for him. "Want some milk?"

He looked at her like she'd lost her mind. "I'm not *five*." He opened the fridge and took out a Dr Pepper. "Are we still fixing the barn and fences Saturday, or…?" He grabbed a cookie and took a bite.

Her grandmother had been incredibly generous to leave the mortgage-free property to her, but she hadn't been the best at keeping things up the last several years. The house wasn't in too bad shape, although little things kept breaking and it definitely needed updating, but the barn and fences hadn't fared quite so well. Her grandmother must have either planned on having the barn fixed or had hired someone to do it and they'd backed out, because the wood and supplies were all there.

"Yes. They're calling for rain Sunday, and I want to patch the holes in the roof and the siding before it gets here. Why? Are you planning a hot date?"

He scoffed and pulled out his phone. He thumbed out another text, then shoved his phone into his pocket again.

"Who are you texting?"

"A friend." He finished his cookie.

"Does your friend have a name?"

He bit into another cookie and spoke around a mouthful. "Layla."

"Jade's niece?" Lucas had gone with her to Jade's house a few weeks ago, and they'd met two of Jade's sweet nieces at the barn, Layla, who was fourteen, and Adriana, who was a few years younger. They were getting ready to go on a trail ride with Jade's husband, Rex, a strikingly handsome rancher with the biggest muscles Juliette had ever seen. That is, until she'd seen Cowboy outside the hospital.

"Yeah. She goes to my school. She's cool for a freshman."

Juliette had talked with Lucas about the birds and the bees a few years ago and had reiterated the importance of being careful when he'd started high school. But in California, he'd always hung out with groups of friends. As far as she knew, he hadn't been into any *one* girl. This was new territory. She treaded carefully, picking up a cookie, trying to act casual and not like she had bigger issues to discuss with him. "Is this a friendship, or are you two an item?"

"Mom." He stuffed the rest of his cookie in his mouth.

She smiled at his exasperation. "What? I'm just asking."

"Whatever. We're friends, okay? Don't get weird about it."

"Okay, no weirdness. I'm glad you're friends. But she's my

boss's niece, and she's young, so please be good to her."

"I'm not a dick." He snagged another cookie.

"I wasn't implying that you are." She didn't want to fight with him, especially now. "I need to talk to you about something. Can we sit down for a minute?"

"Am I in trouble?" he asked tentatively.

He asked that every time she said they needed to talk, and it always made her wonder whether she'd missed something. On the heels of that came a bigger thought. It made sense that guys hated to hear the phrase *we need to talk*. Their reluctance probably came from times like this, when a parent had to talk about something big. "No, you're not in trouble."

His brows slanted. "Are you sick or something?"

"*No*. Why would you ask that?"

"Because the last time you made cookies and said we had to talk was when Grandma Hazel died."

Her chest constricted. "Nobody is dying. Can we please sit down?"

"Yeah, hold on." He put more cookies on his plate before sitting down.

Juliette's stomach knotted as she pulled out a chair and sat down. She worried with her hands, wishing she'd never lied to him regardless of what she'd thought back then.

He ate another cookie, sitting back in his chair. It was hard to believe she was only a little older than he was now when she'd gotten pregnant. She'd felt so grown-up that summer with Seeley, making future plans together, excited about her life for the first time ever. As much as she wanted to hold Lucas when she told him the truth, to try to soften the blow, she couldn't treat him like he was a little boy for this conversation. He was on the cusp of manhood, and he probably felt like he was grown-up, just as she had at that age.

He crossed his arms, drumming his fingers. It broke her heart knowing there was no barrier strong enough to block the hurt she was about to dole out. She'd spent last night and all of today figuring out how to tell him the truth, but now that she was looking at her boy's sweet face, it was hard to remember what she'd come up with.

Her throat felt thick, anxiety prickling her skin. Mustering all of her courage, she said, "Honey, you know how I told you that my parents aren't very nice people and that my father has been known to do some bad things?"

"Yeah. That's why we don't see them."

"That's right. Well, a long time ago, he did something to me that changed the course of my life, and yours, and other people's, too. But I never knew the full extent of what he'd done until last night."

"Does this have to do with that Seeley dude?"

"Yes." She took a deep breath and looked him in the eye. "It has to do with all of us, and with your father." It felt strange calling Josh his father after last night, but nothing about this conversation felt normal.

His brows slanted. "What is it?"

"It's a little complicated. I dated your father when I was your age. We were great friends and we dated for a long time, but I broke up with him right before I interned at Redemption Ranch the summer before my senior year, where I met Seeley. His family, the Whiskeys, own the ranch. They rescue horses and help people who need a fresh start. Seeley was nineteen, and I was sixteen." She swallowed hard. "And we fell madly in love."

"I *knew* there was more to that story," he hissed.

"I told you he was important to me. My father found out

about us, and he was furious. He took me away from the ranch and forbade me from seeing Seeley. He threatened to ruin him and his family and close down the ranch if Seeley ever came near me again."

He sat forward. "Did Seeley take advantage of you or something? Because if he did—"

"*No*," she said adamantly, shutting that thought down. "He's not like that. He always treated me well, and I know you didn't have a great first impression of him, but there's a good reason he was upset with me. Your grandfather didn't like that he was from a blue-collar biker family and not a prominent family like your father's."

"What a dick."

"Yes, he was. I was devastated, and I found out a few weeks later that I was pregnant." She leaned forward and put her hand on his leg, trying not to let the tears that threatened fall. "Honey, Seeley Whiskey is your biological father."

"What the hell are you talking about?" He pushed to his feet. "*No*. I know my father, and that asshole is not him."

"*Lucas.*" She got up, reaching for him, but he stalked away. "I know this is hard to hear, but Seeley *is* your biological father, and he's not an asshole. He didn't even know you were his child until yesterday. We were both lied to."

"Have *you* known all this time that I was *his*?"

"Yes, but—"

"You've been lying to me forever?" he shouted, tears spilling from his eyes. "Did *Dad* know?"

"Yes, he knew, and he loved you as his own from day one. We were trying to protect you."

"Protect me by *lying* to me? What else are you lying about? Are you even my real mother?"

"How can you ask me that? *Of course* I'm your mother. Please let me explain. It wasn't my fault. My father deceived all of us—"

"I don't care what Grandpa did. *You* lied to me! I can't even believe this." He grabbed his head with both hands, keeling over like he was in pain.

She dragged air into her lungs, feeling his pain as her own. "Honey, you have to understand. I got a letter that your grandfather must have either written or had someone else write, but I thought it was from Seeley, telling me that Seeley wanted nothing to do with us, and—"

"And you decided it was better to *lie* to me? This is messed up. You had years to tell me the truth." He stormed out of the kitchen to the front door and threw it open.

"*Lucas John*, do not walk out on me. I am still your mother."

He turned with one foot out the door, the hatred in his eyes slaying her. "Are you? I don't know what to believe anymore."

Her tears sprang free. "Lucas, *please*. There's so much more you need to know. Just let me explain."

"I've heard enough," he snapped. "I'll be in the barn."

"Lucas!" Her heart shattered. She ran out the door, but he was already halfway to the barn.

"Leave me alone!" he shouted, and sprinted through the barn doors.

Her sobs broke free, and she crumpled to the porch, crying for her son's heartache and for the way this would change their relationship. She cried for the teenage girl who had been deceived and for the young man who had loved her and lost them both.

She cried until she had no more tears left.

Then she forced herself to get up and go inside. She washed her face, needing to pull herself together before Lucas came back in. Parenting was so fucking hard.

It was hell not going down to the barn to try to reason with him. But he deserved time to process what he'd learned. Hopefully once he calmed down, they'd talk and she'd be able to explain what had happened.

She tried to busy herself cleaning up and doing laundry, but mostly she worried and paced.

When she couldn't take it anymore, she tucked two cookies into a napkin as a peace offering, put on her boots, and headed down to the barn. Greeted by the scents of hay and horses, where she, too, had always found solace, she called out, "Lucas?"

Her horse nickered, beckoning her like the elegant, liver chestnut Morgan queen she was. Maxine had been her grandmother's last broodmare before retiring several years ago. She was always Juliette's favorite. Juliette petted her, and Maxine pressed her head into Juliette's sternum as if she knew Juliette needed that extra bit of love. As she leaned in to kiss Maxine's head, she realized Warrior wasn't in his stall.

Juliette's stomach bottomed out, and she ran out the back door. "Lucas!" She scanned the pasture, but she knew he was gone. She never let him ride when he was angry. She worried he'd make a mistake, or take too big a risk and get hurt.

She quickly saddled Maxine, hoping she wasn't too far behind Lucas, and cursed herself for not coming down sooner as she climbed on. With her heart in her throat, she leaned forward, guiding Maxine at a fast clip toward the entrance to the trail she and Lucas had ridden most often. But fast wasn't nearly fast enough.

With a tap of her heels, and a "*Hya!*" the horse bolted up the trailhead.

Chapter Nine

AFTER FINISHING HIS evening rounds, Doc checked his phone for the umpteenth time and cursed at the blank screen. It had been a hell of a day, and he'd hoped to hear from Juliette by now. He'd been up half the night sick with worry about how the truth would affect Lucas, and he hated not being there when Juliette broke the news to him. But to Lucas he was an outsider, and he trusted that Juliette knew what was best for their son.

He was still grappling with the fact that he *had* a son and trying to decide what to do about Juliette's asshole father.

He pocketed his phone as he headed out of the clinic to catch dinner at the main house and found Dare and Cowboy leaning against a UTV, their arms crossed, their cowboy hats firmly in place. Last night he'd gone to see his parents after Juliette left and told them what was going on in a furious explosion of hurt and anger and a deep-seated need for vengeance. His parents were as angry as he was at what Juliette's father had done. His mother had shed tears over what Juliette had been through, for the time Doc had missed with his son, and the years they'd missed out on with their grandson. Doc and his father had talked into the night about retaliating against

Juliette's father, and this morning he'd explained the situation to his brothers and Sasha, and they were as angry as the rest of them.

They'd all checked in with him throughout the day, but their hovering didn't bother him this time. This was a lot to deal with, and they were worried about Juliette and Lucas, too. He eyed his brothers curiously. "What's going on?"

"We missed your pretty face." Dare smirked.

"How's Queenie?" Cowboy asked.

Queenie was the name Doc had given the rescue horse who had been in critical condition when she'd come in yesterday. He'd named the other horse Contessa, the regal names chosen to give them back some of the dignity that had been stolen from them. They'd been found tied to trees, left to starve in an empty field. They were emaciated, with varying degrees of cuts, skin infections, hair loss, and injuries. If Doc ever found the fucker who'd done that to them, he'd put the asshole six feet under. "She's strong. She's hanging in there."

"Good, and you?" Cowboy asked. "Any word from Juliette?"

Doc shook his head. "Not yet."

"Then get your ass in the vehicle," Dare said.

"Why? Where are we going?"

"To get some grub," Dare said.

"And don't even think about telling us you're not hungry or you want to be alone, because that shit ain't happening," Cowboy added.

"Anyone ever tell you you're a pushy motherfucker?" Doc asked as they climbed into the vehicle.

Cowboy chuckled. "Just about everyone I know."

"Have you decided what to do about Juliette's old man yet?"

Dare started the UTV.

"Not yet. I called Reggie Steele. He's seeing what he can dig up on him." Reggie had grown up in Trusty, Colorado, a nearby town. He was a private investigator whose brothers were Dark Knights in the Harborside chapter. Reggie had been instrumental in connecting Sully with her biological sister and helping to shut down the cult she'd escaped from. Doc also asked Reggie to find out what he could about Ana, the housekeeper Juliette had given the letters to, and to track down Ana's brother, who had supposedly given those letters to him.

When they pulled up to the main house, Birdie's yellow Camaro was driving into the parking lot, music blaring out her open windows, and she was singing "Can't Tame Her" at the top of her lungs. It was one of her favorite songs.

"I'll catch up with you guys." Doc headed for Birdie's car. His *I'm fine* responses to her texts earlier in the week had finally put an end to them, but he hadn't had a chance to fill her in on what went down yesterday.

She parked and climbed out of her car, belting out the lyrics and dancing, oblivious to the lack of music *and* to Doc closing in on her. She wore bright pink cowgirl boots, a wide-brimmed pink hat, and a one-piece blue-and-white leopard-print shorts romper with flouncy sleeves.

He crossed his arms, chuckling to himself as she swung her hips into the driver's side door, slamming it shut, then threw her arms over her head and began singing a different song. Something about slowing down and making it last as she spun around, nearly colliding with him, and let out a surprised squeal.

"How's it going, Bird?"

"You tell me. You look kind of serious. Is something wrong?

Oh *crap*. Sasha didn't tell you about my date, did she? I'm going to kill her. I told her not to say anything."

"What *date?*"

She barked out a laugh. "I'm kidding! I love doing that to you. You should see your face! But seriously, after everything that went down last weekend, I did you a solid. You're going to thank me. I met the perfect girl for you, and I even got her number."

"Birdie—"

Hands flailing, she said, "Hear me out. You know what they say. The best way to get over a woman is to get under a new one. Or, I guess in your case, on top of a new one, or behind her. Anyway, I know you've gotten around since you and Juliette were an item, but those other women were just extended stays, and I really like this girl. She could be the one."

"Birdie, *stop.*"

"Why? I think you're going to really like her."

"I'm *not* in the market for a woman."

"You always say that, but then you're with someone a few weeks later."

"I'm done with that." He leveled her with a serious stare. "Listen to me. It turns out that kid that was with Juliette at the hospital is my son."

Her eyes bloomed wide. "Your *son?* Holy shitake mushrooms. Really?"

"Yes. His name is Lucas. I didn't want you to hear it from someone else first." He told her the whole sordid story.

"Ohmygod. *Doc.*" She touched his arm. "Are you okay? Is Juliette okay?"

"Yeah. It's a lot to deal with, and I'm worried about them, but I'm looking forward to getting to know Lucas, and Juliette *again.*"

"And pummeling her father, I hope. You must want to tear him apart. *I* want to tear him apart. I bet Dad's ready to mess that bastard up good. I want to know who wrote that letter and what happened to the letters *she* wrote to *you*."

"We don't know any of that yet. But I'm going to get to the bottom of it."

She sighed and shook her head. "A secret baby. A second chance at your first love." Her eyes brightened. "This is like reality TV, only better."

"Can we skip the extra drama, please?"

"Sorry." She reached into her pocket and held her fist out toward him. "I think you need these more than I do right now." She opened her hand, revealing three individually wrapped truffles.

He smiled. "I'm good. Thanks. Let's go eat."

She put the chocolates back in her pocket. "Didn't Dad ever teach you to wrap it before you tap it?"

"*Jesus*, Birdie."

She laughed. "I couldn't resist." She wrapped her hand around his arm as they headed up to the entrance. "God, Doc. You're a *dad*."

"Pretty wild, huh?"

"I'll say. And I'm an auntie." She beamed up at him. "I'm going to be the coolest auntie *ever*. Sasha can be the calm, responsible auntie, and I'll be the one he comes to for dating and fashion advice. He's cute. I bet he's got a flock of girls after him."

"How about we let him get used to the idea that I'm his father before you get him riled up about dating?"

She sighed dramatically. "Fine."

Doc opened the door for her, but instead of walking inside, she wrapped her arms around him, hugging him tight. He put his free arm around her. "What's this for?"

She smiled up at him, looking sweetly impish. "I thought you could use a hug."

"Thanks, Bird." They headed inside.

"I'll always have your back. I guess I need to find a new wingman." As they walked past the two-story gathering space, heading for the dining area, she said, "Since you're off the market, maybe I'll work on finding Dwight a woman." Dwight Cornwall was a retired navy commander and a Dark Knight. He'd worked at the ranch since Doc was a teenager.

"Maybe you can lay off your matchmaking missions, since they never seem to work."

"Where have you been? Sasha and Ezra would never have gotten together if I didn't push her to kiss him."

"I don't even want to know," he said as they walked into the dining area.

Laughter and conversation rang out from around three large farmhouse-style tables and the buffet, where people were filling their plates and chatting. Between Doc's family, the men and women who worked and lived on the ranch, and the clients who were going through their programs, nearly every seat was spoken for. Doc couldn't remember a time his family hadn't eaten a meal with the people they worked and lived with. This was all he knew, and after the summer he'd lost Juliette, it had become his saving grace. This place, these people, his *family*, was all he'd ever wanted.

Until last night.

Juliette had claimed such a big part of him when they were younger, he'd felt like a piece of himself was missing ever since.

As overjoyed as he was that she was back and they had a shot at a second chance, he couldn't shake the feeling that another piece of himself was missing. But while he'd always known exactly what Juliette's missing piece looked and felt like, this new missing piece was elusive. Like a shadow, undefined yet present. Leaving him unsettled and desperate to fill in the blanks, aching to spread his wings and gather his son and Juliette beneath them, so nobody could ever hurt them again.

"Who missed me?" Birdie called out, drawing him from his thoughts.

Several people shouted greetings, Gus's chirpy voice rising above the rest. "Birdie!" He ran over and threw his arms around her. "Did you bring me any chocolate?"

"I sure did." She handed Gus a chocolate, and he tugged her over to the table where Sasha, Ezra, Dare, Billie, Cowboy, and Sully were sitting with some of the ranch hands.

Tiny looked over at Doc and lifted his chin in a silent question. *Any news?*

Doc shook his head, and his father gave a curt nod.

Doc headed up to the buffet and grabbed a plate and a bowl, stepping into line beside his mother, who was perusing her options. Dwight never failed to make something for everyone. Tonight they had beef-and-sausage chili, homemade biscuits, vegetarian lasagna, and an array of salads and other vegetables.

"Hi, sweetheart," his mother said with a compassionate smile. She looked pretty in a green blouse and jeans. "How are you holding up? Any word from Juliette?"

"Not yet." He put some chili in his bowl.

"They have a lot to talk about. It could take all night before you hear something."

He looked at her with new eyes. She had been there for him through his roughest times and shittiest attitudes, had taken his late-night phone calls when he was at his wit's end over one thing or another during college and vet school, and had never once made him feel bad about unloading on her. She had a knack for listening and for easing him off the ledge without pushing or preaching. It was that innate ability that drew the truth from him now. "The wait is killing me. I want to be there for them, and I can't if I'm not physically with them."

"I understand why you feel that way, but giving Juliette the space she's asked for *is* being there for them. The hardest things in life are the ones we can't control, and Juliette has had to deal with more than her share, and from what you've said, it doesn't sound like she's had anyone other than Hazel to help her through in a very long time."

"And that relationship was tainted by her father." That truth tasted bitter.

"That's right. I'm sure a big part of Juliette would love nothing more than to hand over tough conversations like the one she and Lucas are dealing with and let you handle it. But it sounds like she's too strong of a mama bear to do that, which is a good thing. Parenting is hard, sweetheart, but as difficult as this is for you, it's even harder for them."

"I know, and I hate that, too."

She put some lasagna and a biscuit on her plate. "I'd like to throttle her father for the crap he pulled."

"Throttling is too good for that bastard." He grabbed a biscuit, but he didn't think he could stomach anything. As they stepped away from the buffet, he asked the question that had been eating away at him. "I remember what it was like to be a teenager. Those were confusing years, and sometimes anger would come out of nowhere. What if it's been too long? What if I never get a fair shot with Lucas?"

"Oh, honey. With patience, understanding, and love, there's always a way. It might have felt like your anger came out of nowhere, but it didn't. It came from thinking you knew best and wanting to do whatever *you* wanted, rather than what you had to do. That's typical teenage behavior. Lucas's world is going to be turned upside down. He may not want to hear the truth right now, but one day he will, and when he does, that'll be your chance to show *your son* that what that awful man did is *not* how we treat our own."

"I hope I get that chance. What if I fuck it up?"

"You've never messed up anything that you cared about."

"Yes, I did. When I saw Juliette's engagement announcement, I believed it. I should've known she'd been forced into marrying someone else. I should have fought harder."

"Do not fool yourself into believing that. We were all given those facts, and we *all* believed them. We were grossly deceived. And I know you, sweetie. You won't screw this up."

He wasn't so sure. "I know nothing about parenting."

"But you know how to love. The parenting stuff will come. Every teen pushes their parents to see where the line lies between loving them and giving up on them. Your job as a parent is to make it impossible for him to find that line because it doesn't exist. When Lucas tells you he hates you—which he will, because all teens do at one point or another—when he calls you names or says you don't know squat, you set him straight so he knows the pecking order. But you also tell him you love him, so when he rests his head on his pillow at night and his feelings are darting like pinballs from badass teenager to guilt-ridden kid over the things he's said or done, the one *consistent* thing he feels is that he's loved." She touched his cheek. "That's what we've always done with each of you."

As she went to sit with Tiny, Doc thought about the night he'd gotten drunk, intending to hunt down Juliette's father. When Tiny had hauled his ass out of that truck, Doc had fought with everything he'd had, punching and cursing, shouting all the things his mother had just mentioned, and worse. His father hadn't even flinched. He'd grabbed Doc by the shirt, lifted him off his feet, and pinned him against the side of the truck, looking him dead in the eyes as he said, *You think killing a person makes you a man? Think again. All that hate you feel for that motherfucker will turn inward, and you'll be rotting in a prison cell, unable to look in the mirror at the monster you've become. And that sweet girl you love? She won't be able to look at you, either.* Doc had been ornery enough, and drunk enough, to continue shouting horrible things at him. His father had hauled him forward, getting right in his face, and said, *You want me gone? You're gonna have to turn that gun on me, because I love you too damn much to ever give up on you.*

Doc's phone rang, startling him from the memory. He pulled his phone from his pocket, his heart thundering at the sight of Juliette's name on the screen. He put the phone to his ear, turning his back to the others. "Hey."

"Is Lucas there?" Juliette sounded frantic.

His gut seized. "No. Why would he be here? What happened?"

"He was so upset, he stormed out to the barn. I thought he needed time alone to cool off, but when I went down there, he and his horse were gone. I went looking for him on the trails, but it's been almost *two* hours. I thought he might've gone to confront you. But now that I'm thinking about it, you're too far away, and—"

"I'm on my way. Stay there in case he comes back, and don't worry, darlin'. We'll find him." He strode across the room to his father.

Tiny must have sensed the gravity of the situation, because he pushed to his feet, lifting his chin in question.

"My boy's missing."

"I'll rally the men," Tiny said.

Chapter Ten

TINY PUT OUT the word to the Dark Knights that one of their own was missing, and while Cowboy and Dare loaded ATVs onto trucks and horses into trailers, Doc climbed on his motorcycle and sped over to Juliette's, as concerned about her as he was about Lucas.

She ran outside as he climbed off his bike and landed in his arms. "He's never run away before. He hates me for lying."

"He doesn't hate you. He's hurt and confused."

"I shouldn't have let him go to the barn alone, but he was *so* angry. This is all my fault. I was stupid for lying to him for all these years. He'll never forgive me."

Doc took her by the shoulders, his chest constricting at her red-rimmed eyes and pink nose. "You did what you could to protect him, given the information you believed to be true. We'll get that straightened out, but right now we need to focus on finding Lucas. Does he have his phone?"

"Yes, but my calls are going straight to voicemail."

"Okay. I need you to text me any recent pictures you have of him, a picture of his horse, and a list of the places you think he might've gone. I need to know where he practices riding, his friends' names and where they live, any places he likes to hang out."

"I've been thinking about that," she said frantically. "It was stupid to say he'd try to get to your ranch. He doesn't know the area well enough to risk it. I don't think he'd go off the trails."

"It wasn't stupid. He's *fifteen*. At that age every boy thinks he's invincible, and he's running from what he sees as his world crumbling down around him. No place is off-limits. Does he have a best friend? Someone he'd confide in."

"Not really. He was texting with Jade's niece Layla earlier, but I called Jade, and she called Layla's parents. They said she hasn't heard from him, but they'll let me know if she does." She pulled out her phone. "Should we call the police?"

"Not yet. He hasn't been missing long enough for them to do anything. But we've got that covered. The guys are on their way, and my buddy Hazard—Hector Martinez—is a cop. Let's get going on that list. They'll be here soon."

She began thumbing out a list.

As she did that, Doc studied the local trail maps on his phone. "Does he ever go to Devil's Bend?" Devil's Bend was a dangerous ravine.

"No. When we first moved here, Jade and Rex warned us about it, and I forbade Lucas from going there."

Doc knew damn well most pissed-off teenagers would take great pleasure in defying the parent who angered them. But he wasn't about to tell her that, because he didn't know Lucas, and hopefully he was wrong.

Juliette thumbed out the list, and as the roar of engines neared, she sent it, and the photos, to Doc. "I wrote down every place I could think of."

"Great." He scanned the list. "Buck's his coach?" Buck

Waller had been Doc's bull-riding coach when he was a kid.

She nodded. "Yeah. He did such a good job coaching you, it made sense to sign Lucas up with him."

"I'm glad you did. If Buck sees him, he'll drag Lucas's ass back home for sure. I'm forwarding this to Tiny so he can disseminate it to the guys."

When the Dark Knights converged on Juliette's property with trucks, motorcycles, trailers carrying ATVs, and horse trailers, her jaw dropped. "How many people did you call?"

"The whole club. We're not leaving anything to chance." As the guys started unloading the equipment and horses, his parents climbed out of his father's truck. "Come on." Doc took Juliette's hand, heading over to them.

Her gaze flicked nervously to their joined hands, then up at him.

Fuck. They were in this together. Taking her hand felt so natural, he didn't even think before doing it. "Sorry." He released her hand, silently cursing himself.

"I just…Everything is complicated right now. I don't want to make it worse."

"It's fine. I get it." That didn't mean it wasn't killing him not to be able to give her that extra support as they quickly made their way to his parents.

"Juliette, honey." His mother opened her arms and embraced her. "You must be worried sick."

"I am," Juliette said. "Sorry to bother you all with this. I didn't know Seeley was going to call in the cavalry. Although I appreciate it more than you can know. Especially after everything that's happened."

"Darlin', you became family the minute you came to stay on our ranch," Tiny said. "That doesn't go away because of hard times."

"Damn right it doesn't," Dare said as he and Cowboy came up behind them. "Otherwise they'd've disowned me years ago. Get in here, girl." He embraced Juliette. "We'll find your boy."

"Good to see you again, Juliette," Cowboy said, drawing her into his arms. "Wish it were under better circumstances."

"Me too," she said nervously.

"Let's get a move on before nightfall," Tiny said.

"Tiny, I'm taking the trail to the west," Doc said. His father nodded, and as Tiny and his brothers headed for the other men, Doc turned to Juliette. "My mom is going to stay with you in case you need anything. Text me if Lucas shows up."

"I will. Do you need flashlights?"

"No. We've got plenty."

"Lucas doesn't have one," she said shakily.

"He has his phone, and it has a flashlight on it." He pressed his hand to her cheek. "Don't worry. We'll find our boy and bring him home." He kissed her forehead, his chest constricting.

Doc grabbed a headlamp and headed for his horse as Tiny doled out orders. "Take a good look at the pictures I texted you. You see any teens while you're out, ask if they've seen him. Anyone gets a lead, text it in. If you find him, text it in. Hyde and Taz, get five or six guys and check the school grounds, the ranch where he practices, and the surrounding area. I need a handful of volunteers to check any trails around those locations. Otto and Pep, take as many guys as you need to check out neighboring ranches. Manny, grab a few men and head into town. See what you can find there. Rebel and Ezra, check the hangouts on that list. Dare and Cowboy, you take the trails to the east. Check every stream, behind every bush and tree. Teenagers are good at hiding…"

Doc mounted Romeo, and with a press of heels and a *"Hee-ya!"* the horse raced across the pasture. The trail was fairly well worn between brush and trees, allowing him to ride at a fast clip. He scanned the area, but he knew Lucas wouldn't be that close. At fifteen, the first thing Doc would have done was get as far away as possible from whoever or whatever had pissed him off. His gut told him to head for Devil's Bend, so that's exactly what he did.

He followed the trail up a steep incline, calling out Lucas's name as he weaved between thick pines and around scrub and rocky outcrops. He slowed to look in places where he thought Lucas might hide. He squinted into the setting sun as he rode along the crest of the mountain, his thoughts volleying between *Come on, boy. Where are you hiding?* and begging the universe to keep him safe. Now he understood why his father got so pissed off every time they'd run off to do something stupid when they were kids.

When he came to the ravine, at the bottom of which was the creek that led to Devil's Bend, he gave Romeo a minute to study the hillside. Doc kept himself centered in the saddle as best he could, allowing Romeo to find his way down the dangerously steep, rocky incline.

"Attaboy, take your time." He prayed Lucas had gone in the other direction. If not, he sure as hell hoped he was as good of a rider as Juliette claimed, because an inexperienced rider could hurt themself and their horse.

When they finally reached the base, they followed the creek. Doc spotted hoofprints in the dirt, and the muscles in his neck and shoulders tightened. The ravine curved at a sharp angle up ahead where the water pooled and deepened right before the creek dropped like a cliff into a bed of rocks. He hoped to hell

Lucas hadn't tried to take his horse down that cliff.

He quickly weighed his options. As a skilled rider, he could get around that bend and down the hill faster on Romeo, but if Lucas was around the bend, it might spur him into doing something stupid. On the other hand, if his gut was wrong and Lucas wasn't there, he was wasting the last precious minutes of dusk.

Erring on the side of caution, he dismounted Romeo, tied him to a tree, and made his way around the bend. Lucas's horse was tied to a tree, but Lucas was nowhere in sight. *Fuck.* Doc's gaze hit the ground, and he saw boot prints leading to the edge of the fucking cliff. His gut seized, his every muscle tensing, and he prayed Lucas didn't fucking jump.

With his heart in his throat, he went to the edge and peered over it. Lucas was pacing by the creek. *Thank Fucking God.* Doc did a quick visual scan for injuries, taking in his gait and unbroken limbs.

He quickly thumbed out a text to Juliette. *Found him. He's safe. I'm going to try to talk to him.* Then he texted Tiny. *He's at Devil's Bend. Don't tell Juliette that. I don't want her to worry. He looks unharmed. I'll report back.*

Doc looked up at the sky. *Don't let me fuck this up.*

As Doc started to make his way down the hill, Lucas spun around, his eyes narrowing. "What the hell do *you* want?"

Doc held his hands up. "I just want to talk." When he came off the hillside, he said, "Your mom is worried sick about you."

"I don't care," Lucas snapped, his hands fisting as he faced off with Doc. "She doesn't give a shit about me. She's a fucking liar."

"I get that you're pissed, and you have a right to be. Hell, we *all* have a right to be. But that's your *mother* you're talking about, so watch your mouth. She gave up her life to save yours when she wasn't much older than you."

"She didn't give up shit." Lucas's eyes were shooting daggers. "And don't act like you're my *father*. I don't even know you."

"You're right. You don't know me, but I'm hoping one day that'll change."

"Keep dreaming." Lucas walked away. "You're just some asshole who knocked up my mother."

"Oh yeah? Is that what you think?" Doc strode in front of him, blocking his path. He knew he was walking a fine line, but he wasn't about to let Lucas get away with assumptions and bad-mouthing him or Juliette. "You seem like you're pretty grown up, so I'm not going to dumb this down for you. Think you can handle talking man-to-man? Or do you want to act like a child and run away again?"

Lucas crossed his arms, lifting his chin.

It was like looking in a fucking mirror twenty years earlier.

Doc pushed that thought down deep and focused on clearing the air. "I don't know how much your mother told you, but I'm going to give it to you straight. I wasn't just the asshole who knocked her up. I was the asshole who fell so damn in love with her, I couldn't see straight when she was torn from my life. Your mother has owned my heart since she was sixteen years old, and if you think she didn't give up anything to raise you, you're sorely mistaken. She gave up a whole fucking ranch full of people who loved her."

"Yeah, right. That's why you were never in our lives, because you *cared* so much."

"I was never in your life because I didn't know you existed." He took a deep breath, trying to temper his frustration and figure out how to get his point across. "Imagine you had a girlfriend, and suddenly her father shows up with bodyguards and drags her into an SUV, kicking and screaming, and he locks her up like a fucking prisoner in her own home. *That's* what your grandfather did to your mother, all because I wasn't from a rich enough family for him. He threatened to ruin my family if I ever came near her again. I went behind my family's back, risking *everything* we were and everything we had, and I *fought* to see her. Your grandfather told me she was back together with her ex-boyfriend and she didn't care about me. Then he ordered his bodyguards to kick my ass. They left me barely conscious on the side of the road. Don't think for a *second* that I didn't fight for her."

Lucas swallowed hard, and Doc thought he saw a moment of understanding. But it was gone as quickly as it had appeared. "If you two were so in love, why didn't *she* fight for *you*?"

"She *did*, only I never knew it. Your grandfather monitored the phones, so your mother wrote me letters and gave them to a housekeeper to get them to me, but I never received them. That housekeeper gave your mother a letter that was *supposedly* written by me, telling her I didn't want her or our baby. But I never wrote it."

Lucas's eyes narrowed. "If you didn't write it, who *did*?"

"I believe your grandfather either wrote that letter or had someone else write it for him. But it doesn't matter *who* wrote it. What matters is that your mother and I were both deceived. Your grandfather gave her an ultimatum to abort the pregnancy or marry Josh. She married Josh so she wouldn't lose you."

"You're saying my father married her *just* because of me?" Lucas's eyes glassed over, new fury igniting in them. "That's a lie," he hissed. "My father *loved* us."

"Yes, he did. Very much, from what your mother says. And your mother loved him, too, but she wasn't *in love* with him, like she was with me. There's a difference."

"And you just gave up on her? That's not *love*."

"Don't you *dare* question my love for your mother. Her engagement announcement was in the newspaper and all over social media. When I saw that, I thought it was true. You have to remember, your mother *never* got a single message to me in all the weeks after she was taken away from the ranch. I thought she was done with me. What did you expect me to do? Fight for a woman who I thought didn't want me? Let your grandfather ruin my family because I was a lovesick fool?"

"Shut up." Lucas turned away. "I don't want to hear any more."

"I get it. This whole situation sucks. But you need to know that your mom was trying to protect you. She thought I'd written that letter, and she couldn't bear the thought of you growing up thinking you were unwanted by *me*. Don't hate her because she made a decision at sixteen years old based on the lies she was told. If you want to hate anyone, hate your grandfather for doing this to all of us. If I'd known your mother was pregnant, I'd have been there every day of your life, loving you as much as I loved her."

"You don't even *know* me." His voice was low and shaky.

"I don't have to know you to care about you. You're my blood, but even if you weren't, I care about your mom, and by extension, that falls to you." Doc gave that a minute to sink in. "If you think I don't care, you're wrong. I have forty men out there searching for you tonight. But I'm not the one who matters right now. Your mother is, and she's beside herself with worry. How about you text her and let her know you're alive?"

Lucas didn't move.

"Come on, dude. She's spent the last fifteen years raising you, providing for you, and protecting your heart. Surely you can take seven seconds to send a text that'll protect hers."

Lucas's shoulders slumped.

Send the text. Come on, buddy. You can do it.

Lucas shoved his hand into his pocket and pulled out his phone, reluctantly thumbing out a text.

"Attaboy. Now let's get you and that horse of yours home."

"Don't think just because you said all that shit, we're buddies now."

"Understood. Think you can get your ornery ass up that hill?"

Lucas glowered at him. "There's nothing I can't do."

You are a chip off the old block.

As they climbed up the hill, Lucas said, "How'd you find me, anyway?"

"Your mom said she forbade you from coming here. If I was your age and in your shoes, it's the first place I'd go." When they got to the top of the hill, he said, "But the next time you want to disobey your mother, you'd better think long and hard about it."

"Or *what?*" Lucas challenged.

Doc shrugged. "I guess we'll find out."

Chapter Eleven

RELIEF SWEPT THROUGH Juliette anew as she read Lucas's text. *I'm alive.* She stopped pacing her living room and sat down on the couch, trying to calm her racing heart.

"Is everything okay, honey? Was that Doc again?" Wynnie asked.

She shook her head. "It was Lucas." She showed Wynnie the text. "I'm guessing Seeley told him to text me."

"Probably so."

Juliette set her phone on the coffee table. "I wish I knew what Lucas said to him, but I guess I'll find out soon enough. I don't know how you survived five teenagers."

"When we were in the thick of it, there were days I wasn't sure I would. As the oldest, Doc paved the way for the others. He was a cocky jokester back then. When he was Lucas's age, he told us he was going to a friend's house, and he did go see his buddy. But then he told that friend he was going home and went to see a girl. She snuck out, and they fell asleep in her backyard. Tiny had all the guys out looking for him, much like Doc did tonight with Lucas."

"Seeley told me about that when we were teenagers." They'd

shared so many of their secrets, and he was still the only person who knew hers.

"I expect he did. He tried us good back then. He was the first to come home drunk at sixteen. He stumbled into Birdie's room thinking it was his and promptly puked all over her floor."

"*Gross.* Poor Birdie."

Wynnie laughed softly. "Tiny made him clean it up, which made Doc sicker, but it taught him a lesson. Then there was the time he and his friends thought sneaking out to have their own bull-riding contest was a good idea."

"Ohmygosh. I don't remember hearing about that. Did they get hurt?"

"No. Thankfully, Buck Waller caught them before they had a chance."

Buck had been Seeley's riding coach the summer they were together. Juliette would never forget going to the Waller ranch and watching Seeley ride bulls, rope cows, and barrel race. "Buck is Lucas's riding coach, too."

"Then Lucas is in good hands. Sometimes I wonder what kind of trouble Doc would've gotten into if what happened between the two of you had never gone down."

"What do you mean?"

"He took a turn to the dark side after that. He was so very heartbroken, he became angry and secretive. It took years before he came back into his own, and he's never been quite the same since."

Juliette felt a wave of guilt. "I'm sorry."

"Don't be. None of it was your fault, and all kids go through tough times. Each of ours tried us in different ways. If I've learned one thing about life, it's that nothing has the power to toughen you up or break you down like a child does. But you know that better than any of us, honey."

Juliette swallowed hard.

"I am so sorry that we didn't know what your father was doing back then and that you've had to deal with everything alone for so long. I know you had Josh at first, and I'm sorry that you lost him. I wish we could have been there to help you and Lucas get through that, and all the years since." She covered Juliette's hand with her own, squeezing it reassuringly. "I hope you know we're here for both of you, and you can lean on us anytime."

The front door opened, and they both stood as Tiny walked in. "The last of the guys just left. Have you heard anything more from Doc?"

"Lucas texted," Juliette said. "I assume they're on their way back."

"Doc will take good care of him. How're you holding up, darlin'?" Tiny asked.

"Okay. I really appreciate everything you've done for us tonight, and I'd like to apologize for everything my father said and did back then."

"Honey, there's no need to apologize," Wynnie said.

"Yes, there is. I thought about calling you guys a million times over the years. I am so sorry for how awful my father was to you. When he showed up that day to take me away, I was shocked. I didn't have any warning or anything. I don't even know how he found out about me and Seeley, and I promise you, I had no idea he had his bodyguards beat him up."

Wynnie gasped. "He *what*?"

"Oh no." Juliette covered her mouth. "You didn't know?" *Shitshitshit.*

"No." Wynnie looked at Tiny, his face a mask of serious-ness. "You *knew*, didn't you?"

Tiny nodded curtly. "'Course I knew."

"And you didn't stop it?" Wynnie snapped.

"Our boy needed to confront that man to fight for the girl he loved. Stopping him from doing it would've left him with an unchecked box, and he would've lost his mind. Trust me, darlin', those bodyguards got their due."

"And Governor Adkin?" Wynnie asked sharply. "Did he pay for ordering them to hurt our son?"

"No, darlin'. I gave you my word I wouldn't go after that man. That was one of the hardest promises I've ever had to keep, but you were right. We had a ranch full of people who were counting on us. I couldn't risk everything we'd worked so hard for, and I sure as hell wasn't going to risk your trust."

Juliette got choked up. This was the kind of honesty and love she'd never known existed before going to the ranch and witnessing it firsthand. She remembered how affectionate Tiny and Wynnie had been toward each other and the way Tiny had discussed things with Wynnie instead of commanding her, like her own father had done to her mother and everyone else in his life. Tiny and Wynnie had set a standard that Juliette had desperately wanted and she'd known she'd found with Seeley all those years ago.

"Thank you for keeping your word." Wynnie went to Tiny and touched his chest. "But I might have let that one slide had I known what happened to our boy."

"I wasn't taking that chance, darlin'." He put his arm around her and kissed her cheek.

Juliette wiped away a tear.

"Are you okay, honey?" Wynnie asked.

Juliette nodded. "It's just been an emotional night. I don't think I ever told you this, but I never knew what true love looked like until I came to the ranch and saw you two together. The way you treat each other, and everyone around you, is really special. In my family, my father told everyone what to do, and we followed like sheep because we were afraid not to. Or at least I did. I think my mother liked his control."

Another tear slipped down her cheek, and she swiped at it. "I know Seeley and I were young when we were together, but it's important to me that you know he never pressured me or coerced me in any way. He treated me with kindness and respect and love like I'd never known. If anything, he was extra careful where my emotions were concerned."

"Honey, we never doubted that," Wynnie said softly.

"In this family we cherish those we love," Tiny said.

"I feel lucky to have been one of them." Juliette wiped her eyes. "If you have any advice about how to deal with this situation with Lucas, I'd really like to hear it."

"There is a lot for Lucas to process, and until he slows down enough to understand how and why it happened, he's going to be angry," Wynnie said. "He's going to need a safe place to unload, and I'm sure he knows your love is unconditional, which means you'll likely take the brunt of it."

Juliette sighed, not wanting to face it, but that never stopped her before. "That makes sense."

"Unfortunately, Doc represents the things Lucas doesn't want to think about," Wynnie said. "Like his mother lying to protect him and his grandfather being as rotten and devious as he was, and that's a rocky road you and Doc will have to figure out how to navigate. But I have faith in both of you, and my best suggestion is to continue to be honest with him. That will help rebuild his trust, and it may take time, but you'll get there."

"The most important thing that boy needs to hear is that he's loved and that what your father did doesn't change that love," Tiny added.

"Right. Of course. It's all overwhelming."

"We know, honey." Wynnie hugged her. "Would you like me to give you the name of a therapist? For you or for Lucas? Or someone you both can talk to? There are quite a few good ones in this area."

"Yes, please." Juliette gave Wynnie her number, and Wynnie promised to text the information.

Tiny nodded toward the window. "The boys are back."

Juliette's pulse quickened as she followed his gaze to Lucas leading his horse into the barn. "Thank God." Seeley was outside the barn, climbing off his horse. She'd know that horse's markings anywhere. *Romeo.*

"That's our cue to leave." Wynnie took Juliette's hands in hers, gazing compassionately into her eyes. "You're a good mother, honey. It's easy to forget that when you're in the thick of things, and I'd bet you haven't been told that often enough. You and Lucas and Doc *will* get through this, and we are here for you, anytime, day or night, for whatever you need."

Tears welled in Juliette's eyes again as Wynnie embraced her. "Thank you. I really appreciate both of you."

Tiny hugged her and said, "We look forward to getting to know you and our grandson when you're ready."

Our grandson.

She soaked in the warmth of those words as they headed for their truck. Lucas and Seeley were making their way up the lawn. Lucas's eyes were trained on the ground, his expression surly. Seeley was walking his horse, his gaze moving between Juliette and Lucas. She wanted to hug both of them, to know what had been said and what they were thinking and feeling. But she focused on Lucas, closing the distance between them.

"You scared the crap out of me. Thank God you're okay." She hugged him. He didn't reciprocate, which stung, but it was to be expected. "I love you, but don't you *ever* scare me like that again."

"Whatever," Lucas grumbled, kicking the grass.

Her fraying nerves snapped. "It's not *whatever*. Anything could have happened to you out there. Don't you understand that you mean *everything* to me?"

Seeley cleared his throat. "I'm going to give you some privacy and get out of here."

"Can you give me a second?" she asked. "Lucas, please go inside. I'll be right in, and then we're going to talk."

Lucas scowled and stalked into the house.

"What a horrible night." She looked at Seeley, beyond grateful that he was there. "I hope he wasn't too awful to you."

"He wasn't, but you should know that I found him at Devil's Bend."

"Are you freaking kidding me? He is in *big* trouble."

"He's confused, Jule, and he's hurt."

"Are you saying he shouldn't be punished?" she asked incredulously.

"No. I think he needs boundaries. I'm only reminding you because he makes it really easy to see his anger and rebellion instead of his pain, which makes him appear strong. He comes by that naturally to some extent. As you've seen, I can be an angry bastard, but my guess is that he's also watched you hold your chin up for *years*. He seems like a quick learner, but he's still only fifteen, and the world as he knew it is never going to be the same. So maybe he needs to be cut a little slack."

"I *know* he does. I'm just upset. I hate all of this, and even though I was protecting him, it's still my fault. I did this to him."

"We all did, but we'll get through it."

"The question is, will he hate us afterward?" The thought killed her. "Did he say anything that I should know about?"

"Not really, but *I* might have overstepped. I told him everything. He knows what your father did to both of us, and about the letters, and that I confronted your father. The whole shitshow."

"I don't know if that's good or bad," she said honestly. "Did he actually listen?"

"I think so." He glanced at the house and raked a hand through his hair. "Is it okay to give you a hug?"

She looked at the windows and didn't see Lucas. "Yes, *please*. I need one, and he's probably locked in his room planning his next escape."

Seeley held the horse's lead in one hand and opened his arms.

She embraced him, soaking in his strength and surety.

"Nobody warned me how hard it was to be a parent." She pressed her cheek to his chest, holding him a little tighter. "You give birth to this tiny baby who's completely reliant on you, and you build your entire world around them, teach them to be strong and independent, to stand up for themselves and others. I've always prided myself on that with Lucas, because of how my parents tried to control me. But tonight, the way he looked at me like I was the *enemy*, makes me want to tie him down and force him to adore me the way he did when he was little."

Seeley pressed a kiss to the top of her head. "I get it."

She tipped her chin up, looking at him. "I guess that wouldn't be a good parenting move, would it?"

"I don't know about that." He cocked a grin. "I'll be happy to supply the rope."

She laughed and touched her forehead to his chest.

"Do you want me to stick around in case he runs again?"

"No. It's okay." She reluctantly stepped out of his arms, but he took her hand, keeping her close, and she loved that. "Maybe I'll get lucky and he'll be as emotionally exhausted as I am."

"I doubt it."

"Okay, Mr. Bearer of Bad News. Right now is the only time it's acceptable to lie to me. Tell me he will be too exhausted, even if you know he won't."

"I will never lie to you, and we both know teenagers never run out of energy." His brooding eyes softened. "We'll make sure he gets through this, darlin'. I promise you that. No matter how long it takes, we'll never stop trying."

She got teary-eyed again and tried to blink the tears away. "*God*, Seeley. Nobody has ever said that to me but you, and I know if anyone had, I probably wouldn't have believed them. You're back in my life for one day, and I *know* you mean it."

"Of course I do. Is there anything I can do to make it easier?"

She shook her head. "You've done enough. Now it's up to me. Thank you."

"Call me later? Let me know how it goes?"

"I will."

He kissed her forehead and glanced at Romeo. "I guess we'll head out."

"Can I just…?" She reached up and petted Romeo. "He's so big and beautiful." The horse pressed his muzzle into her chest. "I think he remembers me."

"You're unforgettable, darlin'."

Chapter Twelve

JULIETTE STARED AT Lucas's closed bedroom door, remembering when he was thirteen and had first started closing it. It had felt harsh to her at the time. Like a barrier she'd never again be able to breach in quite the same way. But she'd known it was all part of growing up.

Now it felt even more like an insurmountable barricade. She gathered her strength, reminding herself there was nothing she couldn't handle. She hoped that still held true for this new battlefield.

"Lucas," she said through the door. "We need to talk."

He opened the door, but he didn't say a word. He plunked himself down on his chair by his desk, crossed his arms, and scowled.

She sat on the edge of his bed, worrying with her hands, trying to figure out where to start, but her words came without much thought. "I'm sorry I lied to you. I know you don't think I did the right thing, but I made the decision that I thought was best for you at the time based on what I believed to be true."

He looked away.

"You're allowed to be mad and hurt, and you can even hate

me for lying to you." She softened her tone. "But you can't run away, Lucas. Not from me, because I will always drop everything to try to find you, and I will always love you, no matter how much you act out or think you hate me." She paused, giving him a chance to respond, but he remained silent. "And you can't run away from the reality of this situation. Seeley will always be your biological father. Those are the facts, and they aren't going to change."

"How do you even *know* he's my father?" he snapped, turning to face her again. "It's not like you did a paternity test."

"He was the first and *only* person I had ever been with. He is your father, Lucas, and I'm sure you have a lot of questions, so let's talk about it."

He stared stoically at her, his fingers drumming on his arm. "He told me about what Grandpa did."

"I know. Seeley told me he was honest with you about everything." She curled her fingers into the edge of his mattress, channeling her anxiety there.

"Was Grandpa really that much of a dick? Did he really do all those things? Did he keep you locked in the house and find a way to fake that letter?"

"Unfortunately, yes. My father was very controlling, and he was even worse after he took me away from the ranch."

Lucas breathed harder. "Did he really have his bodyguards beat up Seeley?"

She nodded, emotions stacking up inside her. "Yes, that's what Seeley said, and I believe him."

His jaw tensed, and his fingers stopped drumming. "Is Seeley the reason we moved here?"

"*No.* I moved to California because I was forced to, and it never really felt like home. Not the way this house does." *Or the ranch did.* "I was honest with you about how much I missed Grandma Hazel. She was the only person who was always on my side, and I wanted to feel closer to her. When she left us this property, it felt like a sign. I didn't think we'd run into Seeley. He doesn't live in Weston. He lives in Hope Valley."

He stared at her for a long moment. "If we hadn't run into him, would you *ever* have told me the truth?"

She gripped the edge of the mattress tighter. "I wish I could say yes, but I don't know for sure. Maybe not."

His jaw clenched, and he looked away again.

"Lucas, try to see things from my perspective. It wasn't easy keeping that secret from you. There were so many times when I'd look at you and think about how much you looked like or acted like Seeley. But I didn't think he wanted us."

"I get it," he snapped.

"Do you?" she asked sharply. "Because I'm going to be brutally honest about something else right now that I think you need to know. As treacherously hard as this is for *all* of us, now that I know the truth about my father and the truth about Seeley, I'm relieved that it's all out in the open. It was *torture* lying to you. I have lived *half my life* thinking Seeley didn't love me the way he said he did and believing he didn't want you."

Her chest constricted, and she struggled to regain control. "Honey, you are my heart and soul, and thinking your biological father didn't want you killed me every time I thought about it, which was all the time."

He looked away, his lips twitching into a frown the way they had when he was little and on the verge of crying. His arms tightened across his chest. "This sucks. I hate it."

Tears welled in her eyes. "I know. I'm sorry. I hate it, too."

"Everything I thought I knew about our family feels like it

was all a lie. Seeley said you weren't in love with Dad. Is that true?"

Oh God, here we go. "I loved your dad, but I wasn't in love with him, and I know that's confusing."

"I'm not stupid. I know there's a difference, and I'm *always* going to love Dad."

"Of course you are, honey, and you should." She inched forward, aching to take his hand or hug him, but she was afraid he'd push her away and clam up, and she needed him to talk with her. "Nobody wants to take that away from you, and Seeley doesn't want to replace your dad. He just wants to get to know you and to be in our lives."

He sat up straighter but looked down at the floor. "What if I don't want that?"

She felt a fissure forming in her heart at the thought. "Then we'll talk about it, and if you really don't want to get to know him, that's your prerogative."

That brought his gaze to hers.

"But I think you should give him a chance. He lost both of us through no fault of his own. He only found out about you yesterday, and when I called him tonight to tell him you'd taken off, he didn't hesitate to help. He brought his family and all those bikers we saw at the hospital over here to look for you. They came with horses and ATVs and trucks and bikes. *That's* the kind of person Seeley is, but only you can make the decision to give him a chance or not."

Lucas looked down again, kicking the bottom of his boot against the hardwood floor. "Do you still love him?"

"I never stopped," she admitted, more tears brimming. "I'll always love Seeley. Our love was big. It made you."

He looked at her with a mix of pain and sorrow. "Are you

two getting back together?"

"I think we have bigger things to figure out, don't you? He and I have to get to know each other again. We're not the same kids we were, and you come first, Lucas, for both of us."

"I doubt that's true for him," he grumbled.

"I understand why you'd feel that way, but if you decide to give him a chance, I think you'll see otherwise." She wiped her eyes and rubbed the dull ache in her temple. "You know what, honey? You don't have to make that decision tonight. What else would you like to know?"

"Nothing," he said sullenly.

She felt him shutting down. "Okay, but I want you to know that you can talk to me about how you feel. I'm not going to get mad. You have a right to feel whatever you're feeling, but I don't want there to be any more secrets between us."

"Whatever."

She let that go, because there were other things they had to discuss. "We do need to talk about you going to Devil's Bend."

"I can't believe he narked me," he said incredulously.

"He's worried about you. Devil's Bend is dangerous. I can't believe you took Warrior there."

"I didn't take him down the cliff," he barked.

"That's good, because he relies on you to keep him safe, and I know you'd never forgive yourself if he got hurt. I'm not going to punish you this time, but if you do it again, you're going to lose riding privileges, and you can kiss your learner's permit goodbye." She pushed to her feet. "Can I trust you not to take off again?"

"*Mom*," he said exasperatedly.

She smiled. "It's nice to hear I'm your mother again." She leaned down and hugged him. "I love you, Lukey boo." The endearment she'd called him since he was little almost earned a smile. "I'm going to skip dinner and drown my emotions in ice cream. Would you like to join me?"

"I'm not hungry," he said sullenly, and pulled out his phone, focusing on it instead of looking at her.

"Okay. If you need me, I'll be on the porch." She walked out of his room.

"Mom?"

She turned around. "Yeah?"

He hadn't moved from the chair, but at least he was looking at her. "I'm sorry I scared you."

"Thanks, baby. I'm sorry about all of this."

He looked like he wanted to say something, but he just focused on his phone again and said, "Can you close my door?"

She pulled his door closed behind her, glad they hadn't ended up yelling at each other. At least that was something. She grabbed a pint of chocolate ripple ice cream from the freezer and a spoon and snagged a hoodie from the hook by the front door on her way outside. She sat on the porch step and put on her hoodie, then looked up at the starry sky, feeling like she'd been through a war, and gave herself a moment to breathe.

It didn't take long before memories crept in, of sitting on her grandmother's porch swing, talking out her troubles and listening to her stories. Oh, how she'd loved that swing. When she and Seeley were together, they'd sit on it, kissing and making plans for a future that had seemed so real she would have bet her life on it. There was a porch swing at the farm where she and Lucas had lived in California, too, and she used to sit on it with him, telling him stories, but it was never the same as it was here.

She sat on the porch for a long time, eating ice cream, hating her father, feeling sad for Lucas, and for herself and Seeley, throwing silent prayers out to the universe that they'd get through this without Lucas hating Seeley.

When she finished the ice cream, satisfied that Lucas wasn't going to escape and seemed okay, at least for now, she headed down to the barn.

She loved up Maxine before making her way to Warrior. He lifted his big head as she approached. Where Maxine was leggy and graceful and had been a champion driving horse before becoming one of her grandmother's broodmares, Warrior was short and compact, with James Bond confidence and charm and a beauty all his own. He'd been a breeding stallion at the ranch where they'd lived in California but had retired and had been gelded several years ago. He'd always been Lucas's favorite horse, and Juliette had bought him for Lucas's ninth birthday. With a good amount of training, Warrior and Lucas had become inseparable. Warrior was always up for an adventure and loved exploring the hills and arroyos of California.

She eyed the dark mahogany bay horse. "Thank you for keeping my boy safe, but if you *ever* take him to Devil's Bend again, your apple stash will suffer." The horse nickered, and she petted his strong jaw. "I know. He's hard to say no to."

She gave him some extra love before heading out of the barn and calling Seeley.

He answered on the first ring. "Everything okay? How'd it go?"

His urgency, and the fact that he cared so much, made her smile despite the gravity of the evening. She imagined him sitting in his backyard, his elbows on his knees, brooding. "Well, we're both still alive. I'd call that a win."

"That bad, huh?"

"Not really," she said. "There was no yelling."

He exhaled loudly. "Good. I was worried I might've made things worse by being so honest with him."

"You didn't." She started walking up the hill toward the house. "It would've been easier to tie him down and make him adore me, but nobody said parenting would be easy."

"I'm sorry. Was he pissed that I was the one who found him?"

"He didn't say. He did ask if my father was really a dick and if I loved Josh, and I was honest with him about both."

"Sorry about that."

"Don't be. I think we need honesty right now. Lucas made it very clear that Josh was his dad and he will always love him."

"Of course. He's staking his claim. I respect that. I should've told him I didn't want to take Josh's place, but I was focused on making sure he knew how and why the situation had gone down the way it had."

The cadence of his voice told her he was pacing. "I appreciate that. He also asked if you and I were getting back together and if I still loved you."

"Jesus." Seeley was quiet for a second. "What did you tell him?"

"The truth. That I'd always love you, but we have to get to know each other again, and he'll always come first."

"Did that set him off?"

"No. But when I said you wanted to get to know him, he asked what would happen if *he* didn't want that, and I told him we could talk about it."

"Shit." The hurt in his voice was evident.

She stopped near the front of the house. "I'm sorry. It was hard for me to hear that, too, but I don't think he's dead set against getting to know you. It's just a lot to think about all at once."

"Yeah. No shit. For all of us. How can I help make things easier?"

"You're already doing more than you know." She paced in the moonlight. "Being here and talking to us and caring about Lucas is more than I've had from anyone other than my grandmother. I appreciate all of it, and I hope one day Lucas will, too."

"It doesn't feel like enough. I know he needs time, but I want him to know I'm here if he has questions or wants to talk, and I don't want too much time to pass before seeing him again."

I don't want there to be either. "He'll probably have a lot more questions as the reality of it all sinks in. Why don't we see how things go over the next few days? Then we can figure out where to go from there."

"Sounds good. Jule, are you sure you're okay? You can tell me if you're not."

"I'm as okay as I can be, I think. But I'd give anything for a do-over."

"You and me both."

"I keep thinking about what my grandmother said when I got that letter. I was completely inconsolable, and she said it was because my heart had found its voice and that it would always speak louder than my head. She said there would be no quieting those screams, and I'd have to learn to hear past them to do what was best for my—for *our*—baby. I worked so freaking hard to do that, and now I wish I had been too weak."

"Don't do that, darlin'. Don't blame yourself for this. It was all fucked up and out of our control. But you're back, and the truth is finally out there, and if I have my way, you're never leaving again. Or if you do, it's not going to be without me."

She smiled at his vehemence and his undying adoration.

"We *will* figure this out, Jule, and I know it may not feel like it right now, but Lucas loves you, and I have to believe that one day he'll understand why you took the path you did."

"I know he loves me. I just hate hurting him."

"So do I, and I hate how much hurt you've suffered. Do you want me to come over and sit with you so you're not alone?"

"*Yes*," she said honestly. "But you can't. I don't want Lucas thinking it's us against him."

"Oh, man. I didn't even consider that. Sorry. I think I need a parenting handbook."

"Don't we all?"

"I don't know, darlin'. Given the hand you were dealt, I think you've done a hell of a job so far."

"Thank you." She soaked in that praise. "I needed to hear that. It means a lot to me."

"Well, you and Lucas mean a lot to me."

She looked up at the house, not wanting to end the call, but she was worried about Lucas. "I should check on him."

"Okay. I'm here if you need anything at all."

"Thank you."

She ended the call, reveling in his support, and a kernel of longing bloomed inside her. She climbed the porch steps, trying to ignore the wave of guilt washing over her, because while their worlds had been turned upside down, she was so frigging glad Seeley was back in their lives, and she ached to be in his arms again.

Chapter Thirteen

LATE THURSDAY NIGHT Doc sat on Dare and Billie's patio shooting the shit with his brothers, Sasha, and their significant others, wishing Juliette were there. Sully was snuggled against Cowboy's side on a lounge chair, absently running her fingers over his stomach, Billie and Dare were eyeing each other like they couldn't wait to tear each other's clothes off, and Ezra and Sasha were holding hands, while Gus slept on Sasha's lap. They'd made s'mores, and little Gus had chatted up a storm before conking out with marshmallow on his adorable face.

It was on nights like these that Doc used to torture himself with what-ifs. What if things had gone differently that fateful summer? What if they'd been allowed to follow through with their plans? When he'd thought about those what-ifs over the years, what hurt the most was knowing without a shred of a doubt that they would still be together, happy, and in love—and conversely, thinking Juliette had betrayed him. Now that they had a second chance, he wanted to barge into every aspect of her and Lucas's life and stake claim. But he was giving her space to see how things panned out with Lucas, and it was killing him.

He finished his beer and set the empty bottle by his chair, crossing his arms.

"Remember that time Dare wanted to start a band with Doc and Cowboy?" Billie asked, eyeing Dare, who was smirking arrogantly.

"You mean the band that Birdie and I weren't allowed to join because we're girls, despite the fact that I'm the only one who plays an instrument?" Sasha asked.

"That's the one," Billie chimed in.

"I didn't need an instrument," Dare said. "I had great moves, and we had an excellent drummer." He motioned to Doc, drumming his fingers on his arm, and everyone laughed.

"Shut the hell up." Doc uncrossed his arms.

"Poor Birdie's hopes were shot down that day," Sasha said. "She was excited to make band outfits."

"We dodged a bullet with that one," Cowboy said.

"Where is Birdie tonight?" Sully asked.

"She wrangled Rebel into being her wingman, and they went to the Roadhouse," Sasha said.

"Sounds like we might need to take a ride over there," Cowboy said.

"No need," Doc said. "I got wind of her plan and had a talk with Rebel." Rebel was several years younger than Doc, and Birdie was always trying to drag him into one of her plans.

"I love how you guys watch out for Birdie," Sully said. "But, Doc, are you okay?"

"*Fine.* Why?"

"It's just that everyone asked about how Juliette and Lucas were doing earlier, and I realized that nobody asked how you were doing," Sully said. "When I first reunited with my older sister, Jordan, I felt so many different emotions, and I had spent the first few years of my life with her. But you didn't even know you had a child, and now suddenly you do, and he's fifteen, and Callahan said Juliette was your first love, and now she's back. I can't imagine what all of that feels like."

Sully was sweet for asking, but there was a reason nobody had asked. They knew he kept his emotions close to his chest. "It's a lot, but I'm okay. Thanks for asking."

They were all looking at him expectantly, as if waiting for him to say more. *What the hell?*

"Okay, I'm sorry, Doc," Billie said. "I get that you don't like to talk about your feelings, but I'm dying to know if you and Juliette are going to try again."

Doc gritted his teeth, not because he didn't want them to know how he felt, but because talking about it would only make him want it more.

"Inquiring minds want to know," Sasha urged. "Is the extended-stay motel closed for good?"

"Jesus, Sash." Doc shook his head.

"What? I know things are complicated right now, but do you and Juliette still love each other?" she asked.

"Of course they do," Dare said. "When a Whiskey falls, that love is forever. Look at me and Billie and you and Ez."

"Gus and I are thankful for that," Ezra said, leaning in to kiss Sasha, who smiled like he and Gus were her world.

"Look, Doc," Cowboy said. "I admit I'm curious, too, but don't feel the need to show your hand because we're nosy."

With the exception of Sully, who hadn't known them back then, they'd all been there to support him through the worst of those early years, even when he'd barely given them the time of day. They deserved to know the truth. "Well, I do have a

Whiskey heart, so there's that."

"*Yes!* I knew it," Sasha exclaimed. Gus made a sleepy noise, snuggling into her. She brushed her hand down his back and kissed his head, whispering, "Sorry, Gusto."

"Does Juliette feel the same way?" Cowboy asked.

Dare scoffed. "How could she not? It's Doc. He's fucking awesome."

Hell if that didn't make Doc feel good…and a bit guilty for being a dick when he first saw her again. "Thanks, man. I appreciate that."

"You are awesome," Cowboy agreed. "But there's a lot of water under that bridge."

"No shit," Doc said, feeling the need to defend himself. "I know she still loves me, but loving someone and being in love with them are two different things. And yeah, I wish they were here right now. I want to charge into their lives and make both of them give me a chance. But we've got much bigger things to worry about and figure out." Knowing his sister and Billie would probably push for more, he picked up his empty bottle and rose to his feet. "It's late. I'm gonna call it a night."

As he tossed the bottle into the recycle bin, Billie said, "Nice mic drop."

"More like an escape," Sasha said. "I'm happy for you, Doc. I hope it works out."

"Me too," Sully said. "There's a light in your eyes when you talk about Juliette, and there's a tenderness to your voice when you talk about Lucas. I was secretly hoping you still had feelings for her."

He looked at the girl who had been stolen from her family and endured years of horrible things. If any of them deserved an extra reason to smile, it was her. "I don't think there's anything or anyone in this world that could ever take those feelings away. Y'all have a good night."

Doc pulled out his phone as he walked home and texted Juliette. They'd texted earlier, but he was dying to hear her voice.

Doc: *Hey darlin. Still up?*

Juliette: *Yes. My body is tired but my brain is going a million miles an hour.*

Doc: *Mine, too. How'd things go with Lucas tonight?*

Juliette: *It's tense between us, but not as bad as last night.*

Doc: *That's good.*

Juliette: *I know, but I wish I knew how to fix this.*

Doc: *Can I give you a call?*

Juliette: *Yes.*

A smiling emoji popped up.

He called her as he walked down his driveway, and his dogs ran over to greet him.

"That was fast," Juliette said.

"Sorry," he said, petting his pups. "Do you need more time?"

"*No.* I was kind of hoping you'd want to talk."

Well, shit. Now he was grinning like a fool. "What I *want* is to be there with you and Lucas, helping you through this."

"I know you do." She was quiet for a beat. "What about you, Seeley? Don't you need help, too? I mean, last night was a lot. I was a little worried it might make you want some distance, and that would be perfectly understandable."

"Distance is the last thing I want. Don't get me wrong. This *is* big, and obviously we need to get to know each other again, and I want to get to know Lucas. But it's always been you, Juliette. Plain and simple." Worried he'd scare her off, he said,

"But that's not what matters right now. Let's talk about Lucas and see how we can ease the tension between you two."

"Okay, but I want you to know that your feelings *always* matter to me."

He headed up to the porch with the dogs on his heels and sat on the top step. "I'm glad, darlin'." He wanted to barrel down that road, but it was too easy to get lost in the high of Juliette caring about him. "Tell me what happened with Lucas tonight."

She explained how Lucas wasn't mean or disrespectful like he had been last night, but he was distant and sullen. "It's like he doesn't know how to act around me anymore."

"Maybe he doesn't. It's only been a day, and all of our emotions are still raw. The summer all that shit went down, I shut everyone out." He told her how he hadn't opened up to his mother until she'd stopped pushing him to. "It might be easier for Lucas to come to you on his terms."

"You think I should *stop* trying to talk to him about it?"

"Not completely. Maybe let him know you're there if he wants to talk, but try not to push too hard. Not that you are—"

"No, you're right. I am pushing. I can't help it," she confided. "I just want to make things better. Every time I see him, it's *right there*, front and center in my mind."

"I get it. It's like that for me, and I'm sure it is for him, too. He feels like his world has exploded, so maybe you need to show him that his daily life isn't going to change, and you're still the same mom you were two days ago."

"How am I supposed to do that?"

"I'm not sure. Is there a way to show him that even though it feels like his life has imploded, some things aren't changing, like bull riding and school and practicing driving?"

"Yeah, that's a good idea."

"I think he just needs time," Doc said. "Is this how he usually handles stress? Closing himself off?"

"Sort of. He used to share everything with me, but over the last year or so, that's been changing. He keeps things closer to his chest."

"That sounds like typical teenage behavior."

"I know, but I don't have to *like* it." She laughed softly. "But this feels bigger."

"Because it is, but we'll figure out how to get through to him. I don't want him harboring resentment like I did. That's a tough way to live. He needs to know he can trust us, and we have to earn that trust. I'll talk to my mom to see if she has any suggestions."

"Your mom gave me the name of a therapist, and I called to make an appointment. I'm waiting for a call back."

"That's a good start." He petted Pickles. "Can I ask you something?"

"Sure."

"I missed so many years of your lives. I want to know about *all* of them, eventually. But I was hanging out with everyone tonight, and Gus, Sasha's fiancé Ezra's little boy, was running around, chatting about a hundred different things, and making s'mores. He's in kindergarten, and suddenly he climbed into Sasha's lap, curled up with sticky little hands and cheeks, and fell right to sleep."

She laughed. "At that age, it's like they're Energizer Bunnies until their batteries run out. That's so sweet."

"It was, and it made me realize how much I missed with Lucas. I was wondering if you could tell me about what he was like when he was little."

"Oh, *Seeley*, he was beautiful and so freaking cute, it was ridiculous."

He laughed. "I'm sure he was the cutest baby ever born, and I bet you were beautiful when you were pregnant."

"I was round, but he was beautiful."

"I don't believe that for a second. I'm gonna need to see proof. Send me pictures."

She laughed. "Seriously?"

"What do you think?"

"Okay. But you'll see. I was like an Oompa Loompa. Hold on." When her text rolled in, she said, "The first picture was taken the week before Lucas was born. The second was in the hospital the night he was born."

"Let me put you on speaker so I can look at them."

He put her on speaker, and his heart felt like it was going to explode as he took in an image of the fun-loving teenage girl he'd known, standing by a fence wearing black leggings and a sky-blue sweater, her belly round with his baby. Her cheeks were fuller, her hair a little wilder, and she was absolutely gorgeous, but she looked too young and innocent to go through everything that she had. In the second picture, she was gazing at their baby with so much love in her eyes, it made his chest ache. Lucas was impossibly tiny, swaddled in a pink and blue blanket, with a dusting of dark hair.

"I told you I looked awful," she said.

"The hell you did. Baby, you're beyond beautiful, and Lucas was by far the cutest baby ever born. I wish I could have been there to rub your belly and your feet, and feel him kick, and hold your hand when you gave birth. Look at you with our boy." Overwhelmed with emotion, he laughed. "You were so damn young, and you took on the fucking world. You amaze me, darlin'."

"*Seeley*," she said a little bashfully.

"You do, Jule. Tell me what I missed."

"I don't even know where to start."

"At the beginning. You continued going to school after he was born. What was that like?"

"I hated leaving him with the nanny when I went to school, but from the minute I got home, he was in my arms or on my lap."

"Lucky boy. What was his first word? How did it feel to hear him speak for the first time? I want to know everything."

She laughed softly. "His first word was *mama*, and when he said it, I cried."

"I can only imagine."

"I just loved him so much. With all the stress with my parents and the guilt of bringing Josh into it, everything Lucas did felt like a miracle. Like something good came out of all that mess."

"Something better than good. Something wonderful."

"He is wonderful. Although he sure wore me out when he was little. He started walking before he was a year old."

"That's my boy."

"I kind of *love* hearing you say that."

"I'm surprised at how much I like saying it." He'd thrown away the dream of having a family of his own when he'd lost Juliette. He was starting to wonder if fate had a hand in his life after all, and the universe somehow knew she'd come back into it. "Do you have more pictures?"

"Only about a million." She laughed softly. "One sec."

After a moment, his phone chimed, and he scrolled through pictures of Lucas fast asleep lying on his back in his crib wearing one-piece pajamas with horses on them, his tiny hands balled into fists beside his head. There was another of him crawling across a blanket when he was a little bigger, his thighs pudgier, and one of him standing up, holding on to a coffee table, wearing a blue-and-white romper. His hair was thicker, his cheeks chubbier, and his pudgy feet were bare. And another of him sitting on Juliette's lap eating ice cream with chocolate dripping down his chin, flashing an adorable toothy grin.

"These are incredible. Look at him, with those pudgy cheeks and big blue eyes. How old was he in the picture with the ice cream?"

"Three, I think. He loves ice cream."

"Do you still love it?"

"I ate an entire pint last night. Do you remember when we used to raid the kitchen in the main house?"

He laughed. "How could I forget? You were so cute and flustered when Dwight caught us."

"How did he always know when we were in there?"

"My old man and Dwight know everything that happens on the ranch."

"Uh-oh. Do you think they knew about us sneaking into the cabin?"

"I didn't used to think so, but I've learned that nothing gets past Tiny. Tell me more about when Lucas was little. What was he like as a toddler?"

"*Busy.* I swear he got into everything. It was exhausting, and I never knew if I was doing things right. Some days I thought I was the worst mother in the world for bringing him into such a messed-up situation. But then I'd look at him sleeping in his crib, and…Seeley, there are no words to describe the love I felt."

His chest tightened. "I wish I'd been there for both of you."

"Me too. I know you would have loved him as much as I did. He was the sweetest toddler, and he was funny, too. He pronounced things wrong, like *hippups* for hiccups, and he'd ask for *chocolate squirrel* ice cream instead of chocolate swirl. But I think the cutest thing was when he was hungry, he'd say, *I'm honey, Mommy.*"

Doc laughed. "That's adorable. I wish I could have heard him say it."

"I have a video with him saying it. It's a little shaky because I was holding the phone and chasing after him. Give me a sec to find it. I used to pretend I didn't hear what he said, hoping he'd say it again. I know that's awful, but he was so cute. I couldn't resist."

She sent the video, and Doc watched Lucas climbing onto the couch beside Juliette, saying, *I'm honey, Mommy. I'm honey,* in a chirpy little voice. She was clearly trying to stifle a laugh as she said, *What are you?* and a frustrated Lucas said, *Hooonnneeey. I'm honey!*

Doc's heart swelled, and he laughed again. "That's too damn cute. You know I'm going to listen to it a thousand times tonight."

"I told you he was the cutest baby ever. He was a mischievous rascal, too. When he was three, he drew on the walls with crayons, and when he was four he refused to pee in the toilet and would only go outside."

"In all fairness, that's a rite of passage for boys."

"His preschool teacher was not impressed."

Doc laughed, and she laughed too.

"What else did he do?"

"What *didn't* he do?" she said. "There was a period of a few months when he wouldn't wear shoes or socks. That was a fun battle every morning before school, but it wasn't quite as bad as when he was six and decided he didn't like wearing pants."

"I can't blame him for that."

They both laughed. She shared more funny stories about things Lucas had said and done and sent pictures of the first time he'd ridden a horse by himself and his first days of kindergarten and first grade. She told him that when Lucas was in third grade, he'd decided he didn't need to go to school anymore because he was going to be a cowboy when he grew up. "Then there was the time when he was ten and he became enamored with a stubborn old horse named Gray, but Gray wouldn't give him the time of day."

"That's rough for a kid who loves horses."

"You're telling me? It broke my heart, but Lucas was determined to make friends with him, and he didn't want *any* help doing it. He went out to the horse's stall every morning before school with carrots and apples, trying to coax it over to him, and every day after school he'd go to the fenced pasture and try again."

"He's tenacious. That's a boy after my own heart."

"Mine, too, but the horse wasn't having it, and Lucas was frustrated. It was hard to see him so bummed, but he refused to give up. One night I caught him watching a YouTube video on how to make friends with a stubborn horse, and he got *so* embarrassed."

"Why? He was researching. That's a smart move."

"I know. That's what I told him, but he said cowboys should know how to make friends with any horse."

Doc chuckled. "I love his attitude. Did he ever get through to the horse?"

"Yes, after what seemed like forever. The horse finally ate

the treats, and a few days later he let Lucas pet him. Lucas continued going out to see him every day, and a couple of weeks later, Gray started coming to the fence when he saw Lucas heading over. Lucas was really proud of that."

"He should be. I hate that I missed so much of your lives."

"Me too."

"I'm going to do right by him, Jule. That's a promise."

"You already are."

They were both quiet for a moment, and he wondered if she wished she was with him as much as he was wishing he was with her.

"Do I hear crickets?" she asked. "Are you outside?"

"Yeah. I'm sitting on my porch with my beasts."

"*Aw.* Can I ask you something?"

"Of course."

"I know you said you were with everyone tonight. But I don't really know who everyone is anymore. Did you mean your family?"

"Mostly. I was with my brothers and Sasha, and their significant others."

"Are they *all* married now?"

"No, only Dare and Billie. They got married over the summer. Cowboy and his girl, Sully, got engaged in the spring, and Sasha and Ezra got engaged the morning I ran into you at the hospital."

"Wow. You guys have had a busy year. Congratulations to all of them. I'm not surprised Dare and Billie are married. Remember how we used to make bets about when something would happen between them?"

He smiled. "Yeah."

"How did their friend take it? I can't remember his name.

The other daredevil."

"Eddie," he said sadly. He told her about Eddie dying and how it had caused a rift between Dare and Billie for several years.

"That's so sad. They were all so close. I'm glad Dare and Billie have each other now. What about Sully and Ezra? Do you like them for Cowboy and Sasha?"

"Yeah, I do. Very much." He told her about Sully's background and how she'd come to the ranch and about how Sasha and Ezra had gotten together. "They're all really happy. I think they're with the people they were always meant to be with."

"I'm happy for them." She sounded a little forlorn.

"Are you okay?"

"Mm-hm. I just…Do you ever think about what it would be like if my father hadn't ruined everything?"

"Yeah, I do." They were both quiet again.

"It's so unfair. I hate my father for what he did to us."

"You're not alone in that, darlin'."

Doc made his way inside as they talked, and an hour later he was lying on his bed with the dogs, and Juliette was yawning sleepily on the other end of the phone. "I'd better let you go."

"Sorry," she said softly. "I don't want to end the call. I like hearing your voice."

"I don't want to, either, but you should get some sleep. We can talk tomorrow."

"Promise?" She didn't give him a chance to respond. "*Ohmygod*, I did not just say that. I'm hanging up before I embarrass myself any further."

He laughed as the line went dead and said, "I promise, darlin'. Love you."

Chapter Fourteen

DOC AWOKE TO Sadie licking his cheek, Pickles lying across his legs, and Mighty sprawled against his other side. "Mornin', Sade." He kissed her snout and reached for his phone. Mighty gave him the side eye, like he had a hell of a nerve moving when he was so comfortable.

As Doc leaned back against his pillow, Mighty and Sadie settled in, and he opened to the pictures and video Juliette had sent last night. He'd spent half the night looking at them, which had made him even angrier at the bastard who had forced them apart.

He scrolled through the pictures and watched the video a few times, grinning at Lucas's little-boy voice and Juliette's and Lucas's sweet faces. He'd missed so damn much. He thumbed out a text.

Doc: *GM darlin. I woke up with three beasts and not the woman I want in my bed. WYWH.*

Juliette: *I wish I was there too. Three beasts? Sounds kinky.*

He took a selfie with the dogs, and Mighty crawled up to his pillow as he sent the text. Doc ruffled his fur. "Claiming your spot?" Mighty licked him as a heart-eyed emoji popped up on his phone. Grinning, he glanced at the selfie. His hair was a mess, and he looked tired, but he was shirtless, wearing only boxer briefs and his lazy dogs.

Doc: *You're into my beasts?*

An eye-rolling emoji popped up.

Juliette: *Why do you look so hot in the morning when I look like death warmed over?*

Doc: *Not possible. Send me a pic.*

A picture popped up of Juliette flashing a cheeky smile, holding up a coffee cup. Her hair was messy and tangled, her eyes were sleepy, and she looked painfully beautiful.

Doc: *You look good enough to eat.*

He added a devil emoji.

He watched the three dancing dots, as if she were typing, but they disappeared. "Shit." He'd known he was pushing it, but he also knew they were there in their hearts, and she wanted the same thing. His phone vibrated as another text rolled in.

Juliette: *I wish I could meet you at the end of the road and go to our old cabin.*

If he had his way, his cabin would be *their* cabin.

DOC WAS IN his office at the end of the day reviewing the latest scans for two of their rescue horses when his cell phone rang, and Reggie Steele's name appeared on the screen. He wasn't expecting to hear from him so soon. "Hey, Reggie. How's it going?"

"Not bad. I've got an update, but before I get into it, how are things with you? How'd Lucas take the news?"

"Not great, but that's to be expected."

"I'd imagine so. Hopefully he'll come around and realize how lucky he is to have you as a father. And Juliette? How is she holding up?"

"She's hanging in there." She'd texted about an hour ago to say she'd heard back from the therapist and had set up an appointment to speak with her while Lucas was at school next week.

"I'm sorry you all are going through this," Reggie said. "I can only imagine how stressful it is. Let me make your day a little better. I have on good authority that Adkin has been under investigation for corrupt activity for the past two years as part of a broader federal investigation."

"No shit? I haven't heard anything about that."

"You wouldn't. None of it is public knowledge. This is big, Doc. My source tells me it involves more than a dozen people. Adkin is being investigated for using his political influence to gain kickbacks from companies seeking to work with the state, for mail fraud, money laundering, extortion, bribery. The list goes on."

"I *knew* that asshole was dirty. If they've got all that on him, what's the holdup? Why aren't they arresting him?" Doc pushed to his feet and paced.

"They need more proof. You know how lawyers are. If they don't have a slam dunk, they'll be tied up in court for years—or worse, the case will be thrown out. I'm sure the Feds have every base covered, but I put out some feelers with my political connections to see what I can dig up."

"Great. Keep me in the loop. Did you get any info on the housekeeper?"

"Yes. Ana Barbosa has worked for the Adkin family for

twenty-four years, since she was nineteen. She was married when she started working there and went through a contentious divorce a few years later. She has a thirteen-year-old son, a younger brother who's been in and out of jail, and a sister who lives out of the country with her mother, who she sends money to every month."

"Who's the kid's father?"

"This is where it gets interesting. There's no father listed on the birth certificate, but after the divorce, she took out a restraining order against the ex, and it was handled by Adkin's attorney, Wilson Chambers. Curiously enough, the ex was severely beaten shortly thereafter. Sound familiar?"

"Son of a bitch." Doc rubbed a knot in the back of his neck. "You think Adkin is the father of her child?"

"That's my guess. After the restraining order was put into place, she moved into a high-end community and started receiving large sums of money from an aunt overseas. But it turns out there is no aunt. The money's coming from one of Adkin's shell companies. He buried it well. The guy's got a network of shell companies in other countries, each with several intermediary entities. The shell companies act as shareholders to each other, making tracking the true ownership nearly impossible."

"How'd you get this info?"

"You know I can't tell you that, and what I've told you has to stay between us."

"I've got to tell Juliette."

"That's a given. I trust she'll keep it quiet. I'm going to email you a report outlining all of this. One more thing about the housekeeper. She has Tuesdays and Sundays off, and from what I can tell from her financial records, she has brunch at the same café every Tuesday in Boulder."

"You think she meets Adkin there?"

"I didn't have enough time to figure that out yet. But give me a week or two—"

"Thanks, but I'm not waiting a week or two. I want to get this bastard. I'll go see for myself. Is the address in the report? I want the housekeeper's home address, too."

"It's all in there, but as I said, this guy's connections run deep and dirty. If you go in there half-cocked looking for trouble, you're liable to find a hell of a lot more than you're counting on."

"Then you have no idea how much I'm counting on. One more thing. Do you have dates on the brother's jail time?"

"Yeah. It's all in the report."

"Thanks, Reg. I'll let you know what goes down."

After ending the call, Doc paced, formulating a plan as he tried to figure out how to break the news to Juliette. It was one thing to know her father had lied to her and to hear that he had done other bad things. But it was a whole other ball game to be given proof. He texted her.

Doc: *Hey darlin. Got a minute to talk?*

Juliette: *Not really. I'm on my way out the door with Lucas to take him to riding practice.*

Doc: *I have information about your father.*

Juliette: *Can you meet me at the Waller ranch?*

Doc: *I'll be there as soon as I can.*

JULIETTE STOOD BY the entrance of the indoor riding ring

anxiously awaiting Seeley's arrival as she watched Lucas on the other side of the arena. The mention of her father always raised her hackles, especially after learning the extent of what he'd done. She was as nervous about what Seeley had to say as she was excited to see him.

Talking with him last night about how to handle things with Lucas and sharing parts of their lives with him after all these years had reminded her of how right things had been when they were together. They'd always been able to talk about anything and everything, and their insane chemistry had added an intensity like no other. It was all of that, the way he considered her and Lucas first, and all the little things she'd never found with anyone else that had her wanting more.

Like the way Seeley had pushed her to follow *her* dreams, not the dreams her parents had outlined for her, and the way he'd looked after her. She remembered sitting at the creek with him the night she'd told him how controlling her father was. She'd broken down in tears when she'd shared the truth about her mother and how empty she'd felt without her parents' love. Seeley had held her while she'd cried, and said, *Some people aren't built to be parents, but that doesn't mean their children aren't worthy of love. You are worthy of more love than this world knows how to give, and I'll never stop trying to give it to you.*

His words had filled those empty places, and she hated her father for stealing that from her.

But she wasn't going to let her father ruin things now. She pushed those thoughts away and watched Lucas. She loved seeing him with his friends, doing what he enjoyed.

A little while later, she sensed Seeley approaching before she felt his hand touch her back as he leaned in close and said, "I came here to talk about something important. How am I supposed to concentrate with you in those sexy shorts and cowgirl boots?" sending her heart into a wild flurry.

It had been a long time since she'd heard anything like that. She smiled at the mischievous glint in his eyes. His dark T-shirt hugged his broad chest, his hair curling out from beneath his cowboy hat. They'd been so focused on everything with Lucas, she hadn't realized how much she'd missed Seeley's playfulness until now. "Way to make a girl's day."

"Seeing you makes my day." He kissed her cheek, then lifted his chin in Lucas's direction. "How's he doing?"

"Surprisingly well. I was worried that the stress might affect his new friendships and be too distracting for him to ride. You know how dangerous distractions can be."

"Absolutely. I wondered about that, too."

"When I mentioned skipping practice, he got pissed. He was *not* going to miss it, and look at him. He's like a different kid here. He's smiling, talking with the other kids in his group, and listening to his coach."

"This is his outlet. It's good that he has one." Seeley arched a brow. "Being here brings back memories of you watching me ride...and *other* things."

"You mean like Buck banging on your truck window when we were making out?"

He cocked a grin. "Those were some good times."

"Maybe even the best," she admitted. "When I brought Lucas here to meet Buck, I prayed Buck wouldn't remember that particular incident."

"And did he?"

"I don't think so. If he did, he didn't mention it."

"You got lucky." Seeley slid his arm around her waist, pulling her closer. "I'd ask if you want to get luckier, but..." He kissed her temple and whispered, "I already know the answer."

Yes, please.

Just as reality hit with a worry about Lucas seeing them that close, Seeley's arm fell away, as if he'd read her mind, and she mourned the loss of his touch. But she'd always enjoyed giving him a hard time, so she said, "You think you know the answer, huh? Care to fill me in?"

He set a seductive gaze on her that had her heart tripping up. "We both know you want me to take you against this railing, but now's not the time."

"Is that what you think? Guess you're still as cocky as you used to be after all."

He glanced across the ring at the kids heading to the bull pen, and stepped closer to her, putting his hand on her hip, out of view from anyone else. Those dark eyes held her captive as he slipped his thumb under the edge of her shirt, brushing it lightly along her skin, sending shivers of heat rippling through her. "I haven't forgotten your tells, darlin'."

"I don't have tells." She totally did, but he couldn't possibly remember them.

"You're probably right." He lifted his other hand and brushed his fingertip over the corner of her mouth. "This twitch is definitely *not* a tell."

"Nope." *Holy cow. You remembered.*

"And the way you wrinkle your nose when you're lying?"

"I had an itch." She could barely keep a straight face.

"Makes sense." He put his hand on her hip and squeezed, sending prickles of anticipation racing through her. How did he still have that effect on her? "I guess the toe of your right boot hitting the dirt and that wiggling ankle aren't tells, either."

"Sorry to disappoint you, but it's just a habit."

LOVE, LIES, AND WHISKEY

A slow grin spread across his face. "Guess I'll have to learn all your new tells." He lowered his voice. "FYI. I do my best research naked."

The image of him naked popped into her head, and her eyes bloomed wide. She pressed her lips together, blinking rapidly to try to clear the lust from her brain. He chuckled and turned back to the riding ring.

She swatted his arm. "That was *not* fair."

"I was just being honest. Would you rather I lied?"

"Yes."

He looked down as her toe hit the dirt and her ankle began wiggling, and they both laughed.

She bumped him with her shoulder. "Do you really have something to talk to me about, or did you just come here to get me flustered?"

"I do need to talk to you, but I have missed that gorgeous smile."

How could something so simple make her feel so good? "In that case, you're forgiven."

"Do you want to talk here?"

The other parents were sitting by the bull pen, giving them a modicum of privacy, and they had a few minutes before the kids started riding. "Sure. That way we won't miss Lucas's ride."

"I reached out to my buddy Reggie Steele. He's a PI. I asked him to look into the situation for us. What I'm about to tell you might be hard to hear, and it needs to stay between us. You can't talk it over with Jade or anyone else."

"Okay." She crossed her arms, needing a barrier between herself and any talk of her father. "What did he find out?"

"It seems the FBI has quietly been investigating your father for two years for a slew of corrupt activities from kickbacks to money laundering and bribery. They just need more proof before they can take him down for it."

"That's not hard to hear. I always knew he was dirty, and knowing what he did to his own daughter, I wouldn't put anything past him. Did you ask Reggie to track down Ana? She's the one I want to talk to."

"Yes. She's still working for your family."

"Of course she is. It's a cushy job."

"I think it might be more than that. She's got a thirteen-year-old son, and it looks like your father might be her son's father, too."

"*What?* No way. She never liked him. She used to talk about him behind his back, and she hated the way he treated me. She's the one who suggested I write you letters because he had all the phone lines tapped."

"I could be wrong, but there's no father listed on the birth certificate. Did you know she was married when she started working for your family?"

"I don't know. Maybe. Why?" There was a commotion by the bull pen, and she saw one of the girls putting on safety gear.

"A few years after she started working for your family, she got a divorce, and she had to get a restraining order against her ex, which Josh's father handled for her."

"Okay. That doesn't mean anything. Mr. Chambers helped other people my father knew."

"I assumed as much, but her ex was severely beaten shortly after it was filed, which reeks in similarity to what happened to me. There were no suspects, and there was no investigation into the beating."

"*Really?* That does sound similar, but I never saw any hint of an affair between my father and Ana. He didn't pay much attention to the staff. At least not that I saw."

"Do you think you would have noticed?"

She thought about it for a minute. "Maybe not. Between school and friends before that summer, I wasn't home all that much, and when I was, I spent most of the time in my room, and I definitely wasn't looking for anything like that. I can't imagine anyone wanting to be close to him."

"Neither can I, but there are more indications that something is or was going on between them. Your father bought Ana a house in a high-end community, and he sends her large sums of money every month. The money trail is buried in offshore companies, so it appears it's coming from her aunt overseas. Only she doesn't have an aunt overseas."

"Yes, she does. She told me she has an aunt who lives with her mother in Brazil."

"Reggie couldn't find a trace of an aunt. Ana's sister lives with her mother, and the money isn't coming from that sister, darlin'. In fact, Ana sends her mother money every month."

"Are you sure? Maybe Reggie missed something."

"He's been doing this for years, and he's too thorough to miss anything. But I figured we could take a ride out to Boulder and talk to Ana ourselves. She has Tuesdays off, and she goes to the same café for brunch every week. That said, if it's too difficult for you, I can do it on my own."

"It's *not* too difficult. I want to talk to her, and if it's true, then I need to hear it for myself. No offense to your friend, but she was like an older sister to me. She was my confidante and the only person I trusted in that house. I told her everything from the time I was eight years old."

His brows knitted. "Jule, she came to see you right before your father dragged you off the ranch. Did you tell her about us?"

She thought about that afternoon and how Ana had commented about how cute Seeley was and how close they seemed. She even said he looked at Juliette like she was special.

"I did confide in her," she remembered. "But she seemed genuinely happy for me, and she swore she wouldn't tell my father. Could my intuition have been that far off? It can't be possible that *every* adult who was in my life back then was that conniving."

Seeley put his hand on her back, compassion shimmering in his eyes. "Unfortunately, I think we've learned not to take anyone who was involved in this situation at face value."

She felt sick at the idea of Ana breaching her trust like that, but she refused to let that nightmare suck the life out of her like it did back then. She drew her shoulders back and said, "What time can you go Tuesday?"

"Reggie said she's at the café by eleven every week. I think we should get there a little early and stake it out. See if she meets your father."

"Okay. Lucas takes the bus to school, but I should let him know if we're leaving earlier than he does. What time are you thinking? Seven?"

"That works. I think we should be honest with Lucas and tell him where we're going. We don't have to give him details about what we suspect, but he needs to know that we're doing everything we can to get to the bottom of this."

"I agree, and I appreciate you taking him into consideration."

"He's on my mind twenty-four-seven, just like his incredibly sexy mother is."

It had been so long since either of them had been a priority in anyone else's life, her throat thickened with emotion.

"Do you think he'll mind if I stick around and watch him practice?"

"I don't know, but if I've learned one thing about teenagers, it's that they don't always know what's best, and I'd like you to stay and watch our son scare the life out of me."

"Our son," he said low and filled with emotion. His fingers curled around her waist, tugging her against his side. "Do you know how much I want to kiss you right now?"

"Probably half as much as I want you to."

"Good answer."

Why does every little thing you do reel me in? "Seeley, what are we doing? We're supposed to be going slow and getting to know each other again."

"We've always sucked at slow." His lips curved up in a devastating smile. "Besides, this *is* slow for us. If we weren't going slow, I'd've hauled your fine ass into my truck by now and reminded you exactly how much you like that we suck at slow."

"You..." She shook her head. "Don't say another word."

He laughed.

With that sinful thought in her head, she turned her attention to Lucas's practice, trying not to let herself get carried away.

When it came to her and Seeley, she sucked at that, too.

They cheered on the other kids, and Seeley made comments about their form and how well they did. When it was Lucas's turn, Seeley hollered, "Show that bull who's boss!"

As always happened when her son climbed onto a bull, her heart raced and she prayed he wouldn't get hurt. The bull charged out of the chute, and she tried to focus on Lucas and not the emotions stacking up inside her as Seeley cheered him on with pride in his eyes.

"Attaboy! He's got a hell of a grip. Look at him." Lucas was right-handed, and the bull was bucking left. "He's fucking phenomenal."

"Like you were—" The bull bucked Lucas off, and she gasped.

Seeley white-knuckled the metal rail in front of them like he was stopping himself from leaping over it, his jaw clenched tight, eyes locked on their boy. Lucas popped to his feet, and Seeley's breath rushed from his lungs as Lucas ran out of the ring.

"Damn." Seeley put his hand over his heart. "I wasn't expecting that."

"What?" She knew what she felt every time Lucas climbed on a bull, but since Seeley had ridden, too, she wondered what he was going to say.

"Stone-cold fear. He's an excellent rider, but *man*." He took off his cowboy hat and raked a hand through his hair, breathing deeply as he settled it back on his head. "Now I know why my mother used to say she lost a year of her life every time I climbed on a bull."

"At least they wear helmets and face guards now. It's hard to believe I could watch you out there when I was sixteen and not be scared for your life. I thought you were the coolest guy around."

"Well, darlin', you weren't wrong."

She laughed. "You definitely haven't lost that cockiness."

"Maybe you bring it out in me." He leaned in like he was going to kiss her but stopped short. "*Shit.* Sorry."

She couldn't help but love that, too.

As they watched the rest of the practice, Seeley had the same white-knuckled reaction each time Lucas was thrown off. It made her feel a little better knowing she wasn't alone in that fear. When practice ended, they made their way over to the group. Lucas was busy talking with the other kids.

Buck, a barrel-chested Black man and the best bull-riding coach around, headed their way, his gaze moving curiously between Juliette and Seeley. "Well, if this isn't just like old times. Good to see you, Doc." Buck shook Seeley's hand.

"Nice to see you, too, Buck," Seeley said.

Juliette saw Lucas walking their way, his smile replaced with a tight jaw. She hoped she hadn't made the wrong decision by letting Seeley stay.

"They looked good out there," Seeley said. "You've got a good group of riders on your hands."

"They're getting better every day," Buck said.

Lucas joined them, eyeing Seeley. "What're *you* doing here?"

"*Lucas*," Juliette chided.

Buck arched a brow.

"I came to talk with your mother and decided to stay to watch you ride," Seeley explained. "You're a hell of a rider."

Lucas didn't respond.

"That's a high compliment coming from this guy." Buck clapped a hand on Seeley's shoulder.

Lucas scoffed.

"You might want to check that attitude, young man," Buck said. "Doc was one of my best riders back in the day."

Lucas eyed Seeley with new curiosity. "You rode bulls?"

"That's right," Seeley said.

"He didn't just ride," Buck said. "Doc was the junior world champion four years in a row, and hit it again at eighteen."

"Seriously?" Lucas asked incredulously. "Do you still ride?"

"Nope." Seeley shook his head. "I'm a horse guy these days."

"If you'll excuse me, I've got to catch up with a few parents," Buck said. "Good seeing you, Doc, Juliette. Lucas, excellent practice. See you next time."

As Buck walked away, Lucas said, "Why'd you quit bull riding?"

Seeley glanced briefly at Juliette before responding. "Remember when I told you I couldn't see straight when your mother was torn from my life?"

"Yeah...?" Confusion riddled his brow.

"You know there's no room for distractions when you're on the back of a bull. You can put two and two together."

"And you just gave it up?" Lucas asked incredulously. "Just like that, because of a girl?"

"*Lucas,*" Juliette cautioned.

"It's a'right, Jule." Seeley's gaze never left Lucas. "There was no *just like that.* I had been riding bulls since I was eight years old. I lived and breathed for it. But I knew my limits, and I didn't want my parents watching me get gored because my concentration was shot."

Lucas swallowed hard, empathy rising in his eyes. "Did you miss it?"

"Yeah, I did. But not as much as I missed your mom."

That seemed to give Lucas a moment's pause, but then he mumbled, "*Whatever,*" and turned his attention to Juliette. "Robert's having some kids from school over tomorrow night. Can I go?"

"Are his parents going to be home?"

"*Yes,*" Lucas said exasperatedly.

"If we get the work around the property done in time and

you don't give me too much attitude, then sure."

"We have all day Sunday to get it done," he complained.

"They're calling for rain, remember?" Juliette reminded him.

"I can give you guys a hand," Seeley offered. "We can knock out whatever work you need done quicker if there are three of us."

There was a lot to be done, and she could use all the help she could get. But she didn't want to push Lucas. "Lucas, how would you feel about that?"

Lucas's face was so serious as he eyed Seeley, she was sure he was going to say no way. "*Whatever*. It's your house."

"Does that mean you're okay with me helping?" Seeley asked.

"I guess. If it'll get it done quicker," Lucas said.

A smile tugged at Seeley's lips. "Smart man."

Juliette stifled the urge to do a happy dance. It wasn't an open door, but it was a fissure in her wounded son's armor, and she knew Seeley would treat it with care.

Chapter Fifteen

"DOES THIS OLD barn remind you of anything?" Doc asked as he assessed the damage to the barn siding Saturday midmorning with Juliette. Lucas hadn't made it outside yet.

"Only some of the best stolen kisses I've ever had." She looked sweet and sexy, with her cowgirl hat shading her beautiful baby blues from the sun, wearing cutoffs, a salmon tank top that clung to her curves, and worn work boots that told him she was no stranger to doing these types of chores.

"Oh yeah?" He dragged his gaze down the length of her. "I'd like to steal a lot more than kisses right now."

She smiled a little bashfully, and that sweetness only made him want to kiss her more. He really needed to get his mind *off* the things he wanted to do to her. But it wasn't easy. The other night had given him a taste of the woman he'd craved for his entire adult life, and it had only whetted his appetite. The more he learned about her and Lucas, the closer they became, and the stronger that ache to be with her took hold.

Pushing those thoughts away was not easy, but he tried to distract himself. "How was Lucas this morning?"

"About the same, I guess. Maybe a little less tense. He didn't really say much, but he's been texting a lot."

"Probably bitching to his friends about me, and that's okay. He needs an outlet."

"I wish he'd talk to me, but I'm trying not to push."

"He will when he's ready. I talked with my mom a little this morning, and she thinks that in addition to dealing with me being his biological father, part of his struggle is that other than Josh, he's never had to deal with someone else having strong feelings for you, or you having feelings for them."

She sighed. "I know. I'm hoping the therapist can help with all of that."

"Are you sure you don't want me to come with you to the appointment?" He'd offered when they'd talked on the phone last night, but she hadn't taken him up on it.

"At some point, maybe, but right now I think I need to talk to her as much as Lucas does. To figure things out, you know?"

As they rounded the back of the barn, he slid his arm around her waist, drawing her into his arms. "Is that your way of telling me to back off?"

"*No*, as long as we're careful around Lucas, I don't want you to back off."

"Why do you think I waited until we were behind the barn to touch you?" He brushed his scruff along her cheek, and she breathed a little harder. "I'd never do anything to hurt our boy."

"That's about the best foreplay you could ever use on me."

"That's not foreplay, darlin'. It's a promise." She was looking at him so longingly, his restraint snapped. "*This* is foreplay." His mouth came hungrily down over hers in a scorching kiss that had them both going a little wild. He tangled his hand in her hair, backing her up against the barn, grinding against her, swallowing her moans of pleasure. "I've been dying to kiss you since yesterday."

She made a needy sound and pulled his mouth back to hers.

He deepened the kiss, sliding his free hand to her ass, and she bowed against him. He broke the kiss on a growl, trailing kisses down her neck, earning one sinful sound after another. "*Fuck*. Those sounds are killing me." He knew they were on borrowed time and listened for Lucas like they used to listen for Hazel when they were making out in the barn or the yard, as he gently tugged her tank top down just low enough to kiss the swell of her breast, earning a desperate "*Seeley—*" and a rock of her hips, taking his mind to dark, erotic places. Her plea was music to his ears, and he took her in another soul-searing kiss, which had her moaning and arching into him. A door slammed in the distance, and they reluctantly drew back. "Fuck."

"*That* brings back memories."

"So does this." He stole one last kiss. *"Mm-mm."*

"How do you always get me revved up so fast?" She squirmed in her shorts as she adjusted her top.

"It's a gift." He picked up their hats and placed hers on her head. "Would you rather I kept my hands to myself?"

"*No*. I just can't believe we're still sneaking around like teenagers," she said, and they both laughed as they headed around the side of the barn.

Lucas was standing in the middle of the yard wearing a loose T-shirt, jeans, and his cowboy hat, thumbing out a text.

"I need to run inside and freshen up," she said. "Do you think you two will be okay for a few minutes?"

"Of course." Lucas was still focused on his phone, so Doc swatted Juliette's ass as she walked away, earning an adorable glare over her shoulder.

She stopped to talk to Lucas. Doc couldn't hear what she

said, but as she headed up to the house, Lucas pocketed his phone and made his way down to the barn.

"How's it going?" Doc asked.

"*Fine*," Lucas bit out, sounding anything but fine. His gaze moved to Doc's cowboy hat. He made an annoyed sound and tossed his own hat onto the grass.

"Something wrong with your hat?"

"*No*. I don't feel like wearing it."

Doc knew spending the day with him wasn't going to be a walk in the park, and that was okay. He wanted to get to know his son, and the only way to do that was to build trust, which took patience and understanding and the ability to let Lucas's attitude roll off his back. He'd never been great at that, but Dare had given him a few pointers, and he was trying. "This old barn has seen better days. But I love working with my hands. How about you?"

"Not really," Lucas said with a tone that implied Doc had asked a stupid question.

That wasn't quite the love of working with his hands that Juliette had mentioned. "Then it's a good thing I'm here to help cut that work in half. Ready to get started?"

He kicked the grass. "Whatever."

"I'll take that as a yes. Let's come up with a plan of attack and lay it all out so we can plow through it. A lot of this siding needs to be replaced, and the roof and gutters need attention, too."

Lucas met his gaze. "I figured we'd patch the siding."

"I don't know, bud. It looks like it's been patched to death."

"So?" He motioned to a board that was rotted at the bottom. "We can cut above the rot. It'll be fine."

There was no way in hell they'd waste their time doing that, but he didn't want Lucas thinking he was walking into his life and taking over, so he said, "Maybe you're right. Let's take a closer look." They went to inspect the board. Doc pointed farther up. "See where it's warped? You can see a path where the water has leaked from that broken gutter."

"So? It's not rotted yet."

"The key word being *yet*. We can patch it, but a few good rains, and we'll be out here tearing that whole board off. Take a look at some of the others. They're damaged in several places. Don't you think it makes more sense to do it right rather than doing a half-ass job that'll cost us time later?"

"*No*," Lucas complained. "It's gonna take forever."

"It'll take forever *twice* if we do it your way." Doc was starting to understand why his father used to argue for only so long before saying, *We're doing it my way, because it's the right way.*

"Hey," Juliette hollered as she hurried down the hill. She'd changed into jeans and cowgirl boots. "I just got a call from Jade. She's away this weekend, and one of her clients has an emergency. I need to go take care of it. I'm sorry, Seeley, but can we reschedule? I don't know how long I'll be gone."

"You can go take care of whatever you need to. Lucas and I can handle this by ourselves. Right, Lucas? Get ahead of the rain?"

Lucas set his jaw. "Yeah. We've got it."

"Okay. If you're sure." Juliette glanced hopefully between them. When Lucas didn't complain, she said, "Great. Hopefully I won't be too long." She went to hug Lucas.

"*Mom.*" He stepped back, out of her reach.

Doc wanted to say something, but he bit his tongue.

"Sorry. I forget you're not a kid anymore." She smiled playfully. "But in my heart, you'll always be my baby boy."

"What*ever*. Just go." Lucas turned away.

Juliette looked amused. "I'll be as quick as I can. There's food and drinks in the fridge."

"I brought a cooler full, but thanks. We'll see you later."

She mouthed, *Is he okay?*

Doc nodded, tossed her a wink, and headed over to Lucas. "A'right. Let's get a handle on this."

As they walked around the barn inspecting the siding, every time Doc pointed to a board that needed replacing, Lucas argued or grumbled.

"We'll knock it out as quickly as we can," Doc promised.

Lucas did not look convinced. "It'll take twice as long to measure and cut all the boards."

"Not if we do it my way. I know a trick that'll speed things up. Do you have tools?"

"Yeah."

"A sawhorse?"

"No."

"No problem. I brought one. Grab your tools, and I'll get mine and the sawhorse from my truck." Doc set up the sawhorse beside the wood planks and other supplies.

Lucas came out of the shed wearing a leather toolbelt with a hammer hanging from it, carrying two hand saws and a box of nails. He put the saws and nails in the grass by Doc. "What now?"

"You tell me. If I weren't here, what would you do next?"

"I'd cut the rotted pieces off and patch 'em."

Doc chuckled. "Well, since I don't want to do this twice, how about we tear off the rotted boards so we can replace them?"

They worked in silence for a while, but eventually Doc tried to break the ice. "You've obviously done stuff like this before. How'd you learn to do it?"

"YouTube."

Doc tossed a board onto the discard pile. "You're lucky you have that at your fingertips. I had to follow my old man around the ranch and help him fix everything from the time I was yay high." He held his hand out beside his thigh.

"I'd've rather done that," Lucas said sharply.

Doc realized his mistake. *Shit.* "I'm sorry, Lucas. I wasn't thinking. That must've been awful losing your dad when you were so young."

Lucas clenched his jaw, prying the board from the barn aggressively with the claw hammer.

"What was your dad like?"

Lucas eyed him skeptically.

"I'd really like to know," Doc said. "He was an important part of your life, but you don't have to tell me about him if you'd rather not."

He tugged the board free and tossed it onto the pile. "He was awesome. A big-time lawyer. Smarter than *anyone* I've ever known." He said *anyone* with venom, like it was a dig at Doc.

"He sounds like a great guy."

"He was the greatest."

"What kind of things did you do together?" It was a tough question, since Lucas had been so young when Josh was killed, but Doc was curious, and he wanted Lucas to know he didn't see Josh as the enemy.

"Stuff." Lucas tugged nails from another board, his jaw tightening the way Doc's did when he didn't want to talk about something.

Doc pulled another board free, gritting out, "You're lucky.

Some kids don't have great parents to do stuff with. Look at your mom."

Lucas didn't respond.

Doc tried to make small talk a few more times, bringing up bull riding, cattle roping, and the horses at the ranch, but each and every time he was met with silence. They worked in that uncomfortable silence, tearing off boards and tossing them into a pile, for a long time.

As Doc pried off the last rotted board, Lucas wiped the sweat from his brow and said, "I need a drink." He turned to head up to the house.

"Grab my cooler from the truck. I could use one, too." Doc tossed the board on the pile.

Lucas retrieved the cooler and set it in the grass, opening the top. "Are you fu—"

"What's the matter? You don't like Dr Pepper? Toss me one, will ya?"

Lucas grabbed a can from the cooler, his eyes narrowing. He beaned it at Doc as hard as he could.

Doc dodged it. "What the hell was that for?"

"*Dr Freaking Pepper?*" Lucas said angrily.

"You don't like it?"

"You think I don't know what you and my mom are doing?" he yelled. "I know this was a freaking setup. She didn't have an emergency. She just wanted us to spend time together."

"Whoa, Lucas. We would *never* do that to you."

"Yeah, right. Like she didn't tell you that Dr Pepper is my favorite soda?"

"I promise she didn't. It's been my favorite since I was a kid. You can ask anyone who knows me." He held his hands up in surrender, closing the distance between them. "Listen, buddy."

"I'm *not* your buddy!" Lucas crossed his arms, his fingers drumming.

Doc's chest constricted. "You're right. I'm sorry. This is a tough situation for all of us, and we're in it because people lied to us. We're not going to make this harder on you by making shit up or forcing you to spend time with me."

"Then that's even worse," he hollered, but there was pain in his voice this time. "That means..." He turned around and cursed.

"What, Lucas? What does it mean?"

He spun around, his watery eyes shooting daggers. "I don't *want* to have anything in common with you."

That cut like a knife, taking Doc aback. "Okay. Would you mind telling me why?"

"Because it's not fair to *him*."

"To—"

"My *dad*! He didn't like horses or anything that had to do with ranching. He didn't like working with his hands or getting dirty, and he's not here to even *try* to find something we could have in common. I don't want to..." He dragged his forearm over his eyes, wiping tears, and turned away. "Never mind."

His pain was so raw, it broke Doc's heart. Suddenly Lucas tossing off his cowboy hat made sense. Doc lowered his voice, talking more gently, but not so cautiously that Lucas would think he was treating him like a child. "Lucas, nothing will ever take away the bond you and your dad had. It wasn't what you had in common that mattered. He helped you become the person you are today. He was there for those formative years, loving you, changing your diapers, putting you to bed, teaching you life lessons that you didn't realize you were learning. People are made to learn and grow. More people than you can ever remember will come in and out of your life, and you'll have things in common with a lot of them. But that won't steal anything from what you and your dad shared."

"I don't even remember *what* we shared." His voice cracked, his back still to Doc, his shoulders rounded in defeat. "I just pretend to, because I know I loved him and he loved me, but it feels like a story someone told me. What does it say about *me*, that I can love him and forget those things?"

Shattered for his son, Doc stepped around him so he could see his face. "It says you loved him deeply, and you were awfully little when you lost him. No four-year-old is thinking they have to memorize a face or an activity because they might never see the person they're with again. You were a little kid living in the moment like you should've been. Nobody expects you to remember more than that, and I've got to believe Josh is watching over you with pride in his heart, because from everything your mom has told me, and from what I've seen, you're a hell of a strong, caring kid."

He scoffed. "Strong people don't cry."

"Who sold you that line of crap? You think I've never cried? You think I didn't cry when I lost my grandfather, or your mom, or found out I had a son?" That brought Lucas's eyes to his, but only briefly. "Let me tell you something. You can be tough as nails and cold as ice, and as you've witnessed, I can be both, but it doesn't make me stronger."

"You seemed pretty strong to me."

Doc shook his head. "That was me at my weakest. What you saw was insecurity. I was hurt and humiliated because I thought your mother had thrown me away."

Lucas met his gaze again, blinking away his tears.

"Strength comes from a hundred different things, Lucas. It

comes from confidence and compassion and honesty. It doesn't matter if you're crying or yelling as long as it's honest emotion. It's understandable that you can't remember things about your dad, but your mom has pictures from the years he was alive. She can share those memories with you, and we can *all* help keep them alive. She shared some with me the other night on the phone."

"About my dad?" he asked disbelievingly.

"Mostly about you, but also about him, and it made me even more grateful that you had a mom and dad who loved you when I didn't know you existed."

Lucas's eyes narrowed skeptically. "You really don't hate him?"

"No. I really don't."

"If I were you, I'd hate him if he married the girl I loved."

"How can I hate a guy who stepped up to raise my son?" He let that sink in. "I don't want to pretend the first fifteen years of your life didn't happen, and I don't want to erase or replace your memories. I'd like to think as we get to know each other, we could make new and different memories. I hope one day you'll see the things we have in common as something we can build on instead of reasons to dislike me."

Lucas shook his head, swiping at his tears until his cheeks were dry.

"You can push me away and refuse to see me if you want to. That's your right. And if you don't ever want to have a relationship with me, that's your choice. But you should know that no matter how many times you buck me off, it won't keep me from coming back and trying again. Whiskeys don't give up on family." He clapped a hand on Lucas's shoulder. "And like it or not, big guy, you are my family."

Lucas opened his mouth as if he were going to speak, but closed it again.

"Listen, the last thing I want is for you to feel like you're stuck being around me today. If you need space, I get it. You can go hang out at the house. I can finish this work by myself."

Lucas looked at the wood pile, and the barn, as if he were mulling it over.

"If you're worried about what your mom will say, I don't think she'll mind. She knows how difficult this is. Hell, it's hard for all of us."

"I know she'd understand, but she'll try to make me talk about it."

Doc smiled, knowing she would. "That's because she loves you, and if you're sad or in pain, she is, too. It's a parental thing." One Doc hadn't ever grasped as clearly as he did when he'd seen Lucas get bucked off that bull yesterday. "You think your mom likes to talk things out? Try having a psychologist for a mother. She still tries to get me to talk about my feelings all the time, and I'm thirty-five. Then there's my younger brother Dare and our buddy Ezra. They're both therapists, and if they get a whiff of me being under any extra stress, they try to talk it out, too. I'm surrounded by people who talk shit out, and you know what?"

"It's way too much talking?" Lucas asked with a hint of amusement.

"It is a lot, and that's a hassle, but they've helped me through some of my toughest times. I'm grateful that they're talkaholics, because if it weren't for them, I'd be an angry, reclusive dick most of the time."

"I guess you win. I've only got my mom talking at me."

"Talking *with* you, not at you." Doc looked up at the barn.

"So, you want to finish this barn with me, or are you heading inside? Either is fine."

"I'll finish it. I don't want to disappoint my mom."

"Good man." Doc gave a curt nod. "I'd like to say you got that work ethic from me, but since we just met, I guess you got it from your mom." He grabbed a Dr Pepper from the cooler. "Still thirsty?"

"Yeah."

Doc tossed him the can. "Next time you have something to say, lay it on the line. Don't try to break my skull with a can."

"Sorry about that." He kicked the ground.

"It's a'right, but don't do it again." Doc opened a can of soda and took a drink. "Best soda ever."

Lucas's lips twitched into a semi-smile. "We can agree on that. Just don't tell me your favorite cookies are mint chocolate chip."

What the...? "Did your mother tell *you* all of *my* secrets?"

Lucas's eyes widened. "Are you freaking kidding me?"

Doc laughed. "Stranger things have happened. Drink up. Then I'll show you my trick to making this work go fast."

"Hiring someone else to do it?" he asked hopefully.

"I didn't know you were a dreamer."

Chapter Sixteen

LUCAS WAS PRETTY quiet as they replaced the siding, but he didn't fight Doc on every little thing, and Doc took that as a good sign. Juliette texted to say she'd be a while, and Doc reassured her that things were okay on the home front. When they took a break to eat lunch, in between Lucas thumbing out texts, Doc got him talking about his horses and what he liked about bull riding.

Clouds rolled in as they got back to work, but when the sun cut through, it was stifling. Lucas had been squinting against it all day. Doc wanted to tell him that wearing his hat didn't have to mean anything about the two of them, but he kept that to himself because, thankfully, Lucas was more receptive to talking while they worked the second time around, and he didn't want to rock that boat. He kept the conversation light and stayed away from anything too personal, until Lucas stopped working to send about his fifth text in ten minutes, a grin curving his lips.

"Girlfriend?" Doc asked.

"Not really."

"Do you want her to be?"

Lucas shrugged and pocketed his phone.

"I'll take that as a no."

"I didn't say that," he griped.

Sounded like Doc struck a nerve. "Well, I haven't been your age in a long time, but I remember *knowing* when I wanted someone to be my girl. A shrug means you're not sure, and that's okay."

"That's *not* what it means."

"No?"

"*No*. It means I don't want to tell you."

"Fair enough." Doc grinned. "But you just did."

Lucas rolled his eyes.

"Hey, I'm not going to lecture you or ask a million questions. But I will say this. How you're seen in the eyes of girls starts now, and you've got two choices. You can treat girls with respect, think of their well-being before your own, and be the guy who sets the standard for how they *should* be treated. If you do that, every girl will want to go out with you. Or you can be the guy whose reputation for being a dick supersedes him when he enters a room. That's a tough rep to shake in a small town like this."

"Which were you?"

"At your age? I was a cocky-ass bull rider with a long line of girls after me. I was the guy who set the standard." Doc took off his hat and wiped his brow. As he set it back on his head, he said, "But I know you don't want to have anything in common with me, and hopefully you won't follow in my footsteps, because after all that shit went down with your grandfather, when I gave up bull riding and went to college, I became the other guy for a while. Ghosting women, not caring if their feelings were hurt." He picked up a board and set it in place.

"That was a long time ago, but I still regret it."

"Then why'd you do it?"

"Because I'd had my heart broken once, and I wasn't about to go through that nightmare again."

They worked in silence for a few minutes, before Lucas said, "Are you still a dick?"

"No, and I haven't been for many years."

"What changed?"

He met his son's gaze, mulling over his answer, and remembered something his father had once said when a kid who had been emotionally abused by his parents and put into the foster care system had come through one of the ranch's programs. That kid's confidence had been driven into the ground, and Tiny had said, *Parents don't realize how much power they have. If you ever have a family of your own, you'll have moments when your kid does stupid shit, and you'll want to tell them as much. Especially when they're in those belligerent teenage years. But you bite your tongue and choose your words carefully, because kids learn from every word you say, and every word you don't. They're going to make hundreds of mistakes, and it's up to you to help them learn from them. Never forget that a single sentence can change a kid for better or worse, and if you repeatedly tell them they're less than anything, they'll believe you.*

Doc chose his words carefully and honestly. "My old man sat me down and said he'd heard I was going down a slippery slope that wasn't going to end well, and he reminded me that I had two choices."

"So you decided to set the standard?"

"Yes, but on my own terms. I didn't want to be a dick, but I also didn't want to get tangled up in a relationship. So instead of ghosting them, I was honest up front about not looking for anything long term. As I got older and realized what setting the standard really meant, I started putting more energy into making sure the women I was with had a good time and felt good about themselves. More importantly, I made sure they knew my lack of commitment wasn't a reflection on them."

"And they bought that?" He looked skeptical.

"It was the truth, so yeah. It's always best to lead with honesty."

A while later, as they finished installing the last board they had, they were still two boards short. "We made good time. Nice work."

"Thanks." Lucas squinted up at the remaining gaps in the siding. "But we're two boards short."

"Yeah, I know. I don't suppose you have a lumber pile hiding somewhere."

He shook his head. "Mom's afraid of snakes getting into them."

Doc remembered the time they'd seen a snake in the woods, and she'd jumped onto his back without warning. He laughed. "That she is. We've got plenty of this type of lumber at the ranch. I'll call my brother and have him bring us a couple of boards. We need some gutter, too. What about the fence? Think we need any additional supplies?"

"No. The wood for the barn was here when we moved in, but my mom had everything we need for the fence delivered. It's over there."

"Okay. Give me a sec." Doc made the call, and Cowboy answered on the second ring.

"Hey, Daddy. How's it going?"

"Better than it's gonna be for you if you don't cut that shit out. You busy?"

"Depends. What do you need?"

"We're two boards short with the siding on the barn, and we need some gutter." He explained exactly what they needed, and Cowboy said he'd bring it over. "Thanks, Cowboy. See you soon." He pocketed his phone. "Okay, we're all set."

"*Cowboy?* How many brothers do you have?"

"Just the two, Cowboy and Dare. I've also got two younger sisters, Sasha and Birdie. We all live and work at the ranch except Birdie."

"Y'all have weird names."

"My brothers and I go by our road names. Our biker names. Dare's real name is Devlin, and Cowboy's is Callahan."

His brow furrowed. "And is Birdie a biker?"

"No. Her given name is Blaire, but trust me, she's Birdie through and through. She is the youngest, and she's always marched to her own beat."

"Why doesn't she live at the ranch?"

"She doesn't want to. She lives in Allure and owns Divine Intervention chocolate shop with our aunt and a family friend."

"That's cool."

"Yeah, she's good at it, but I can't imagine working anywhere other than Redemption Ranch."

"My mom told me a little about the ranch, but I don't know what *you* do there."

"Let's load the old boards onto my truck, and I'll tell you." They began carrying the boards. "I'm a veterinarian, like your mom."

Lucas was reaching for a piece of wood and stopped midway. "Seriously?"

"Pretty wild, huh? It's all I ever wanted to do. Your mom said you've been into horses since you were little. Those are two beauties in your pasture. Do you know what you want to do when you grow up?"

"I don't know, but not *that*."

That was a far cry from the horse-loving answer he'd expected. "Well, you've got plenty of time to figure it out." As they carried another load to the truck, he said, "I knew from the time I was a little kid I wanted to help horses. The ranch has been in my mom's family for generations."

"Did you always live there?"

"Yeah. It was only a horse rescue until my dad came through town and fell in love with my mom. She was getting ready to start graduate school at the time. He's from Maryland, and he never went back. He started working for my grandfather at the ranch."

"Seriously? He *never* went home?" He loaded up his arms with more planks.

"Yeah. I mean, he visited, but never went back for good. He and my mom are the reason the ranch helps people now, too. My old man was hiring ranch hands who had been in prison or had gone through recovery for drugs or alcohol. He was trying to give them a helping hand to find their footing, but they kept not showing up for work and falling back into their old ways."

"That's what happens when you hire dumbasses."

Doc stopped walking. "Hey, don't do that."

"What?"

"Don't judge people."

"You gotta be stupid to do drugs or end up in prison."

Doc shook his head. "No, you don't. Sometimes it's the circumstances you were brought up in. It's stealing to put food on the table, or growing up in a house full of drugs, where there's no escape, or suffering a life event that throws them over the edge, like grief or losing their job and their house. You can't know what someone has been through until you've asked."

"Well, you said they fell right back into old habits. What does that tell you?"

"The important thing is what it told my parents." Doc picked up another load of wood. "My father realized that many of the people he was hiring had no family or friends. No support system. They'd lost their support while their lives were in turmoil, so after they left the ranch each night, they had no one telling them they'd done a good job, or they were better than where they came from. They had no purpose."

Lucas tossed the wood he was carrying into the truck. "What does that mean?"

"It means they were working to make ends meet, but they had no connection to that work. It was just a job, and it wasn't helping them heal the relationships they'd lost or find their way back into society. Luckily, my parents realized those people needed more than money. They needed help and guidance. They needed a purpose for the work they were doing on the ranch, and they needed a reason to work on themselves, too."

"I don't get it." Lucas tossed another plank into the truck bed.

"After my mom graduated and did all the things she needed to do in order to open a practice, they expanded Redemption Ranch to help people as well as horses. They added therapeutic services and came up with programs to help people of all ages. Even kids your age." As they grabbed a few more planks, he said, "Our clients live and work on the ranch, and they attend therapy to work on themselves. But if you ask me, one of the most important things that our ranch does is give them a sense of family."

"But they're paying you, right? That's not really family."

"Clients don't pay a penny. We run on grants and donations." He tossed the last board into the truck. "They become family because when you live and work together, that's what happens. I can't remember a time when there weren't twenty or thirty people around our tables at mealtime."

He crossed his arms. "You *eat* with them?"

"Our whole family does, and so does everyone who works or lives there, and some people who don't."

"What do you mean?"

"Well, Birdie comes by when she can, and my cousin Rebel is there all the time. And anyone who works at the ranch or goes through one of our programs is family by the time they leave, and they're always welcome back. Even if only for a visit."

"That's so weird." They headed over to get drinks.

"It's not traditional, that's for sure." Doc grabbed a bottle of water from the cooler and tossed one to Lucas. "But we've helped hundreds of people find a new lease on life, and many have stayed on even after they were done with the program."

"So, your mom *and* Dare are therapists on the ranch?"

"That's right. Ezra, too." He took a drink. "He went through one of our programs as a kid after his mother abandoned him and his father. He became a therapist to help other kids, and he and his little boy, Gus, have lived on the ranch for years. Now Ezra's engaged to my sister Sasha. She's an equine rehabilitation therapist, which means she helps the horses heal."

"What does Cowboy do?"

"He manages the ranch hands. Our team also includes a residential manager and a cook, two on-call physicians, and a handful of other staff, and they're all family."

"That's a *lot* of people to call family."

"It is, but it's good to have family. You should come by sometime. I'll show you around, and you can decide for yourself. We work hard, and we give each other shit, but we play hard, too. We've got a paintball field, and everyone plays. Even my parents and Gus, who's only five."

Lucas choked on his water and coughed. "You let him play paintball?"

"Heck yeah. We never leave anyone out. We're all careful with him, of course."

"I wasn't allowed to play until I was thirteen."

Doc grinned. "We run things a little differently at our place. If you come by, you can meet Dare's wife, Billie. She teaches kids your age to ride motocross. She's got a racetrack on the ranch."

Shock shimmered in his eyes. "No *way*. Do you think she would teach me to ride?"

"Probably, but you'd have to get the okay from your mom."

"She lets me ride *bulls*. She'll probably be thrilled about me riding a motocross bike."

Doc knew Juliette might have hesitations because of what happened to Eddie, but Lucas didn't need to hear about that. Billie would keep him safe. Doc would make sure of it. "You're probably right."

They finished their waters, and as they tossed the empty bottles into the cooler, Cowboy's truck pulled down the driveway. "There's Cowboy. No pressure, but if you want to meet one of your uncles, he's a pretty great guy."

Lucas's expression turned wary. He lowered his eyes and kicked the grass. "Was he one of the people looking for me the night I took off?"

"Yes, but we've all been there. Remember what I said about

not judging people?"

Lucas nodded.

"He's never walked in your shoes. He's not going to judge you just because your life was turned upside down and it was overwhelming. Remember, he puts his jeans on the same way you do. One leg at a time. And by the way, I've seen Cowboy cry. You'll understand why that's astonishing when you see him."

That earned a smile, and they headed for the truck.

Dare practically flew out the passenger door, shouting, "Have no fear. Your coolest uncle is here." He ran across the grass and did a flip in the air, holding his cowboy hat on his head as he did it.

"Whoa!" Lucas exclaimed.

"That's Dare," Doc said with amusement. "He's the biggest daredevil *and* show-off you'll ever meet."

"*He's* the therapist? Look at all those tattoos." As Cowboy climbed out of the truck, his tank top showing off his massive muscles and breadth, Lucas's eyes nearly bugged out of his head. "There's no way you saw that guy cry."

"Don't let his size fool you. He's got a big heart behind all that muscle. And for the record, there are only two times when size matters. The first is if you run up against a guy Cowboy's size, swing first and pray later."

Lucas laughed. "And the second?"

Doc eyed him. "You're not old enough to worry about that yet. Come on." He strode toward his brothers. "Thanks for bringing the wood, guys."

"Your wood always did come up short." Dare laughed at his own joke. Lucas and Cowboy joined him.

"Very funny," Doc said. "Which one of us produced an

awesome kid? Oh yeah, that'd be me. Now stop talking crap and say hello to Lucas."

"Hi, Lucas. I'm Dare." He sidled up to Lucas and hiked a thumb at Doc. "He's almost as bossy as Cowboy. Was he a pain in your butt all day?"

Lucas's gaze flicked to Doc, then back to Dare. "*Nah*. He's been pretty cool."

That surprised Doc, but damn, it sure felt good to hear it.

"That's good, because I'd hate to have to kick his ass," Dare teased.

Doc arched a brow. "You and what army?"

"He's secretly terrified of me," Dare said to Lucas.

"Of your smell, maybe," Cowboy said.

Lucas laughed.

It was good to see him less on edge.

"How's it going, Lucas? I'm Cowboy, and I'm really happy to meet you."

"Hi." Lucas fidgeted with his tool belt, his gaze flicking briefly to Doc.

Loving that he trusted him enough to look to him for reassurance, Doc gave a slight nod. *I told you it'd be okay.*

Cowboy motioned to the pasture. "Those your horses?"

"Yeah."

"They're beautiful," Cowboy said.

"Thanks." Lucas pushed his hands into his front pockets.

Knowing Lucas was a little uncomfortable, Doc said, "Thanks for bringing the supplies. Let's get them unloaded. We've got a lot more work ahead of us, and Lucas has plans for tonight."

"What's left to do?" Dare asked.

"Patch the roof, fix the gutters, and repair the fence on the other pasture," Doc said.

Dare and Cowboy exchanged a glance, and Dare said, "Why don't we take the roof and gutters while you two fix the fence? Knock it out twice as fast?"

Lucas looked confused. "Don't you have better things to do than work?"

"We're never too busy to help family," Cowboy said.

Lucas's eyes narrowed, his gaze shifting between Cowboy and Doc. "Did he tell you to say that?"

Doc wasn't surprised he was skeptical, and he was glad he wasn't afraid to voice his concern directly to his brothers.

"No, sir. That's how we were raised," Cowboy answered. "Family first, then playtime."

Dare nudged Lucas. "Plus, roof work has two things I love. Getting my hands dirty, and driving Cowboy batty by doing flips on the roof."

As Dare headed for Cowboy's truck, Lucas said, "Will he really do that?"

Doc said "Yes" at the same time Cowboy said "Over my dead body."

LUCAS WAS FRIENDLIER as they worked on the fence, asking questions about Dare and Cowboy and the ranch. Doc was enjoying it. In no hurry to finish the work, he did everything he could to keep Lucas talking as they replaced and repaired the fencing.

By the time they finished, they were hot and sweaty, and still, Doc was sorry to be done. But it was getting late. Juliette had texted to say she'd be back soon, and Lucas was excited to see his friends.

"I really appreciate your help," Doc said to Cowboy and Dare as they got ready to leave.

"Yeah, thanks a lot," Lucas said. "The fence took a lot longer than I thought it would. We never would have gotten done in time for me to see my friends tonight if you guys hadn't helped."

Dare and Cowboy glanced at Doc, knowing he could have finished it in half the time had he wanted to.

"That's ranch work for you," Cowboy said.

"I'm glad we got a chance to meet you, Lucas," Dare said. "You should come by the ranch sometime and hang out with the cool kids."

"You have kids?" Lucas asked.

"Dude." Dare held up his palms in disbelief. "I meant *us*."

Lucas grimaced. "Aren't you like thirtysomething?"

"Is he calling me old?" Dare didn't wait for an answer. "Seriously, though, you should come to the ranch and hang out."

"You can check out our horses and the paintball field," Cowboy suggested.

"I'll show you the obstacle course where I've spent a lifetime whipping their butts," Dare offered.

Worried Lucas might get overwhelmed, Doc stepped in. "I already extended an invitation for Lucas to come to the ranch. I'm sure when he's ready, he'll let us know."

"Right, of course," Dare said. "No pressure."

"We'd better get going. I want to take Sully to the movies tonight," Cowboy said.

"Who's Sully?" Lucas asked.

Cowboy grinned. "She's my fiancée. You'll like her. She's a

sweetheart, and a horse whisperer."

"As opposed to my wife, Billie, who's a badass and a Dare whisperer," Dare said.

"Why is everything a competition with you?" Cowboy asked as he and Dare climbed into the truck.

"Are they always like that?" Lucas asked with amusement.

"Pretty much." Doc watched them drive away.

"It's freaking hot out here."

Lucas pulled off his T-shirt, and Doc was struck speechless at the sight of the necklace he'd made with his grandfather hanging around his son's neck. He hadn't seen it in so long, he felt a tweak in his chest, remembering his grandfather's strong hands helping him with the tools they'd used as they'd made it. There was a knot representing their strong family bond above two horse heads that faced each other, with silver bands protectively winding around them and through their manes, coming together in a point at the bottom. Doc had seen those bands as their family protecting the horses. But that night in the lake, Juliette had said the horses represented him and her, and the necklace formed a heart. That was the first time he'd noticed the heart shape. His grandfather had loved the horses as much as he'd loved his wife, and as the necklace shimmered in the sunlight, Doc wondered if his grandfather had seen that heart all along.

"Something wrong?" Lucas asked.

Doc broke his stare. "No. Where'd you get that necklace?"

Lucas touched the metal charm. "It was my mom's good luck charm. She wore it every day for as long as I can remember."

His thoughts stumbled again at the idea that she'd continued wearing it when she'd thought he wanted nothing to do with her and Lucas. "And she gave it to you?"

"Yeah. When I started bull riding, as my good luck charm. Why?"

"I'm not sure I should tell you. I don't want anything happening to that necklace."

Lucas's jaw tightened. "You gave it to her, didn't you?"

"Yes, I did. My grandfather and I made it when I was a little kid. I never took it off until I gave it to your mom. But that necklace is between you and her now. Please don't let me ruin that for you."

Lucas wrapped his fist around it, his brows pinched.

"Please don't destroy it or throw it away. If you don't want it, I get it. You can give it back to your mom or give it to me, but *please*. My grandfather is gone, and that necklace means more to me than you can imagine."

His jaw ticked. "It can't mean that much. You gave it away."

"I gave it to the girl I thought I was going to spend my life with."

"But you thought she dumped you. Why didn't you ask for it back?" Before Doc could respond, Lucas said, "*Wait*," remorsefully. "You couldn't, right? Because of her stupid father?"

"Yeah, but even if I could have, I wouldn't have asked for it back."

"Why not if it's so important to you?" he challenged.

Doc's pulse ratcheted up, like it had the night he'd slipped the necklace over Juliette's head and said, *You and me forever, darlin'*. "I made a promise when I gave it to her, and from that moment on, it was no longer mine."

Lucas was silent for a beat, still clutching the charm. "Well, do you want it back?"

"No. I'm glad she gave it to you, but it's okay if you don't want it."

"I'm keeping it," he said sharply, and let go of the charm. "Like you said, it's between me and my mom now."

Doc breathed a sigh of relief. "Okay."

Lucas's shoulders relaxed, and he looked relieved, too. "Thanks for helping me today."

"Anytime."

Lucas touched the charm again as Juliette came down the driveway. "I won't do anything bad to the necklace. It's not your fault I didn't know about you."

"It's not your mom's fault either. She really thought she was protecting you."

He looked down at the ground. "Whatever."

"She loves you, Lucas. Don't *ever* doubt that."

Juliette climbed out of her truck, eyeing them with concern. "Is everything okay?"

"Yeah," Doc said.

"We got everything done," Lucas said anxiously. "Can I still go to Robert's?"

She looked toward the shed. "Wow, the barn looks brand-new. I thought you were going to patch it, not redo the whole thing."

"We'd just have to do it all over again after a few good rains," Lucas said, parroting what Doc had said earlier. "The fence is done, too. Doc said the gate was too rickety, so we rebuilt it. Can I go?"

She looked at Doc incredulously. "That's amazing, and yes, you can go, Lucas, but we need to talk about your curfew."

"Midnight," Lucas suggested.

"*No.* Ten thirty," Juliette offered.

"*Mom.* Nobody goes home that early. Eleven thirty."

"Eleven," she countered.

"Eleven fifteen," Lucas pushed.

Doc tried to keep a straight face. The kid had game.

"Fine, but that means you're ready to leave at eleven fifteen, not twenty minutes after I get there."

"Okay. Can we go as soon as I shower and change? Everyone's going to be there soon."

"I'd like to shower first."

"Come *on*, Mom. You take forever," Lucas complained.

"I can drop him off on my way home," Doc offered. "I mean, if that's okay with you and Lucas."

"Lucas?" she asked.

"Fine, whatever. Give me fifteen minutes." He ran into the house.

"You sure you don't mind driving him?"

"Not at all." Doc took in the dried blood and dirt on Juliette's jeans. "That must have been quite an emergency. Are the animals okay?"

"They're going to be fine, but it was awful," she said. "Three horses got out last night, and they found them right before Jade called this morning. Two were tangled in barbed wire, and the third had a fractured leg."

He drew her into his arms and kissed her. "Damn, darlin'. You should've told me. I would've come help."

"The owners were there. I called a service we use sometimes, and they sent a tech out. We were fine. Besides, I thought you and Lucas could use the time together. How did it go?"

"Up and down, but overall I think we made some headway. He's struggling with liking me and the fact that we have things in common."

"I wondered if that was going to be a problem because you and Lucas are so alike, and he and Josh were not alike at all. But Josh loved him. I'll talk with him."

"We talked about it, and you should know that he doesn't remember Josh or the things they did together. He only pretends to. I think that's mostly what scares him about being around me. Josh is the only dad he's ever known, and Lucas feels like he's betraying him."

"Our poor boy." Her words were drenched in worry. "This is all *so* hard. I really hate my father for what he's done."

"I know, darlin'." He hugged her again. "Lucas and I talked about it, and I reassured him that I don't want to replace Josh. I also suggested that you tell him stories about him and Josh and the things they did together. We can all help keep those memories alive for him."

"That's a great idea," she said softly. "My heart breaks for Lucas. This is so much for him to deal with."

"It's a lot for all of us, but we'll get through it. It's going to take time, and a lot of talking, which he doesn't love. But like I said, we made some headway today, and that's a good thing. He also met Cowboy and Dare today."

"Really? I love your brothers, but how did that happen?"

"I called them when we ran out of wood. They brought some over, along with a few other things, and stayed to help. Lucas got a kick out of Dare's antics."

"He was okay with meeting them?" she asked with surprise. "It looked like things were tense when I drove up."

"That wasn't because of them. My brothers helped Lucas open up this afternoon. Things were tense because I saw him wearing the necklace I gave you, and I asked about it."

"Oh my gosh. I'm sorry. I should've told you—I should've told *him*—but he's had it for so long, I didn't even think about it."

"It's okay. We talked about it, and I told him if he didn't want to keep it, I'd understand. But he wanted to keep it."

Her brows shot up. "That's a good sign, right?"

"I hope so, but who knows with a teenager."

"Tell me about it." She sighed.

"I have a better idea. How about we set our worries aside for a few hours, and you let me wine and dine you tonight while Lucas is with his friends?"

A smile bloomed across her beautiful face. "Seeley Whiskey, are you asking me on a *real* date?"

"Yes, darlin', I believe I am."

"Then I believe I'm accepting."

Lucas flew out the front door, looking sharp in jeans and a short-sleeved button-down shirt, his damp hair curling around his ears. "Ready to go?"

"Look at you," Juliette said. "Is Layla Braden going to be there?"

"*Mom.*"

"Hugh and Brianna's daughter?" Doc asked.

"Yes. Can we go, please?" Lucas asked.

"The Bradens are friends of mine. You'd better be good to her," Doc said.

"Have you seen her uncle Rex?" Lucas asked. "He's as big as Cowboy. I know better than to do anything to piss him off."

"That's smart, but it'd be smarter if you mind your manners regardless of who's watching out for her."

"Yeah, I know," he said exasperatedly. "Be the guy who sets the standard."

"What does that mean?" Juliette asked.

"Nothing," Lucas said.

"Got your learner's permit with you?" Doc asked.

"Uh-huh. Why?"

"Because you're driving." Doc tossed him the keys.

He caught them, his eyes wide with excitement. "Really? I get to drive your truck?"

"Yup. But if you're not ready to leave that party at eleven fifteen like your mom said, you'll never drive it again." He winked at Juliette. "See you later."

As he and Lucas climbed into the truck, Lucas said, "You're seeing my mom later?"

"I asked her to dinner. Is that okay with you?"

"I guess." He put the key in the ignition and cracked a mischievous grin. "Just remember to mind your manners or it'll never be okay again."

Chapter Seventeen

JULIETTE HEARD SEELEY'S truck outside and hurried into the bedroom to take one last look at herself in the mirror. She'd never been this nervous about a date. Not that she'd been on all that many, but she'd been on enough to feel the difference. She was excited to spend time alone with Seeley. She couldn't stop thinking about how quickly they'd gotten swept up in each other behind the barn and how badly she'd wanted to do more. But that anticipation was mixed with worries about Lucas, and she was trying to find a balance. Even if only for tonight.

She gave herself a quick once-over. She didn't own many dresses, but she'd chosen her favorite: a gauzy seafoam-green sleeveless dress. It had a deep V neck and gathered at her waist, with tiny buttons running from the center to the hem just above her knees. She was a little worried she might be overdressed, but she wanted to look pretty for Seeley. She'd paired it with cute Western boots and pulled the sides of her hair up, leaving it loose in the back, with a few tendrils in the front.

The doorbell chimed, sending her heart into overdrive. With a deep breath, she headed out of the bedroom and answered the door. Seeley stood on her porch, devastatingly handsome in a gray-blue short-sleeved button-down, tattoos snaking out from beneath the sleeves.

"Hi." She sounded as nervous as she felt.

His gaze slid appreciatively down the length of her, making her even more nervous. "Damn, darlin'. I feel like a horse kicked me in the chest. You are too beautiful for words."

She covered her racing heart with her hand. "I think that horse might've kicked me, too."

A low husky laugh tumbled from his lips, and he leaned in and kissed her, bringing a wave of his deliciously rugged scent.

"I was worried I might be overdressed."

"You look great. That dress reminds me of the frilly white skirt you were wearing the first time we met. You were the prettiest girl I'd ever seen then, and now you are the most gorgeous woman I've ever seen."

You remember what I was wearing? "You always knew just how to sweet-talk me."

"As I recall, it was my dirty talk that lit your fire."

She had a feeling her heart would be racing all night. She grabbed her purse, and as they headed for his truck, she gasped in disbelief. In her driveway sat the faded black-and-silver truck Seeley had driven the summer they were together. "You still have Tiny's old truck."

"Yeah. She's not going anywhere."

He opened the passenger door and helped her in. She watched him walk around the front of the truck, feeling like a giddy teenager all over again. *A giddy teenager with a son who may or may not have been a jerk to Seeley when he dropped him off at his friend's house,* she reminded herself.

"How was Lucas?" she asked as they drove away from her house. "He didn't give you any attitude, did he?"

"Nah. He was fine, and he's a careful driver."

"Probably extra careful since he was driving your truck," she said.

"Probably." He glanced at her. "He did say he liked driving with me because I don't use a fake brake or grab the dashboard."

She laughed. "I might have done that a few times."

"My mom used to do the same thing. He asked if I'd take him driving again."

"Really? That's great. But don't feel any pressure to do it."

"I'd like to, if you don't mind. I'll take any time I can get with him."

Happiness bubbled up inside her.

"He said he has riding practice three times a week. Barring an emergency at the ranch, I can pick him up Wednesdays and Fridays after practice and take him out driving. If he wants to do a few hours of driving on Saturdays, I can make that work, too. I have church on Tuesdays, and I try to go riding with the guys when I can on Sundays."

"Are you sure that's not too much of a commitment? I don't want you to feel trapped."

He reached across the seat and took her hand. "I can't think of a better way to spend my time than getting to know our son."

"I love that you want to, but I worry that spending too much time together might be harder than you think. You're not used to a teenager's attitude, and what if it's too much for him?"

"I can handle his attitude, but you're right. I don't want to overwhelm him. How about if we take it one day at a time? See how it goes Wednesday, and go from there?"

"That sounds like a better idea."

"Great. I forgot to mention earlier that when we were talking about the ranch and my family, I invited him to come over when he's ready. I told him there was no pressure, and I know it might take some time, but it's an open invitation for both of you."

"Thanks, but how did Lucas respond?" She was surprised by how much they'd talked while she was gone. Lucas must have felt safe with him, because he was excellent at shutting down if he was upset.

"He asked a lot of questions, but he didn't say much about coming over. We'll play it by ear."

"Okay." Thankful things went well, she tucked those thoughts away as they drove out of Weston. "Where are we going?"

He squeezed her hand. "You'll see."

They chatted as he drove into Hope Valley, and when he turned into Redemption Ranch, an anticipatory thrill ran through her. "Are you wining and dining me at your place?" That sounded perfect to her.

"No. I have something a little more fun in mind."

He parked at his house, and as he helped her out of the truck, his dogs scampered off the porch to greet them, their tails and tongues wagging. They petted them, getting lavished with sloppy dog kisses that made Juliette laugh.

Seeley whistled. *"Enough."* Sadie and Pickles went to his side, while Mighty pushed his snout between Juliette's legs. "Hey, that's *my* girl." He redirected Mighty. "Sorry about that."

My girl sent a shiver of delight through her. "It's okay."

Seeley grabbed a flashlight from the glove compartment of his truck and took her hand, leading her around the house.

"Where exactly are we going?" she asked.

"You'll see."

The dogs trotted beside them, but Seeley stopped in the backyard and petted them again. "I love you guys, but you can't come with me this time." He straightened to his full height and in a stern voice said, "*Porch*," and pointed toward the house. The pups doubled back toward the house.

"That's impressive."

"Show them love and teach them right from wrong, and they'll listen most of the time. Like kids, I'd imagine."

"Most of the time," she agreed. "Unless they're mad and they disappear to a dangerous ravine."

"He's a good kid," Seeley said as they walked across the wooden bridge.

He turned on the flashlight, and they made their way into the woods. Seeley held branches to the side and helped her over fallen tree trunks and rocks, like he had all those years ago, when they'd ventured into the same woods to be alone.

"This is where we went on our first date," she said. "When you told me about how your grandfather used to take you camping, and you and your brothers would chase each other around a boulder and play boss of the boulder and moonlight tag."

"I think you're mistaken. This is the place I took my first and only serious girlfriend."

She smiled as he guided her around two trees and tried to process what he'd said about her being his only serious girlfriend. That couldn't be true, could it?

"I wanted so badly to share the most meaningful parts of my life with her, and that night, I learned exactly how sheltered of a life she'd led," he said. "She'd never played boss of the boulder or moonlight tag."

"You taught me to play that night." She remembered how

much fun they'd had, running wild in the woods, laughing, hiding, and climbing that big boulder, and how she'd ended up in his arms, which was where she always wanted to be.

He lifted the flashlight to the boulder where they'd played. "Let's see if you've gotten any better at it."

Her heart skipped. "You want to play boss of the boulder and moonlight tag?"

"Darlin', you went from being an overprotected teenager to being a mother when you were just a kid yourself, skipping right over the carefree times you were due." He cocked a grin. "Unless you've outgrown the need for fun, that's exactly what I want to do. But with you in that gorgeous dress, we should probably skip boss of the boulder."

"Moonlight tag it is, then," she said excitedly. "Turn off your flashlight and count to fifty. I'll hide."

He turned around and started counting. She let out a giddy shriek and ran through the dark, searching for a hiding place. She ran through groups of trees, circling spiny bushes, and zigzagging, trying to confuse him with her footsteps as he counted out, "Thirty-five, thirty-six…"

She tiptoed through the darkness and hid behind a tree beside the boulder, holding her breath as he called out, "Fifty!" She listened to leaves rustling with his steps, her pulse sprinting.

"Where for art thou, Juliette?" he called out.

She clamped her mouth shut to keep from laughing.

"Oh, Juli*ette*," he said in a singsong voice, closing in on her. "It's your *Romeo*."

She tiptoed in the other direction, and a twig snapped beneath her boot. She stilled, squeezing her eyes shut and holding her breath, listening for his footsteps. She didn't hear him coming and took another step. As her boot touched the ground, his arm swept around her waist. She shrieked as he hauled her against him, both of them laughing.

She squealed again, turning in his arms. "I *let* you win, Whiskey."

"Uh-huh."

"I did! Who wouldn't want a handsome cowboy catching them?"

"You'd better only want *this* cowboy catching you," he growled.

"I see you're just as possessive as you used to be."

"Only over you, darlin'." His mouth covered hers in a kiss of laughter and lust and everything in between. He drew back and ran his finger down her breastbone to the buttons on her dress. "Look at you, so beautifully tempting."

"Kiss me."

He kissed her deeper, more devouringly, and slid his hands down to her butt, crushing her against his enticingly hard body. *"Jesus,* Jule," he said. "We've got to stop, or I'm going to ravage you right here and now." He gave her a chaste kiss. "Close those pretty blue eyes of yours and count to twenty-five."

"You mean fifty?"

He flashed a coy grin. "I don't need that long." He swatted her ass and jogged into the darkness.

They played a few more rounds, laughing like kids when they caught each other and getting lost in ravenous kisses between turns. As they were now. His kisses went from urgent and possessive to exquisitely slow and sinfully sensual. Every slide of their tongues sent a wave of heat through her, and she moaned. He made the sexiest guttural noise she'd ever heard.

"I'm really trying to be a gentleman, but you in *this* dress, making those noises. You're killing me, darlin'."

"Maybe I don't want you to be a gentleman."

"You don't, huh?" He ran his thumb along her lower lip. "Do you know how many nights I fantasized about this sexy mouth?" Her pulse quickened, her breaths coming faster as he kissed the swell of her breasts. "And these beautiful tits?"

Craving his dirty talk like an addict, she panted out, "*Tell me.*"

"Too fucking many nights, with my cock in my hand, thinking about kissing you." He kissed her feathery light as he opened the top buttons of her dress and ran his finger between her breasts. "Touching you." He unhooked the front clasp of her bra and pushed a cup aside, palming her breast, his thumb teasing her nipple. "Tasting you." He lowered his mouth, sucking her nipple to the roof of it.

"*Ohgod—*"

He teased her with his teeth and tongue. A needy whimper tumbled from her lips, and he took her in a punishingly intense kiss that sent spirals of desire coursing through her. They groped and pawed, and she went up on her toes, kissing *him* harder. His hand snaked under her dress, into her underwear. "Damn, baby. So wet for me. Your pussy misses me."

He pushed his fingers inside her, zeroing in on that secret spot that had her crying out. He silenced her with a tantalizingly demanding kiss, his talented fingers stroking, his thumb teasing her where she needed it most, taking her right up to the verge of combusting. She clung to him, chasing that high as he tore his mouth away, and sealed his teeth over her neck, sucking so *hard*, she cried out, spiraling into oblivion. He captured her cries in a ravenous kiss as she rode out her pleasure. As she started coming down from the peak, he sent her soaring again, kissing her until she went soft against him, trying to catch her breath.

He rubbed his scruff along her cheek, and she reached for the button on his jeans. He touched her hand, stopping her. "Not yet, darlin'. I promised to wine and dine you, and I'm a man of my word."

She could do little more than stare at him as he fixed her bra and buttoned her dress, reveling in the way he took care of her.

He slid his finger under her chin, lifting her face, and kissed her. "Moonlight tag just became my favorite game."

"Mine, too."

He took her hand and turned on the flashlight. "Let's go, beautiful. I've got a surprise in store for you."

Chapter Eighteen

"REMEMBER THAT GIRLFRIEND I told you about?" Doc asked as he led Juliette through the trees.

Her stomach clenched. "What girlfriend?"

"My sheltered, first and only serious girlfriend."

Relief brought a smile. "Yes."

"Those games I taught weren't her only firsts in these woods. She'd never even skipped stones, so I brought her up here to the lake where I grew up dicking around with my brothers and sisters and showed her how to do it. She was the cutest thing, sinking stones, and getting so frustrated she stomped her foot."

"It was *hard*," she said, loving that he remembered, and then decided to play along with his storytelling. "I mean, that's what I heard."

He laughed and pulled her into a kiss. "That was one of my favorite memories."

When the lake came into view, she was shocked to see a red-and-white cooler on a blanket a few feet from the water's edge, just like the night he'd surprised her when they were teenagers.

"*Seeley.*" She turned to look at him, and her breath caught in her throat. He was holding a bouquet of freshly picked wildflowers, also like he had that warm summer night so long ago. His dark eyes were tender and as hopeful as her heart. But it was this whole special night, and what she realized he'd done for her, that had her getting so emotional, her voice came out barely a whisper. "You re-created our first date."

"I *was*, until we dove into that extracurricular activity."

She laughed softly. "That was my fault, wasn't it?"

"It's *us*, darlin'. As real and honest as ever." He handed her the wildflowers and kissed her. "I know I promised you wining and dining, and you look so beautiful, I'm sure you were expecting to go to a nice restaurant. But I didn't want to sit in a room full of strangers making small talk where you'd worry about seeing one of Lucas's friends or their parents and word getting back to him if we're holding hands or kissing. I told him we're having dinner together, but still."

"You told Lucas? I thought we were keeping this between us."

"I know, darlin', but he heard me say I'd see you later, and when we got in the truck, he asked about it. It didn't feel right to lie to him. Should I have?"

"How should I know? I haven't dealt with this before." The Seeley she'd fallen for years ago had been painfully honest, and she appreciated that he respected their son enough to be honest with him, too, but she had no idea whether Lucas would feel the same. "What did he say?"

"I asked him if it was okay, and he told me to mind my manners, which is exactly what I told him to do with Layla. I also reiterated that he needed to be ready at eleven fifteen when you pick him up or he'd never drive my truck again."

"I don't know if I'm more shocked or relieved that he was

okay with us having dinner. But I am pleasantly surprised that you told him to mind his manners and supported me about his curfew."

"I will always support you." He squeezed her hand. "And let's go with relieved about Lucas giving us the okay. I don't want there to be anything fake in our lives. I brought you here because I wanted to get to know the real you, not some stilted version. I wanted a chance to just be *us*. To talk or kiss or simply sit together without worrying about who might be watching."

She thought about how nervous she'd been when he'd picked her up tonight and how that anxiousness had fallen away when they'd come to the ranch. She didn't know if he was right, and she'd worried that Lucas might hear about something that could upset him, but it didn't matter. The fact that he took it into consideration meant the world to her.

"I'm glad we're here. It's absolutely perfect."

"You might not think so after you see what I brought for dinner. I was nervous about leaving hot food out here for so long, so I went with sandwiches, cheese and crackers, fruit, and wine."

"I still think it's perfect. I love that you thought to do all of this, and I love the reasons we're here."

He exhaled with relief and drew her into his arms. "Good. I'm hoping when the dust settles, you and Lucas will see how good we can all be together, and we'll have years of wining and dining ahead of us."

"We really do suck at going slow. I can't believe I'm saying this after only a week, but I hope so, too."

They sat by the water eating dinner, drinking wine, and talking.

"You know Lucas and his friends are probably playing Seven Minutes in Heaven, or whatever kids play these days." He ate a bite of his sandwich.

"I *know*. Don't remind me. He's growing up so fast, and dealing with all of this will make him grow up even faster."

"He'll get through it. But let's not spend our evening worrying about what's to come. We'll handle whatever comes up as best and as honestly as we can. But tonight I want to know what you've been doing for all these years and how the hell you're still single." He leaned against her shoulder. "And don't tell me you've been too busy to date. I might buy that when Lucas was little, but you must've had plenty of guys to choose from over the years. Has there been anyone special in your life?"

She swallowed the bite of sandwich she was eating. "I *have* been busy raising our son, and in California I also had my veterinary practice to run. But I dated here and there, and there were a couple of guys who I thought could lead to something serious."

"Why didn't they?"

She shrugged. "Life got in the way, or they wanted something I couldn't give."

"Such as?"

"One of them wanted to eventually move overseas, and I didn't want to. I've always been a small-town girl. That's where I'm most comfortable, and the idea of moving to a foreign country with Lucas wasn't appealing to me at all."

"I'm glad you didn't. What about the other guys?"

"There was only one who I would have even considered getting more serious with, but he wanted more kids, and I couldn't have them."

"That must've been hard. I'll understand if you don't want

to talk about this, but when you found out you couldn't have kids, did you and Josh consider IVF or think about a surrogate or adopting?"

"The short answer is no. Josh wanted to father a child, which meant adoption was out, and he didn't like the idea of a surrogate. We were so young, I didn't even think about IVF. We never even went through any kind of testing to see why we couldn't get pregnant. But honestly, a baby was his last-ditch effort to save our sham of a marriage. I would have given it to him if I could have, because he stepped in when I needed him for Lucas, but I wasn't happy, and we both knew forcing the issue wasn't the right thing to do."

"What about the other guy? Did you love him? Couldn't you have tried with him?"

"We weren't there yet, and being with him would have been *nice* and comfortable, but it wasn't like it is with us. I've never felt the spellbinding chemistry that you and I have with anyone else. You kind of ruined me for other men with that."

He grinned. "I'm not sorry for that."

"Neither am I, now that we're here."

"What about Lucas? How did he handle meeting those guys and the end of those relationships?"

"He never met them. He'd already lost Josh. I couldn't take a chance of him getting attached. I wasn't going to introduce him to anyone who I wasn't one hundred percent sure I wanted in our lives." She sipped her wine, debating asking the question that had been nagging at her. But if ever there was a time she should not hold back, it was now. "Before I fall any harder for you, I need to ask you something."

"Anything, darlin'."

"Are you asking about IVF and the other alternatives because you hope to have more children?"

"That wasn't why I was asking. I wanted to understand what you've been through. But would I want to raise more children with you? Baby, I would happily raise a houseful of kids with you, like we dreamed about, whether they're biologically ours or not. But that's not a dealbreaker for me. I am incredibly lucky to have you and Lucas in my life. I don't need anything more to be happy." He leaned in and kissed her. "So feel free to fall harder for me. Fall at breakneck speed. Let me know if you need a push."

She laughed. "As if I ever had a chance in hell of *not* falling for you?"

He kissed her again. "What other questions are swirling around in your beautiful brain?"

"Hm." She pretended to think about it, but in reality it took no thought at all. "Has there ever been anyone special in your life, other than me?"

"No." He finished his glass of wine and set it down, his jaw tightening.

She popped a grape into her mouth, waiting for him to say more. When he didn't, she said, "Why not?"

"My family will tell you I never let anyone get close enough to become special, and they wouldn't be wrong. Losing you hurt like hell. I never wanted to go through that again. But I don't think that's the only thing at play. I think when things are *right*—chemistry, friendship, values, future dreams—everything falls into place, and we don't have an ounce of control over it. You and I are proof of that. All it took was hearing the truth to unearth and unleash all those emotions in both of us, and I don't know about you, but I couldn't ignore them if I tried."

"I think we both know that I can't hold back with you,

either."

"I like that about you." He put his hand on her leg and kissed her.

"So, you really never had any long-term relationships? Not even in college?"

"No. My brothers say I'm like an extended-stay motel."

"That's awful."

He laughed. "Yeah, but it's accurate. I'm not a dick about it. I tell women up front that I won't catch feelings for them, and I treat them well."

She was curious about his dating life and pried with a tease. "Wining and dining all the single ladies around town?"

"Not all of them, but dinner and drinks are expected when you're dating. I don't bring women to the ranch to hang out or back to my place, and I don't take them to the Roadhouse with the guys. I keep that part of my personal life separate from my family and club life."

"That's surprising. Your family and the club were always such a big part of who you were."

"They still are. That's why I protect them. There have been women who thought they could get under my skin, and they got clingy. I don't need any of them showing up at the ranch or the Roadhouse and making a scene."

"*Oops*," she said, remembering the scene she'd made, and they both laughed.

He squeezed her leg. "Darlin', you're the exception to my every rule."

They finished eating and talked more about their lives. Seeley told her about the ways the ranch had grown and how they'd expanded the back of the veterinary clinic to include better surgical and recovery rooms. He shared stories about his family, the silly things he and his siblings had done, and the ways they'd supported each other over the years. She'd always wished she'd had a sibling to lean on, and hearing those stories made her wish Lucas had one, too.

She told more stories about Lucas, and they talked about her veterinary practice in California and the ranch where she and Lucas had lived. They reminisced about her grandmother and the time they'd spent with her when they were teenagers and talked about a hundred other things, sharing smiles, laughter, sorrows, and lots of delicious kisses.

They were lost in one of those kisses now, sitting in the moonlight, filling each other up with the years, and the love, they'd missed. It felt as easy and right as it had on their very first date. He'd re-created this beautiful night just for her, and she wanted to re-create one of her favorite parts just for him. "I need a second," she whispered as she drew back. She pulled off her boots and socks, earning a curiously sexy grin.

"What're you doing, darlin'?"

"Re-creating another memory I'm quite fond of." She pushed to her feet and started unbuttoning her dress.

He flashed a wolfish grin.

She'd never seen anyone undress so fast. As the last of her clothes hit the ground, he scooped her into his arms, running into the water with her as they laughed. She shrieked when the cold water hit her skin. She wrapped herself around him as he walked them in deeper. "I don't remember it being this cold!"

"I'll warm you up."

His mouth came coaxingly down over hers, their slick bodies sliding against each other, friction and desire setting her body aflame. His hardness pressed temptingly against her, and he lifted her up, aligning their bodies, and lowered her onto his thick cock, filling her so completely, sparks radiated outward from her core to her fingertips and toes.

They devoured each other, surrendering to their passion, thrusting to a frantic beat, like they'd never get another chance. He fisted one hand in her hair, sending an erotic sting of pain and pleasure coursing through her, and her thoughts spun away. She moaned, and he drove into her harder, deeper, so perfectly, every pump of his hips took her closer to the edge. "*Seeley,*" she panted out, wanting to say so much more, but every thrust stole her breath.

"I know," he gritted out. "We're fucking perfect together. Always have been."

Her fingernails dug into his shoulders, and a low, sexy growl rumbled up his throat. Their hungry sounds sailed into the darkness, water splashing with their efforts.

He grabbed her ass with both hands, holding it so tight she was sure he'd leave marks, and she hoped he would. She wanted to see his handprints on her skin tomorrow, to know this was real and not a dream. *God*, she'd missed this, *them*, their raw, visceral connection. It seemed unfathomable that she'd gone so many years without him, when every second he was inside her, she felt like she needed him to breathe.

"Look at me," he gritted out, a primal hunger gleaming in his eyes. "Tell me you're *mine*. We'll figure the rest out. Just *tell me* you're *mine*."

Oh, her heart! "I'm yours, Seeley. I've always been yours."

He tugged her mouth back to his, kissing her so passionately, driving into her so exquisitely, she soared into ecstasy. Her cries and his curses flew from their lips like thunder, their climaxes going on and on. She clung to him as they thrust and ground, kissing and moaning, wishing she could stay in his arms forever.

As they came down from the high, trying to catch their breath, she was floating on a cloud of pleasure. Reveling in his strong arms around her, in their bodies connected as one, she touched her forehead to his, and he murmured, "*Jule. My Jule.*"

The rawness in his voice brought her eyes to his, and her breath caught at the slew of emotions brimming in them.

"It's always been *you*, darlin'. You're the only person who could ever tear me to shreds or heal me in a single breath. The world was cold and gray without you. You are my light, my fucking heart, and you completely, utterly *own* me."

She teared up and opened her mouth to speak, but love whirled inside her like a sandstorm, stealing her voice. But she didn't need it, because as her heart bubbled over, he kissed her again, slow and deep, drawing all that love to the surface, and she showed him better than words ever could.

AFTER TWO MORE mind-numbing orgasms and dozens of glorious kisses, Seeley used the blanket to dry her off, the same way he had all those years ago. Only this time they weren't silly kids. There were years of heartache between them and a world of questions ahead of them, which made his caring touch feel even more intimate and meaningful.

Juliette felt high as they dressed and headed out of the woods hand in hand. She carried the wildflowers he'd picked for her, and he carried the cooler and blanket, letting the moonlight lead the way this time.

She was still on cloud nine when the dogs greeted them in

Seeley's yard. They lavished them with attention, and the pups trotted beside them as they walked through the yard.

"I know you have to pick up Lucas, but if you can spare a minute, I have something I want to show you."

"Okay." They headed into his house through the doors off the back deck, and she felt like she was seeing it for the first time. She'd been so stressed the night she'd been there, she'd missed how warm and inviting it felt. "Your home is really beautiful. I love all the stone and wood. But I have to admit, I was bummed that you tore down the old cabin. Not that I blame you, after everything that happened."

"That was a difficult time." He led her into the bedroom, where there were candles ready to be lit and tin cans filled with wildflowers on every surface.

An incredulous and enamored, "*Seeley,*" fell from her lips.

"I thought we might end up here. Don't get the wrong idea. I don't want to go back to being the kids we were, but making love to you in that old cabin, lying on the floor making plans, and just..." He cleared his throat. "Those are some of my happiest memories. I thought it would be nice to re-create it when I showed you this." He pulled back the area rug in front of the bed, revealing the scuffed and worn floorboards with the heart and their initials he'd carved into them when they were kids.

She couldn't believe her eyes. "Is that...?"

"It's the original floor from the old cabin. I refinished the rest of it, but I couldn't bring myself to get rid of that. Even through all the anger, all the shit with your father and your marriage, and every sign telling me you played me, some part of me couldn't accept it. We felt too big for you to turn your back on. We felt *unfinished,* and I just couldn't do it."

Tears burned her eyes, her voice cracking. "You were so angry when you saw me at the hospital. I can't believe you kept anything that reminded you of us. I thought you hated me."

Pain rose in his eyes. "In that moment, I might have."

That hurt, even though it was warranted. She'd felt the same way at first, thinking he'd dumped her knowing about the pregnancy.

"Darlin', when I saw you, my head and my heart had been at war for the past sixteen years. I did a damn good job of bottling up the pain and longing and the anger and confusion, but seeing you again broke my ability to hold it in. My emotions erupted like a fucking volcano, and I had to get away from you before I lost it. I'm sorry for what I said."

She shook her head, stepping closer. "It's okay." She wound her arms around his neck. "That's behind us now. I'm sorry you were so tortured, but I'm so freaking *happy* you didn't forget us."

"I could no sooner forget us than I could be done with you."

Her heart felt like it might burst as his arms circled her, and he sealed those words with a long, sensual kiss.

Chapter Nineteen

DOC AND JULIETTE sat in his truck Tuesday morning across from the café in Boulder watching Ana, a thick-waisted woman with olive skin and dark shoulder-length hair. She had arrived at the café alone nearly twenty minutes ago, looking sharp in a black skirt and cream-colored blouse, and was seated outside at a table for two. Every passing minute felt like an hour, making the tense situation even more excruciating. Doc was used to staking out people and confronting assholes. He'd done it more times than he cared to count with the club. But while his gut was burning with a need for vengeance against Juliette's father, his heart burned with worry for Juliette. She'd had a tough morning before she'd even left the house.

When she'd told Lucas where they were going, he'd wanted to go with them to confront his grandfather if he showed up. She'd told him maybe one day he could do that but that she needed to find out what really happened first. Doc knew that wasn't an easy conversation for either of them. Now she was strung so tight, she held her breath every time someone walked into the café. He was concerned she might break if her father showed up to meet Ana.

He glanced at his blue-eyed beauty, so fucking thankful she'd come back into his life with Lucas, but his chest constricted at her pinched brows as she stared out the window, her hands curled tightly into fists. He should've insisted on coming alone.

He reached across the seat and pried open her fingers, interlacing them with his. "You don't have to do this."

She whipped her head to the side. "Yes, I *do*. I want answers."

"I know you do." He squeezed her hand. "But I can see how hard this is for you. We can leave, and I can get those answers for both of us another day."

"I'm *fine*."

He arched a brow.

"*Okay*," she relented. "Maybe I'm not fine, but I need to do this. If my father shows up, I want to look them both in the eye and hold them accountable for what they've done."

He kissed the back of her hand. "I admire your strength, darlin'. It's not going to be easy."

"It'll be a heck of a lot easier than what they put me through."

He hoped that was true.

When they returned their attention to Ana, the waitress was standing by her table. Ana looked at her watch and said something. The waitress nodded, and as she walked away, Ana grabbed her purse and fished around in it, pulling out her phone. She thumbed out a text and then set the phone on the table and took a sip of her drink. As she set down her glass, she picked up the phone and put it to her ear, a smile gracing her face as she spoke. Her smile faltered, her shoulders slumping.

"Uh-oh," Juliette said.

Ana shielded her face from the other customers, looking

toward the parking lot, and giving Doc and Juliette a front-row seat to what looked like a heated discussion. She ended the call and *shoved* her phone into her bag.

"Someone pissed her off," Juliette said as Ana squared her shoulders and flagged down the waitress.

They watched her pay, and when she got up to leave, Doc said, "Looks like she got stood up."

"Good. Then we can talk to her sooner." Juliette reached for the door handle.

Doc grabbed her arm. "Not here. Since your father didn't show up, we're moving to plan B, remember?" Plan B entailed following Ana until they could speak with her alone. "If you confront her in public, you're not going to get anything out of her. All it'll do is alert your father to what we're doing."

She sank back against the seat with a sigh. "Okay. Let's follow her."

Doc kept his distance as they followed Ana's car from the café to the bank, the gas station, a gift shop, and finally to her neighborhood. They parked down the street and waited for her to go inside.

"Want to go over our plan one more time?" Doc asked.

She shook her head. "It'll make me more nervous. Are you one hundred percent sure that her brother was locked up when I wrote those letters?"

"Yes. According to the reports, he was serving a one-year sentence for possession of illegal drugs."

Her eyes narrowed with determination. "Then I'm as ready as I'll ever be."

Doc stepped out of the truck and came around to help her out, but she was already on her feet. He took her hand, and they made their way down to the lavish brick Colonial.

"This looks like a smaller version of my father's house," she said with disdain as they ascended the porch steps. She took a deep breath and rang the doorbell.

Ana opened the door, and her ready smile faltered, her dark eyes filling with disbelief. "Juliette."

"Hello, Ana," Juliette said with a hint of wistfulness.

Doc wasn't surprised to hear her heart slipping out.

"It's..." Ana's gaze moved curiously between him and Juliette. "It's so good to see you, honey." She embraced Juliette. "I had no idea you were in town."

Doc wondered if Ana felt Juliette bristle or if he and Juliette were so connected that he sensed what she was holding back. As Juliette stepped out of her embrace, he offered his hand, purposely using his given name to see Ana's reaction. "Hi. I'm Seeley Whiskey."

Ana blinked several times before shaking his hand with a sweaty palm. "*Seeley*. It's nice to meet you."

He gave a curt nod.

"I was hoping we could come in and visit for a minute," Juliette said.

That's it, baby. Be kind before going in for the kill.

"Of course. Gosh, it's been so long." Ana led them into a plush living room with expensive furniture. On an end table and on the mantel over the fireplace were several framed photographs of Ana and a boy at various ages, assumably her son. "Can I get you something to drink?"

"No, thank you," Juliette said. "We can't stay long."

Ana stood before a love seat and motioned to the other couch. "Please, sit down."

Doc picked up one of the photographs as they sat down. "Is this your son?"

"Yes." She folded her hands in her lap. "That's my Rolando."

"He's a good-looking boy." Doc put the picture back on the end table.

"Thank you. He's my pride and joy. Juliette, how are you, sweetheart? You look beautiful. How is your Lucas? He must be fifteen or sixteen by now?"

"He's fifteen, and he's doing great. No thanks to my parents," Juliette said with an edge to her voice.

Ana wrung her hands, shaking her head. "I felt horrible about the way your father treated you."

"Did you?" Juliette asked pointedly.

"Yes, *of course*," Ana said imploringly. "That was such a difficult time, and you and I were so close. My heart broke for you. Don't you remember?"

"Yes. I thought we were very close. That's why I'm here, actually. Do you remember the letters you said you gave to your brother to give to Seeley?"

"Yes," Ana said far too casually.

"I never got them," Doc said, drawing her eyes to his. "But you already know that, don't you?"

"I don't understand." Her gaze darted back to Juliette, and to her credit, she *almost* pulled off a confused expression. "You got his letter, Juliette. You *know* he got the letters and wrote back to you."

"I got *a* letter that you said was from Seeley."

"I didn't write that letter." Doc leaned forward, pinning a dark stare on Ana. "We know your brother never saw the letters, either. He was locked up when that went down. Now, how about you tell us the truth?"

"*Juliette*," Ana pleaded. "As I said, I felt horrible about what your father did."

"Not horrible enough to stop him," Juliette snapped. "What did you do with my letters, Ana? Did you give them to my father?"

Ana looked down at her wringing hands. "I didn't have a choice."

"You always have a choice," Doc gritted out. "Who wrote that letter to Juliette?"

With her eyes trained on her hands, she said, "I didn't have a choice."

"*You* wrote the letter?" Juliette pushed to her feet, her hands fisting. Doc rose beside her. "How could you do that to me? I trusted you!"

Ana stood, her breathing hampered, her eyes darting between them. "You know how your father is."

"Yes, but now I know how *you* really are, too." Juliette's voice escalated, tears welling in her eyes. "I didn't want to believe that you'd deceive me. You ruined *years* of my life. You made me feel used and hateful toward Seeley. You encouraged me to marry a man I didn't love. Why did you do it? *Why* did you trick me?"

Tears streaked Ana's cheeks. "Your father said being with Seeley would ruin your life."

"And you *believed* him? You saw me crying day and night, and you sat there pacifying me with lies, telling me you wished you could do something to help, while you were *behind* it all? You said you hated the way he treated me. You said he was despicable."

"You don't understand," Ana said. "I had to say those things so you wouldn't find out about us." Her eyes widened, and she snapped her mouth closed, realizing her mistake.

"*Us*, as in you and my father?"

"I've said too much already." Ana backpedaled, fear rising in her eyes.

Juliette's eyes narrowed. "You deceived me to save your relationship with my father? Your *affair*? Are you still sleeping with him?"

"You don't understand," Ana said harshly. "We love each other."

Juliette scoffed. "Are you kidding me? After everything he's done? That man doesn't know what love is, and you're as bad as he is. How could you do this to my mother?"

"Your mother is not a good person," Ana snapped.

"Neither are *you*," Doc bit out. "Did you know I went by the house to try to talk to her father and change his mind after he took her off the ranch?"

Ana nodded, her face contorting as more tears fell.

"You knew?" Juliette bit out. "You heard me begging my father, day after day, for five minutes with Seeley, for *one* phone call. Did you know my father had his henchmen beat Seeley up?"

"*Yes*," Ana croaked. "I'm sorry."

"You make me sick." Juliette turned away.

Doc touched Juliette's hand reassuringly as he shot off questions at Ana. "Did he threaten to fire you if you didn't help him?"

"No," Ana said just above a whisper. "But he would have ended our relationship, and he said you were bad for her. I loved Juliette. I didn't want her life to be ruined."

"He *lied*," Doc gritted out. "And because of what you did, I missed out on being there for Juliette when she was pregnant and when she had our son. I missed out on fifteen years—*fifteen years*—with the woman I love and our son because *you* wrote that letter." He stepped closer. "I'm going to take him down and put him behind bars, and you're going down with him."

"But I didn't do anything illegal," Ana pleaded.

"You sure as hell did." Doc held her stare, making sure she heard every word he spoke. "You committed fraud, Ana. You falsely represented a material fact with the intent to deceive Juliette, and you cost her years of emotional stress." He was reaching with the extent of the law, but he could tell by her fearful stare and trembling hands that she was buying it. "Your actions made her keep our son from *me*, and now that the truth has been exposed, our son has to deal with the psychological pain of what you have done. You and her bastard of a father will both be held accountable."

The blood drained from her face. "I can't go to jail. Rolando needs me."

"Maybe you should've thought of that before you tricked a sixteen-year-old girl into changing her entire life based on a lie."

"*Please.* I'm sorry!" Ana begged. "Please don't do this to me."

Doc sensed she was the key to taking down Juliette's father. He pushed harder, needing to break her. "How many times did you hear Juliette say those very words to her parents?"

Ana's breathing hitched, tears flooding her cheeks.

"You deserve everything you're going to get," Doc warned, and exactly as he'd anticipated, she lost it.

Sobbing, she clasped her hands together beneath her chin. "*Please.* I'll do anything. I can help you take him down. I know things."

"Well, then, maybe you and I *can* strike a deal." He glanced at Juliette, who was fuming a few feet away, and hoped she'd read his silent message to go along with his fishing expedition. "What do you think, Juliette?"

"I think she hurt me more than I can ever forgive her for." She turned a cold stare on Ana. "And I think she knows everything that goes on in that house."

"I do! *Please*," Ana said. "I'll tell you everything I know. Just don't send me away from Rolando. Your father has a safe where he keeps the documents he doesn't want people to find. It's in Juliette's old bedroom, under the floorboards beneath the bed."

"In my *room?*" Juliette asked with disgust.

"Yes. He said it was the only place people wouldn't look," Ana explained.

"What does he keep in it?" Doc asked.

"I don't know." Ana looked between them, shaking her head. "He gives me documents and notebooks, and I put them in the safe. I never look at them. I never have. I don't want to know what's in there. But if you tell him I told you, he'll do something bad to me. He's done *really* bad things to people. I've overheard him talking about it with Mr. Chambers."

Bingo. "Tell me about *those* things," Doc demanded.

Ana lifted her chin, her damp eyes holding his stare. "Not unless you promise not to tell him who you got the information from and not to come after me."

"I promise *I* won't." *But I can't speak for the Feds or Juliette.* She looked pleadingly at Juliette.

"I won't, either, *if* you tell us everything you know. Then I *never* want to see you again." Juliette's icy tone cut through the air like a knife.

JULIETTE WAS SHAKING when they finally headed back to the truck. Ana had confirmed their worst suspicions and then some. Not only did she say she'd overheard conversations revolving around bribery and extortion, but she'd also heard the esteemed governor talking about having people *taken care of* before his last election. Seeley had pushed her to elaborate, but she said she didn't know and feared the worst.

So did they, which was only one of the reasons why, as Seeley helped Juliette into the truck, it took all of her strength to hold her shit together. His jaw was clenched tight, his every muscle rigid, like he was ready to hunt her father down and tear him apart.

She didn't blame him. The full scope of her father's evil manipulations cut so deep, she could hardly process them. Coupled with the realization that Ana, the woman she'd trusted with all of her secrets, had set the wheels in motion to ruin her life, had hurt, anger, and shock stacking up inside her.

She tried to hold it all in, mentally preparing herself for Seeley to let his rage out, to hiss a threat toward her father or Ana or both of them. After the restraint he'd shown with Ana, he was due a release. But when he turned those angry eyes on her, they softened, and he didn't yell or curse. He gathered her in his arms, holding her tight, and said, "Let it out, darlin'. I've got you," chipping away at her armor.

She felt like a boiling pot ready to blow. Struggling to remain in control, she choked out, "*I'm fine.*"

"You're strong, darlin'," he said softly, holding her tighter. "But you just heard horrible things about your father and the awful truth about the one person you thought you could trust. You're not okay."

Her restraint snapped, rage pouring out. "I'm just so freaking angry! Did you *see* her? She didn't even feel bad about lying to me." She pushed out of his arms, swiping at her tears. "She spewed empty words, trying to save herself. And my father? I always knew he was corrupt, but he's a *monster*. I can't even feel sorry for my fucking mother. She knows everything that goes on in that house, the same way Ana does. I'm sure she knows about their affair and all the awful things my father has done. But she enjoys her lavish lifestyle too much to do a damn thing about it. She turns a blind eye to all of it, the way she did to me."

"I'm sorry, darlin'." He pulled her back into his arms.

"How could my awful parents have created me? They're heartless." She buried her face in his neck.

He held her for a long moment before drawing back, framing her face in his big, warm hands, and set his loving eyes on her. "They brought you into this world, and you got only the best parts of them. Your father is smart, and your mother is beautiful. But you have Hazel's heart, darlin', and it's too pure to be soiled by the likes of them."

She gathered up those sentiments and tucked them away. "How do you always know what to say to make me feel better?"

"It's called honesty." He kissed her softly, wiping her tears with his thumbs. "I'm proud of you, baby. You said your piece, and you didn't hold back."

"Lotta good it did me. I don't even know where we go from here."

"Home, so Lucas doesn't worry about you."

She deadpanned. "You know what I mean."

"There's nothing I want more than to go after your father with everything I have and make the bastard pay. But I'm not willing to put you and Lucas in his line of fire."

"What more can he possibly do to us?"

"How can you ask that after what he's done to us and everything Ana told us?" he said heatedly. "Your father sold you out to protect his ego, and he's got a hell of a lot more at stake with the new information we have."

"*Ugh.* You're right. He's a total self-centered asshole, and I wouldn't put anything past him. The best thing I ever did was get him out of our lives. I don't want to put Lucas in his sights, either. I just hate him *so* much, I can taste it. I want to go after him like Harley Quinn or Beth Dutton and show him he didn't break me."

"Baby, we're going to get vengeance. I promise you that. I want him to suffer for what he's done to us. I want to strip away his last shred of dignity, and let the world see him for the worthless piece of shit he is, but we need to be smart about it so he can't tie anything back to you."

She rubbed her hands together. "So, we *are* going after him?"

"Damn right we are, and he'll never see us coming."

Chapter Twenty

JULIETTE WAS GLAD for the long drive back to Weston. She needed time to wrap her head around what they'd learned. But when they reached her street, she was still toying with what to tell Lucas.

"You doing okay, darlin'?" Seeley asked.

"Yeah. I was just thinking about Lucas. He's going to want to know what we found out. I don't know how much I should tell him."

Seeley put his hand on hers. "We're leading with honesty, but that doesn't mean he needs all the gory details. He needs to know we're handling it, so he doesn't worry about it."

"That's what I was thinking. I do want to tell him about Ana. It's a good lesson in not trusting people at face value."

"Maybe you should talk to the therapist about how to present that first? He's such a tough kid, and he's so protective of you. I fully support teaching him not to take people at face value, even if I'm kind of one of those people right now. But with everything he's dealing with, I don't want to make him unjustly tougher or too untrusting. That's a hard way to grow up."

She felt a pang of sadness, knowing he was talking from experience.

He turned into her driveway and said, "I'm really hoping that as he gets more comfortable with me, he'll realize his world is still safe. Safer, actually, now that you both have me and my family and the club watching over you, and he'll be able to go back to just being a kid, where his biggest worry will be getting a zit before a date."

She laughed softly. "I barely remember those years."

"Because yours were cut short." He pulled up beside her truck and lifted his chin in the direction of the barn. "Whose horse is that?"

There was an unfamiliar horse tied to a post outside the barn. "I don't know, but I'm going to find out."

They climbed out of the truck, and as they headed down to the barn, Seeley said, "It probably belongs to one of his friends. As I recall from the night he took off, he has a few friends who live nearby."

"I'm sure it is, but Lucas knows he's not allowed to have friends over when I'm not home."

As they neared the barn, she heard a girl giggling and froze. She grabbed Seeley's arm, whispering, "Did you hear that? He's in there with a girl."

He chuckled.

"Don't laugh," she whispered harshly. "What if they're messing around?"

"Then we should give them some warning so we don't embarrass whoever he's with."

She rolled her eyes, earning another chuckle. Juliette cleared her throat loudly, then practically shouted, "Come on, Seeley. I'll show you the horses."

He shook his head, whispering, "Real subtle, babe."

"You said to give them a warning," she whispered, then loudly announced, "Let's go into the barn."

"Okay," Seeley said loudly, playing along.

She mouthed, *I hate this*, and he laughed.

"Mom, why are you shouting?" Lucas called out from Warrior's stall.

"I didn't know I was," she said as they made their way to the stall, where she was relieved to see Layla taking a selfie with Warrior. "Hi, Layla. How are you?"

"Hi, Dr. Chambers." She tucked her long dark hair behind her ear, smiling sweetly. She looked cute in brown riding pants, black boots, and a white T-shirt with IN MY HORSE GIRL ERA in colorful seventies-style letters down the front. "Hi, Doc."

"It's nice to see you, Layla," he said. "How's it going, Lucas? What are you guys up to?"

"Layla was on a trail ride and stopped by," Lucas explained a little nervously. "We were hanging out and talking while I did my chores."

"I hope that's okay," Layla said. "I probably should have texted first."

"It's fine, honey," Juliette said. "Although next time, Lucas, maybe you can text me and let me know."

"Okay," he said, visibly relieved. "Sorry."

"It's okay."

"Do your parents know you're here, Layla?" Seeley asked, surprising Juliette with the fatherly question.

"Uh-huh," Layla said cheerily. "I texted my mom when I got here, since I hadn't planned on coming over. She said it's fine if I stay awhile."

"Mom, since Layla's already here, can she stay for dinner? I was thinking we could order pizza." He barely took a breath before adding, "Doc can stay, too, if he wants."

That was the first time Juliette had heard him address Seeley by a name, and she liked that he chose Doc instead of Seeley. It sounded familiar. Friendlier. Though she wondered if Lucas had called him that because Layla had. In any case, she was elated that he suggested Seeley stay for dinner, even if she had a feeling it was his way of keeping her out of his and Layla's hair.

"What do you think, *Doc*?" Juliette said teasingly.

"I've got church tonight, but I can't think of a better way to spend my time until then." The twinkle in his eyes told her how pleased he was by the invitation. "Dinner's on me."

"You don't have to do that, but thank you," Juliette said.

"You go to church at night?" Lucas asked with confusion.

"Not the kind of church you're probably thinking of. Church is what we Dark Knights call our weekly club meetings."

"Oh, cool." Lucas turned a charming smile on Layla. "Do you want to ask your mom if you can stay? I can ride home with you before dark to make sure you get there safely."

Layla beamed. "I'd love to. Thanks."

About a dozen emotions swirled through Juliette as Lucas chatted up Layla while she texted her mother, earning the type of sweet smiles that come only when a young girl is crushing hard on a boy. She hadn't been prepared to watch Lucas grow up so fast, but her heart felt full seeing him so happy.

"What kind of pizza do you like?" Seeley asked.

"What kind do you like?" Lucas asked Layla.

She shrugged. "Anything except onions and anchovies."

"Pepperoni sound good?" he asked.

She nodded, eyes bright.

"We'll have pepperoni, please," Lucas announced.

"Got it." Seeley looked at Juliette. "Do you still like mushrooms?"

"I can't believe you remembered." She shouldn't be surprised, given that he'd remembered everything else about their relationship.

Seeley winked. "Why don't we let them finish up with the horses?"

She didn't know if he wanted to give Lucas and Layla a minute alone, or if he wanted a moment alone with her, but the way he was looking at her told her it was probably both. "Good idea. I have a few things to do before dinner. We'll meet you guys up at the house."

"Okay," Lucas said. "Wait. Doc, are you still taking me driving tomorrow?"

"Sure am. I'll pick you up after your riding practice."

"Cool. Thanks."

After Juliette and Seeley left the barn, Seeley said, "Our boy's got game."

"Yes, he does. But Layla's only fourteen, so he'd better not have too much game."

"I'll talk with him about that when I take him driving tomorrow."

She was floored at how naturally Seeley was taking on fatherhood. "Do you think he invited you to dinner to keep me busy?"

"Hell yes. He's no dummy. But I'll take it." He draped his arm over her shoulder, hugging her against his side as they neared the house. "Gotta love those baby steps."

AN HOUR LATER, Doc and Juliette were sitting at the kitchen table, eating pizza and chatting with the kids. It was strange to think that a few hours ago, he and Juliette were confronting Ana. Juliette was strong, but there was so much to consider with going after her father. Doc didn't just want to hold off on calling Reggie to protect her and Lucas from any backlash. He also wanted to give Juliette time to let the truth sink in, in case she had second thoughts down the line.

He had to leave to get ready for church soon, but he was enjoying sitting with his hand on Juliette's leg under the table, watching Lucas act cool with Layla, talking about his bull riding and playing off the falls like they were no big deal. Layla was adorably smitten with him.

This was one of those moments he didn't want to forget. The first time his son asked him to stay for dinner, and he'd learned that it was also the first time Lucas had ever had a girl over. He wanted nothing more than to stay all evening, to laugh and joke with them. To hold Juliette long after Layla went home and Lucas was sleeping safe and sound in his bed, to make sure *she* felt safe, too. Talking over the phone was great, but it wasn't the same as having her in his arms.

"I'd love to see you bull ride sometime," Layla said, drawing Doc from his thoughts.

Lucas's smile lit up the whole damn kitchen. "Maybe you can come to my next competition."

"That'd be fun. Christian told my parents he wants to ride a bull," Layla said, referring to her mischievous little brother, who was about Gus's age. "My mom was like, *no way*, and my dad said Christian was going to be too busy racing cars." Hugh was a professional race car driver.

"Lucky kid. That would be awesome," Lucas said.

"I hope he doesn't learn to race. Christian's a *maniac*." Layla took a drink of her soda. "I swear he doesn't know how to sit still, which is great for Cami, because she's *always* chasing him around." Her little sister, Camryn, was an adorable, chubby-cheeked toddler.

"Doc used to ride bulls," Lucas said, eyeing him over his glass as he lifted it to his mouth.

Layla's eyes widened. "You did?"

"Yeah, when I was much younger. It was a lot of fun."

"He was good, too," Lucas bragged, surprising Doc, and by the look on Juliette's face, surprising her, too. "He was the junior world champ *five* times."

"*Wow*," Layla said. She nudged Lucas. "I bet you can be a world champ if you try."

Lucas sat up taller, eating up the compliment.

"He's better than I ever was," Doc said.

Lucas gave him a disbelieving look. "You thought I was that good?"

"Dude, you were awesome." Doc could see him struggling with that praise, his lips twitching like he wanted to wear it proudly, but that big heart of his was holding it back.

"I think you're both pretty great," Juliette said.

"You have to say that. You're my mom," Lucas said, and they all laughed.

"I do *not*," Juliette insisted.

"Whatever," Lucas said. "Layla competes in horse shows, and she's really good."

Doc was impressed with his swift pivot, but the admiration

in Lucas's voice told him it wasn't only a pivot. He wanted them to know she was special. As if her being there wasn't like a neon sign.

"I would've loved to have competed when I was your age," Juliette said.

"Why didn't you?" Lucas asked.

"I didn't have the time to dedicate to it," Juliette said.

Doc squeezed her leg under the table, knowing the truth. Her father hadn't allowed it, but she probably didn't want to get into that with the kids.

"It does take a lot of time, but I love it," Layla said.

"She has a competition in a few weeks," Lucas added. "I want to go. Is that okay, Mom?"

"I don't see why not. I'd like to go, too," she said.

"That sounds like fun. My sister Sasha used to compete," Doc said. "What's your discipline?"

"Junior dressage," Layla said, and went on to tell them about the events she'd won and how her whole family, including her grandfather and all of her cousins and aunts and uncles who lived in the area, tried to come to her competitions.

Doc hoped that one day Lucas would be able to say the same thing about their family.

Chapter Twenty-One

DOC SHOWED UP for the last half of Lucas's riding practice and enjoyed the hell out of watching him interacting with the other kids as well as seeing him ride. He was surprised by how those little moments took hold of a part of him that he hadn't realized was there for the taking.

He took pictures of Lucas riding and sent them to Juliette with the caption *He's amazing.*

Juliette: *Like someone else I know.* She added a smile emoji surrounded by four hearts.

She'd met with the therapist that morning and had really liked her. She'd told Juliette it sounded like they were handling things with Lucas well, keeping open communication but not pushing. They had a lot of ground to cover, but Juliette would continue to see her weekly, and she was going to talk with Lucas about talking with her as well. Doc had been glad to hear she'd advised Juliette to take some time to think about the situation with her father and Ana before making any moves. He'd shared the information with his father and brothers last night after church, and they'd agreed that he needed to be careful so nothing could come back on Juliette.

Doc had spoken with his mother earlier to see if she had any advice about how to handle things with Lucas during their driving lesson this afternoon. She'd reminisced about what it had been like to ride in the car with him and his brothers when they were learning to drive and how different it had been from teaching his sisters. Apparently Doc and his brothers weren't very talkative, had tried to play the music too loud and drove too fast, while his sisters would talk the whole time, pointing out cute boys walking by, only occasionally putting the pedal to the metal.

Doc sent the pictures of Lucas to his family in a group text.

Doc: *That's my boy.*

Mom: *I'm having heart palpitations.*

Tiny: *Chip off the old block.*

Dare: *He's a badass like his old man.*

Cowboy: *Make sure he keeps that helmet on.*

Dare: *We didn't wear helmets.*

Sasha: *That explains a LOT.*

Birdie: *What a little heart stealer! Are there any hot guys my age there?*

Birdie: *I would make a cute buckle bunny.*

A bunny emoji popped up from Birdie.

Tiny: *Over my dead body.*

Doc gritted his teeth, thumbing out, *B, you're banned from all bull-riding events.*

Birdie sent an eye-roll emoji.

Sasha: *Don't worry, Birdie. I'll sneak you in.* She added a winking emoji.

Cowboy sent an angry emoji.

Three laughing emojis popped up from Birdie.

Birdie: *Y'all are so easy to rile up. As if I'd ever chase a man?!*

Mom: *That's my firecracker.*

Sasha: *When can we meet Lucas?*

Birdie: *After the way Doc acted when we saw them at the hospital, Lucas is probably afraid we're all jerks.*

Dare: *Not all of us. He knows I'm cool.*

Dare: *And Cowboy's pushy.*

Laughing emojis popped up from Birdie and Sasha.

Doc: *When he's ready he'll let us know. I've got to run.*

He pocketed his phone and watched the rest of Lucas's practice. Lucas had a rough ride his third time around. Doc held his breath when Lucas was thrown to the ground. But he popped up quickly and headed out of the ring.

When practice ended, Lucas put away his gear and headed over to Doc. "Hey."

"Great practice. How'd it feel?"

"A'right, except when the bull turned back." Turning back was a bucking pattern in which the bull bucked in one direction and made a sudden move in the opposite direction. "I don't know what happened. I knew he was gonna do it. He's got a history of turning back."

"Cut yourself some slack. That's how you learn." As they headed to the truck, Doc said, "I always wanted to ride the bulls that never showed patterns."

"Why?"

"They kept me on my toes. Ready for anything. Focusing on my grip and moving with the bull—keeping my free hand up, getting over its front end when it reared, and keeping my butt down when he kicked up his hind legs—and not what I thought he was going to do made me a better rider."

Lucas's brow furrowed. "I focus on all that, but I'm usually trying to anticipate what's next."

"Some riders do best that way, and you might be one of them. But consider this. Yesterday Layla didn't plan on coming over, right?"

"Yeah. So?"

"She changed her mind while she was out, and when she showed up, how'd you feel?"

"Great, but what does that have to do with bull riding?"

"Because if you'd known she was coming over, you might've had time to get nervous, and it could've been awkward when she got there, and you wouldn't have been at your best, right?"

"I guess."

"Well, animals are like people. They have their own brains. Their thoughts can change with the wind. If you're too focused on what you expect to happen, you're not ready for the unexpected. Last night proved you're damn good at handling the unexpected."

Lucas grinned as they stopped by the truck. "Yeah, I am."

"If you want my advice, practice on the bulls that challenge you to hone your basic skills, because you can't control the bull, but you can control your grip and your form."

Lucas nodded. "That makes sense. Thanks."

"Ready to roll?"

"Hell yeah."

Doc tossed him the keys. "Try not to kill us."

He scoffed. "I'm a great driver."

"Don't get too cocky. You haven't tried parallel parking this beast yet."

AFTER THEY'D DRIVEN around town for a while, Doc was satisfied that Lucas was driving as carefully as he had the other night. He gave him directions on some larger roads, heading through Allure to Hope Valley. "Watch your speed on town roads."

"'Kay."

"You know, there are perks to being related to me."

"Driving lessons?"

"Yes, but also, now that you know Birdie's my sister, which means she's your aunt, the next time you go in there"—he pointed to Birdie's chocolate shop as they drove past—"you can charm some chocolate out of her."

Lucas grinned and stopped at a red light.

As they passed the park, Doc said, "That's where they hold the Festival on the Green."

"What's that?"

"A weeklong event with live music and a sea of tents where people sell all types of things. They have a huge fireworks display when it's over. The ranch and the club have booths there every year. People come from all the neighboring towns. Maybe we can go next year."

"Fireworks are cool, but why would a ranch or a motorcycle club need a booth at a festival?"

"Take the next left, and remember to watch the oncoming traffic." After Lucas navigated the turn, he said, "That's how we spread the word about the ranch's programs, and my father founded the Dark Knights and made it our mission to keep the residents and businesses of Hope Valley and the surrounding areas safe. So it's good to let people know we're around."

"How do you keep them safe?" he asked as he drove along a larger road.

"Lots of different ways. We work with schools to stop bullying and raise awareness about mental health issues and drug and suicide prevention, and we patrol certain neighborhoods. Keep an eye on the seedier operations that are known to be connected to troublesome activities."

"Like drugs?"

"Sometimes. If you want to check us out and meet the guys, the ranch is hosting the club's Ride Clean anti-drug event in a few weeks. There'll be food and games, horseback riding, all sorts of fun stuff. No pressure."

"So, you guys are like badass do-gooders?"

Doc laughed. "You could put it that way."

Lucas gripped the steering wheel tighter. "Do you ever do bad things?"

"Let's just say we do whatever it takes to keep the good people of our community safe."

"I'm taking that as a yes," he said with a rascally grin. "Why were you at the hospital that day we saw you? We saw a bunch of bikers in the parking lot."

"That was our annual fundraising event for the hospital called a Reindeer Ride. We go on a ride with the club dressed up for the holiday so people pay attention. It's a gentle reminder for the community to give back to the hospital and medical staff that's there for them every day, rain or shine. People donate money for the hospital and gifts for the kids who are in it. After the ride, we visit with each of those kids and give out the presents."

"Why? I mean, I get the fundraising, but why give kids gifts in the middle of summer and not at Christmas?"

"Because some of them won't live that long," Doc said carefully.

"Oh." Lucas swallowed hard, readjusting his hands on the wheel tighter. "That sucks."

"Yeah. It's really sad." He told Lucas to take the next right, giving him a minute to digest what he'd said. "Each time we do an event like that, it reminds me to be grateful for every little thing I have."

Lucas's brow furrowed, as if he was thinking that over as he drove down the street.

"You're doing great. Take the next right." After Lucas turned, Doc pointed up ahead. "See that building with the motorcycles parked out front? Pull into that parking lot."

Lucas did as he asked and stopped in front of the building. Doc watched him taking in the brick wall with the words DARK KNIGHTS painted above the club emblem—a skull with dark eyes, sharp brows, and a mouth full of jagged fangs—and HOPE VALLEY CHAPTER painted below.

"Is that your church?" Lucas asked.

"That's our clubhouse."

"Can I go in? Does it have a bar inside?"

Doc was surprised by his interest. "Sorry, but kids aren't allowed inside. If you ever prospect the club, you'll see for yourself what it looks like."

Lucas's gaze shifted to the open garage bay, where Rebel was working beneath the hood of a classic car. "Is this your club's auto shop?"

"No. My cousin Rebel rents that bay for his classic car restoration business."

"Cool."

Rebel ducked out from under the hood and strode toward the truck with a curious expression. "What's going on, Doc?" His dark hair hung nearly to his eyes as he looked at Lucas, and said, "Hey."

"Hi," Lucas said.

"Rebel, this is"—Doc was surprised by how *my son* hung on the tip of his tongue, but he didn't want to make Lucas uncomfortable—"Lucas. Lucas, this is my cousin Rebel."

The glint in Rebel's eyes told Doc he'd already made the connection. "How's it going, Lucas?"

"Not bad. Is that an old Mustang?"

"Sure is. Sixty-five convertible GT. You like old cars?" Rebel asked.

"Heck yeah," Lucas said excitedly.

Rebel looked at Doc. "You got time for him to take a peek?"

"Sure."

"Really?" Lucas's eyes shimmered with joy. "I gotta park!"

Lucas's excitement was contagious as Rebel showed off the Mustang. When Rebel let him sit in it, he raved about how cool the car was, and asked Doc to take a picture. He listened intently to every word Rebel said when they looked under the hood, and asked questions about the engine like a real gearhead.

"How'd you get into doing this?" Lucas asked.

"My family owns a restoration business in Salvation Falls, which is in Upstate New York. I grew up doing it from before I could see over the hood of a car."

"So why are you here?" Lucas asked.

"I went through a messy divorce and needed to get away. Couldn't think of a better place to get out of my own head than with my cousins." Rebel clapped a hand on Doc's shoulder.

"We're glad you did," Doc said.

"Are you a biker, too?" Lucas asked.

"Hell yeah," Rebel said. "It's in my blood, just like Doc and the rest of the guys. My old man and his buddy founded the

Salvation Falls chapter."

Rebel took them behind the building, showing Lucas more classic cars he was working on. Lucas was like a kid in a candy store, taking pictures of each one, rattling off questions and car facts. Doc knew he was getting a glimpse at the kid he'd been before having his life turned upside down. He hoped one day soon Lucas could get back to being that kid.

When they got back on the road, Lucas talked up a storm about the cars he'd seen and how cool it was that Rebel got to work on them.

"Dare's into restoring old cars, too. He's got a bunch of them in his garage."

"On the ranch?"

"Yeah. We can drive by if you'd like." That had been his plan all along. "We don't have to go in, but that way you'll know where I live in case you ever need anything."

"Okay."

Doc gave him directions.

"Layla said she's been to the ranch a bunch of times for events. She said it's cool."

"It is cool. We've known her family forever. They've got a big family, like ours. Layla's grandfather Hal Braden is one of my old man's closest friends. I was glad you offered to ride home with her last night. It's always best to think of your girl's safety before anything else."

"She's the coolest girl in school and definitely the prettiest. If I want to set the standard, I've got to aim high, right?"

Knowing Lucas had listened to his advice filled Doc with pride. "That's right. Between us guys, were you two really just hanging out when we showed up, or were you making out?"

"We were hanging out." His lips tipped up in the corner.

"But I kissed her when I took her home."

Doc laughed. "I figured you might. Were you nervous?"

"No."

"You're braver than I was. I remember being nervous at your age."

"Really?" Lucas didn't take his eyes off the road. "I was nervous. I really like her."

"I know you do, and she obviously likes you. Kissing is okay, but y'all are young. I know it doesn't feel that way, and you probably want to do a whole lot more. But nothing good comes from rushing things. Part of setting a standard is waiting until you're both ready for more, which hopefully won't be for a few years."

"I'm just glad I got to kiss her. I'm in no hurry to do more."

For the love of God, please let him hold on to that feeling for a few more years.

"Good. I know you probably want to brag to your friends, but—"

"No, I don't," Lucas said urgently. "She's too special. I don't want to embarrass her. She's the only person I really talk to about anything important. We trust each other. I don't want to mess that up."

Doc remembered having that feeling with Juliette when they were teenagers. "That's great, and it's really smart not to mess it up. Trust is hard to come by."

"I know." He was quiet for a beat. "Did you know her dad isn't her biological father?"

"Yeah, I did." Hugh and Brianna had met when Layla was little, and he'd adopted her after they were married. "Why?"

"I was just wondering if you knew. She never knew her real father, and she loves her dad. I mean the dad she has now."

"That's good, because I know Hugh loves her very much."

Lucas was quiet for a minute or two. "I told Layla."

"Told her what? Watch your speed."

He slowed down. "You know. That you're my father."

Doc tried to hide his shock. "What'd she have to say about it?" He wasn't sure he wanted to know the answer.

"That I was lucky. She said she knows lots of kids who would love to have you as a father."

Relief swept through him. "That's good to hear." He wanted to ask how that made Lucas feel, but he was worried he might clam up.

"She said I look like you. That's why I told her. I also told her I didn't want to like you, but you're kind of hard to hate."

A low laugh slipped out, and to his relief, Lucas smiled. "I'm glad to hear that."

Doc reveled in that breakthrough. When the ranch came into view, he said, "There it is."

"That's where you met my mom?" Lucas asked with a mixture of tension and intrigue.

"Yeah."

Lucas gripped the steering wheel tighter. "Can we drive through?"

"Sure, but you've got to go real slow. Vehicles don't own the roads at the ranch. The animals and people do."

"Okay." Lucas turned into the entrance and slowed way down, nearly to a stop, pointing up at the Redemption Ranch sign. "Why is the *R* backward?"

"Good question. The people who come here are trying to move past wherever they came from or the things they've done. The backward *R* represents where they are when they get here. They're kind of stuck looking back. The forward-facing *R* represents them when they leave, moving forward, heading in the right direction."

Lucas drove under the sign, taking in the sprawling ranch before them. "This place is huge."

"A couple hundred acres." As they made their way along the main road, Doc said, "My vet clinic is down that road."

"Can we drive by?"

"Sure."

Doc pointed out the well-horse and rehab barns. There were a few ranch hands milling about, and Sasha and their father were talking in front of a rehab barn.

"Is that big guy one of the clients? He looks like he was in prison." As he said it, Tiny looked over and held up a hand, indicating for them to stop. "Should I pull over?" Lucas asked nervously.

"Yes. That big guy is my father, which means he's also your grandfather. He's rough, and he's gruff, but he's one of the fairest, toughest, and most loyal men you will ever meet, and he was out searching for you that night you took off, so show some respect."

"Sorry," Lucas said remorsefully as he pulled over. "Does everyone here know I'm your kid?"

"Pretty much. He and my sister are heading over, but if you'd rather not meet them, I can get out to talk to them."

Lucas stole a glance at Tiny and Sasha and sat up a little taller. "It's okay. You don't need to."

"Okay." Doc lifted his chin to Sasha and Tiny as they came to his window. "Hey, guys, this is Lucas. Lucas, this is my sister Sasha and my father, Tiny."

"Hi," Sasha and Lucas said in unison.

"Nice to meet you, son," Tiny said. "For a minute there, I

thought I was seeing things. You look a lot like Doc did at your age. You flew the coop the other night like he used to, too."

Lucas glanced nervously at Doc. Doc gritted his teeth, sure Lucas was offended by his father's correlation, but before he could string two words together to soften it, Tiny spoke.

"With any luck, you'll grow up to be a hell of a man, just like my boy is." Tiny smiled. "Welcome to the family, son. I look forward to getting to know you."

"Thanks," Lucas said. "It's nice to meet you, too."

"Doc said you're a great bull rider like he was," Sasha said.

Surprise rose in Lucas's eyes. "I guess so."

"Let us know when your next competition is," Sasha suggested. "We'll come cheer you on."

"Um...*okay*," Lucas said tentatively.

Worried he was overwhelmed, Doc said, "We'd better get going."

"It was really nice meeting you, Lucas. I hope we see more of you," Sasha said.

"I do, too," Tiny said, then more sternly, "You drive safe now, you hear?"

"Yes, sir," Lucas said.

Tiny gave a curt nod, and as he and Sasha stepped back from the truck, Tiny crossed his arms, his thick fingers drumming.

As they drove away, Lucas exhaled like he'd been holding his breath that whole time. "Your father is a finger drummer, too."

"Yeah," Doc said with a grin. "He is."

"Weird."

"Sure is." Doc showed him the clinic, and as they drove back toward the main road, he pointed in the direction of his own house. "I live down there. Want to see my place?"

"I guess."

When they got to his house, Lucas instantly spotted his other truck. "Is that your old truck?"

"Yeah, it used to be my father's."

"Why do you need two trucks? Why don't you sell one?"

"That truck isn't going anywhere. It's my old man's legacy. But I needed a double cab and something more reliable I could take on longer trips to pick up horses." The dogs barreled out of the woods beside the house. "And they're my beasts."

"Whoa. Are they all yours?" Lucas asked excitedly.

"Yep. Sadie's the Irish setter, Mighty is the black Lab, and Pickles is the one barking up a storm."

"I always wanted a dog, but my mom said she had her hands full with me and the horses. Can I get out and pet them?"

"They'd love that, but how about you put the truck in park and cut the engine first?"

Doc had never seen the dogs so enamored with anyone. They sniffed Lucas up and down, and Sadie whined for his attention despite the fact that he was showering her with it. Lucas didn't just play with the dogs; he turned into a whole different kid, laughing and loving them up, tossing sticks, and cheering them on as they ran to retrieve them.

"Do you leave them out all day?" he asked, tossing a stick for Pickles.

"No. They come in and out as they please. They have doggy doors."

Lucas looked up at the house. "This place is cool, back here in the woods."

"There's a creek behind the house and a lake up in the woods. When I was a little kid, my grandfather used to take me camping back there."

"I've never been camping." He threw another stick for the dogs. "I think Mom's afraid to go camping because she's never gone."

That saddened him, but not because he thought Juliette was afraid. She loved the outdoors. He was sad she'd never gone. "Is that something you want to do?"

He shrugged. "Kinda, *yeah.*"

"I'd be happy to take you both camping sometime. Here or somewhere else if you'd like."

Lucas didn't respond as the dogs barreled over with sticks in their mouths. Sadie plunked down beside Lucas, and he threw the other dogs' sticks again.

Doc wanted to get through to him, but he knew better than to push. "I have something I think you might find cool. It's from when your mom was here that summer. Mind coming inside for a second?"

"I guess not."

The dogs followed them in, sticking to Lucas like glue as he walked through the living room, trying awfully hard to look like he wasn't checking out the pictures of Doc's family. "What'd you want to show me?"

"It's this way." He led him to the bedroom and lifted the area rug, showing him the heart with his and Juliette's initials carved into the floor.

Lucas looked at it with confusion.

"There was an old cabin here the summer your mom and I met. We used to hang out there, and I carved that into the floor of that old cabin right before your grandfather yanked her out of here. When I tore down the old cabin years later and built this house, I couldn't get rid of it. It's one of the only tangible things I have from that summer."

"Why are you showing it to me?"

"Because I want you to know that I'm not just some asshole who knocked up your mom."

LUCAS WAS QUIET on the way home, and Doc feared he might have overwhelmed him. After they'd left his house, he'd seemed interested in seeing the rest of the ranch. They'd driven by the main house, the paintball field, and each of his family member's houses.

When they pulled down the driveway, Doc said, "I hope seeing the ranch and meeting Sasha and my father weren't too much for you."

"It wasn't. The ranch was cool. That paintball field is huge."

"It's a good one. Sasha and Cowboy love paintball. Every few years they expand the field."

"That's awesome." Lucas parked by Juliette's truck, and after cutting the engine, he stared down at the keys and said, "Do you think Sasha meant what she said about coming to watch me ride?"

"She wouldn't have suggested it if she didn't. My family—*our* family—doesn't fake anything well. What you see is what you get. Sometimes it's suggesting to go see you ride, and other times it's calling you out for being a dick."

Lucas eyed him cautiously. "But your dad welcomed me to the family, and he doesn't know me."

"Because that's how he feels. You're half Whiskey, which means you're Tiny's blood. In our family, that's all that matters."

"What if they think I'm a jerk?"

"I can tell you without a shred of doubt that we all think that about each other at one time or another."

Lucas smiled.

"Look, you're a good kid going through a hard time. But even if you weren't a good kid, and you were stealing or treating people badly, you're *still* family, and we don't turn our backs on family. Not if you're a jerk some days, or if you're going through a rough patch and need to be handled with kid gloves, or if you're turning into an asshole and need to be tough loved."

Lucas looked down at the keys in his hand again.

"I'm sure the idea of a big, loud, welcoming family seems weird and overwhelming because it's been just you and your mom for a very long time. But you can trust that the love we will show you is real. Your mom was out of our lives since she was sixteen, but when you went missing, my family showed up for her. No questions asked. My father rallied the club, and my mother sat with your mom until you were safely home."

"I didn't know your mom was there." Lucas looked at him again.

"I know. She and my father left when we were down by the barn. Everything about our situation is new for you and your mom and for me and my family. We're bound to have ups and downs. But how boring would life be if it was easy all the time?"

Lucas almost smiled. "I never thought about that."

"As I said before, family means everything to us, and they're going to be there for you in good times and bad. Honestly, if you choose never to meet the rest of them, they'd still show up for you."

Lucas fidgeted with the keys again, nodding.

"Look, there's no pressure. We're not going anywhere. We're Hope Valley born and bred, and we'll be there until we're buried six feet under."

"Will they be there for my mom if her father comes after her?"

Christ, you've got way too many worries for a kid. "Your grandfather isn't going to come after her."

"But my mom said you guys are going to make sure he pays for what he did, and that he'll go to jail for the other bad things he did."

"We are, and he will, eventually. But that's not something you need to worry about. We would never do anything that would lead to him coming after your mom. Your grandfather can't hurt any of us anymore, okay?"

Lucas nodded.

"Any other worries you want to talk about?"

He shook his head.

"Come on, let's find your mom."

As they got out of the truck, Juliette came out the front door, looking like a ray of sunshine in a yellow tank top, her hair bouncing with each exuberant step, her hips swaying in sexy cutoffs, and those cowgirl boots that made Doc want to toss her in the back of his truck and make out with her like they were carefree kids.

"I'm glad to see you're both in one piece," she said. "You were out so long, I was starting to worry."

"He's a lot more fun to drive with than you are," Lucas said. "We went by his clubhouse, and I met his cousin Rebel, who showed me a bunch of classic cars."

"Really?" she asked.

"Doc showed me the ranch, too," Lucas said.

Her eyes widened. "Wow. How'd that go?"

"Good," Lucas said. "I met his dad, Tiny, who's not tiny at all, and his sister Sasha, who's really hot."

"*Lucas,*" she said with amusement.

"What? She is hot—for an older girl."

Juliette nudged Doc. "No wonder he thinks you're more fun than me."

"That's not why," Lucas said. "Doc doesn't slam his foot on a fake brake or grab the dashboard like you do."

She and Doc laughed, and she said, "Yeah, yeah."

"He did great today," Doc said, knowing she'd realize he meant overall, not just driving.

"See? I'm a good driver," Lucas said cockily.

"But you do need to watch your speed," Doc corrected. "Vehicles are dangerous machines."

"I will." Lucas handed him the keys. "Thanks for taking me."

"Let me know if you want to do it again."

"Can we?" Lucas asked Juliette. "Do you mind if he takes me driving again?"

"I would hate for you to be forever traumatized by my fake braking," she teased.

"I can pick you up Friday after practice," Doc offered. "I can also do a few hours Saturday. Your pick, or we can do both."

"I want to do both," he said. "I told Layla I'd try to hang out with her this weekend, but I can do that after we go driving, and, Mom, Robert invited me to spend the night Saturday. Is that okay?"

"Sure, as long as his parents will be home."

"They will." Lucas shoved his hands into the front pockets

of his jeans, looking nervously at Doc. "Do you think next weekend you could take me driving through the ranch again and maybe I can meet some more of your family?"

Doc's heart soared, but he tried to play it cool. "Absolutely. How about we have your mom meet us there next Saturday afternoon and I'll show you both around? You can join us for dinner, and we can kick Dare's and Cowboy's butts in paintball. Maybe have a bonfire afterward if you're up for it."

Lucas looked hopefully at Juliette. "Can we?"

"Sounds fun to me. I'd love to see everyone again," she said.

"Awesome. I'm starved. Is there still leftover pizza in the fridge?" Lucas said.

"Yes," Juliette said, and Lucas ran up to the house. She turned a curious gaze on Doc. "Did you add kid whisperer to your résumé when I wasn't looking?"

"I'm as surprised as you are. I thought we'd drive by the ranch so he'd know where it was, but he asked if it was okay to drive through it."

"*Wow.* I'm floored."

"I think Layla had a little something to do with his change of heart. He told me that he told her I was his father."

"He *did*? He must really trust her. He doesn't even want to talk to the therapist yet. He said he doesn't need to."

"He may not right now. Kids are pretty resilient. But we shouldn't give up on him talking to a professional. Maybe wait a couple of weeks and then bring it up again."

"That was my plan. I'm glad he trusts Layla, but if they're that close, their relationship could progress quickly, and she's way too young."

"They both are. But the reality is, we can't control what they do. All we can do is teach Lucas respect for himself and for her, guide him in the right direction, and hope that if or when they do more, they're safe."

"Lucas is proof that passion can obliterate safety. Did you talk to him about yesterday?"

"Yeah. They weren't fooling around in the barn, and he's in no hurry to do more than kiss."

"He *kissed* her?" She put a hand over her heart. "My baby boy is growing up too fast." She looked up at the sky. "I'm not ready for any of this."

"There's nothing we can't handle."

"We," she said a little dreamily. "I like how that sounds."

He stepped closer, wishing he could pull her into his arms, but they were in view of the windows. "Then I hope you love how this sounds. Saturday night, you on the back of my motorcycle, dinner and dancing at the Roadhouse, and a slumber party at my place."

"A slumber party, huh?" she teased. "Will there be snacks?"

"Darlin', if you agree to stay over, then I'll have my favorite snack, and I'll happily be yours."

"Seeley Whiskey, you do know how to entice a woman."

"Well, you deserve to be spoiled on your birthday."

Her brows shot up in surprise. "I can't believe you remembered. Did Lucas mention it? He always makes me cinnamon toast for breakfast on my birthday and gives me a homemade card."

"He didn't mention it. I told you I haven't forgotten a single thing about you, but it sounds like I better up my game. So what do you say?"

"I say I can't wait. But I haven't ridden on a motorcycle or been to a bar or gone dancing since you took me to the Roadhouse for lunch that summer."

The biker in him was thrilled she hadn't warmed another man's back, but his heart was eating up the rest of what she'd said. "You've never gone on a date to a bar?"

"Nope."

A slow grin slid into place. "Is it bad that it makes me happy knowing no other man has held you close on a dance floor?"

She laughed softly. "I'd be disappointed if it didn't."

He couldn't resist taking her hand and leading her around to the other side of the truck, out of eyeshot from the house. "I missed you today, and if I don't get to kiss you right now, I'm pretty sure I'm going to lose my mind."

"We wouldn't want that to happen."

As she wound her arms around him, he lowered his lips to hers, kissing them both breathless.

Chapter Twenty-Two

JULIETTE HAD BEEN a little nervous about riding on Seeley's motorcycle, but her nerves didn't stand a chance against the thrill of being wrapped around his back, the vibration of the engine working its magic as the world sped by. The feel of his muscles flexing against her chest and beneath her hands was intoxicating.

Heck, the man himself was even *more* so.

When she'd seen him straddling his shiny black bike in faded jeans, wearing his leather cut over a black T-shirt, tattoos snaking out from beneath the sleeves, her entire body had ignited. She'd seen enough hot guys in her life to know it had less to do with his incredible looks and more to do with the heart that beat within his broad chest.

The heart that had welcomed their son without hesitation and had never fully closed to her.

The crisp evening air whipped over her skin as they turned off the main road, heading for the Roadhouse. Seeley had told her his siblings would be there. He said he wanted to give her a chance to get to know them again before introducing Lucas to everyone next weekend. She was excited and nervous to see everyone again.

By the time they arrived, she felt freer and lighter than she had in years. The rustic building hadn't changed. It still had a long front porch and an orange neon ROADHOUSE sign above the front door.

He cut the engine and took off his helmet as he climbed off the bike, raking a hand through his thick hair. He set his helmet down and helped her take off hers. As she shook out her hair, the lascivious look he gave her made her body vibrate anew.

"*Mm-mm.* You on my bike is too hot to pass up."

As he straddled the bike, facing her, she laughed. "What are you doing?"

"Getting a taste of what's mine."

He pushed his hands into her hair, drawing her mouth to his in a penetrating kiss. His tongue slid over hers, possessing more of her with every stroke. She was arched forward, kissing him harder.

"Now, *that's* a kiss. No wonder Juliette got pregnant."

Seeley broke the kiss on a curse, and it took a minute for Juliette's brain to catch up. When it did, she was flooded with embarrassment. Doc was glowering at Birdie, who was standing beside the bike smirking. She looked like a cute Madonna throwback in a white lace bustier and denim microskirt, with jagged layers of lavender tulle hanging from the hem to just below her thighs. A pearl choker circled her neck, along with several long necklaces, and she wore fingerless, elbow-length white gloves.

"Hi, Birdie," Juliette said.

"Hi! Are you guys coming or what? I mean coming *into* the bar. I don't want to know about—"

"*Birdie,*" Doc warned, climbing off the bike.

Birdie held up her gloved hands. "Hey, I'm not the one inspecting her tonsils with my tongue."

Juliette laughed as Doc helped her off the bike.

"Don't encourage her," Doc said as he locked the helmets to the bike.

"Damn, girl," Birdie said. "You look hot."

"Thanks." She'd worn her favorite jeans and boots and a short-sleeved copper shirt that laced up between her breasts, making her boobs look amazing.

"That's a killer shirt. I don't blame Doc for wanting to take you right here and now. I'm surprised you made it out of your house. If I had boobs like that—"

"*Jesus*, Birdie. That's enough," Seeley scolded, and draped his arm over Juliette's shoulders as they headed inside.

Juliette couldn't help laughing. Birdie had been so young when they knew each other before, but she'd always pushed Seeley's buttons. "You look great, too, Birdie. I love your skirt."

"Thanks. I made it." She wiggled her hips. "Hopefully it'll be a man magnet tonight."

Seeley turned a dark stare on Birdie. "Can you pretend you're not out to find a guy for one night?"

Birdie planted a hand on her hip. "I don't go out to find guys. I go out so they can find me. Now, if you'll excuse me." She threw open the door and strutted into the bar.

"I swear that girl's gonna give me gray hair."

Juliette laughed. "She's a grown woman with a vibrant personality. Don't try to tame her."

"I don't want to tame her. I want to protect her."

And there it was, one of the things she loved most about him.

As they made their way inside, the music and the din of

people dancing, playing pool, gathered around the bar, and cheering on a girl riding a mechanical bull brought a rush of adrenaline.

Seeley kept her close as they weaved through the crowd and around packed tables. Juliette noticed a large number of men wearing cuts with Dark Knights patches scattered throughout the bar, like there had been way back when, and memories rushed in. She'd been so young and in love, their lunch dates at the Roadhouse had felt like a dream, and the few times they'd had dinner there, the bar had been hopping, and she'd felt the same sizzling energy then that electrified the air tonight.

But one thing *had* changed.

Back then the other Dark Knights had been watching over them. Now it was Seeley's keen eyes trailing over the crowd, slowing for a beat when he spotted Birdie chatting up two guys. Juliette could feel tension rising in him, his arm tightening around her as he shot those men a warning glare, and they took a step back. She felt bad for Birdie, but she was also in awe of Seeley and how hard he loved the people in his life.

She noticed a few people looking at them with curious expressions, and her nerves flared. Given what Seeley had told her about his dating history, she assumed they were wondering if she was his fling for the next few weeks. Her stomach twisted at the thought of him with other women. But they'd both lived full lives, which had included other men and women. More importantly, their hearts had stayed connected through unbearable heartache. There was no room for jealousy in a love like theirs.

She spotted his siblings sitting at a table just ahead. Cowboy had his arm around a petite beauty with shoulder-length golden-brown hair and a warm smile. She looked to be about

Birdie's age and was gazing at Cowboy adoringly. Sasha was cozied up to a handsome man with jet-black hair, olive skin, and chiseled features, and Billie stood beside Dare's chair holding a tray of glasses and chatting with them.

Dare looked up, catching Juliette watching them. He pushed to his feet and called out, "There's the man of the hour and the beautiful birthday girl!" sparking a round of *happy birthdays* from everyone.

Juliette looked at Doc in elated shock. "You told everyone?"

"You deserve to be celebrated, darlin'." He kissed her, and she couldn't stop smiling.

"Get over here." Dare pulled her into an embrace. "I'm glad you're here."

"Thanks. Me too."

He put his hand on Billie's back and said, "You remember my beautiful wife, Billie?"

"I do. It's good to see you. I always knew you two would end up together."

"This one didn't give me a choice," Billie said, eyeing Dare lovingly.

"Yes, I did," Dare said. "I said you could marry me or I could marry you, but either way, we were gettin' hitched."

They all laughed.

"Jule, you know Cowboy and Sasha." Seeley pulled out a chair for her and said, "This is Cowboy's fiancée, Sully, and Sasha's fiancé, Ezra."

"It's nice to meet you both," Juliette said, a wave of awkwardness moving through her as her gaze connected with Sasha's. Sasha had been there when she'd yelled at Seeley about Lucas at the ranch. She had been the calm, centered sibling years ago, and she had that aura about her now as she watched them settle into their seats. Juliette tried to break the ice. "I can't believe all of you are getting married. Congratulations."

"Thanks," the four of them said at once.

Billie said, "I have to get back to work. Doc, Juliette, what can I get you? I'm bringing these guys appetizers and drinks."

Seeley put his arm around Juliette's. "Do you still like loaded potato skins and wings?"

"I love them. *Finger food is life*," she said, parroting what they'd said as teens, earning a laugh and a kiss, which also made her a little nervous in front of everyone. She wasn't sure how much his family knew about their current relationship, and she wanted to clear the air with Sasha. She also didn't want to have too much alcohol since they'd taken the motorcycle, but she needed a little liquid encouragement and allowed herself one drink. "I haven't ordered a drink in forever. What's good but not too strong?"

"Margaritas!" Birdie said as she plopped down into a chair beside her.

"Yes!" Sasha and Sully agreed.

"I guess I'm having a margarita," Juliette said.

"I'll have my usual," Doc said.

As Billie walked away, Juliette bit the bullet and gazed across the table at Sasha. "Sasha, I'm a little embarrassed and wanted to apologize for making a scene that day at the ranch when I yelled at Seeley about Lucas."

Sasha waved her hand dismissively, her dirty-blond hair hanging loose over her shoulders. "Don't worry about it. I've seen worse, and this guy"—she pointed to Seeley—"needed a kick in the ass."

"Especially after the way he spoke to you at the hospital," Birdie said. "I wanted to kick his butt."

Seeley pulled Juliette closer. "Birdie gave me hell for it, and Sasha gave me crap for what I said that day at the ranch."

"Thank God," Juliette said with a sigh, and everyone laughed. "I thought you guys might hate me for it."

"No way. He told us what you guys have been through, and I'm *so* sorry," Sasha said. "That's awful."

"I'm sorry, too," Birdie said. "You know, for all those years, we weren't even allowed to say your name, because Doc would lose his shit, and we never knew why. Now that I know the truth, I want to kick your father's butt."

"You and me both," Juliette said, noticing Seeley and the guys exchanging serious glances she couldn't read. But she sensed they were in agreement of wanting to do the same.

"I'm really glad I finally got to meet you," Sully said. "I grew up in a cult, and I know how it feels to have the person who should protect you not only fail to do so but put you in harm's way. I know your situation was different, but they're kind of the same. If you ever need somebody to talk to, I'm a pretty good listener."

"You're a great listener," Cowboy said, and kissed her temple.

Juliette didn't know the extent of abuse Sully had suffered at the cult, but Seeley had alluded to enough for her to guess, and she knew that even admitting as much as she did probably wasn't easy for Sully. "I appreciate that, and one day I just might take you up on it."

"We're all here for you and Lucas," Sasha said. "He's a cutie, by the way. I met him the other day when he and Doc came by the ranch. He looks so much like Doc did at his age, it made my dad's head spin."

"Sash, Lucas thinks you're hot," Doc said.

Ezra hugged Sasha against his side. "The boy has good taste."

"I heard he's got a thing for Layla Braden," Cowboy said.

"He does, and I'm not ready for it," Juliette said as Billie brought their drinks. "Thanks."

"Your food will be right up," Billie said.

"Give me some sugar, Wildfire." Dare pulled Billie down for a kiss and slapped her ass as she walked away, earning a glower over her shoulder.

"Layla's a cutie, too. I could see them together," Sasha said.

"She's a sweet girl," Juliette said. "Lucas spent the day with her and her family at the Real DEAL, that total immersion exploratory park. It's supposed to be educational, but they had so much fun. They were there all day. Apparently the place has everything you can think of from hands-on survivalist activities, marine biology labs, and a bunch of other things that all have to do with science. Of course Lucas's favorite part was the race track. He's such a speed demon."

"He gets that from me," Dare said.

"Where is Lucas tonight?" Sully asked.

"Spending the night at his friend's house," Seeley answered. "Which means I get Juliette all to myself." He kissed her temple.

"Not yet, you don't." Birdie popped to her feet. "Girl time! Let's go dance!"

Sasha and Sully got up in a flurry of excitement.

"Juliette, stop ogling my brother and get your butt out of that chair." Birdie took Juliette's hand, tugging her up to her feet.

"Oh! I didn't know you meant *me*," she said.

"We can't do girl talk in front of the guys," Birdie said.

"*Birdie*," Seeley warned.

Birdie rolled her eyes, tugging Juliette toward the dance floor with Sasha and Sully.

"Tell us everything," Birdie said.

"What was it like for you out in California? It must have been so hard," Sasha said.

"What's it like being back after all this time?" Sully asked. "Does Lucas know about you and Doc?"

And so it began.

They danced as they talked, and while it started out sounding like an interrogation, it quickly morphed into something else. Something she hadn't realized she'd needed. The girls were empathetic and asked questions that only other women would know to ask, and they seemed to genuinely care about what she and Lucas had been through. Birdie and Sasha shared the worries they'd had about Seeley over the years. They explained that they really hadn't known what had happened, and they told her how they'd known he'd harbored love for her for all this time because he'd become so closed off after that summer.

Their serious conversations were interspersed with laughter and hugs as they teased each other, and the girls joked about how possessive the guys were, watching them like hawks while they danced. Juliette knew that, at least for Seeley, it wasn't because he didn't trust her, but rather because he didn't want anything to happen to her or any of them. She loved that about him, but with the girls, she saw the humor in it, too, because the guys' eagle eyes were peeled.

They danced and laughed until they were too hungry to keep going. Then they joined the guys at the table, chowing down on finger food, enjoying easy conversation, fun banter, and smooches from their men. Which Birdie never failed to comment on, and *wow*, did Juliette feel good. She'd lost touch with her high school girlfriends after moving to California, and it had been hard to find new friends there, because she was a seventeen-year-old married mother, and most girls her age were still in high school or out partying. She hadn't realized how much she'd missed having girlfriends until now. She felt like she'd found a true sisterhood. A tribe of women friends who talked about *real* things and understood that life could be treacherously hard but also irresistibly beautiful. And they not only believed in deep, soul-searing love, but they were rooting for her and Seeley and Lucas as hard as she and Seeley were.

As the night wore on, her new girlfriends convinced her to ride the mechanical bull, which was an embarrassment but fun as hell. Seeley and everyone else cheered her on for the five seconds she lasted. She couldn't stop laughing after falling off, and Birdie hollered, "Attagirl! Show that floor who's boss!" making her laugh even harder.

Seeley helped her up and pulled her into his arms. "I think you'd better stick to riding your cowboy." He smothered her laughter with a merciless kiss that drew whistles and shouts from the crowd.

Now she was in his arms on the dimly lit dance floor, dancing to "What if I Never Get Over You." His hands were warm on her back, his body brushing sensually against hers. They were surrounded by couples, but he was looking at her like she was the only person in the entire room. Her heart was so full, she was sure he could feel it beating between them.

"Are you having a good time, darlin'?"

"I'm having the *best* time. I love being here with you, getting reacquainted with your brothers and sisters, and getting to know their partners. This is what I'd always imagined for us."

"Me too. I still can't believe you're right here in my arms. And I get to have you all to myself tonight." He kissed her softly, his gaze moving slowly over her face.

"What?"

"You're so beautiful, it almost hurts to look at you."

She rolled her eyes, shaking her head.

"I'm serious, darlin'. When we were apart, even when I was trying *not* to think of you, I'd wonder how you'd changed over the years. No matter how I pictured you, whether it was heavy or thin, short hair or long, you were always beautiful in my mind's eye. No one could ever hold a candle to you."

Not for the first time, and she knew not for the last, the honesty in his voice took her breath away. "Seeley Whiskey, are you telling me that at sixteen I ruined you for all other women? Because I'm thinking there should be a trophy for that."

"Oh, there is, and you're going to get all nine inches of it."

They laughed, and he kissed her again.

"But I do have a little something for you. I hate that I missed so many birthdays and Mother's Days, but I look forward to being here for all that are yet to come." He pulled a small velvet bag from his pocket, and there in the middle of the dance floor, he presented her with the most beautiful white-gold diamond-studded infinity necklace that hung vertically, with a heart-shaped aquamarine at the bottom. "Happy birthday, darlin'. I hope I got Lucas's birthstone right."

She teared up. "You did. It's beautiful." He put it on her, and then he kissed her. She choked out, "Thank you," and he held her a little tighter.

She rested her head against his chest, holding him tighter, too, as they danced through the end of the song. When "Ready to Be Loved" came on, it was a faster song, but they continued swaying to their own silent beat. They gazed into each other's eyes, and he whispered the lyrics to her. As he sang about how he was used to hiding his feelings and wanted to risk it all with her, how he'd been hurt and had never let anyone in, and how he was ready to let it all go to be loved by her, every word made her heart feel even fuller.

It was no wonder she'd never been able to connect with any other man. She and Seeley were soul mates. Two halves of the same heart, and their beautiful son had all the best parts of both of them.

Chapter Twenty-Three

"FINALLY," DOC SAID between urgent kisses and greedy gropes as they stumbled through his front door, trying to fend off the dogs, who were as excited to see them as they were to be alone.

Mighty shoved his big head between them. Doc pushed him away, gritting out, "*Get outta here*," but Pickles and Sadie were on their other side, doing the same thing, tails wagging, big bodies rubbing against them.

Juliette laughed. "It's like having three toddlers. They missed you."

He let out a frustrated growl, but she was right. They'd waited all day to see him, and they deserved attention. He stole another kiss before crouching to give the dogs some love. They ate it up.

Juliette watched him with a dreamy expression. "Who knew watching you love on those dogs could be an aphrodisiac?"

"Sorry to cut you short guys, but you're on your own tonight." He pushed to his feet and snagged her hand, reclaiming her mouth as they hurried into the bedroom. He kicked the door shut behind him, but Pickles bullied his way in, leading the pack, and as Doc and Juliette tumbled to the bed, the dogs bounded up beside them. *"Christ."*

Juliette cracked up, and he tried to usher them off the bed and out of the room—a riotous event that took far too long. She was still laughing when he finally closed the door. "I wish I'd videoed that!"

"You think that's funny, huh?" He locked eyes with her as he tugged off his boots and socks.

"*Yes*," she said between laughs. "They sleep with you. They were laying claim to their territory."

He stripped off his shirt, and her gaze moved appreciatively over his chest, her laughter quieting as he strode toward her, opening his jeans. "Maybe so, but you're my territory, and I'm going to stake claim to every inch of your body." He pulled off her boots and socks. "I've been thinking about all the things I want to do to you."

"You have?"

"Damn right I have, and it's a long list. Your pleasure is my new obsession. I'm going to taste every inch of your body. Starting here." He kissed the tips of her toes, and she giggled. He kissed the top of her foot and around her ankle. Her breathing hitched, her eyes darkening. "Mm. You like that." He did it again, and she bit her lower lip. "You are so damn sexy."

He took her hand, bringing her up to her feet. Holding her gaze, he unlaced her shirt and trailed his fingers over her necklace and the swell of her breasts. He drew her shirt over her head, tossing it to the floor. Her bra followed, and he looked his fill. "So beautiful." He brushed his fingers teasingly over her nipples, and her breath hitched. "I'm going to lick and suck these gorgeous tits until you come so hard, they hear you screaming two towns over."

A whimper escaped her lips, making his cock ache for her. "You like that, don't you?"

"*Yes*," she said in one long breath.

A husky growl climbed up his throat. "I have missed my dirty girl." He cupped her cheek, dragging his thumb over her lower lip. "I want to fuck these lips while we're in the shower and see your big blue eyes staring up at me while I come down your throat."

The breath rushed from her lungs. "You *have* thought about this."

"Oh yeah, baby. More than you know."

"*Tell me*," she begged. "I want to know your fantasies."

He flashed what he knew was a lecherous grin at her eagerness. "You mean our realities?"

"I hope so," she said so damn sweetly and hungrily, it nearly did him in.

"Christ, baby." He crushed his mouth to hers, kissing her rough and deep. He rolled her nipple between his finger and thumb and broke the kiss to see the flames in her eyes. "We have years to make up for." He nipped at her lower lip. "Remember how we used to talk about making love in the barn without getting caught?"

She nodded. "Uh-huh."

"I'm going to strip you naked in the barn and bind your wrists to the crossties on either side of the aisle." Her eyes widened. "Then I'm going to lick your pussy until you come down your legs."

"I want that," she panted out.

"Does it make you wet thinking about that, baby?"

"Yes."

"Fucking right it does." He rubbed her through her jeans

and took her in another passionate kiss. She ground against his hand, and he tore his mouth away. "Just thinking about you tied up, at my mercy, coming on my mouth, makes my cock hard as steel. Feel it."

She palmed him through his jeans. "*So hard.*"

"When you're tied up in that barn, I'm going to fuck you so good, you're going to beg me to do it every night, right there, where anyone can walk in and see us."

"We'll do it at night," she said breathily, and so fucking eagerly he could barely contain his need for her.

"*Maybe,*" he teased.

Her wicked grin had him stripping off her jeans and panties and running his hands up her legs. "Look at you. So fucking pretty." He pressed a kiss to her glistening pussy. She moaned, and he slicked his tongue along her wetness, all the way up to her clit, teasing her there until she said, "*More.*"

He rose to his full height. "Your pussy is so fucking sweet." He teased her with his fingers, loving how hard she was breathing and the way her body trembled with need. He crushed his mouth to hers, his tongue sweeping and devouring. She moaned, sucking his tongue, sending a bolt of heat straight to his dick. "Taste how sweet you are." He brought his glistening fingers to her lips, and she opened her mouth. He placed them on her tongue, and her lips closed around them, sucking as he pumped them. "That's my girl. That's going to be my cock."

He pulled his fingers out of her mouth, teasing her pussy again. "Do you want to suck my cock, baby?"

"*Yes,*" she pleaded, blushing.

He dragged his tongue along her lower lip. "On your knees, my dirty darlin'." He stripped off his clothes as she dropped to her knees. She reached for his cock, those big blue eyes gazing up at him as she teased him with her tongue, licking up and down the length of him and around the broad head. Every slick of her tongue had his cock jerking.

He tangled his hands in her hair. "Wrap those soft lips around my cock and show me how much you missed it." She did as he asked, taking him in deep. *"Fuuck."* He pumped his hips, and she chased her mouth with her fist, squeezing as she sucked. "That's it. So fucking good." She closed her eyes, working him faster. "Eyes on me, darlin'."

Her eyes opened, and fucking hell, they glowed with pleasure as she sucked and stroked. "What a stunning sight you are, loving my cock." She smiled around his dick and grabbed his hips, giving him full rein like she used to, her eyes egging him on. He ran with them, thrusting fast and deep. "Give me your throat."

She angled her head back, opening her throat for him. He slowed his pace, loving the way it squeezed around his dick. "Fuck." With every thrust, she pulled him in deeper. "That's it. You take me so well." He quickened his efforts. "You want my come, baby?"

Heat flashed in her eyes, and she nodded, grabbing his balls with one hand. He gritted out a curse, thrusting faster. A mix of challenge and pleasure stared back at him as she gently squeezed his balls, sending heat searing down his spine, and his release shot down her throat. *"Fuck...Jule...Fuck."*

She stayed with him as his body jerked through the last of his release. She licked her lips, and as he lifted her to her feet, she said, "I've missed that, too."

She knew just how to get to him. He took her in a brutal kiss that left them both a little hazy. "Time for another birthday present, baby." Moving behind her, he grabbed her ass, caressing the soft globes. "Tell me this gorgeous ass is mine."

"It's yours. I'm all yours."

He spun her around to face the mirror over the dresser and guided her hands to it, watching them in the mirror. "Look at my girl, so trusting." He held her gaze in the mirror as he grabbed her ass cheeks, spreading them slightly, and brushed his thumbs between them. "Has anyone else touched you here?"

Her eyes flamed. "Never."

There was no hiding his greedy grin. "Watch me make you come." He sank down, loving those globes with his mouth and hands, earning moans and whimpers. He licked her pussy and spread her cheeks, licking *all* of her.

"Seeley, please."

As he feasted on her pussy, he moved one hand to her clit and used his other to tease that forbidden entrance. *"Ohgod, Seeley...Don't stop..."* He licked and teased, making her legs shake and her pussy drip. *"Oh. Oh. Yes. Yes. Yes! Seeley—"* His name flew from her lips like a fucking prayer. He pushed to his feet, driving his cock into her in one hard stroke. She cried out, the shrill noise laden with pleasure, drawing a curse from his lungs.

"Eyes open," he demanded, and her eyes flew open. "Hold tight and watch me love you."

She clung to the dresser, watching as he pounded into her, her eyes shimmering with desire, her cheeks flushed, and her beautiful tits and silky hair bouncing. *"Feels...so...good,"* she said, pressing her hands flat against the dresser.

"Your pussy is so damn tight and hot, and look at your gorgeous tits. Fuck, baby," he gritted out. "You're a goddamn dream."

He reached around her, stroking her clit with one hand and rolling her nipple between his finger and thumb with the other. She moaned, arching into his hand. He pinched her nipple, and she lost it, crying out as she shattered around his cock, her inner muscles pulsing, her hips thrusting. Clenching his teeth against the need to come, he gritted out, "That's it, baby. Drench my cock."

A long moan sailed from her lips as she started coming down from the peak, her head dropping between her shoulders. "We're not done, sexy girl." He lifted her upright and put his hand to the base of her neck and collarbone, holding her there. "Watch what you do to me." He quickened his efforts, and she reached back, digging her nails into his hips.

"Yes. *More*," she pleaded, and put her hand over his on her neck, squeezing slightly.

"*Fuck.*" He tightened his grip, thrusting harder, working her clit with his other hand. "Look at you, giving all of yourself to me."

His heart, his body, his fucking *soul* had existed for this woman before he even realized she was willing to be just as wild as she used to be with him.

Only with him.

That kernel of truth had him wanting—*needing*—even more.

"Play with your tits." He watched her fondle them, teasing her nipples, and his cock ached for release. He clenched his teeth, staving off his orgasm. "Fucking hell."

This was too good, too fucking hot. He wanted to burn the image of her playing with her tits into his mind, etch the image of him claiming her into her heart. "One day I'm going to come all over those beautiful tits."

"I want you to," she panted out. *"Oh God.* Seeley. *I'm...so...close."*

He worked her clit faster, thrusting impossibly deeper, and sank his teeth into her shoulder, sending her crashing into another climax, her pussy squeezing his cock like a fucking vise, sending bolts of heat down his spine. His climax rocketed through him. *"Fuuck—"*

They pumped and ground, their gasps, moans, curses, and growls ringing out like feral animals, unable to get enough. He'd never come so hard or for so long. Their bodies grew slick with sweat, jerking and thrusting through the very last tremor of their releases. She went boneless against him. She looked drunk on him, high on them, and he was right there with her. Their eyes connected in their reflection, her neck pink from his hand, her lips curving into the sweetest, sexiest smile he'd ever seen.

He kissed her neck, wanting to say so many things, but as he turned her in his arms, his voice was silenced by the raw emotions gazing back at him, mirroring the all-consuming ones he was struggling with. He was so full of them, so consumed with love for her—and Lucas—he had to stop himself from overwhelming her. He bit back the urge to tell her he wanted them there with him, in his house, surrounded by people who loved them and would protect them if ever he wasn't around.

Instead, he brushed his lips over hers and kissed her, wondering how he'd ever survived a day, much less sixteen years, without her in his life.

DOC AWOKE TO the feel of Juliette's warm lips trailing

down his stomach and the dusky predawn light peeking through the curtains. He was already hard. He'd been dreaming of her, reliving the three times they'd made love last night.

He ran his fingers through her hair. "What a nice way to wake up."

She wrapped her delicate fingers around his erection and tipped her beautiful face up with a sweet smile on her lips. "Like you said, we have lots of time to make up for." She dragged her tongue slowly from the base of his dick to the tip, swirling it around the head, setting off sparks beneath his skin. He sucked in a breath through gritted teeth. She grinned victoriously and said, "We only have a few hours before I have to pick up Lucas, and I intend to take full advantage."

"Lucky me," he said as she lowered her mouth over his cock. "Christ, baby."

He tangled his fingers in her hair, rocking his hips to her efforts, soaking in every sinful sound, the feel of her hand chasing her mouth along his shaft. She moaned around his cock, and his hips shot up, the head hitting the back of her throat. She gagged, jerking back.

"*Fuck*. Sorry, baby. I should've warned you. You just felt too good." He rubbed her jaw, but she was *laughing*.

"Remember when you did that the first time I blew you?"

The memory came back to him, and he laughed. "Shit. Yeah. God, I thought I'd died and gone to heaven that night in the hayloft. You were so innocent, but so *hot* for me."

"You thought you'd died and gone to heaven, and I felt like Santa came early." She began stroking him again, dragging her tongue around the head of his dick. "All you had to do was look at me, and I nearly combusted." She took him in deep, working him in slow, tight strokes, her teeth and tongue driving him out of his fucking mind. "When I finally got to touch you, I couldn't get enough."

She sucked and stroked, sending waves of pleasure crashing over him, taking him right up to the brink of release. He yanked her hair, and his cock slipped from her lips. "Your mouth was made for my cock, baby, but I'm too greedy for you. I want to be buried deep inside you when I come. Get your pretty little ass up here and ride your cowboy."

She climbed up his body, and as she sank down onto his cock, she moaned, and he gritted out, "*Fuck.*" He grabbed her hips, holding her in place and gyrating his hips. Her hair fell in tangled locks over her breasts, the necklace he'd given her shimmering against her skin.

"Your cock was made for me," she said with a seductive glint in her eyes.

"Fuck yeah, it was." He eased his grip, and as they started moving, she arched her back and palmed her breasts. "You spicy little minx. You know just how to drive me wild."

"I've got a few tricks up my sleeve." She smiled coyly, caressing one breast as she slid her other hand down her stomach to the apex of her sex.

"Better be careful, darlin'. I might never let you leave."

Chapter Twenty-Four

"THIS IS *AWESOME*," Lucas exclaimed, petting his new best four-legged friend, Sadie.

It was late Saturday afternoon, and Seeley was showing them around the ranch. They'd just come from the rope-climbing course that Tiny had built for Dare and Billie when they were kids, which Lucas had thought was the coolest thing he'd ever seen, until he saw the five-acre motocross racetrack Dare had built for Billie after he'd graduated from college.

"I can't believe he built an entire racetrack for Billie when she wasn't even speaking to him," Lucas said. "I know you said they were both messed up after losing their friend, but if he built this for *me*, I'd talk to him again no matter what."

"Sometimes it's not that easy to move on," Seeley explained, looking unfairly handsome in a dark tank top and jeans, his strong arms and tattoos on display, his cowboy hat perched on his head.

"But if she wasn't even talking to him, *why* build it for her at all?" Lucas said.

"Because on Billie's thirteenth birthday, Dare promised he'd build her one, and a Whiskey's word is as good as gold." Seeley gave him a serious look. "You need to remember that. You're half Whiskey. If you make a promise, you stand behind it. No matter what happens with the other person."

"Even if they want nothing to do with me?" Lucas asked.

Seeley nodded. "That's right. It's not about what anyone else does. It's about being true to your word. But in Dare's case, he fell in love with Billie when they were kids, and when a Whiskey gives away his heart, it's forever. There's nothing he wouldn't do for her." He winked at Juliette.

Her heart skipped.

It had been a busy, wonderful week since they'd gone on their date at the Roadhouse and she'd had the sheer pleasure of waking up in his arms, and it felt like they'd *all* turned a corner. She and Lucas were back on solid ground, talking more and even joking around a little like they used to, and Lucas and Seeley were enjoying their driving lessons.

Juliette was enjoying getting to see Seeley after those lessons, when he'd stick around to spend time with them. Lucas usually headed off to do his homework and text with his friends, but that was fine with them. It gave them time to talk and steal a few kisses. They'd even managed to sneak in two lunch dates at Grandma's Kitchen, a local diner they'd gone to as kids. They'd ended up back at his place tearing off each other's clothes, which she'd also thoroughly enjoyed, and when Lucas went to hang out at Layla's house last night, they'd stolen another few hours alone.

Things were looking up.

"So Dare fell for Billie when they were kids, and you fell for my mom when you were teenagers," Lucas said, petting Sadie as if he hadn't casually mentioned Seeley's feelings for her.

They'd been careful not to even hold hands in front of him.

Juliette didn't think he knew they were a couple, even if they were spending a lot of time together. But they were already in so deep, maybe it was time to clue Lucas in, so he didn't feel duped. She'd have to talk to Seeley about it later.

"That's right," Seeley said.

"Is that a Whiskey thing, too?" Lucas asked, drawing her from her thoughts. "Falling in love when you're young?"

"Guess so." Seeley laughed. "Sasha and Ezra shared their first kiss as teenagers, too, and neither of them ever fell for anyone else." He glanced at Juliette, and he didn't have to say a word for her to hear, *like us.*

Lucas looked out at the track again. "Dare really set the standard for Billie, didn't he?"

"He sure did," Seeley said. "But if you think this racetrack is cool, wait until you see the new racetrack and clubhouse he built for her."

"He built her another one?" Lucas's eyes were wide saucers. "Why? This one's huge."

"Because it's also too close to their house, which is right up that path." He pointed to a dirt path heading back toward the rest of the ranch. "The kids she teaches aren't residents at the ranch, and we all know how mischievous kids can be. Come on. I'll show you."

"This place is so cool," Lucas said as they followed Seeley across the grass. "No wonder you've never wanted to live anywhere else." He picked up a stick from the ground, and Sadie barked. "You wanna play, girl?" Sadie's tail wagged, her eyes trained on him. "Watch, Mom." He threw the stick, and Sadie sprinted after it, snagged it off the ground, and darted back to him. "Attagirl!"

Juliette had wondered how it would feel to be on the ranch

with Lucas. She worried it might be uncomfortable for him or for her as memories rolled in, but it wasn't. Even after all these years and after hollering at Seeley a few weeks ago right there on the ranch in front of Sasha and whoever else had been in earshot, being there *still* felt like coming home. Somehow the ranch made everything feel calmer, better, happier. It was still the only place where she could truly let down her guard and just *be*. It didn't make a lick of sense, but that's how she felt, and sharing it with Lucas made it that much better.

She watched him playing fetch with Sadie and chatting with Seeley as they made their way across the property, and a memory crept in. During one of her and Seeley's cabin rendezvous when they were teens, she'd asked him why he thought Redemption Ranch had been able to help so many people. After explaining all the tangible reasons, like competent therapists, well-rounded programs, and a family atmosphere, he'd said, *But my grandfather used to say this land had a touch of magic in it.*

Seeing Lucas so carefree made her wonder if there was some truth to that.

A massive racetrack and a large clubhouse came into view, and Lucas nearly lost his mind with excitement. There was a young guy wearing a cowboy hat who looked to be eighteen or nineteen watching two people racing around the track, flying over bumps and jumps and onto raised flat platforms and ramps.

"Hey, Doc," the guy said.

"Hey, Kenny. This is"—for a split second, Juliette saw Seeley wrestling with how to introduce them—"Juliette and Lucas."

"Hi," Juliette said as Lucas said, "Hey," and petted Sadie,

who was happily holding her stick in her mouth.

"Dare told me y'all were coming by. It's nice to meet you." Kenny shook their hands. "I hear we might play paintball later."

"I hope so," Lucas said.

One of the racers flew up a ramp and did a flip on the bike. Juliette gasped.

"Whoa! That was cool," Lucas exclaimed as the other racer followed in the first racer's wake, also doing a flip. "I want to learn to do that."

"*Lord, help me,*" Juliette said more to herself than to anyone else.

Seeley put a hand on her back and said, "It's a little safer than bull riding."

"It's only as safe as the rider," Kenny said. "Lucas, if you're thinking of learning, Billie was a professional motocross racer. She'll make sure you're as safe as you can be, but it's up to you to listen to what she teaches you. These bikes aren't toys."

"I know. Doc told me about their friend," Lucas said more seriously. "Do you ride?"

"Kenny's been riding for more than a year," Seeley said. "He's doing an exhibition at the Ride Clean event next weekend."

"You should come check it out," Kenny said. "It's really cool. I did my first exhibition at the event last year after I finished going through one of the programs here."

Surprised, Juliette glanced at Seeley, who nodded almost imperceptibly.

"You were in a program?" Lucas asked with a furrowed brow.

"Yeah, look." Kenny pulled out his wallet and withdrew a gold card, handing it to Lucas.

Lucas read it aloud. *"Member of the Redemption Ranch Family."* He turned it over. *"If Lost, Please Return to."* He looked up and handed it back to Kenny. "I don't get it. It has the address and phone number of the ranch."

"Everyone who goes through our programs receives one, so they know they always have a safe place to come back to," Seeley explained.

"Oh." Lucas seemed to mull that over. "Kenny, what did you do to end up here?"

"I took a neighbor's Beamer out for a joyride with their daughter. It was stupid, because my parents had already taken away my license. But I did a lot of stupid stuff back then."

"Why?" Lucas asked.

"I don't know. I was pissed. We had to move for my dad's job, and my girlfriend back home broke up with me, and then she hooked up with my friend. It was a lot."

"So you came *here?*" Lucas asked.

"I didn't want to come here. My parents forced me to. I was pissed, but it was either that or get arrested for stealing the car. Looking back, I'm glad I ended up here. If I hadn't, I'd probably still be doing bad shit." He looked at Juliette. *"Sorry."*

"It's okay," she said, glad he was sharing his story with them.

"Anyway, this place saved me from myself," Kenny explained. "Dare was my therapist. His family, and the rest of the people here, they're the best. I didn't want to leave when I finished the program. Now I'm going to community college, riding with Billie, and working with Cowboy. It's awesome."

Billie and Dare were speeding toward the finish line, nose to nose. "Hold on a sec," Kenny said. "They're wicked competitive." His gaze moved between the stopwatch and Dare and

Billie as they crossed the finish line. "They're so frigging fast."

Their bikes fishtailed, kicking up dirt, causing Sadie to bark.

Lucas petted her. "They're *so* cool."

Dare and Billie climbed off their bikes and took off their helmets. "I *nailed* you, Mancini," Dare said.

Billie smirked. "Yes, you *did*, but that was this morning, and I just beat your sorry butt."

Dare laughed and smacked her ass. She scowled, and he tugged her into a hard kiss. "I love you."

"You still lost," she teased. They headed over, grinning like they were on top of the world.

"Hey, Juliette. Hey, Lucas," Dare said. "Did you see me beat Billie?"

"You guys were incredible," Lucas said.

"*I* was incredible." Billie leaned closer to Lucas like she was sharing a secret. "Dare was mediocre, but don't tell him that."

Lucas laughed.

"I'm Billie, by the way. *Mediocre's* wife. It's nice to meet you, Lucas."

"You too." Lucas looked a little awestruck. "What do I have to do to learn to ride?"

"He's got the Whiskey adrenaline bug, huh?" Dare asked, giving Seeley an approving nod.

"Oh, yeah," Seeley said. "You should see him ride a bull. The kid's a natural."

Lucas beamed at his praise, which warmed Juliette's heart.

"Have you talked to your mom about riding?" Billie asked.

"Yeah," Lucas said with a grin. "She's cool with it."

Billie looked at Juliette. "Yeah?"

"There's no stopping him," Juliette said, glad Billie had thought to check with her.

Billie eyed Lucas. "Then we'll talk."

"Awesome." Lucas was absolutely glowing, as he had when he'd first talked about bull riding.

"Kenny, how much did I win by?" Billie asked.

"Dream on, Mancini." Dare crossed his arms, dipping his chin with a serious expression. "Go ahead, dude. Give her the news."

"I hate to say this." Kenny paused, dragging out their anticipation. "But you were three-tenths of a second behind her, Dare."

Billie's arms shot up. "*Yes!* I am the reigning champ!"

Everyone laughed.

Dare pointed at Billie. "We're going again." He looked at Juliette and Lucas. "You guys are sticking around, right? Dinner and we're beating you in paintball later?"

"You wish," Lucas said.

"I see you're a dreamer like your old man," Dare teased. "I hear you like old cars. I'll show you my garage and the cool cars I have."

"Seriously?" Lucas asked.

"Hell yeah." Dare draped an arm around Billie. "Come on, beautiful. Time to lose."

As they headed back to their bikes, Kenny told Lucas about Dare's affinity for cars, and as he filled Lucas's head with dreams of classic cars and motocross, Seeley leaned closer to Juliette and whispered, "I think our boy likes it here almost as much as you did when you first showed up."

"I like it even more now."

SEELEY SHOWED THEM around his veterinary clinic, and as he explained how the rescue process worked, Juliette thought about their teenage dreams, of working together to save horses and raising their own family. It was funny how, as kids, everything had seemed not only possible but as if by dreaming it, their futures were cast in stone.

"Can we see the rehab horses?" Lucas asked as they left the well-horse barns.

"It's not easy to look at horses that have been abused and neglected. We might want to skip the rehab horses," Seeley said.

"I've seen plenty of sick animals," Lucas objected. "Right, Mom? I've gone with you a bunch of times."

"You have, but Seeley's right. A sick animal is very different from one that has been abused or neglected," she explained. "It can be heart-wrenching, Lucas."

"I can handle it," he insisted. "I want to see them. I want to see the work they do here."

She looked at Seeley. "What do you think?"

"I think if he says he can handle it, we should let him try. But, Lucas, I've been around horses like some of the ones you'll see since I was a little boy, and I *still* have a hard time seeing the horrible shape our rescues are in. So promise me if it's too much, you won't try to tough it out. There's no shame in walking away."

Lucas set his jaw. "I swear, but I'll be *fine*."

"Okay, let's head over," Seeley said. "But the horses can be skittish. You'll want to talk softly, approach slowly, and don't make any sudden movements."

"I can do that." When they got closer to the rehab barns, Lucas pointed to two horses in a small paddock. "Why aren't they with the other horses in the pasture?"

"That's Posey and Dream. Posey, the Appaloosa with the chestnut coat and white splash along her hips, is blind in her right eye, and her left eye was removed because of an infection."

"That sucks," Lucas said.

"Yeah, especially since her eye could have been saved if her previous owner had cared for her properly." Seeley's voice held a bite, which Juliette understood.

"That's awful," he said. "Now she can't go out to pasture or see anything ever again. Someone should do *that* to the previous owner."

"I don't disagree," Seeley said. "But Posey's safe and loved now, and blind horses *can* be put in pastures with other horses. You need special fencing and to make sure the grounds are safe, but Posey's still skittish around some of the other horses, and she's bonded with Dream. For now it's best for her to be with the friend she trusts."

"That makes sense."

"There's Sully." Seeley motioned to another paddock, closer to the barn, where Sully was walking a horse. "Come on, I'll introduce you. She's walking Goldie."

"Is that Cowboy's girlfriend?" Lucas asked.

"His fiancée, yeah."

"I met her last weekend when Seeley and I were at the Roadhouse," Juliette said. "She's really nice. You'll like her."

Lucas approached the paddock carefully and waved to Sully.

Sully waved and walked the horse over to them. The bay mare had innumerable scars on her shoulder and hind quarters and a bandage around its right front leg, but there was light in her eyes. "Hi, you guys. It's nice to see you again, Juliette, and you must be Lucas. I've heard a lot of wonderful things about you."

Lucas looked curiously at Juliette and Seeley.

"Why are you looking at us like that?" Juliette asked. "You're a great kid, and you know it."

"Whatever." He turned back to Sully. "Cowboy said you're a horse whisperer."

She petted Goldie's cheek. "I do love them. How about you? Do you like horses?"

"Yeah," Lucas said easily. "We have two, Warrior and Maxine, and I grew up around them in California."

"You're lucky," Sully said sweetly.

Knowing what Sully had been through, Juliette felt a pang of sadness for her new friend. She wanted to climb over the fence and hug her.

"How did Goldie get all those scars?" Lucas asked.

"She had a few not-so-nice owners, and she was rescued from being sent to a slaughterhouse." Sully looked lovingly at the horse. "But she's doing great. We were about to go back to the barn. Where are you heading?"

"To the rehab barn," Lucas answered. "I'll get the gate for you."

Sully led the horse through the gate, and Lucas closed it behind them.

"Would you like to lead Goldie?" Sully offered.

Lucas's eyes lit up. "Yeah. Can I?"

"Sure," Sully said. "But don't go too fast."

He took the lead, pride shimmering in his eyes as he led Goldie toward the barn, and asked, "How long do you walk her?"

"She's recovering from a bowed tendon, and she's up to about fifteen minutes twice a day," Sully said. "We'll gradually increase that until she's good as new."

They walked into the barn, and as Lucas and Sully led Goldie into her stall, Seeley slid his arm around Juliette's waist and said, "Is it just me, or does he seem really comfortable here?"

She looked at Lucas, petting Goldie and chatting with Sully. "He does."

Seeley whispered, "That's the magic of the ranch."

When Lucas went into the stall, Seeley pressed a kiss to her temple and lowered his arm.

"I told you I could handle it," Lucas said a few minutes later when he came out of Goldie's stall. "Sully said you're not sure what Goldie has been through."

"Unfortunately, that happens a lot. It's not uncommon for owners to abandon their horses," Seeley said.

"Maybe I'll become a horse vigilante when I grow—" His words were lost to a pained expression as he gazed over Juliette's shoulder.

She followed his stare to Sasha leading a severely emaciated horse through the side door. It was covered with scars from recent and old wounds, and its ribs and spine protruded sickeningly.

A sad sound fell from Lucas's lips.

"Oh, honey," Juliette said, her heart breaking for both the horse and for her son.

Seeley put one hand on Lucas's shoulder, his other on Juliette's back. "We can go."

"*No.*" The pain in Lucas's voice was palpable. "The horse can't *go*. I'm not gonna leave just because it's hard to see it."

"I'm sorry," Sasha said softly. "I didn't know you were in here."

"It's okay," Seeley said. "Lucas, look at me."

Lucas looked at him, his jaw tight, his sad eyes shimmering with determination, but glassy, as if he were struggling against tears.

"Remember the first time I came to your house? When you found me and your mom arguing?"

He nodded.

"Earlier that day we'd rescued Queenie, the horse Sasha is leading, and another horse, Contessa. They'd been tied to a tree in an empty field and left to starve for who knows how long. Queenie was in critical condition, but she's a fighter, and with our love and care, she *survived*."

"Can't you feed her?" Lucas's voice cracked.

"We are. I promise she's getting the absolute best care. She's already gained weight."

"Not enough. Feed her *more*," he pleaded quietly.

Juliette was proud of him for respecting the rules Seeley had given him earlier about rescue horses and not shouting.

"We can't. If she eats too much too fast, it could kill her. Do you trust me to take care of her?"

He nodded, his brows pinched.

"Good. She's on this ranch, which means she's your family now, too. Would you like to meet her?"

Lucas nodded again.

"Okay, but horses are intuitive. They respond to our emotions. If you're sad or mad, they'll sense it and react to it," he explained. "Take a minute to get ahold of your emotions."

Lucas breathed deeply.

"That's good, honey," Juliette said. "Just relax."

Lucas shook out his hands, and after a big exhalation, he said, "Okay. I'm ready."

They went to the horse, and Seeley spoke softly and stroked

her neck. "Hi, sweet Queenie. How's my beautiful girl?" The horse nickered. "Go ahead and pet her, Lucas. Show her some love."

Lucas lifted a shaky hand and petted her.

"That's right. Now look in her eyes and tell me what you see."

He studied her as he petted her. "She looks calm and happy. I think she likes being petted."

"She doesn't just like it. She needs it," Seeley explained. "When she got here, she was terrified. Her eyes were sunken and dull. They were *hopeless*. She wouldn't lift her head or even look at us. Unfortunately, there's no quick fix for this kind of trauma. But with patience, love, and the right medical care, she'll plump up, and her energy will return. This time next year, she'll be a whole new horse."

Lucas's lips twitched into a smile. "Hear that, Queenie?"

"Attaboy," Seeley said. "One of the best things you can do for a horse like Queenie is fill her with confidence and encouragement and show her love. There's a good chance she's never been shown tenderness before coming here. Tell her how great she's doing, how strong she is, that she's safe."

"She's going to have a great life," Sasha said. "We make that promise to the horses who come here, and when they're healthy and rehomed, they leave with a plaque with their name on it for their new stall. We call it their badge of dignity, giving them back what was stolen from them."

"That's cool," Lucas said. "Can I help you get her settled in her stall?"

"You sure can," Sasha said. "Her stall is on the side of the barn." They headed down the hall that led to the other side.

Juliette touched Seeley's hand. "Thank you. You explained

everything so beautifully."

"I've been doing this a long time, and it's never felt like that." He rubbed the back of his neck.

"What do you mean?"

"I don't know. Like I better not fuck up, because how Lucas sees animals *and* people who are suffering, how he'll treat them, was hanging in the balance."

She hugged him. "We are so lucky to have you in our lives."

"I'm the lucky one, darlin'."

Lucas wasn't scarred by what he'd seen. He wanted to meet all of the rehab horses and hear each of their stories. As they left the last horse, he said, "Now I really do want to be a horse vigilante." He pointed to a door. "What's in there?"

"Tack for the horses." Seeley pushed the door open.

Cowboy and Sully were inside kissing, and they startled apart. "Oh. *Hey,*" Sully said, pink cheeked. "Callahan was just…helping me reach something. On the…*up there.*" She pointed at the ceiling.

Cowboy's Cheshire-cat grin said otherwise.

Sasha and Juliette stifled laughs. Seeley arched a brow.

"How about you knock next time?" Cowboy pulled Sully into his arms, and she buried her face in his chest.

"Come on, Lucas. We'll see the tack room another time." Doc closed the door.

"Mom, did you and Doc ever get caught making out in the tack room?" Lucas asked.

"*No,*" she insisted.

"We were too clever for that," Seeley said.

"*Seeley!*" she chided, and heard a chuckle behind them. She turned around and saw Cowboy and Sully following them out.

"What?" Seeley said. "He obviously knows we did more

than kiss. I mean, he does exist."

"Yes, but we don't have to admit it," she said, which made Sasha laugh.

As they left the barn, Tiny and Wynnie drove up in a UTV. On Tiny's lap was the little boy Juliette had seen with Sasha at the hospital, who she now knew was Ezra's little boy, Gus. Sasha and Ezra had shown her pictures of him at the Roadhouse.

"Sugar!" Gus yelled as he scrambled off Tiny's lap and ran toward Sasha. He was adorable in little cowboy boots and shorts, his dark curls bouncing around his cherubic face.

"Doc, did he call her *Sugar?*" Lucas asked.

"Yeah. That's Gus, Ezra's boy. He picked it up from how Dare used to talk to women," Seeley said. "Don't even think about calling a woman that."

"I got to steer the UTV!" Gus bragged.

"That's great, Gusto." Sasha tousled his hair. "Thanks, Dad."

"In a few years he'll be coming out with me before dawn to check on the ranch," Tiny said as he and Wynnie climbed out of the vehicle. His long gray beard brushed his chest, and he wore a blue bandanna tied around his hair, which was pulled back in a ponytail.

"Which means I'll be sending Tiny out with extra biscuits," Wynnie said.

"That's Tiny's favorite time to check on the ranch," Gus announced. "Because everyone else is still asleep, so we can make sure everything's shipshape and have special time with the horses!"

"That used to be my favorite time, too," Sasha said. "It's also a special time for you and Tiny."

"Guess what else?" Gus said excitedly. "Tiny and Wynnie said I can call them Grandpa and Grandma even though you and Dad aren't married yet!"

"We also said he could choose whatever names he wanted to call us," Wynnie said as she made her way toward Juliette and Lucas.

"I like Grandma and Grandpa," Gus said.

"*Aw*, I love that, Gusto." Sasha looked at her parents with so much love, Juliette could feel it.

Wynnie smiled warmly as she and Tiny joined them. "Welcome back to the ranch, son, Juliette," Tiny said.

"Thanks," Lucas said.

"It's been a long time," Juliette said. "The place looks amazing."

"We're glad you made it. It's nice to see you again, honey." Wynnie hugged her.

"It's nice to be here," Juliette said. "Lucas, this is Seeley's mom, Wynnie."

"Hi," he said.

"Hi, honey. I've been aching to meet you. Are you a hugger?"

"I guess," he mumbled.

She hugged him and said, "You can call me Wynnie or Grandma or anything you want. I'm so *happy* to finally meet you."

"You too," he said a little tightly.

"Gus, remember I said we were meeting some special people today?" Sasha asked, and he nodded. "This is Juliette and Lucas." She looked at Lucas and said, "This is Ezra's son, Gus."

"Hi, Gus," Juliette said. "It's really cool that you got to steer that UTV."

"Hi!" Gus looked up at Lucas. "Sugar said we're cousins! I don't have any other cousins. Do you like the ranch? I grew up here. I can show you cool places, and if you don't know how to ride a bike yet, Sully can teach you. I just learned how. Daddy won't let me ride it anywhere alone yet, but I bet he'd let me go with you! We can go exploring, and you can go on trail rides with us to the meadow. Will you be eating with us, too? Dwight makes yummy food."

Lucas's brows knitted, his jaw tightening. He looked at Juliette with contempt.

Oh God. This is too much for you. She tried to ease the tension without causing a scene. "Lucas, don't you want to say hi to Gus? He's excited to meet you."

"Hi," Lucas gritted out, and crossed his arms, his fingers drumming.

"Excuse us." Juliette leaned closer to Lucas, and as Sasha guided Gus a few feet away, Seeley stepped closer to Lucas, who turned his back to the group. "Sweetheart, what's wrong?" She noticed his lower lip trembling.

"We were alone for all those years," he fumed. "And you *knew* I had family the *whole* time!"

Guilt consumed her. "I'm sorry. I tried to explain why I did that."

"Lucas, you have to remember that we all were deceived, and your mom was protecting you in the best way she knew how," Seeley said.

"I *know*. I get it. I'm not *mad* at her. I'm just…" He looked between them, his eyes tearing up. "It's *so* unfair."

"I know, buddy," Seeley said. "It's unfair for all of us."

"It's not only unfair to the three of you," Tiny said as he walked around Juliette and planted his feet in front of Lucas, in his worn jeans and leather cut over a T-shirt. "What your *other* grandfather did was downright dirty, son, and it affected all of us. We're all hurt and angry. What he did makes him a miserable person, but it doesn't have to make you one."

Lucas swiped at a tear. "I *hate* him."

"Then you're among the right company, because I don't think anyone on this ranch feels any differently," Tiny said firmly. "Now, you listen to me. You're our blood, and we take care of our own."

"Nobody can take you away from Doc or any of us ever again," Wynnie said.

Lucas's jaw ticked, and so did Seeley's, his dark eyes full of emotion.

"The way I see it, you've got a choice to make," Tiny said. "You can stew on that hatred, and close yourself off like Doc did for all those years and lose more time with the people who want to get to know you. Or you can accept that what's done is done, decide not to let that hatred eat you alive, and start moving forward. Get to know your family."

Lucas blinked away tears. "How can I just let it go? It sucks."

"That's the million-dollar question, isn't it?" Tiny's mustache lifted with his grin.

"You start by realizing you don't have to hold it all in," Wynnie said sweetly. "You can talk to any of us, or a therapist. We know plenty of those. It doesn't matter who you talk to. You just have to get that hurt out of your heart so you can begin to heal."

"You can talk to a friend you trust or your girlfriend," Tiny suggested.

"I don't have a girlfriend," Lucas said.

Tiny shook his head. "Boy, if you think I don't know Layla Braden is your girl, you've got another thing coming."

Lucas shot an accusatory look at Juliette and Seeley.

Seeley shook his head, holding up his hands in surrender. "It wasn't me, buddy."

"Or me," Juliette said.

"I've got eyes and ears everywhere," Tiny explained. "That's how I keep the people I love safe. If I'd known you were Doc's boy, I'd've come for you and your mom long ago. But if that'd been the case, I have a feelin' Doc would've beat me to it."

Lucas looked at Seeley with a small smile, and Seeley said, "Damn right I would have."

"Lucas, honey, it's okay to be upset and even to feel betrayed by me," Juliette said. "I'm upset at myself for not seeing through my father's ruse and realizing that Seeley would never have turned his back on us."

"I know it's not *your* fault. You were just a kid." Lucas looked at Tiny, Wynnie, and the others. Cowboy had his arm around Sully, and Gus was standing in front of Sasha with his back against her, her hand resting on his belly, watching them.

Juliette was glad their expressions were empathetic and not judgmental.

"I'm sorry," Lucas said. "I didn't mean to..." He shrugged. "Sorry."

"It's okay," they all said.

"No, it's not," Lucas said. "Tiny's right. I can't let what my grandfather did to us ruin the chance I have to get to know all of you. Gus, I'm sorry I wasn't very nice to you."

"That's okay," Gus said. "Sometimes when I'm sad, I'm not nice, either. But Sugar and Daddy love me anyway."

Sasha patted his stomach. "That's right, Gusto. Everyone

has hard times."

"So, what do you say, Rodeo?" Tiny asked, lifting his chin at Lucas. "You want to drive us up to the main house, and we'll meet your parents there for dinner?"

Juliette's heart swelled at the care they were taking with him.

"You'll let me drive the UTV?" Lucas asked excitedly.

"I offered, didn't I?" Tiny took Wynnie's hand and lumbered toward the vehicle. "Come on, now. You still gotta meet Dwight and the others."

Lucas ran over to the UTV as Tiny and Wynnie climbed into it, and Gus called out, "Can I come?"

"You bet," Wynnie said, motioning for Gus to climb onto her lap.

Tiny eyed Lucas. "We got precious cargo in here, Rodeo. You drive slow now, you hear?"

"Yes, sir." Lucas called out, "See y'all up there!" and drove off, grinning.

Juliette exhaled, feeling like she'd been holding her breath that whole time.

"You okay, darlin'?" Seeley asked.

"I am now. Your parents are really something."

"Yeah, they are. It took everything I had not to say more to Lucas, or to hug him and tell him how much I love him and how sorry I am for all of this bullshit. But I was worried it would embarrass him and make things worse."

"That's how I felt, too," she said.

"Your boy has got a lot of feelings to work out," Cowboy said. "Might want to think about a therapist."

"Juliette tried. He doesn't want to speak to one yet," Seeley said.

"I hate my frigging father for doing this to him," Juliette said. "Seeley, you were right to give me time to think about going after him. As much as I want my father to pay for everything he's done to us, I can't do that to Lucas. The minute we give Reggie the information we got from Ana and the FBI gets a search warrant, it'll be all over the news. And you know how the media is. Lucas doesn't need that kind of circus."

"We're on the same page, darlin'. Reggie knows we have something that will take that bastard down. He's waiting to move on it until we're ready."

"That's smart," Cowboy said. "Those media hounds will open up a can of worms, and you'll be in the spotlight for months."

"Can't you guys do what you did for me?" Sully asked.

Juliette looked curiously at Seeley. "What did you guys do for Sully?"

"We kept her whereabouts out of the media," Doc explained. "But this is different. Sully was in hiding. Nobody knew where she was. We're too big a part of the community. I will figure out how to keep you and Lucas safe before we do anything more." He drew her into an embrace and kissed the top of her head. "Parenting is fucking *hard*."

"That's the understatement of the year," she said.

"But you know what?" His lips quirked up. "I can finally kiss you without worrying Lucas will see us."

As he pressed his lips to hers, Sasha said, "The tack room is free, if you want to take it for a spin," making them all laugh.

Chapter Twenty-Five

THE FLAMES FROM the bonfire danced in a gentle breeze, sending sparks crackling against the night sky. The din of conversation and laughter hung in the air, serenaded by the soft sounds of Sasha's guitar and Gus's chirpy voice as Ezra helped him make s'mores. Doc stood by the cooler, taking in the familiar scene of his family and friends around the bonfire. Only this time, his *family* included Juliette and Lucas. This was how it was always supposed to be.

He might be getting ahead of himself, but it sure didn't feel that way.

For the first time since that awful summer, he finally felt whole again, like all the broken pieces of himself had come back together stronger than ever. Not even the emotional turmoil they were all dealing with or the need for vengeance that was eating away at him could steal that sense of completeness. He'd make sure they all got the help they needed, and he'd find a way to take down Juliette's deceitful fucking father while protecting Lucas and Juliette if it was the last thing he did.

He glanced at Juliette, sitting by the fire wearing one of his sweatshirts, her eyes shimmering in the moonlight. She flashed that easy smile that never failed to hit him square in the center of the chest. She looked so comfortable, to an observer it would seem like she'd never left as she chatted with Billie, Sasha, Sully, and Simone Davidson, one of their employees. When Doc had introduced Lucas to Simone, Lucas had been as surprised to learn she'd gone through their program and had remained on to work at the ranch as he had been about Kenny, Hyde, and a handful of their other employees he'd met at dinner.

He looked at Lucas on the other side of the fire, laughing at something Kenny, Rebel, Dare, or Hyde, had said. For all the heartache Lucas had shared earlier, he had laughed a lot tonight and had clearly enjoyed the banter around the dinner tables in the main house. It had taken some time for him to loosen up and realize it was safe to be himself. Meeting that many people in one day would be a lot for anyone. But with a little encouragement, he'd come out of his shell, and by the time they'd finished dinner, he'd set up motocross lessons with Billie on Sundays and he and Kenny were heckling Doc and his brothers like it was old hat.

"Hey, Tiny," Lucas called across the fire.

Tiny lifted his chin in acknowledgment.

"If I get my license to drive a motorcycle next year, can I prospect the club?" Lucas asked.

Tiny's mustache split with a big-ass grin.

"Tiny Whiskey, do *not* answer that," Juliette said. "He's *not* driving a motorcycle at sixteen."

"Come on, *Mom*! Doc and Dare and Cowboy did!"

She looked expectantly over her shoulder at Doc.

He shrugged, laughing. Sasha tapped Juliette's knee, and Juliette turned away.

As he reached into the cooler to get her soda, his mother

sidled up to him.

"Things never get dull around here, do they?" she said with a knowing smile.

"They sure don't."

"I spent some time talking to Lucas earlier. He's a special young man. He's got a big heart, like you and Juliette, and big hearts feel everything deeply."

"Yeah. That's what worries me."

"I think he's going to be okay. Things like this aren't fixed in a day or a week, and even after they've been dealt with and you all move forward, it might arise again and again. Like what you and Juliette have dealt with over the years. You never know when it'll hit. But that's how life goes."

"At least I'm with them now. I can help."

"And they can help you, too. Being around family is good for them. I noticed Lucas is wearing the necklace you and Grandpa made."

Doc smiled. "You saw that, huh?"

"I never thought we'd see it again."

"Neither did I. I was shocked to find out Juliette had kept it, much less had given it to Lucas after everything she thought had gone on."

"How does that make you feel?"

"Happy. Proud to see him wearing it." He gazed across the yard at Lucas before meeting his mother's gaze again. "And so damn grateful, I feel like my chest is going to explode."

She laughed softly and leaned into his shoulder. "That's the best feeling, honey."

"It's pretty wild. I'm glad he has that necklace. It's part of me and Grandpa. Did I tell you Juliette gave him my middle name, too?"

"No." She smiled. "Isn't that something? It's not surprising though."

"It surprised the hell out of me."

"I'm sure it did. What I mean is, you and Juliette had a special bond as teenagers that reminded me of me and your father. We were older, of course, but the love was the same."

"In what way?"

"Every way. You filled gaps in each other's lives that weren't just physical or rebellious. Don't get me wrong. You two lusted after each other like starving kids who couldn't get enough, but you helped each other grow, and you encouraged each other to figure things out. You helped her become stronger, more confident, and you showed her what it was to be loved."

"She was confident and strong when I met her. That was one of the reasons I was so drawn to her."

"She most certainly was, but you helped her grow to become even more so. She helped you in the same ways."

"Are you saying I wasn't confident? Because I beg to differ."

"No. You were *overly* confident, if not a bit cocky. You had direction and friends and all the hallmarks of a happy life. But your father and I always felt like you were a little unsettled. Searching for something. You'd had plenty of girlfriends, and that never seemed to settle whatever it was we were seeing. Then Juliette came to the ranch, and everything changed."

He grinned. "She definitely knocked me for a loop."

"Yes, she did. We were concerned when we first realized how close you two had gotten and how fast it happened, because she was not quite seventeen, and that's awfully young."

"I tried to keep my distance."

"We know that, too. During that week when you were trying to hold back, you were as tense and restless as a bull in the chute, dying to break free and conquer." She smiled. "Well, we won't go there."

"*Please* don't. But how did you know I made it a week?"

"Oh, honey. You were oblivious to everything around you except her, but we weren't."

"Why didn't you stop me?"

"You can guide your kids, but you can't stop them. If we'd told you she was off-limits, you'd have only wanted her more. But we could tell it was deeper than a summer fling for both of you. It was like looking into the eyes of two horses that had been rescued. Your eyes got clearer and brighter, and you and Juliette had this aura, this energy that I swear threw sparks. When we saw those changes in you, we knew you'd found your one and only."

"I wasn't looking for a relationship, much less to fall in love, but she knocked my boots off."

"That's how love happens. When your father rolled into the Roadhouse the first time, I had plans for graduate school and then building my career off the ranch. I wasn't looking for a gruff and gritty, possessive, tatted-up biker. But your father, like each of you, has his own brand of charm, and I was a goner by the end of our first date."

Doc had heard the story a million times. Tiny had walked up to her in the Roadhouse, taken one look at her, and said, *Hey there, darlin'. I'm Tiny Whiskey, and I'm going to be the last man you ever go out with.* The fact that he was indeed the last for a strong woman like his mother said a lot about his father, who had been raised by a heavy-handed misogynist biker who believed women should be seen and not heard.

"Any regrets?" Doc asked, though he knew the answer.

"Honey, your father is a brilliant, big-hearted hunk of a

306

man who came from a horrible situation and tries to make the world a better place every day of his life. How could I regret giving my heart to a man as special as that?"

"I hope Juliette feels that way about me someday, and I hope Lucas feels as proud to have me as a father as I am to have you and Dad as my parents."

"I think they both already do," she said. "They may not be ready to admit it, but I can feel it, and I can see it in the way they look at you."

"Thanks, Mom. Any parenting advice?"

"I could fill your ears, honey. Parenting is the hardest and the best thing you'll ever experience. Some days you're sure you're doing everything right, and others, you feel like you're sledding down a hill on a bed of razor blades."

He laughed. "Ain't that the truth."

"But that's what makes the good times even sweeter. Keep following your heart, honey. You're doing great so far." She looped her arm around his. "Shall we?"

As they made their way back to the fire, Birdie's car pulled into the lot. "About time your sister arrived."

His mother went to sit with Tiny, who had Gus on his lap, and Doc headed for Juliette. He handed her the soda and kissed her tempting lips. As he drew back, he caught an imploring look from Juliette and froze. *Fuck. Lucas.* He turned to see if Lucas saw them kiss and caught the same worried expression from Sasha and Cowboy.

"Try not to look so guilty," Ezra said under his breath.

Lucas was staring right at them.

"Doc, you look like you did when you were six years old and you got up in the middle of the night and opened everyone's Christmas presents," Tiny said.

Fuck. "Lucas, your mom and I were going to tell you we've gotten close—"

"Give me a break," Lucas said. "You've been telling me you love my mom in one way or another since we first met. Did you really think I wouldn't put two and two together? My mom never texts with guys or hangs out with them. You think I don't hear you guys on the phone late at night? And you're always at our place."

"We should've told you right away," Juliette said. "But we didn't want to make things more complicated. I'm sorry."

"Mom, *chill.* It's not like you lied to me," Lucas said. "You always tell me when you guys are going out. Knowing you're together makes it easier than guessing."

"So, you're not upset?" Juliette asked.

"No." Lucas looked at Doc. "He's cool. Besides, he *is* my father. It'd be weird if you were kissing some other dude."

Relief swamped Doc, and he laughed. "Thanks, bud."

"Thank goodness." Juliette got up and hugged Lucas.

"*Mom,*" he complained, and everyone laughed.

Juliette headed back to her chair as Birdie breezed into the group wearing high-waisted floral bell-bottoms and a sleeveless peach crop top, carrying a small bag from her chocolate shop. "Sorry I'm so late. I can't believe I missed dinner *and* paintball!" She planted a hand on her hip, her gaze trailing around the fire and landing on Lucas. "Aha! There's my cutie-pie nephew!" She strutted over to Lucas, who was kind of checking her out, and said, "Hi! I'm Birdie, your coolest aunt!"

"Hey."

"Don't *hey,* me. I've missed out on fifteen years of hugs. Stand up and give me a hug like a cool nephew." She waggled the bag. "I brought you chocolate."

"You are a cool aunt." Lucas stood and hugged her.

"The coolest," she corrected. "I wasn't sure if you were allergic to anything. I stayed away from nuts, but are you allergic to anything? Tell me now before you eat something you shouldn't."

"I'm not."

"Good!" she exclaimed. "There's a bunch of different chocolates in there. If you have a favorite, tell your aunt Birdie, and I'll hook you up. But if you hate them all, you can either lie to me or show up at my chocolate shop and we'll make something you love."

"That's awesome," Lucas said. "Thank you."

"I think Aunt Birdie wants you to share those with your mom," Juliette said.

Lucas flashed a grin. "I think Doc can afford to buy you your own chocolates."

Everyone laughed.

"You're gonna fit right in here," Birdie said.

"He already does," Dare said.

There was a flurry of conversation, as Birdie talked a mile a minute, asking Lucas how he liked the ranch and chatting about everything he'd seen and done, bringing everyone else into the conversation. She asked if Doc was annoying when he gave him driving lessons, and Doc was glad to hear Lucas say he wasn't, but Birdie proceeded to tell Lucas stories about when Doc had taken her driving and had apparently annoyed the heck out of her.

"You did everything you could to push my buttons," Doc chimed in.

"Well, *duh*," Birdie said. "I had to entertain myself somehow." She continued her inquisition as she made s'mores, egging on Lucas to eat the ones she burned.

Lucas didn't seem to mind.

"So, when can we see you on the back of a bull?" Birdie asked.

"Yeah, when can we?" Sasha asked.

"I would like to see you ride, too, son," Tiny said. "It's been a while since I've seen a competition."

"Can I go, too?" Gus asked.

"Of course, buddy," Ezra said.

"We'd like to cheer you on," Sully said. "Right, Callahan?"

Cowboy nodded. "Absolutely."

"Really? *All* of you?" Lucas's eyes brightened.

Everyone talked at once, excited to see him ride. Doc's emotions were running high, and Juliette appeared just as delighted. Leaning closer in his chair, he hugged her against his side.

"I'm competing in the Carlisle Ranch Rodeo in two weeks," Lucas said with elation. "It's a small competition, not a qualifier or anything. But if I win the bull-riding event, I get five hundred dollars and a belt buckle."

"Five hundred bucks?" Birdie asked. "Heck, maybe I should start bull riding!"

"*No,*" Doc, Dare, Cowboy, and Tiny all said at once.

Birdie narrowed her eyes and said, "That only makes me want to do it more. You know, Lucas, I do hold the record for the longest ride on the mechanical bull at the Roadhouse."

Lucas laughed. "You're right, Doc. She's totally a Birdie, not a Blaire."

They all laughed.

"Juliette," Dare said. "Can you send us the info for his competition?"

"I don't have anyone's number. I'll give it to Seeley, and he can text it to everyone," Juliette said.

"I'll give you their numbers," Doc said. "You should have them anyway."

"Okay," she said softly, but he could see how pleased she was by the suggestion.

"Good idea," Dare said. "You never know when she'll need us to come kick your ass."

The guys laughed. Doc shook his head.

"Are you guys really going to come watch me ride?" Lucas asked.

"Heck yeah!" Birdie exclaimed.

There was more excitement and conversation, and when it finally calmed, Cowboy reached for Sully's hand and said, "Sully and I have an invitation to extend as well."

All eyes turned to him.

"Sully and I would like to cordially invite you to our wedding."

Birdie squealed. "You picked a date?"

"We're going to do it on the same day we got engaged. On our birthday, April seventeenth, at midnight," Sully said.

"*Midnight?*" his mother asked.

"We know that might be too late for some of you," Sully said. "That's why we thought we'd have a celebration dinner beforehand."

"It'll only be family, and Treat Braden is officiating," Cowboy explained. Hal Braden's son Treat was a real estate mogul who lived in Weston. He'd also married Dare and Billie. "Jax is making Sully's wedding gown, and he and Jordan are flying in for the ceremony." Sully's brother-in-law was a world-renowned wedding gown designer.

"Ansel and his mom, Gaia, are flying in, too," Sully said. "I can't get married without my childhood best friend and the woman who took care of us on that awful compound."

"Well, I did say family, darlin'," Cowboy said.

"Oh, Callahan, of course you did." Sully leaned in and kissed him. Then she turned back to the everyone else, and said, "But if any of you would rather skip it, we understand."

"You must be kidding if you think we'd miss your wedding. Midnight it is!" his mother announced, and a round of cheers rang out.

"Am I the only one who wants to know *why* you're doing it at midnight?" Sasha asked.

Cowboy and Sully exchanged a loving glance, and he said, "Because we fell in love during our late-night walks, and we want to exchange our vows in the moonlight."

"That's so romantic," Juliette said a little dreamily.

Birdie exclaimed, "We have to plan a bachelorette party!"

As commotion rang out, Doc pulled Juliette closer, whispering, "Our wedding will be even more romantic."

He kept her close, her eyes widening with surprise, as he'd known they would. But he could no sooner hold that truth back than he could keep from falling head over boots in love with her all over again.

"Wipe that look off your face, Peaches." He brushed his lips over hers, whispering, "You know you're going to be my wife one day," and he sealed those plans with a kiss.

Chapter Twenty-Six

THE CARLISLE RANCH was bustling the afternoon of the rodeo competition. Crowds enjoyed a variety of food vendors, games for kids, live music, and dancing. The arena was packed, the anticipation palpable, as Lucas and the other young riders prepared to compete. Lucas would be competing in barrel racing, bareback bronc riding, and bull riding, and he was stoked. True to their promises, all of the Whiskeys showed up to cheer him on, along with Kenny, who had made fast friends with Lucas the night of the bonfire two weeks ago, and Layla. They'd gone to see Layla's competition last weekend. Lucas had proudly cheered her on and had been raving about her win ever since.

Juliette was elated to see so many people there to support him. She hadn't made it to the stands yet. She'd wished Lucas luck and hugged him, telling him how great he was going to do, while silently praying he wouldn't break his neck. Now she was waiting for Seeley, who was talking with him and Buck.

With the exception of last Saturday morning when Seeley had the ride and rally before the Ride Clean event, he'd been to all of Lucas's practices the last two weeks. With some prodding from Lucas, he'd also managed to take him driving *six* times. On three of those occasions, they'd ended up calling Juliette to meet them at the ranch for their big family dinners.

Lucas was loving spending more time there. Juliette hadn't realized how much he'd needed a bigger circle. They'd met Seeley after the ride and rally, and while he oversaw events, Lucas had hung out with Kenny and Layla, and Juliette had spent time helping the girls with the events they were managing. Lucas had his first motocross lesson last Sunday, and of course her young adrenaline junkie was hooked. He even got Seeley on a bike, which Billie said was a miracle. Motocross had never been Seeley's thing. But she had a feeling nothing was off-limits for him when it came to spending time with Lucas.

She looked for them now, but they were no longer where they'd been talking with Buck. She spotted Lucas and Seeley having a private, and what looked like a serious, conversation. Seeley was standing in front of Lucas with one hand on Lucas's shoulder. She wondered what was being said, but she wasn't worried. So much had changed the last few weeks, she knew whatever it was, Seeley was handling it with equal amounts of tact and love. He'd become Lucas's other *person*—the loving, protective father she'd always known he'd be—and because of that, Lucas was thriving.

They all were.

That was why she was so torn. She desperately wanted her father to pay for what he'd done, for the years she, Seeley, and Lucas had lost and the trauma he'd put them through. Two weeks ago, she'd asked Seeley *not* to make a move because Lucas was having such a hard time. Now she didn't want him to call Reggie because Lucas was finally settling in.

Was this the universe's way of telling her there were more

important things to worry about than vengeance?

Seeley and Lucas looked over, drawing her from her thoughts.

She smiled at them, feeling like the luckiest woman on earth, despite what her father had put them through. She had a second chance with the man she adored, and he and their son were finally right where they belonged. *Together.*

She went to them, needing to give Lucas one last hug for good luck. "I love you so much, and I'm so proud of you." She squeezed him a little tighter before letting go. "Go out there and show them what you're made of."

"I will." He looked out at the stands and waved to everyone who had come to see him.

They all waved back, and Layla and Kenny held up a banner they must have brought with them that read LET'S GO, RODEO! Layla shouted, "You've got this, Rodeo!" The nickname Tiny had coined for him had caught on, and Lucas answered to it proudly.

His fist shot up in the air victoriously, but it was his heart-stopping, ear-to-ear smile and the memories of her and Seeley doing practically the same thing in this very arena a lifetime ago that had Juliette reaching for Seeley's hand, praying Layla wouldn't be too big of a distraction for Lucas while he was riding.

"Lucas, remember what I told you," Seeley said firmly.

Lucas nodded curtly. "I've got this. Don't worry." He headed for his coach.

"What did you tell him?" Juliette asked as they headed for the stands.

"To keep his mind on the bull, not his girl."

"Good, but that's probably easier said than done at his age.

Should I be worried? Because I am."

"Nope. When you used to watch me, I wanted to impress you, and I was even *more* focused on staying on the bull. When I told him to keep his mind on the bull, he said nothing was going to stop him from winning." He leaned down and kissed her. "Then he said he had big boots to fill."

She melted inside and stopped in her tracks. "He said that?"

"Yeah," he said with an almost silent laugh, and pulled her into his arms. "I think we're almost over the hump, darlin'."

"I hope you're right, but he *is* a teenager, so let's not count our chickens yet."

"I'm counting mine. Every damn one of them." He kissed her again.

Birdie hollered, "Get a room!"

They made their way over to sit with the others.

"Is our boy ready and focused?" Tiny asked.

"He is," Seeley said. "And he's thrilled that y'all are here."

"We're thrilled to be here," Dare said.

"This brings back memories," Wynnie said. "I'm already nervous."

"You and me both," Seeley said as they sat down in front of his parents between Dare and Cowboy. He took Juliette's hand. "It's a whole different rodeo from this side of the gate."

Tiny patted his shoulder and said, "Better get used to gritting your teeth, son. Watching your boy on a bull never gets easy."

The announcer's voice boomed through the speakers. Seeley took Juliette's hand as the din of the crowd quieted and the event began. Juliette filled with a mix of exhilaration and trepidation as they watched kids compete in barrel racing, tie-down roping, saddle bronc riding, and bareback. The horses were beautifully strong and the riders, focused and athletic. The sounds of hooves pounding dirt, the snapping of ropes, and the cheers of the crowd heightened the excitement. But nothing topped the sounds of Seeley's family and their friends cheering on Lucas like he was king of the rodeo.

He took first place in barrel racing and second in bareback. As he climbed onto a bull in the chute, Juliette could hardly hear her own thoughts for the whoops, cheers, and whistles ringing out for *Rodeo*. Even Gus was cheering his heart out. She squeezed Seeley's hand.

"He's got grit, darlin'. He's got this," Seeley said reassuringly, and lifted her hand to kiss her knuckles.

"I know" came out as nervous *and* hopeful as she felt.

The bull exploded out of the gate, bucking and twisting, and Juliette held her breath. *Come on, baby. Stay on. That's it.* As the seconds ticked by, Lucas clung to the rope, holding one hand in the air, his body jerking and flailing with the bull's powerful and unpredictable bucks, rears, kicks, and spins as it tried to throw him off.

Juliette's heart pounded as the tenths of seconds flashed on the clock and Lucas fought to stay on the massive animal. The eight-second buzzer sounded, and they all shot to their feet, shouting and cheering. Seeley hugged Juliette as Lucas leaned into his hand and kicked his leg over the bull to dismount. The bull reared and twisted, sending Lucas flying head over feet. The crowd gasped as he landed on his back like a rag doll.

"*Getupgetupgetup*," Juliette begged, but Lucas lay as still as steel. Panic flared in her chest and she reached for Seeley, but he was already gone. She saw him leaping over the railing, tearing across the dirt toward Lucas as medics appeared and other men wrangled the bull.

She ran down the stands with Cowboy and Dare flanking her and realized Tiny was ahead of them, blazing a path through the crowd. As they rushed around the ring, she couldn't see Lucas. The medics and Seeley were leaning over him. *Ohgod. Please! Please let him be okay!*

Seeley and a medic helped Lucas to his feet, and Lucas's arms shot up, and he turned toward the crowd triumphantly. The air rushed from Juliette's lungs, relief flooding her as the crowd erupted into applause, cheers, and whistles.

By the time they made it to Lucas, the medics had finished their evaluation, and they were talking with Seeley. Juliette ran straight to Lucas, looking him up and down. "Baby, are you okay?" Behind her, the guys were asking the same thing.

"I'm *fine*. Did you see me ride? I'm in the lead!" he exclaimed.

"We all saw it," she said. "I'm so proud of you, sweetheart, but are you sure you're not hurt? What happened out there?"

"I got the wind knocked out of me. It's not a big deal," Lucas said, as the rest of Seeley's family caught up to them.

"You didn't get the wind knocked out of you," Seeley said sternly, and turned to Juliette and the others. "He got knocked out. The medics cleared him, but we're going for a CAT scan, just to be on the safe side."

"Aw, come on!" Lucas complained. "I'm not even dizzy."

"You were knocked *out*?" Juliette asked with renewed panic. "Why did you say you got the wind knocked out of you?"

"Because I knew you'd freak out," Lucas said.

"That's my *job*, Lucas. I'm your mother."

"Lucas, honey," Wynnie said. "It's always better to be safe than sorry."

"Tiny, tell them I'm fine," Lucas pleaded.

"Son, your parents are *both* doctors. They know what's best," Tiny said firmly.

Lucas rolled his eyes. "They're animal doctors."

"Hey, you were out long enough that I want to be sure you're okay. We're *going*," Seeley said, leaving no room for negotiation.

"Dude, you don't mess with head injuries," Dare said. "Trust me on that, Lucas. Billie still has gaps in her memory from a head injury she got over a year ago."

"*Fine.* I'll go, but can we just stay for the awards?" Lucas asked as cheers rang out for the last bull rider.

As Lucas turned to watch the show, Juliette looked at Seeley, and said, "What do you think? You said the medics cleared him?"

"They did. They said if he gets a headache or feels nauseous, dizzy, or has trouble breathing or chest pain, we should take him in. But he was *out*, Jule, and it took a bit for him to come around. We can let him stay for the awards, but I'd feel better if we get him checked out right after. I'll ask Cowboy to take Warrior back to your place."

The crowd exploded with excitement, and Lucas shouted, "I won! *Mom! Doc!* I won!" He threw his arms around Juliette *and* Seeley. "Congratulations, baby!" Juliette said as Seeley said, "You did it, buddy! King of the rodeo!"

With the entire arena cheering him on, the Whiskeys louder than all the rest, Lucas made a beeline for Layla.

Chapter Twenty-Seven

DOC HADN'T BEEN able to shake the uneasy feeling he'd had since seeing Lucas lying lifeless on the ground. Lucas had tried to tough it out, proudly accepting his awards and congratulatory embraces, but then he'd told them his head hurt, and they'd come directly to the emergency room. It was nearly eight o'clock, and Lucas was sitting on the exam table, his long legs dangling off the side, his arms crossed and his fingers drumming while they waited for the doctor to come in. The triage nurse had taken his vitals and put a cervical collar on him, which made him look even younger and more vulnerable than he was.

"How's your head, buddy?" Doc asked.

Lucas shrugged. "Still hurts. Can I take this thing off? My neck doesn't hurt."

"No, honey. They said not to," Juliette said.

"Let me see how much longer it's going to be." Doc got up and opened the curtain.

Mandy, the nurse he'd dated, was walking by and stopped when she saw him. "Doc? Hi. What're you doing here? You okay?"

Shit. "Hi, yeah. My son fell off a bull." *Son* came out without any thought, and he realized his mistake. He prayed Mandy wouldn't make a scene.

"Your *son*?" she whispered. "Are you *married*?"

"No. My girlfriend, Juliette, and I just reconnected after sixteen years. I didn't know about him." He didn't know what the right thing to do in this moment was, but he knew Juliette could hear him talking to a woman, and he didn't want her to worry. He stepped aside, allowing Juliette to see who he was talking to, and prayed this wouldn't go south. "Juliette, this is Mandy. We went out a while back. Mandy, this is Juliette and our son, Lucas."

"*Oh*," Juliette said a little awkwardly. "Hi."

"It's nice to meet you." Mandy looked between Doc and Juliette, and a small smile appeared. "You're a lucky lady. Doc's a great guy. I wondered why his heart was never up for grabs, but now I understand. I'm glad you've reconnected. I hope you're not hurt too badly, Lucas."

"Thanks," Lucas said.

Relief swept through Doc. "Thanks, Mandy."

She nodded. "Take care."

As she walked away, Doc pulled the curtain closed instead of going to look for the doctor and took Juliette's hand, addressing her *and* Lucas. "Sorry about that."

"It's okay," Juliette said. "We know you had a life before we got here, and she was nice about it."

"Yeah, who cares?" Lucas said.

The curtains parted before Doc could say anything more, and in walked Dr. Chen, a tall thin woman in her early fifties with straight black hair and wire-framed glasses whom Doc knew from the many years they'd been working with the hospital for their fundraisers. "Doc," she said with surprise. "I wasn't expecting to see you in here."

"Hi, Dr. Chen. This is my girlfriend, Juliette Chambers, and our son, Lucas."

Surprise flickered in her eyes for only a second before she caught it and schooled her expression. "Well, it's a pleasure to meet you both, although better circumstances would have been nice." She smiled at Lucas. "Lucas, Nurse Jacob told me you are a heck of a bull rider, but a bull got the better of you on your dismount, and you landed on your back. Is that right?"

"Yeah, but I won the competition," he said proudly.

"Congratulations. Did you hit your head when you fell?"

"I'm not sure, but I don't think so. I hit the ground, and the next thing I knew, Doc and another guy were looking down at me asking if I could hear them."

"He landed on his back," Doc said.

"Okay," she said. "Lucas, do you remember everything that's happened since your fall?"

"Yeah. I argued with them about coming here. Then I got something to eat, and I accepted my awards, but my head hurt, so we came here."

Dr. Chen looked at Doc and Juliette. "Mom? Dad? Does that sound about right?"

"Yes," they both said.

"Good. Lucas, are you in any pain?"

He pointed at his head. "My head hurts."

"On a scale of one to ten, one being no pain and ten being the worst pain imaginable, how would you rate your pain?"

"Five, maybe."

"And do you hurt anywhere else? Your arms, legs, back, neck?"

"Not really. My upper back is a little sore, but it doesn't

really hurt."

"Can you rank it on a scale of one to ten for me?"

Lucas's brows furrowed. "Three, I think."

"So, bad enough to be annoying, or worse?"

"It's not annoying. It's just sore."

"Okay. That's not unusual after an incident like yours. I'm going to do a quick exam, and we'll see what's going on." She put on gloves and did a neurological exam, and then she checked his reflexes and had him scrunch his shoulders and wiggle his fingers and toes. She moved behind him and palpated his back, asking if it hurt when she touched certain areas.

Lucas didn't seem bothered by any of it.

She loosened the cervical collar and began examining his neck. "Does this hurt?"

"No," Lucas said.

She repositioned her fingers. "How about this?"

Lucas shook his head. "No."

She continued feeling around. "Tell me if anything hurts. Even a little." Her brows knitted. "How long have you had this lump on your neck?"

"I didn't know I had a lump," Lucas said.

"Have you been sick recently or had a cold or a toothache?" she asked.

"No," Lucas said.

"Then it could be from the fall," she said. "Does it hurt when I apply pressure?"

"No."

Doc thought back to Lucas's practice last week. He'd taken a hard fall, and Doc had checked him out, but he didn't remember anything unusual on Lucas's neck at that time.

Dr. Chen refastened the cervical collar and had him lie

down so she could complete her exam. When she was done, she took off her gloves and addressed Doc and Juliette. "I don't feel any broken bones, but I'd like to get some blood work and a CAT scan of Lucas's head and neck and X-rays of his back, so we can make sure there's nothing going on that we should be concerned about. Nurse Jacob will bring in the orders, and then you can go up to radiology."

"They're going to do them now?" Lucas asked.

"It might take them a while to get to you, depending on how many other patients there are, but yes, they'll do them tonight. Then you'll come back to see me for the results."

"Are you concerned?" Doc asked. He'd watched closely as she'd examined Lucas, and he didn't see any neurological or motor deficits. Whatever she felt in his neck didn't seem to bother him, either, so he wasn't overly concerned, but he wanted to hear it from her.

"He had a traumatic fall. I'd be remiss if I wasn't," she said. "Let's get the tests done so we can see if we have cause for concern, and we'll go from there."

Doc should have known better than to ask. Of course she couldn't give the all clear without seeing the test results. "Right. Of course."

"Thank you, Dr. Chen," Juliette said.

"Can I take off the collar now?" Lucas asked hopefully.

"I know it's uncomfortable," Dr. Chen said. "But to be on the safe side, I'd rather you kept it on until after we have the results."

Lucas groaned.

NEARLY THREE HOURS later, they were back in the emergency room waiting for Dr. Chen to give them the results. It had been a long night, and they were all on edge. Lucas had been texting all evening and complaining about having to sit around. He was bored, tired, and irritated with the cervical collar. On the upside, his headache had subsided. Doc's family had been texting him and Juliette to check on Lucas, so he'd started a group thread that included his family and Juliette to keep everyone up to date. He'd asked Cowboy to take care of Juliette's horses, and Dare and Billie were checking on his dogs.

Lucas looked up from his phone. "Can I go on a trail ride tomorrow with Layla and her cousin?"

"We're sitting in the emergency room waiting to see if you have a head injury," Juliette said. "Don't you think we should wait to get the results before making plans to go horseback riding?"

"I don't have a head injury," Lucas snapped. "My headache is *gone*. I'm not even dizzy. Please?"

"Why don't we ask Dr. Chen after we get the results?" Doc suggested.

"Whatever." Lucas thumbed out another text.

Doc took Juliette's hand. "You okay? Do you need anything? A drink? Something to eat?"

She shook her head. "I'm just ready to get the results and go home."

"Me too," Lucas said without looking up from his phone.

Doc wished they were all going to the same home. "What about you, Lucas? Are you hungry? Thirsty?"

"No. I'm good. Thanks."

When Dr. Chen came in, she smiled warmly and said, "Good news, Lucas. We can take off that uncomfortable collar."

"*Yes.* Thank you," Lucas said, and they all breathed a sigh of relief.

Dr. Chen removed the collar and set it down. "The CT scan of Lucas's head was clear, as were the X-rays, so there's nothing to worry about there."

"See?" Lucas said. "I told you I didn't have a head injury. Can I go on the trail ride tomorrow?"

"Sure," Juliette said.

"We did find an enlarged lymph node on the right side of Lucas's neck that I think you should get checked out," Dr. Chen said.

"Lucas, if you have mono, I'm going to kill you," Juliette said. "Does that still mean weeks off school?"

"I don't have mono. I'm not sick," he snapped.

"I ran a monospot with the blood work and have ruled out mono," Dr. Chen said. "The rest of the labs were normal, and I didn't feel any other swollen nodes. I'm not sure what's causing this, which is why I'm recommending you get it checked out. I've provided names of a couple specialists on your discharge paperwork." She handed Doc the paperwork.

A specialist? Doc mentally ran through the possible causes of swollen painless lymph nodes.

"Another doctor? Just for that?" Lucas asked.

"Don't worry. It's not happening tonight," Dr. Chen reassured him.

"They can be caused by lots of things, like viral infections and sore throats," Juliette said. "Maybe you're coming down with something."

"It's probably nothing," Doc said to reassure them. "But we'll get it checked out. Thank you, Dr. Chen."

"Let me feel it." Juliette got up and felt Lucas's neck. Concentration lines deepened across her brow. Doc could tell she didn't like what she felt, but she managed a small smile. "Yeah, it's probably nothing. We'll follow up and get it looked at."

"Can I still go horseback riding tomorrow, Dr. Chen?" Lucas asked.

"Absolutely," she said. "Try to land on your feet when you dismount."

He smiled. "I will."

"You might be sore tomorrow from your fall. Tylenol or Motrin should help," Dr. Chen said.

"Thank you, Dr. Chen," Juliette said, her voice heavier than before. "Ready, Lucas?"

"Yeah. Can I get a Dr Pepper from the vending machine on the way out?" Lucas asked as he and Juliette walked out.

Doc hung back and touched Dr. Chen's arm, stopping her from walking away. "Robin, between you and me, should we be worried?"

Her expression turned apologetic. "If he were my child, I'd get him in right away."

Doc managed a nod, and as she walked away, he quickly scanned the paperwork for the referrals. *Dr. Michael Santowski, Pediatric Oncologist* and *Dr. Bethany Rodgers, Pediatric Oncologist.*

His stomach plummeted. He looked down the hall at Juliette and Lucas pushing through the doors to the lobby, and a million thoughts hit him at once, his gut twisting. Emotions swamped him, making it hard to breathe. *Pull your shit together.*

He forced himself to focus, mentally batting the painful thoughts away. He needed to figure out how to break the news to Juliette and how they'd get Lucas to an oncologist without scaring the ever-living-fuck out of him.

Chapter Twenty-Eight

IT WAS AFTER midnight when they finally got home. Juliette was a mental mess and trying not to show it, which was as exhausting as the rest of the day had been.

"I'm whipped," Lucas said as they walked in the door. "I'm going to bed."

"Okay, sweets. Do you want some Tylenol for your back?" Juliette asked.

"Nah. I'm good, thanks."

"Come here." Juliette hugged him a little tighter than usual. "Congratulations on your wins. I'm really proud of you."

"I am, too," Seeley said. "Mind if I steal one of those hugs?"

"You're gonna steal one anyway," Lucas said, and Seeley embraced him. "Did you ever end up in the hospital after a bull ride?"

"No, but I probably should have a time or two. When I was growing up, if you remembered your alphabet and didn't have a bone sticking out, you carried on. But ask Dare next time you see him. He got hurt so often, he had an ER bed with his name on it."

Lucas laughed. "I bet. The night of the bonfire, he told me

about the crazy stunts he's done on his motorcycle. Standing up riding on the highway? Jumping over buses? Is that true?"

"Yes. And don't get any ideas," Seeley warned.

"Don't worry. I'm not that big of a risk taker. I told Layla about how fun the bonfire was. Do you think we could invite her to the ranch for one some night?"

"I think that's a great idea," Seeley said.

"Cool." Lucas yawned. "G'night."

"Night, buddy."

"Good night, honey," Juliette said. She waited for Lucas's bedroom door to close before looking at Seeley. She felt her maternal mask cracking.

He took her hand, drawing her into his arms, and she closed her eyes, soaking in his comfort and praying her fears were unfounded.

"It's been a hell of a night." He kissed the top of her head. "Let's sit on the porch where we can talk."

They went outside and sat on the top step. "I miss the porch swing," she said. "We had one in California at the farm where Lucas grew up. We used to sit on it, and I'd tell him stories or sing to him. In the evenings, he'd lay down with his head on my lap and fall asleep." Her throat thickened. "I would sit there for hours before carrying him to bed."

Seeley put his arm around her, pulling her closer. "I'll build you a swing, darlin'."

She rested her head on his shoulder, avoiding the inevitable. She didn't want to voice her worries for fear of making them real. She was well aware that her reasoning made no sense. Her clients had played the avoidance game plenty of times about their ailing animals. But she didn't care if it made sense or not, her mama's mind wasn't ready to go there. "Lucas did great today, didn't he? It meant the world to him that everyone showed up to cheer him on."

"It meant the world to them, too." He kissed her temple. "Talk to me, darlin'."

"I *am* talking to you. Did you see how big Lucas's smile was when they called him up to the stage? He strutted up there like a proud peacock, and when he looked at Layla, I swear I could see her swoon."

"He's going to be okay, darlin'," he said softly, and held her a little tighter.

"Of course he is," she said too cheerily. "He has to be."

"I know this is hard to talk about, but we need to. I checked him out after a fall at practice last week, and I didn't feel anything unusual on his neck. That means this popped up quick. What did his lymph node feel like?"

The words stuck in her throat.

"It's okay, baby. Take your time," he said.

"It was *hard*," she said quietly, as if that would somehow make it less real. "It didn't move when I pressed on it. You know that's not good."

He was quiet for a beat. "We're not going to jump to any conclusions, but she referred us to pediatric oncologists."

Gutted, Juliette sank back, and her face went cold. "*Seeley*" fell shakily from her lips, eyes stinging with tears.

He cradled her face in his hands. "Listen to me, darlin'. We don't know anything yet. His blood work was normal. She checked his other lymph nodes, and they weren't swollen. We are *not* going to assume the worst. Do you understand?"

She nodded, struggling to keep her tears at bay.

"My cousin Bones—*Wayne*—is an oncologist in Maryland. I'm going to call him and see what he can tell us."

"Okay. Can you call him first thing tomorrow?"

"No. This is our boy. I'm going to call him now."

"You can't call him this late," she said.

"He's family. He'd expect nothing less." He kissed her and hugged her, then pushed to his feet, pulled out his phone, and made the call. "Hey, Bones. Sorry to call so late." He paused, listening. "I need some advice…" He walked away as he explained what was going on.

Juliette pulled her phone from her pocket, her heart racing as she opened the browser and typed, *What does a hard, painless, enlarged lymph node in the neck mean?* Her thumb hovered over the search button. She knew what she'd find, but she hoped to be surprised by something less terrifying. She glanced at Seeley. His back was turned, the phone still pressed to his ear, his other hand balling into a fist.

She glanced at her phone again, debating the search, and her grandmother's voice whispered through her mind. *There's nothing you can't do, Juliegirl. Get ahead of the devil so he can't sneak up on you. Get your ducks in a row, then cut them off.* That was the advice she'd given Juliette when she'd told her she was leaving with Lucas and stopping all communication with her parents. She'd taken her advice and had gotten her and Lucas squared away before severing the toxic relationship with her parents.

She needed to get ahead of this devil, too.

She tapped the search icon and held her breath as the results popped up. She scanned the page, phrases hitting her like knives to the heart. *Possible cancer or lymphoma…Lymphoma or another type of cancer should be investigated…* It became harder to breathe with every line she read.

But she knew the internet was loaded with misinformation,

so she went to the Mayo Clinic website, a reference she trusted. She read about healthy swollen lymph nodes being tender, the size of a pea or a kidney bean, sometimes larger, but usually painful. Lucas's lymph node was the size of a walnut and painless.

She continued reading about all the usual symptoms she knew she'd find, like how they're associated with runny noses, sore throats, and fever. She read about general swelling of lymph nodes throughout the body, which could be indicative of an infection or an immune system disorder.

But the doctor had only found one swollen node.

She read a list of bulleted symptoms and stopped cold at *hard, fixed, rapidly growing nodes, indicating a possible cancer or lymphoma.*

With her heart in her throat, she skimmed to the section that talked about when to see a doctor. Her gaze held on the third bullet. *If the lymph nodes feel hard or rubbery or don't move when pushed on.*

Nonono. No! Fuck no.

She quickly navigated to the types of cancer associated with such lymph nodes. *Leukemia. Lymphoma. Other cancers that have metastasized to lymph nodes.*

Metastasized. The word made her feel sick.

She scanned the symptoms of leukemia. *Pale skin, red spots on the skin, bone pain, bruising, shortness of breath, dizziness, weakness, weight loss, fatigue.* And the symptoms of lymphoma. *Night sweats, coughing, itchy skin, shortness of breath.* She scanned the other related symptoms, hope rising in her with each one, because Lucas had none of the symptoms mentioned.

She clicked another link, reading about five-year survival rates and cure rates, which, depending on the type of cancer, ranged from sixty-five to ninety percent. It sounded like a fucking crapshoot.

It was all too much.

"A'right," Seeley said, drawing her attention. "Thanks, man."

She shoved her phone into her back pocket, pushing away the crapshoot statistics, clinging to the fact that other than one swollen lymph node, Lucas was healthy. "What did he say?" she asked as Seeley neared the porch.

"He told me what we already knew," he said solemnly. "A firm, immovable lymph node in the neck *could* indicate certain types of cancer but not to worry until we know for sure. He said the doctor will probably order a biopsy, which is the only way to get definitive results."

Biopsy magnified in her mind.

"He suggested we see Dr. Santowski. He said he's a leader in the field. He also said we shouldn't go online to look this up, because it'll only scare the shit out of us."

"Too late." She went to him. "And he's right. It scared the shit out of me. Every result mentioned cancer, but I looked up the symptoms of leukemia and lymphoma, and Lucas has *none* of them. Not a single one. They mentioned other types of cancer, but without any symptoms, maybe this is a fluke, and the lymph node will shrink on its own. I mean, stranger things have happened, right?"

"We can hope, darlin'." He drew her into his arms, but he didn't sound convinced. "The good news is that if caught early, the diseases he mentioned are highly curable."

She didn't think sixty-five percent sounded highly curable, but she didn't have the bandwidth to do more research or talk about it. "Did he say anything else?"

He shook his head, still holding her tight. "No, baby."

The sadness in his voice told her he wasn't telling her everything, but she knew he was protecting her. Part of her wanted to push, to get every little detail so she would know what they might be up against. But a bigger part of her, the part that needed to stay strong for Lucas, the part that couldn't afford to go down a rabbit hole that might shred her to pieces, didn't want to know.

She didn't care if that made her seem weak or stupid. Right now, she *was* weak, and maybe she *needed* to be stupid. She already knew too much. She was scared out of her fucking mind. She melted into him, wearing the safety of his arms like armor. "Will you stay with me tonight?"

He gazed down at her with troubled eyes. "There's nothing I want more than to stay with you, but what about Lucas?"

"I don't think he'll mind. You're a big part of our life, and he likes it that way. But if you're worried about it, we can get up before he does, and he won't know you stayed over."

"Okay, darlin'. I'll stay." He lowered his lips to hers in a slow, sensual kiss. "You must be exhausted."

"I am, but my brain is on fire."

"Let's go inside. I'll run you a warm bath. It'll help you relax." His brows slanted. "You do have a tub, don't you?"

"*Yes*," she said with a little laugh. "But you don't have to do that. That is, unless you're willing to climb in with me."

His wicked grin told her he had planned that all along. "Remember how you used to dream about having a big Jacuzzi tub in the cabin, because your grandmother used to let you use hers?"

"I can't believe you remembered that."

"I told you, you're unforgettable." He slung his arm around

her. "Come on. My baby mama needs pampering."

"Is that what I am to you? Your *baby mama?*" she teased as they headed inside.

"Darlin', you're so many things to me, I don't even know where to start."

On the way down the hall, she stopped to listen outside Lucas's door. "I think he's asleep."

They peeked into his room. Lucas was lying on his back with his phone on the mattress beside him. The covers were pulled up to his belly. His necklace hung to one side, twinkling in the light from the lamp on the nightstand. She remembered when she'd given that necklace to him. She'd wanted him to have a piece of Seeley, and she'd thought Seeley's good luck charm could help keep him safe, too. If only it were that easy.

"Look at our perfect boy," Seeley said quietly. "He was made of the purest form of love there is."

There were no truer words.

"I won't let anything happen to him, darlin'," he whispered. "If he's sick, we'll make sure he gets whatever treatments he needs. If he needs an organ, I'll give him mine. I will do whatever it takes, *always*, for him and for you."

Choking up, she turned and wrapped her arms around him. "I don't want to think about any of that."

"I'm about to help you with that." Seeley pulled Lucas's door closed, took her hand, and led her into her bedroom. "I want you to relax while I fill the tub." He looked around her bedroom and snagged a candle from her dresser. "Do you have any more of these lying around?"

"Just one." She pointed to the nightstand on the far side of her bed.

He reached for the candle, but stopped short, picking up the framed photo of her and Lucas instead. "Look at you two with that baby goat." He smiled, studying the picture. "When was this taken?"

"When Lucas was three. It was his first time at the petting zoo." In the picture, she was crouched beside Lucas, looking at him, and he was caught mid-giggle, petting the goat.

"So you were twenty." He ran his finger over the picture. "You're both so beautiful. Look at his little pudgy cheeks and hands. He liked the goats?"

"He loved them. But he called them *boats*." She laughed softly. "He had trouble with *G*s for a while."

Seeley smiled. "That must've been adorable."

"It was pretty darn cute."

"I wish I could go back in time and be there with you. I missed so much. I'll never know how it felt to kiss those pudgy cheeks or hear that infectious toddler giggle kids have." His jaw tightened as he set the picture down. He cleared his throat, turning a tender smile on her. "I'm glad I'm here now. I'll never miss another thing." He picked up the candle. "Okay, sweet girl, your bath will be ready momentarily."

He winked and headed into the bathroom, leaving her with so many emotions, it was hard for her to separate the gratitude for their coming together from the guilt of her keeping Lucas a secret from him for so long.

She was still thinking about that and stewing over what Lucas was going through, when they climbed into the tub. She nestled between Seeleys thick thighs, leaning back against his chest. The lights were off, the candles flickering on the counters, and moonlight streamed in through the window.

Seeley gathered her hair over one of her shoulders, kissing the one he bared. "Close your eyes and relax."

She closed her eyes as he bathed her, his hands moving down her arms and over her stomach. It felt good. Soothing. But her mind was still racing. "I can't stop thinking about Lucas."

"I know. Me too."

"He's going to freak out when he hears he's seeing an oncologist."

"I've been thinking about that." He kissed her neck. "I think we should keep things as normal as possible. There's no need for him to worry until we know what we're dealing with. Once you make the appointment, say it's a *doctor appointment*. Keep it general."

"But he's smart. He'll know when we get there."

"And at that point we'll explain that we wanted him to see a specialist who looks at swollen lymph nodes all day long because they're the most qualified to figure out what's going on."

"That's a good idea. He'll understand that." She took a deep breath and blew it out slowly, feeling a little better.

He kissed her shoulder, cupping water in his hands and pouring it over her breasts. "Now, how about you close those beautiful baby blues again, and let me redirect that pesky fire from your brain to other, more appropriate places?"

"I like the sound of that."

She closed her eyes, and his warm lips trailed up her neck. "Your mind can only think of one thing at a time. Think about me kissing you." He slicked his tongue along the shell of her ear and sucked the lobe into his mouth, sending rivers of heat slithering through her. "My hands on your body." He kissed her neck as he cupped her breasts, teasing her nipples, sending prickles of desire chasing over her skin. One hand moved between her legs, teasing her where she needed it most. She gasped, rocking against his talented fingers. "Think about my mouth on your pussy."

He worked her clit faster, his cock pressing temptingly against her back. He caressed, kissed, sucked, groped, and teased, distracting her in the most glorious ways, driving her out of her freaking mind. He rolled her nipple between his finger and thumb as he teased her clit, sending heat searing through her core and drawing a whimper. *"Oh...God."*

"That's it, darlin'. Let me hear those needy sounds," he said huskily, and sank his teeth into her neck at the same time he pinched her nipple. Spikes of pleasure shot through her, and *"Seeley,"* flew from her lips like a plea. She tried to turn toward him, but he held her in place.

"Not yet, beautiful." He continued his masterful assault, quickening his efforts between her legs, lavishing her breast with gropes and tweaks, bringing her to the verge of orgasm. His mouth was a sinful storm of taunts. Biting, sucking, and kissing. Need coiled hot and tight deep inside her as she writhed and moaned, splashing water over the sides of the tub. "My greedy girl. You're so ready to come, you're shaking."

"Yes. Please."

He pushed two fingers inside her, using his thumb on her most sensitive nerves, and she gasped at the shock of pleasure it brought. He stroked and teased until her entire body vibrated with desire. He sank his teeth into her neck, pinching her nipple and doing something magical with his fingers, sending a hailstorm of white-hot sensations raining down on her. She cried out, but he reached up and turned her face, capturing the sounds with his mouth as waves of pleasure consumed her, and the world spun away.

When she finally started to come down from the peak, her

body still trembling, he said, "Time to ride my cock, baby," his dirty words revving her up again. He turned her in his arms, sending water over the side of the tub, and held her hips, his dark eyes eating her up as she perched on her knees above his hard length. "You're too damn tempting."

He pulled her forward, sending another wave splashing onto the floor, and lifted her higher, his fingers pressing into her flesh as she straddled his mouth, and—*Holy hell.* How was this even possible? She grabbed the wall to keep from tipping over as he used his tongue and teeth in ways she never thought possible. Her body was flaming inside and shivering outside from the cool air on her wet flesh, but she didn't care. She could barely hold on to a single thought. She wasn't even sure she was breathing as her orgasm crashed over her. She clamped her mouth shut to keep from waking Lucas, and Seeley shifted, lowering her onto his long, thick cock. She gasped, pleasure consuming her like wildfire as he pumped and thrust, sending them both careening into a world of ecstasy so bright and hot, she couldn't imagine anything more perfect.

As they came down from their high, he gathered her in his arms. "Come here, my sweet forever girl," and took her in a slow, passionate kiss, showing her how wrong she was. Because every moment with him was more perfect than the last.

Chapter Twenty-Nine

JULIETTE PUSHED THE pitchfork through the shavings in Warrior's stall, thinking about Lucas, as always. Only today she was remembering how cute he'd been at four years old, with his plastic pitchfork, tiny cowboy boots, and felt hat, helping her muck a stall at the farm. He'd been so excited to help take care of the horses, he'd rattled on the whole time about how happy they'd be with their clean stalls. He'd complained about a lot of things in his life, but taking care of the horses had never been one of them. She tried to focus on that, but her fucking mind veered into dark, terrifying territory. The Land of What-Ifs. Her chin trembled, tears threatening, but she fought them with everything she had, refusing to go there.

He's going to be fine. He has to be.

That had become her mantra.

She had always considered herself strong. When Lucas was growing up, she'd kept her chin up and had never let him feel her inner turmoil. When she'd left Josh, she'd told everyone she was fine, when leaving him and truly being on her own for the first time in her life had been the second-hardest thing she'd ever done. The first was the day she'd turned her back on her heart and married the wrong man. When Josh was killed, it had broken something inside her *and* Lucas, but she'd forged on, putting on a brave face and hiding her grief to remain strong for her son. She'd convinced herself there was *nothing* she couldn't handle.

But the last eleven days had tried her on every level.

They'd met with Dr. Santowski, a pleasant enough man with kind eyes and a straightforward demeanor, and Lucas hadn't freaked out when he'd realized he was an oncologist. He had no reason to worry. He trusted Juliette and Seeley's explanation of wanting quick and accurate answers from a specialist. When Dr. Santowski ordered a biopsy, the word *cancer* never left his lips, and Lucas had taken it in stride as part of the process to get those answers.

But Juliette knew what they were trying to rule out, and trying to act like everything was normal while waiting for the results of the biopsy had her breaking down at the strangest moments. Thankfully, she'd been holding her shit together in front of Lucas, but other times, like when she was doing dishes or taking a shower, she'd hide away and cry. Last weekend, while they were having dinner at the ranch, Lucas was having a grand time, boasting about his motocross practice with Billie and sharing how excited he was that Layla was joining them for a bonfire afterward. But all Juliette could think about were the what-ifs.

What if he has cancer? Will he be able to do all the things he loves? What will his treatments be like? Sixty-five to ninety percent had trampled through her mind, demanding her attention and drawing the most terrifying questions of all. *Will he still be here in a month? Six months? Six years from now? Or is this the beginning of the end?* She'd had to excuse herself to hide in the ladies' room until she could regain control of her emotions.

Seeley had been her anchor.

They'd decided not to hide the fact that he'd stayed over that first night, and Lucas had been surprisingly okay with it. She was glad, because Seeley always knew exactly what to do or say to help her feel better. He held her when she was sad, reassured her incessantly without losing patience, checked in with her during the day, and always found little ways to make her smile. Every day he left them a little something—a tin can full of wildflowers in the kitchen, a bouquet of them in her truck, chocolates for Lucas on his pillow, a framed picture of Lucas riding a bull at practice on their coffee table, or Lucas's favorite, a picture of him and Layla making s'mores at one of their bonfires.

But Seeley's gifts went far beyond the tangible. At night they talked, made love, or lay in each other's arms, comforting one another, reminiscing, making jokes, or spinning hopeful tales.

Lucas may not realize it, but Seeley had become his rock, too. He showed up at every one of Lucas's riding practices, joined him at motocross practices, took him driving three times a week without fail, and together they worked around the ranch fixing little things. They talked a lot and heckled each other often. She'd caught them in hushed conversations a few times, and when she'd asked what they were talking about, Lucas had said, *guy stuff*, and Seeley hadn't breached that confidence.

She didn't think it was possible to fall more in love with Seeley than she already was. But boy had she been wrong. Watching him nurture their son and build a strong relationship with him built on trust and love was the most beautiful thing she'd ever seen. And the best part was, she could tell Lucas loved him, too.

Seeley had spent nearly every night with them since that first night, and he'd been bringing the dogs with him, which Lucas loved. The dogs followed Lucas like he was the Pied Piper, and slept on his bed. Monday night Lucas asked if he could watch the dogs while Seeley was at church on Tuesday, and he'd been thrilled when Seeley dropped them off before his meeting. But as much as he loved having the dogs and Seeley at their house, when they'd spent the night at Seeley's house last weekend, Lucas had enjoyed it even more. He'd gotten up early to check on the rehab horses with Seeley, and at Gus's request, they'd brought his bicycle to the ranch, and he'd ridden to Sasha and Ezra's house, so he and Gus could ride their bikes together up to the main house for breakfast.

There was definitely something magical about being around the Whiskeys and the energy at the ranch that had reeled their son in, just as it had her. The Whiskeys had been rallying around them, creating a new kind of normal for her and Lucas. One filled with family and friends and all the support they could ever need. The girls texted her often, and it was wonderful to have real girlfriends who cared about her and Lucas. Last Sunday, several of his family members had gone on a trail ride with them and Lucas and Layla. Lucas still hadn't stopped talking about how much fun they'd had.

Juliette's therapist was helping her navigate the pressure of waiting for the results of the biopsy, but not as much as Seeley and his family were. She'd quickly learned that there was no substitute for a loving family, and she thanked her lucky stars that Seeley's had accepted her and Lucas so completely.

Now she was praying for those lucky stars to align for Lucas.

They were meeting with Dr. Santowski later this afternoon to get the results of his biopsy.

Her chest constricted just thinking about it.

He's going to be fine. He has to be.

She hoisted a pitchfork of manure into the wheelbarrow.

"Juliette?"

She peered out of the stall and saw Wynnie by the open barn door. She looked pretty in a colorful sweater, jeans, and her ever-present cowgirl boots. "I'm in here." Juliette set the pitchfork against the wall and wiped her hands on her jeans as she stepped out of the stall.

"Hi, honey. I looked for you up at the house, and thought you might be down here."

"I was in a mucking mood."

Wynnie drew her into her arms, holding her a little longer, and tighter, than usual. Juliette had gone so many years without hugs from anyone other than Lucas, she hadn't realized how much she'd missed them, and she was grateful for the extras.

"I can understand that," Wynnie said. "It's a hard day for everyone. I made you some of that lemon cake you were so fond of the other night. I left it on your kitchen table."

"*Aw*, thank you. That was really nice of you." She'd eaten three pieces the other night. "I swear, I'm either stress eating or unable to stomach a thing lately."

"There's a lot of that going around in our family right now." Wynnie touched her hand. "How are you holding up, honey?"

She pressed her lips together, shaking her head, and shrugging. "Doing the best I can. You know. I keep telling myself he's going to be fine, and that works for a while. Until it doesn't, and then I'm bawling in the bathroom or pulling over on the highway to wipe my tears."

"Oh, sweetheart." Wynnie squeezed her hand. "I've been doing the same thing. But we're all putting positive energy out there, hoping and praying for the best. Whatever happens today, we'll get through it together. All of us."

Tears sprang to Juliette's eyes, and she fanned her face. "I'm sorry."

"Sweetheart, it's okay to cry." Wynnie embraced her again, speaking softly. "You've got a mountain of worry in your heart. Let it out, baby girl."

That made her cry harder. "I just...I'm so scared. What if it's bad news?"

"Then we'll deal with it. Doc has been gathering information, talking to doctors, finding out who the best physicians are for *every* possible outcome."

"He *has*?" She drew back, wiping her eyes. "Why didn't he tell me?"

"Because he loves you, and he doesn't want to worry you. He's hoping for the best, like the rest of us, but he wasn't going to walk in there today unprepared. He wants to be strong for you and Lucas, and the only way he feels like he can do that is to be ready for anything."

Guilt swamped her, drawing more tears. "*I* should've been doing that. I'm his mother, and I didn't think to do it."

"Honey, you're doing everything you can to keep your head above water in a very trying time. But I understand how you feel. You and I are a lot alike. We've had different journeys, but we're strong, hearty gals who are used to dealing with the ups and downs of life on our own. I helped my father run the ranch and helped him grieve my mother. The woman he loved his entire life. It was not easy, and when Tiny came into my life, letting him take the lead and take care of me went against everything I knew. But he showed me how we were stronger together. Sometimes Tiny needs to lean on me, and other times I need to lean on him. And occasionally we do things without mentioning them to each other, because we know they're best handled that way. That's *love*, sweetheart. You and Lucas are Doc's world. It's okay to let him do the heavy lifting right now. Doc needs that as much as you need to cry in the shower and muck the stalls."

Juliette swiped at her tears. "I know you're right, but I keep thinking about all the years I wasted when Seeley and Lucas could've been together, and now we're dealing with *this*. I feel so guilty."

Wynnie took her by the shoulders, holding her gaze, and said, "Listen to me, sweetheart. We don't even know what *this* is yet. What we do know is that *nobody* blames *you* for those lost years. Not Doc or me, or Tiny, or anyone else. You and Lucas are our treasured gifts, and nothing will *ever* change that."

Overwhelmed with emotion, tears spilled down her cheeks as she choked out, "Thank you," and embraced Wynnie.

"You're family, sweetheart, and in our family, that bond is unbreakable."

Chapter Thirty

THE HOURS PASSED too slowly, giving Juliette far too much time with her own thoughts. She finished mucking the stalls and doing the other chores Lucas would normally do after school. Then she baked mint chocolate chip cookies for him. Seeley called twice, asking if she wanted him to come over, but she knew he had animals to care for, so she'd said she was okay.

Fifteen minutes after the second call, he was in her driveway, and she'd never been more thankful to see anyone in her life.

Her heart skipped as she went out front to meet him. "I told you that you didn't have to come over."

"What can I say? You're a sucky liar." He wrapped her in his arms. "I love you, Jule, and I'll always know when you need me."

She kissed the center of his chest, reveling in the depth of his love before meeting his warm gaze. "I love you, too, Seeley, and I hope I always know when you need me."

"Not a minute goes by when I don't need you." He pressed his lips to hers in a tender kiss. "Want to take a walk?"

"A walk?"

"Yeah, you know, that thing where you put one foot in front of the other, breathe in the crisp fall air, appreciate the beauty around us."

She gave him a deadpan look.

"Come on, darlin'. Let's get out of that pretty little head of yours." He took her hand, tucking her against his side as they walked away from the house.

"Your mom came by this morning."

"She told me she was going to when I saw her earlier. Was that okay?"

"It was more than okay. I love your mom. I needed the visit with her. Hazel used to be my touchstone when I needed motherly love, but it was all long distance because of my parents. I never let myself think about how hard it was without a loving mom to help me through life and motherhood. But when your mom hugs me, it brings it all home, and I realize how much I really missed not having one." She got teary and wiped her eyes. "I'm sorry. I'm just overtired."

He drew her into his arms and held her. "You're scared, love, and that's okay." He kissed the top of her head.

She gazed up at him. "Are you scared?"

"I'd have to be heartless not to be." He tucked her beneath his arm again, and they walked along the grass.

"Your mom told me you've been talking to doctors."

"I have."

"Why didn't you tell me?"

He hugged her against his side. "Because we don't know what we're dealing with yet. I don't need to fill your head with potential treatment plans and possible outcomes that may never be necessary." He kissed her temple.

"Then why do all that research?"

"Because I can't control the outcome, and I had to do something."

She rested her head against him as they walked, her heart hurting for both of them.

"Know what that research taught me?" he asked.

"What?"

"To be grateful for every minute we have together, every smile, every time you give me a look like I'm out of my mind or Lucas rolls his eyes and grumbles *whatever*."

"Does that mean you're worried we'll get bad news?"

"No, darlin'. It means I never want to take my forever girl or our beautiful son for granted. Let's leave the worrying for when we see the doctor and spend the time we have thinking happier thoughts."

God, she loved him. She'd been so lost in worry, she never would have thought of taking a walk. But as they walked across the grass, talking and soaking in the afternoon sun, gazing out at the mountains in the distance, she realized his calming presence, and getting away from the place she'd been stewing, was exactly the comfort she needed.

By the time Lucas got home from school, she felt more at ease.

Lucas was thrilled to find the cookies she'd baked, and as he chowed down on them, he said, "All we need is some Dr Pepper, and this would be perfect."

"We'll pick you up some on the way to the doctor's office," Seeley promised. "But we better get going so we're not late."

"Okay." He grabbed a few cookies, and as he put them in a napkin, he said, "Layla and I are going to hang out on Halloween, and her mom said she'd take us shopping sometime to get costumes."

"That sounds fun," Juliette said, and they headed out.

As they climbed into Seeley's truck, Lucas said, "I did something today."

"That sounds nefarious," Seeley said. "Should we be concerned?"

"What kind of *thing?*" Juliette asked.

"I asked Layla to the Snow Ball."

Seeley cocked a brow, eyeing him in the rearview mirror. "That's not code for something dirty, is it?"

"*Seeley,*" Juliette chided.

"What? Do you know all the teen slang these days?" he asked.

She rolled her eyes.

"Like I'm really going to announce something dirty to my parents?" Lucas shook his head, smiling. "It's the winter dance."

Juliette whipped her head around, unable to believe her ears—about his casual tossing out *parents* and about the dance. "You're going to a dance?" He'd never wanted to go to dances at his old school.

"Yeah. With the coolest girl in school," he boasted.

"Congrats, buddy," Seeley said. "That's awesome. When is it?"

"The last day before winter break."

"This is so exciting," Juliette said, taking his change of heart as a good sign from the universe. "We'll need to go shopping to get you nice clothes. What do kids wear to school dances nowadays? Do you need a suit? I bet Layla's excited. You'll have to match your shirt or tie to her dress, so we should wait to go shopping until you know what she's wearing."

"Whatever," he said. "Can I drive to the dance?"

"You know you can't," Juliette said.

"Come *on*," Lucas complained.

"Sorry, bud, but you can't drive with a teenager in the car when you've only got your learner's permit," Seeley said as he pulled up to a convenience store. He put the car in park and pulled out his wallet. "You want anything, darlin'?"

"No, thanks."

He handed Lucas a five-dollar bill. "Go get your soda."

"Thanks." Lucas snagged the cash and climbed out of the truck.

"Our boy got hit by Cupid's arrow." Seeley reached for her hand. "We're in trouble now."

She smiled. "He's *so* happy."

"As well he should be. He and Layla are crazy about each other."

"I know, but what if—"

Seeley put his finger over her lips. "No what-ifs. Let's bask in his happiness. He deserves it, and so do we." He leaned forward and kissed her.

Forty minutes later they were led into Dr. Santowski's office and told he'd be right in. There was nothing particularly threatening about the office, but as they sat in front of the large wooden desk, the room felt ominous. There were abstract paintings on the walls and a framed drawing that was so simplistic, it looked to be done by a child. A black line started at the bottom left of the canvas and turned into a dark, scribbled tangle with a single bumpy line coming out the other side, angling upward and then forming a spiral. On the other side of the spiral, it became a single line again, and as it reached toward the upper-right corner, it bloomed into a stunning array of colorful bubblelike petals and green leaves.

Hope.

That's what the drawing said to her, but it didn't ease her nerves. Lucas was sitting between her and Seeley texting, which for some reason was making her more nervous. "Lucas, put your phone away, honey."

"One sec." He continued thumbing out a text.

Seeley's arms were crossed, his fingers drumming anxiously. He nudged Lucas, nodding to the phone. "Come on, bud. You heard your mom."

"*Fine*. We'd better get out of here in time for practice."

She'd been so sidetracked, she'd forgotten he had practice today. "We should have plenty of time," she said as the door opened, and Dr. Santowski walked in. He was a thin man, mostly bald, with serious, kind eyes. Juliette tried to read his expression, but he looked the same as he had the first time they'd met. Serious and kind.

"Sorry to keep you waiting," he said as he closed the door.

"No problem." Seeley stood, offering his hand. "Thanks for seeing us."

The doctor shook his hand and went around the desk, lowering himself into his chair. "How are you feeling, Lucas?"

Lucas shrugged. "Fine."

"Good." He looked at Seeley and Juliette, and something in that steady gaze made the hair on the back of her neck prickle. "I've looked over the biopsy results. Lucas has Hodgkin's disease, which is a type of lymphoma."

Tears sprang to Juliette's eyes. The room spun, and she struggled to keep herself in check, wanting to scream *No! You have the wrong kid!* but needing to be strong for Lucas. She knew he didn't have the wrong kid, regardless of how hard she'd tried to bury her head in the sand, and now Seeley's arm was wrapped protectively around Lucas, the tips of his fingers brushing her shoulder. *You knew, too. That was why you did all that research.*

"What is that?" Lucas asked.

"It's a type of cancer that affects your lymphatic system, but it's very responsive to treatment and highly curable."

"*Cancer?*" Lucas snapped. "I don't have cancer. I'm not sick. Look at me. I'm fine."

Juliette put her hand over his. "It's okay, Lucas."

He yanked his hand away. "No, it's *not*. He's *wrong*. Do another test."

"I'm sorry, Lucas, but the biopsy was conclusive," Dr. Santowski said gently, leaving no room for argument. "It's not uncommon for kids your age to find a swollen lymph node as their first indicator that something is wrong and not to have any other symptoms."

"*No*. You're wrong," Lucas insisted. "I *don't* have cancer."

"Lucas, look at me," Seeley said sternly, turning his entire body toward Lucas, keeping one hand on his shoulder, and holding his gaze.

"This is messed up, Doc," Lucas said shakily.

"This *is* messed up," Seeley said with all the love, compassion, and strength a father should show. "No kid should ever get cancer. I know this sounds scary, but you're *strong*. You're a frigging bull rider, buddy. There's *nothing* you can't get through, and your mother and I, and everyone else in our family, will be by your side every step of the way."

"*Every* step of the way," Juliette reiterated.

"We'll fight this together, and we'll *beat* it. Okay?" Seeley said.

Teary eyed, Lucas said, "What if we don't? What if I...?" Tears slid down his cheeks, breaking Juliette's heart.

"That's *not* going to happen," Seeley said, putting his arms around him, then reaching for Juliette, too, as she got up and hugged Lucas. Seeley put his arms around both of them, his body, their armor against the awful unknown.

As tears fell from Lucas's eyes, drawing her own, Seeley held them tighter, their great protector. "We're going to beat this. Don't you doubt that for a second," Seeley said, as if he truly believed he could control their son's fate.

She desperately wanted to believe he could.

He held them until Lucas stopped crying, and his grip eased. Then he put one hand on Lucas's shoulder, the other on hers, his gaze moving reassuringly between them. "Are we ready to make a plan of attack, so we can beat this thing?"

She and Lucas nodded. She was so glad Seeley was there, because she was afraid if she tried to speak, more tears would fall.

Seeley squeezed Lucas's shoulder. "We've got this, Rodeo."

Why did the nickname make her want to cry again?

She took her seat as Lucas sat back. He set his jaw and crossed his arms, drumming his fingers, looking like he did at four years old at Josh's funeral, when he was consumed with grief and shock and trying so hard to be brave.

Seeley put his arm around Lucas again, the tips of his fingers touching Juliette's shoulder, and addressed the doctor. "What's next?"

"I'll order a PET scan, which is like the CAT scan you had, Lucas, but we'll look at your whole body to see if any other lymph nodes are affected. That will allow us to stage the cancer and determine a treatment plan…"

Chapter Thirty-One

AFTER A FEW fitful hours of sleep, Doc glowered at the clock, as if it were at fault for it being four o'clock on a fucking Monday morning. It had been five days since they'd learned Lucas's diagnosis. His PET scan was scheduled for tomorrow morning, and while they were keeping things as normal as possible, Doc was struggling inside. He needed to get out of his own head.

He slipped quietly out of bed, trying not to wake Juliette, quickly showered and dressed, and pulled on a flannel shirt over his T-shirt as he headed upstairs to check on Lucas.

When Lucas had asked if they could bring their horses to the ranch and spend the weekend there, Doc had been thrilled. That was what he'd wanted all along, to have Lucas and Juliette in the one place he knew they'd be surrounded by love and support. As far-fetched as it was, he hoped his grandfather was right, and some of the ranch's magic might help heal Lucas and kill the motherfucking cancer. He'd grasp at every fucking straw there was if it would heal his boy.

The door to Lucas's room was ajar for the dogs.

Doc peered in, and his heart thudded a little harder. Lucas

was fast asleep with Mighty on one side of him, his arm over Sadie, and Pickles lying at his feet. Mighty lifted his head at the silent intrusion, and Pickles didn't move a muscle, but he was eyeing Doc.

Doc had been thinking a lot about the way the dogs had sniffed Lucas so fervently the first time they'd met him, how Sadie had whined even while he was playing with her, and the way they stuck to him like glue. He had no doubt the dogs had known something was off with Lucas.

Why the fuck didn't I?

As a medical professional, he knew it was an unfair correlation, but it didn't fucking matter. It was how he felt.

He made his way downstairs and headed outside, filling his lungs with the brisk October air. He walked down his driveway and along the narrow road until the trees gave way to grass. Then he cut along the hill, gazing out at the pastures on his way to the rehab barns. A few horses were visible in the distance. That sight usually calmed him, but today he was too angry.

Tortured.

He turned away and looked beyond the barns and pastures, over the treetops, to the mountains in the distance. They were every bit as majestic against the predawn sky as they always had, but the beauty and sense of freedom they'd held his entire life had dulled with Lucas's diagnosis.

The whole fucking world had.

When he entered the barn, the familiar smell of the horses finally brought a modicum of solace. He made his way from one stall to the next, checking the horses, giving them extra love, and taking stock of the good he'd done. He'd hoped to take the edge off his anger, but as he walked into Queenie's stall, she nickered, turning her bright eyes on him, and he felt a stab of guilt.

"Morning, sweet girl." He petted her, wondering if she'd hoped Lucas was with him.

Lucas had been visiting Queenie every time he was at the ranch. Two weekends ago, he'd been chomping at the bit to visit the healing horses with Doc in the morning, and he'd enjoyed it so much, he'd been excited to do it again. But this past weekend, after he got the news of his cancer, he hadn't wanted to.

Doc didn't blame him. Queenie had come a long way in the month since Lucas had first met her, but the rehab barn was a heart-wrenching environment, and Lucas had enough heart-wrenching things of his own to deal with.

They all did.

Queenie pushed her muzzle into Doc's chest. He scratched behind her ears, trying to muster a smile or a positive word, but he was grappling with guilt and worry.

"She knows you're troubled."

Doc was startled by Tiny's voice, but he didn't turn around. He didn't want his father to see his pain. "Isn't it a little early for you to be here?"

"I could ask you the same thing." He walked into the stall and stood beside the horse, giving himself a head-on view of Doc, studying him.

Doc studied him right back, remembering years ago, standing in a barn with his unflappable father beside a horse they weren't sure was going to make it. His father's hair had been long then, too, but dark like Dare's. His father had barely left the horse's side in the twenty-four hours since it had arrived at the ranch. Doc had asked him why, and his father had said, *The horse is scared. I'm giving her a reason to fight.* Doc hadn't understood how sitting there would do that. His father's answer was simple. *Love is the cornerstone of hope. Nurture the heart, and the mind and body will thrive.*

His father looked at the horse. "How's she doing?"

"Good." It was a pat answer, because Tiny kept close tabs on all the horses. He knew exactly how well she was doing.

"And you, son?" His dark eyes found Doc's again. "How're you holding up?"

"Fine." Knowing the horse would feel his rising tension, he walked out of the stall.

Tiny followed, closing and locking the stall. He put a hand on Doc's shoulder, applying enough pressure to set Doc's legs in motion to walk with him out the back door of the barn. He planted his boots in the dirt and crossed his arms, facing Doc head-on. "You sure about that?"

Fuck no. "As good as to be expected."

"Then you're doing better than I am. My grandson is going through a hell of a health scare, and I'm downright angry about it. He's too damn young to deal with this shit."

"You think I don't know that?" Doc barked, as if Tiny had accused him of not caring. He knew that's not what Tiny had meant, but that didn't stop his heartache from pouring out. "You think I wouldn't give my life to save him from all of this? To save Juliette from worrying?" He paced angrily. "He's a fucking *kid*. He should be thinking about kissing his girl, and Halloween costumes, and the fucking Snow Ball dance, not PET scans and treatment plans, and worrying about whether his hair is going to fall out. You should have heard the questions he asked his doctor. It broke my fucking heart."

He turned away from Tiny, tears burning his eyes. "And what fucking good am I? I can save a ranchful of horses, but I can't save my own son from going through this or the woman I love from suffering."

His father's heavy hand landed on his shoulder again, hauling him into his arms.

"I'm *fine*," Doc bit out, trying to pull away, but Tiny was a strong bastard, and he locked his arms around him.

"The hell you are. We're all about as *fine* as rabbits caught in a rattler's nest."

"*Fuck.*"

"You need to holler? I'll listen. You need to beat the hell out of something? I'll hang a bag for you to beat on. You need the open road? I'll ride with you. You got a lot on your shoulders, son, but you don't have to carry that burden alone. We're all here to help."

He knew that to his core. Not just with family and the people on the ranch, but with the brotherhood, too. Tiny had mentioned what was going on with Lucas at church last night, and every man in that room had offered to help.

"This fucking disease." He pushed free, pacing. "I thought if I knew what was coming, I could handle it. But Jesus, Tiny, he's my *kid*. My flesh and blood." He pounded his chest with his fist. "I just fucking found him, and now…"

"What're you saying, Doc? You said this is a highly curable disease even if it's later stage."

"I fucking *know*, but this is science, Tiny, not magic. We don't know what stage he has or how his cancer will respond to treatment. We don't know if his hair will fall out or if he'll get sick from treatments. Did you know being male is a higher risk factor than being female with this disease? *Yeah*. How fucking great is that?" Tears streaked down his cheeks. "And Lucas, my amazing kid, who was just coming into his own and coming to grips with me being in his life, is withdrawing from everyone. Did you notice Layla wasn't here this weekend?"

"I did."

"He said she was busy, but I *know* he's pushing her away. All I want to do is help him, and I feel so fucking useless. Last night Juliette was in tears because when we were in the hospital and the doctor mentioned the swollen lymph node, she told Lucas she'd kill him if he had mono. No amount of talking will take away her guilt, and she didn't do a damn thing wrong. She just said what hundreds of parents have probably said. How can I fix that for her? How can I make her see that Lucas didn't take the comment to heart, and neither should she?"

He dragged his forearm across his eyes, gritting out a curse.

"I know it doesn't feel like it, but you're doing exactly what they need. You're listening and reassuring. You're there for them when they need you."

Doc scrubbed a hand down his face. "It doesn't feel like enough."

"It never will."

"That's not helpful," he barked.

"It's honest, son. Before you found out Lucas was sick, did you feel like you were doing enough for them?"

That felt like a lifetime ago, but he thought about it and realized he hadn't felt like anything was enough. "No."

"That's love, son. No matter the situation, good or bad, when you love someone, you never feel like you've done enough. The only thing besides this family and the club you can count on in life is that things change, and if you love your partner, your kids, and your friends, then you're going to continue changing with them and for them. That's how you make sure they have what they need and what they don't even know they need."

Tiny stepped closer and said, "Now, as far as your boy goes, I do have one piece of advice. I don't have many regrets, but I do carry one about my brother Axel." Axel was Tiny's youngest brother. He'd passed away more than a decade ago from lung cancer. "You know he was a rough and tough Nomad who worked hard and played harder. Axel battled demons, and took them out on himself."

"Yeah. But he cleaned up his act eventually."

"That's right. But by then he was already so damaged. He lost his first love in a motorcycle accident. He was driving, but the accident wasn't his fault. The guilt though?" Tiny shook his head. "He wore it like a second skin and spent years running himself into the ground, drinking, using women, trying to outrun the pain."

"Why are you telling me this?"

"Because you know what we do here. The ways we help people."

Doc nodded, understanding dawning on him.

"I knew Axel was fucking up, and when he didn't want to talk about it, I let it go. If I'd tried harder, given him a purpose, gotten him to talk to someone, to stay here, to take part in our world, maybe things would've turned out differently. Maybe he'd've let himself be loved, and he'd've had a chance to know *his* son."

"You can't know if trying harder would've helped."

"Exactly. That's why it's my regret and why my advice to you is this. If you feel Lucas pulling away from the people he loves or the things he enjoys doing, don't let him. Fear can chew a person up and spit them out. You do everything you can to give that boy a reason to fight. You figure out the things that will make him want to take part in life. It doesn't matter if they're big or small. You get him involved, and most important-ly, you keep talking to him, even when he doesn't want to hear your voice anymore, and you never stop."

Doc thought back to those painful years after Juliette was ripped from his life, when he'd tried to push everyone away, and his parents were constantly pestering him. His mother would show up on campus and say she happened to be in the area and she'd take him to lunch, or his father and Manny and a handful of other Dark Knights would drag him out for a motorcycle ride. And his parents always needed help with something: rescuing a horse, fixing a fence, or helping with the rehab horses. He'd thought they were shorthanded on the weekends. But looking back, his father had used those times to get him talking, and his mother would often show up in the rehab barn and get him talking, too.

An idea took hold, and he looked at his father through new eyes. "Like you did for me?"

Tiny cocked a grin. "I have no idea what you're talking about, son."

"*Uh-huh.* Thanks for the talk. I needed it."

"You okay? You want to take a walk or get some coffee?"

"No, thanks. I'm afraid I need a rain check, if that's a'right. I've got something I want to take care of back at the house." As they headed around the barn, Doc decided to ask the questions he never had. "When all that went down with me and Juliette, you had to know we were sneaking off to that cabin. Why didn't you stop us?"

"Because I raised you to respect women, and she was a bright, mature young lady. I wasn't worried that you were taking advantage of her, and you two were crazy in love. That's rare, son. I wouldn't steal that from either of you."

"I'm glad you didn't, but why didn't you tell Cowboy and Dare and everyone?"

"At the time we'd thought she'd dumped you, and you were heartbroken. You didn't need your siblings giving you shit about it, and with what went down with her father, we thought the less it was talked about, the better."

As they walked up the hill, Doc couldn't stop thinking about the way his parents had been there for him without letting on that *that* was what they were doing. When they came to the road that led to his place, he said, "Hey, Pop, thanks for not giving up on me."

"Don't count your chickens," Tiny teased with a chuckle.

"RODEO, WAKE UP."

Lucas groaned, and Sadie licked his face.

Doc shook his shoulder. "Come on, buddy. Get up."

Lucas squinted at the clock as Pickles and Mighty crawled over him, tails wagging. "*Why?* It's five thirty in the freaking morning."

"I know. I need your help before school."

"For *what?*"

"To help me grab some lumber from our stockpile. We're going to build your mom porch swings."

"*Now?*"

"No. We're going to gather the wood and get set up in the workshop behind the barn. It'll take a while for us to get them built." Doc tossed him his jeans. "Hurry up. It's a surprise."

"Why not buy her one?"

"Because we're not *lazy*." That earned a smile. "And we're going to make them special."

He sat up to pull on his jeans. "Them? Like more than one?"

"Yup. We're building two since sometimes we stay at your place, and sometimes we stay here."

He grinned. "She's gonna be so happy, but you know you're spoiling her by building two, right?"

"Just setting the standard, bud. Now get dressed, brush your teeth, and meet me downstairs in five minutes. I'm going to feed the dogs."

"Wait." Lucas stood up to button his jeans. "Can I help you build both of them?"

"That's the plan."

"But how can we do it without her knowing? I'm at school all day."

"We'll be crafty. When you stay here, we'll get up before she does and put in an hour of work. The nights we go driving, we'll sneak in more time. We'll get 'em done."

"Cool."

"Meet me downstairs, and try not to be too loud. We don't want to wake your mom." He slapped his leg, letting out a soft whistle, and the dogs jumped off the bed, following him downstairs.

THE DOGS CAME along for their adventure. As they sifted through the woodpile, Doc pointed out the boards that were warped or not suitable for building and explained why, teaching Lucas as his father and grandfather had taught him. Lucas asked a dozen questions about how they were going to build the swings, how long it would take, and how Doc learned to build in the first place. As Doc shared stories of his youth, telling Lucas about his father and grandfather teaching him how to build, how to care for the animals, and how to take care of the ranch, Lucas's curiosity turned to enthusiasm, and that enthusiasm was contagious. Doc felt lighter and less stressed with every story he shared, weaving humor into them to see his boy smile.

Before they knew it, the wood was chosen and stacked neatly in the workshop, ready for them to begin their project. They couldn't yet, since Lucas had to go to school, but they headed back to the house in higher spirits. Doc wondered if his father had known Lucas wasn't the only one who needed a purpose beyond the norm, but just as the thought hit, he realized the answer.

Tiny had always known exactly what he and his siblings had needed. Doc hoped, in time, he'd learn to have Lucas's back in that way, too.

"Can you pick me up after school today?" Lucas asked. "We can tell Mom we're going driving and get started on the swing."

"I'm glad you're excited, but I don't want to lie to her, even about this."

"Then we can tell her the truth without revealing the secret."

Doc arched a brow. "How are we going to do that?"

"If we say we're going driving, it's the truth if you let me drive. And we can tell her we're working on a secret project together. That's not a lie."

"That's not a bad idea. She'd probably enjoy a little time alone tonight."

"And we can pick up dinner on the way home, so she doesn't have to worry about cooking."

"You sneaky boy. That's a great idea."

Lucas grinned. "Cool."

"You do realize that you've shown your hand, right?"

"What do you mean?"

"Now that I know you're sneaky, I'm going to have to read between the lines when you get your license and want to take the car out for a spin. I can't have you saying you're going for a ride, then taking your girl parking."

Lucas rolled his eyes. "Kids don't go parking anymore."

"Better brush up on your poker face," he said as the house came into view. Juliette was sitting on the front step, holding a coffee mug. "Your mother and I can spot *that* lie a mile away."

Lucas's boyish grin returned.

Juliette pushed to her feet, looking too damn beautiful in curve-hugging jeans and a red flannel shirt over a clingy white top that accentuated her gorgeous figure. The dogs ran to greet her. She bent to pet them, smiling at Lucas and Doc. "Where did you two sneak off to?"

"Nowhere," Lucas said with a guilty grin that made him look like he got caught with his hand in a cookie jar.

"I've got a project I needed some help with, so I got him up early and dragged his ass out with me."

"Oh? What kind of project?"

"Woodworking," Lucas said. "It's super boring, but Doc said he'll show me how to build stuff if I help."

She looked at Doc approvingly. "That's great."

"Doc said if I help him with the project for an hour after

school, he'd take me driving. Is that okay?" Lucas asked.

"We'll pick up dinner afterward, and you can have the evening to chill," Doc offered.

"This project sounds better by the minute," she said. "But, Seeley, are you sure you can get away?"

"Barring any emergencies, it should be fine."

"Okay, sure."

"*Yes!* I'm starved. I'm gonna go eat before we leave for school." He and the dogs bounded up the porch steps and into the house.

Doc swept his arm around Juliette, tugging her into a hug. "Good morning, beautiful."

"He's been so grumpy and quiet lately. What kind of spell did you cast on him this morning?"

"He's a teenager who just had his legs kicked out from under him. I gave him a distraction to focus on. It was Tiny's idea, actually."

"Remind me to thank him." She wound her arms around his neck and said, "I'll thank you properly later tonight."

As he lowered his lips toward hers, he said, "I'm holding you to that promise, darlin'."

Chapter Thirty-Two

JULIETTE HAD A grueling day taking care of one veterinary emergency after another, running from Weston to Allure to Trusty and back, only to be called to Trusty *again*. She hadn't minded all the running around when she'd first taken the job working for Jade, but lately everything was taking a toll.

She'd thought getting the good news that Lucas's cancer was Stage IA would take their worries away. Stage IA meant it was found in only one lymph node, he had no other symptoms, and it had a cure rate of ninety percent. But while they all felt a surge of relief and hope, it didn't quell their worries. Lucas was having a port put into his chest next Friday and then starting treatment a week from Monday. He would undergo two to four cycles of chemotherapy. Each cycle lasted four weeks and included two infusions. He'd have one day of chemotherapy, followed by two weeks of rest for his body to recover before having the second infusion.

It was overwhelming to think about, and even though the doctor said some people don't experience harsh side effects, there was a looming laundry list of them. Juliette knew from the things Lucas had said in the doctor's office that he was stressing out about possibly losing his hair, getting sick from treatments, and being exhausted. On top of that, he hated that he'd have to take a break from motocross and riding practice. The fact that competition season was over was no conciliation for a kid who'd planned on practicing throughout the year.

Not that Lucas was talking about any of that. He avoided talking as much as he could these days. Although he did ask if he could be homeschooled during chemotherapy. The doctor had suggested he try to maintain as normal a routine as possible. They'd agreed to take it one day at a time and see how he felt after his treatments before making that decision.

At least it was Friday. Juliette could make an early dinner and turn off her brain.

She opened the fridge and scanned the shelves, searching for the chicken she'd taken out to defrost. She rummaged through the shelves and drawers. "Where is—" *Shit.* She'd forgotten she didn't have chicken in the freezer, and she'd planned on stopping at the grocery store on the way home.

Wasn't that the icing on her frustrating *cake* of a day?

She'd wanted to make chicken Parmesan, one of Lucas's favorite dinners. He'd been so down lately. The only time his mood lightened was at bull riding or motocross practice or when he and Seeley worked on their woodworking project. Even going driving didn't excite him like it had a few weeks ago. Riding practice was canceled today because Buck had to go out of town, which pretty much guaranteed that Lucas would be in a shitty mood. Seeley was still going to swing by to take him driving, which might lighten his mood a little. She realized that would be the perfect time for her to run to the grocery store.

Boring dinner thwarted.

She heard Lucas come through the front door and the familiar *thud* of his backpack hitting the floor. She held her breath, waiting to see what kind of mood he was in.

He headed straight for the pantry.

"Hi, honey. How was school?"

He snagged a bag of chips and shrugged as he plunked down in a chair and tore open the bag. "What's for dinner?"

She closed the refrigerator, happily announcing, "Chicken Parmesan."

"Okay," he said flatly.

His phone must have vibrated, because he pulled it out of his back pocket, read a text, and set it on the table without responding to the message. She'd noticed he'd disregarded several texts lately, and that was worrying her, too. "Do you want a drink with your chips?"

"No thanks." His phone vibrated again, and he turned it face down on the table.

"Is that Layla?"

"Yeah." He shoved a chip into his mouth.

"Don't you want to respond to her?"

"Not right now."

She wanted to ask if something had happened between them, but she thought better of it and said, "Halloween is next weekend. Do you know when her mom is taking you shopping for costumes?"

"We're not doing that anymore."

Her heart sank. "*Oh*, I'm sorry."

"It's not a big deal. She's going to a party, and I don't want to go."

"Why not? You had so much fun at the last one."

"It's just not my thing."

Now she had to ask. "Did something happen between you and Layla?"

"*No.* Can't I change my mind about a stupid party?" He pushed to his feet and threw the rest of the bag of chips in the trash.

"*Lucas,*" she chided.

"What?" he snapped.

She stopped herself from lecturing him about throwing out food and said, "I know you're going through a lot right now, and I get that you don't want to talk to *me* about it, but I think you should talk to somebody."

"I'm *fine.*" He stalked out of the kitchen, and she followed him into the living room.

"Lucas, it's okay *not* to be fine. None of us are fine right now. I'm talking with a therapist, and it's helping me. I think it could help you, too."

"I don't *need* a freaking therapist," he snapped. "What's she going to do for me? Is she going to take away my cancer? Is she going to make sure my hair doesn't fall out? Or I don't feel like shit when I have chemo?"

His words severed her heart. "No," she said softer. "But she can help you deal with everything you're feeling."

"I *am* dealing with it," he said sharply.

"No, you're not. You're bottling it up, and I'm worried about you."

"*Please* stop pushing me." His chin trembled, his words shooting out fast and vehemently. "Not everyone deals with shit as well as you do. I *just* found out I have cancer, so excuse me for not feeling like going to a party and pretending everything is normal, or wanting to spill my guts to a stranger." Tears spilled from his eyes. "*Nothing* is normal. It's never gonna be normal again, and I need to deal with it *my* way. On *my* terms."

"I'm sorry, baby," she said, her own tears falling. "I didn't mean to push you. I'm just worried about you. I don't want you to get so overwhelmed you...give up."

"Give up?" His brows knitted. "Are you worried I might hurt myself or something?"

"No." She didn't even realize she'd been worried about that until now. "I don't know. I guess, maybe. This is the hardest thing any of us has ever had to deal with, and I love you so much, I don't want anything more to happen to you."

"*Mom*, I promise I'd *never* do anything like that. I'm not a quitter, and I'd never do that to *you* and Doc. I know if I ever felt that way I could come to you guys, but I don't. I just need to deal with this my way."

"Okay," she choked out. "I'm sorry." She drew him into her arms. "I'm sorry. I love you."

He returned her embrace. "I love you, too."

"I'll try not to push you anymore, as long as you know I'm here if you ever do want to talk."

He held her tighter. "I know."

Two quick knocks sounded at the door, and they both looked over as Seeley walked in. "Hey."

Lucas stepped out of her arms, wiping his eyes.

Seeley's brow furrowed. "Is everything okay?"

"It is now, I think," she said. "Lucas?"

Lucas nodded. "Yeah, we're good. And if you're worried about me offing myself, don't be. I'd never do that."

"I wasn't worried about that." He looked curiously at Juliette. "What happened?"

"I was worried about him, and I didn't realize I was pushing him so hard to talk about everything that's going on. But Lucas reminded me that we all handle things differently."

"Are you sure you're okay?" Seeley hiked a thumb over his shoulder. "Do you want me to take off and give you some time alone?"

"No, we're fine," Lucas said adamantly. "She's not going to push me, and if I need to talk to you guys, I will. I promise."

"In that case…" He cocked a grin. "Go get your hiking boots or sneakers on, throw a few clothes into a backpack, and let's get out of here. We're going on a fuck-cancer camping trip."

"What?" Juliette asked at the same time Lucas said, "We *are*?"

Lucas was *smiling*, and oh, how Juliette had needed to see that!

"Yes, we are," Seeley said. "I think we all can use a weekend away from our worries. I've got everything ready and waiting at my place."

"Cool!" Lucas said. "Where are we going camping?"

"The place my grandfather used to take me. He was your great-grandfather. I figured you might want to have something to tell your kids about when you're my age."

God, this man…

"What about our horses?" she asked.

"Cowboy's going to come by later to pick them up and take them to the ranch. Lucas, I've got an extra pup tent if you want to invite Layla. I'd be happy to talk to her parents and reassure them that you will *not* be sneaking into that pup tent."

Juliette's heart squeezed. What a perfect way to bridge the gap they'd noticed between the kids.

Lucas pushed his hands into his front pockets. "Thanks, but I'd rather it was just us."

Her stomach sank. She didn't know if he was pushing Layla away, if it only seemed like he was, or if they'd broken up and he was embarrassed to admit it, but either way, she felt a pang of sadness for him.

"You sure, bud?" Seeley asked.

Lucas nodded. "Yeah."

"Okay. Go get your stuff, and then you're driving."

"Awesome!"

As Lucas ran toward his bedroom, Seeley went to Juliette and slid his arm around her, pulling her into a kiss. "Are things really okay between you two?"

"I think so. He's a good communicator when he wants to be. He put me in my place. He's really struggling, but he wants to handle it his way. He still does not want to talk to a therapist."

"He gets that from me. I fought my mom tooth and nail after all that shit went down. We'll keep our eyes and ears open. I think he'll talk when he's ready to."

"I know. I just wish I could make it all go away."

"You're preaching to the choir, darlin'." He kissed her.

"It was really sweet of you to plan this camping trip."

"With his moods lately, I was a little worried he wouldn't want to go. I wasn't sure you'd want to, either."

"I've never been camping. I think it'll be fun."

"Good, and since Layla's not going, Lucas will have his own tent." He grabbed her butt, holding her tight against him, and like a match to kindling, her body heated. "Once he's asleep, I get you all to myself."

"Just me and the big bad wolf?" she teased. "How will I *ever* survive?"

THEY PICKED UP the camping gear at Seeley's house and hiked a long way, weaving between trees and around brush and boulders. The farther they hiked, the more Lucas opened up, sharing how great it felt to be away from everything and asking Seeley about his hikes with his grandfather. Juliette felt lighter, too, silently musing that they were like trees shedding their leaves.

Eventually they came to a lake, but while Juliette knew it had to be the same lake she and Seeley had gone to, it had taken a lot longer to get there, and nothing about their surroundings looked familiar. As they unpacked their supplies, Seeley waved a flashlight. "This is for telling scary stories by the campfire later."

"That sounds fun," she said.

"You were afraid to watch the movie *Scream* with me," Lucas said. "I don't think you'll like telling scary stories when it's pitch-black out here."

"Hey, your mom might not like horror movies, but she's still tough." Seeley put his arm around her. "Right, darlin'?"

"Darn right," she said, secretly worrying that Lucas might have a point. But there was no time to dwell on that, because the guys were getting ready to set up the tents.

They weren't those easy vinyl pop-up tents she'd seen on social media. These were canvas, and they looked ancient. They dumped the supply bags onto the ground, and out tumbled poles, connectors, ropes, stakes, and a bunch of other stuff that looked like way too much hardware for two tents.

"What is all this stuff?" Lucas asked.

"I think they're the parts we need to set up the tents." He

picked up a pole, eyeing the other parts littering the ground. "This'll be an adventure. I haven't set one of these up since I was a kid."

"I can help," she offered.

"It's okay, I got it," Seeley said.

"Then I'll help Lucas."

"I want to set up my own tent," Lucas said. "Besides, you've never even been *in* a tent."

"He's got a point," Seeley added.

"Neither has *he*," she insisted. It was like they got into the wilderness and turned into cavemen.

"Yeah, but it's in my blood," Lucas said.

How could she argue with that? Especially when he said it bursting with pride, and hearing it brought a shine to Seeley's eyes. "Whatever," she teased, and took Wynnie's advice, letting them do their thing while she collected sticks for a campfire. She got a kick out of listening to them egging each other on and racing to see who could figure out how to erect their tent first.

They ended up helping each other. When they were done, Seeley showed them how to make a campfire as the sun went down, while doling out lessons in fire safety. He taught them about checking for local fire restrictions, never lighting a fire if it's too windy or too dry, clearing the area of any flammable brush, and making sure to bring enough water, or having a natural water source nearby to put out the fire afterward. Hence, the lake.

"And when you put a campfire out, there are three steps to follow," he explained. "Douse it with water, mix the water with the embers, and as my grandfather always said, *douse it again, because Mother Nature's a finicky gal.*"

Watching Seeley teach their son the things he probably

would have taught him years ago had he been given the chance warmed her heart. He was firm but kind, making sure Lucas knew these were serious lessons.

"And when you think it's completely out, stick your bare hand in it," Seeley said. "If you feel any heat, the fire isn't out, and you need to do it all over again."

"That sounds dangerous," Juliette said. "He could get burned."

"That's why it's a three-step process," Seeley said. "Too many people do a half-ass job of putting out campfires. That's how many forest fires are started. If you know you can't walk away until you've put your bare hand in the remains, you tend to take the time to do it right. You got that, Lucas?"

Lucas gave a curt nod. "Douse it, mix it, touch it."

"Attaboy," Seeley said.

They cooked hot dogs over the fire and enjoyed the potato salad Dwight had sent along. They made s'mores and had a contest to see who could stack theirs the highest. They cracked up as they tried to fit the monstrosities into their mouths and ended up with chocolate and marshmallow all over their faces. Seeley pressed his chocolate-marshmallow lips to Juliette's cheek, getting her all sticky, which Lucas thought was hilarious.

"You think that's funny, huh?" She got up and went to kiss him.

He jumped to his feet, walking backward, waving his hands. "No way."

"Oh, there's a way!" She lunged toward him, and Lucas took off running.

She chased him, and he hollered, "Doc! Save me!" Seeley ran after them, but he grabbed Lucas from behind. "What the…? Traitor!"

Seeley laughed, and Juliette sauntered over making kissing sounds.

"No!" Lucas was cracking up, throwing his body from side to side, trying to break free. "Doc, lemme go!"

"No can do, buddy."

Juliette planted a sticky kiss on Lucas's cheek, and then she planted one on Doc's. Big mistake. He went after her, and so did Lucas. The three of them ended up tumbling to the ground in a heap of flailing limbs, bursting with laughter.

She couldn't remember the last time she or Lucas had laughed so hard.

They washed up using lake water, and now they were telling stories in the moonlight.

Seeley held the flashlight by his chin, illuminating his face in the creepiest way, and spoke in a low voice. "There used to be a club for kids eight to ten years old called Young Hikers. They'd go hiking on the weekends and stay overnight in the wilderness with a camp counselor, who was usually a kid in their twenties. One warm September night, a group of kids were hiking the Appalachian Trail, and there was a boy named Tommy, who befriended another kid named Jimmy. The boys became close, sticking together during the entire three-hour hike. Jimmy even showed him the thin leather necklace he wore as a good luck charm. Tommy had never had a good luck charm, and since his birthday was coming up, he made a mental note to ask his parents for one. That night they were staying in a log shelter that had cots along both walls and rough openings in the walls for windows, but there was no glass, and there was no door."

He paused, the sounds of crickets chirping and animals scurrying under the brush breaking the silence. "After dinner, they played some games and told ghost stories around the campfire, like we are. The counselor told a story about a werewolf that lived in the woods and ate children. That made the kids a little nervous, but he reassured them that he was only kidding, and then he told a bunch of silly stories that put them at ease. When they got up to go to bed, the counselor teasingly told them to be sure to check under their cots for the werewolf. The kids were like, *yeah, right*, laughing him off. But Tommy was still a little nervous, so Jimmy said he'd sleep in the cot next to his. They stayed up as late as they could, talking until they both fell asleep."

Seeley's gaze moved between Juliette and Lucas, who was as riveted by the story as she was. "The next morning, Tommy woke up excited to see his new friend, but Jimmy's bed was empty, his backpack was gone, and most of the kids were outside already. Tommy quickly ran outside to find Jimmy. When he didn't see him anywhere, he asked the other kids if they'd seen him. But they had no idea *who* he was talking about. It was like Jimmy didn't exist. But Tommy knew his new friend was not a figment of his imagination. The counselor told them to get their things together because they were heading out soon, so Tommy went back into the shelter with the other kids to change out of his pajamas and grab his backpack. But Jimmy didn't return to the cabin. Tommy's stomach started hurting, his nerves made him shaky, and when he picked up his backpack, the contents fell out because he'd forgotten to zip it closed. He scrambled on his hands and knees, collecting his things as the other kids ran outside with their backpacks. When he reached under Jimmy's cot, he felt scratches in the wood floor. He looked closer, and saw they were claw marks."

Seeley's voice went lower, sounding eerier. "Tommy's heart

was pounding, fear prickling his skin. He quickly looked under his cot, but there were no scratches in the floor. He ran around checking under each of the other cots, and there were no scratches under any of them. He jumped frantically to his feet to go tell the counselor, but the counselor was already standing in the doorway. Tommy ran to him, but before he could say a word, the counselor bent down, bringing his face inches from Tommy's. That's when Tommy noticed Jimmy's leather necklace hanging around the counselor's neck, and when the counselor asked what was wrong, Tommy saw that he had fangs."

"Whoa!" Lucas said, and started laughing. "That was awesome!"

Juliette's chest was so tight, it hurt. "That was terrifying. Lucas, are you going to be okay sleeping in your own tent tonight?"

"*Yes.* It was just a story." Lucas glanced at Seeley and said, "I told you she'd get scared."

Seeley laughed and put his arm around her. "Don't worry, darlin'. I can take down a werewolf."

"I'm not *scared.*" She shrugged out from under his arm. "I just wanted to make sure Lucas was okay."

"Uh-huh. Right, Mom." Lucas grinned.

"*Whatever,*" Juliette teased. "I've got a scary story for you. Keep making fun of me, and I'll go find a werewolf to gobble you up."

"A'right. That's enough," Doc said with a laugh, and handed Lucas the flashlight. "Your turn, bud. Make it a good one."

Lucas held the flashlight under his chin, eyeing them, and spoke as low and creepily as Seeley had. "One time there was a kid who fell off a bull, and he found out he had cancer."

Juliette's and Seeley's smiles plummeted.

"I'm *kidding!*" Lucas exclaimed. "But you should see your faces." He laughed.

"Lucas, that's not funny," she said, worried. "Do you want to talk about it?"

"*No.* I know having cancer isn't funny, but that kind of *was* the perfect scary story. I mean, Doc told a story about werewolves. At least mine is real."

"Buddy, your cancer isn't just a story to us," Seeley said.

"I *know.* I get it. I'm not stupid. But isn't this our fuck-cancer camping trip?" he asked. "I know you love me, and this scares the crap out of all of us, but it's *my* cancer. Can't I try to make it not so horrible in my own head? I mean, if I can't be sarcastic about it, then it's just this awful thing that I can't stand to think about. And that sucks even worse."

Juliette took a deep breath, struggling to understand and keep her emotions at bay.

Seeley held her a little tighter and said, "Did it make you feel better to joke about it?"

"*Yes,*" Lucas insisted. "But not if it gets you guys mad."

"We're not mad," Juliette said. "You caught us off guard, that's all. We worry about you."

"Mom, remember when I was sick last year and puking all over the house? I had that awful fever, and you were really worried about me, remember?"

"How could I forget? I had to clean up all the puke trails, and you could barely hold your head up, so yes, I was worried."

"I called myself the barf train, remember? As sick as I was, joking about it made me feel better. That's all I was doing. I didn't mean to worry you guys."

She remembered him calling himself the barf train and

realized she had to separate *her* feelings from what their son needed. "It's okay. You're right, honey. You're the one who has cancer, and you should be able to say the things that make it easier for you to deal with."

"Just give us a little warning next time, will ya?" Seeley pushed to his feet and ruffled Lucas's hair.

"Yeah, sure. *Wimp*," Lucas teased.

"Wimp, huh? We'll see who the wimp is when you're stuck alone in the dark." He took the flashlight from Lucas. "Time for some flashlight tag."

"Yes!" Lucas popped to his feet. "I've never played. Are there rules?"

"Yeah. No phone flashlights, and whoever is *it* counts to twenty-five before searching." Seeley handed Juliette the flashlight and said, "You're it. *Let's go, Lucas!*"

Juliette was still processing what Lucas had said, but as they took off running, their voices and Lucas's laughter cut through the air, embracing her like a gift. *A gift.* That was exactly what Lucas's shocking story was. He *was* dealing with his disease after all, and that gave her a little window of hope that he wouldn't push them, and everyone else, away completely.

Chapter Thirty-Three

"DOC, WAKE UP."

Doc startled awake at Lucas's whisper and sat up. "What's wrong?" It was Monday. Lucas had gotten a port put in his chest on Friday, and they'd stayed at Doc's for the weekend. He was starting chemotherapy in a few hours.

"Nothing," he whispered. "It's five o'clock. We gotta go work on our project."

Doc realized he was already dressed in a hoodie and jeans. "Buddy, we've got to be at the hospital in a few hours for your first treatment. Sure you don't want a break?" They'd worked on the swing a few nights last week and again Saturday and Sunday mornings. One of the swings was almost finished.

"Yes. I want to finish one in case I get too sick to help."

Doc's chest constricted. Last night when Lucas asked if they could stay at the ranch for one more night, Doc had thought he was just tired. Now he understood his real motivation. "A'right."

"I already put the dogs out. Meet me downstairs in five, and be careful not to wake Mom," Lucas whispered, and headed for the door.

Doc grinned at his parroted words as Lucas walked out, closing the door behind him.

"He's as bossy as you are," Juliette said sleepily, rolling over onto her stomach.

Lucas had been so sullen and withdrawn lately, Doc had been worried about how stressed Juliette was. He'd surprised her with a massage at a local salon yesterday and had gifted Sasha and each of the girls the same, so she wouldn't be able to beg out of it.

"I love that about him." He nuzzled against her neck. "How's my girl this morning?"

"Nervous and worried, but hopeful."

"He's going to be okay, darlin'. I can feel it." He kissed her cheek. "Love you. Try to go back to sleep. We'll meet you at the main house for breakfast at seven."

Ten minutes later, he and Lucas were heading down to the workshop with the dogs. Lucas was bundled up in a hoodie under his jacket, but Doc ran hot, and he was fine in a Henley under his flannel shirt.

November had blown into Hope Valley with brisk air, clear skies, and worried hearts. Lucas had gotten his port installed the morning of Halloween and had wanted to lie low. Doc helped run the Dark Knights' Trunk and Treat event, as he did every year, and Juliette and Lucas had stopped by, but they didn't stay long.

Lucas had been pretty quiet all weekend, which wasn't surprising, since he was on the cusp of starting treatment. Juliette offered to pick up Layla so they could spend some time together, but Lucas said she was busy. It had been weeks since they'd seen each other outside of school, but Kenny came by and hung out with him for a little while yesterday. That seemed to do him some good, but what helped the most was their family rallying around them. They kept mealtimes light and fun in the big house, spent time playing with the dogs, and kept their evenings low-key.

"How're you feeling?" Doc asked as they crossed the lawn toward the workshop.

"Scared, but don't tell Mom, okay?"

Glad Lucas was comfortable enough to tell him the truth, and wishing he could take that fear away, Doc agreed. "Are you afraid it'll hurt?"

"Not really. I read about other kids who have gone through it. They all say different things, but nobody said it hurt."

Doc had figured he'd be reading up on it online. "What did they say?"

He shrugged. "Some say they had more energy afterward because of the medicine they gave them with the chemo, and others said they went home and slept. I don't really know what I'm afraid of. I'm just scared."

Doc slung an arm over his shoulder. "It's okay to be scared. We're all a little scared, but we know you're going to be okay."

He nodded. "Ninety percent chance."

"You're going to be fine, Lucas. You might get sick and tired, and you might lose your hair, but you're going to come out the other side of this, and you're going to have a long, happy life driving me and your mom crazy."

He smiled, but he stopped walking and turned toward Doc with a tentative expression. "Do you regret finding out about me?"

"Hell no. That's something you *never* have to worry about. Why would you ask that? Do I act like it?"

"*No,*" he said quickly. "But you didn't sign up for all this worry."

Fuck. "Lucas, I love you with every ounce of my being, whether you're sick or healthy, annoying or sweet, a good guy or a total prick. None of that affects my love for you. I wouldn't trade a minute we've had for anyone or anything in this world. Do you understand that?"

Lucas nodded, his chin trembling. "I wouldn't, either."

Doc hauled him into an embrace. "You and your mom are the best things that have ever happened to me. My love for you is unconditional and unwavering. Don't ever doubt that."

Lucas nodded against his shoulder. "I love you, Doc. I'm really glad you're my dad."

Now they were both teary-eyed.

JULIETTE WAS WAITING in front of the main house at seven on the dot, and she looked as beautiful as ever in a brown suede jacket over a pretty gunmetal-blue sweater that made her eyes *pop* and what Doc had learned were her favorite jeans. The ones with a small tear under the right knee. They'd become his favorite, too, for the way they hugged her in all the right places. He whistled at her as they approached, and the dogs bounded over to her.

"You're such a flirt," she said lightly, but there was no missing the anxiousness in those baby blues.

"Only with you, darlin'. You look gorgeous." He kissed her.

"Thank you. You don't look so bad yourself." She hugged Lucas. "Morning, sweetheart. Did you have fun?"

"Yeah," Lucas said sullenly. "We're almost done with the

first part of the project."

"That's great. How're you feeling?" Her gaze trailed over his face, and Doc knew she could see the worry in his eyes, too.

"Hungry."

"I bet," she said.

"Let's go eat." Doc pulled the door open, and the dogs and Lucas ran inside. He and Juliette followed them in.

When he took Juliette's hand, she whispered, "Is he okay?"

"He will be."

As Lucas walked into the dining area with his four-legged sidekicks, applause broke out, and everyone pushed to their feet, whistling and shouting, "You've got this!" and "We're pulling for you!" Stunned, Doc took in the large banner hanging across the back wall that read GOOD LUCK, RODEO! and tried to calm the dogs as his family, their employees, and even the clients Lucas had met converged on Lucas with hugs and well-wishes.

Juliette turned to Doc and said, "Did you do this?"

"No. I'm as surprised as you are." He glanced at his parents, waiting for their turn to hug Lucas, watching him with so much love, it emanated off them. Tiny looked over and winked, his words coming back to Doc. *Love is the cornerstone of hope.*

"First bull riding, and now this? Talk about street cred," Birdie said, and hugged Lucas tight. "You're the toughest kid I know."

"Yeah, he is." Dare hugged him. "You're going to kick cancer's ass, dude."

"Damn right he is," Cowboy said, wrapping his thick arms around Lucas's lanky body. "This is tough, Rodeo, but you're tougher."

"You're going to crush it," Sasha said, tugging Lucas, who was grinning and damp eyed, into her arms. "You've got this,

Lucas." Gus hugged his legs and said, "I love you. The medicine's gonna make you better."

"Love you, too, buddy," Lucas choked out as Ezra put his arms around all three of them and said, "We love you, Rodeo. I'm here if you want to talk."

Doc got choked up as Lucas was passed from one caring person to the next, and then those loving arms found their way to Juliette, and she was surrounded by words of encouragement. Eventually, that support made its way to Doc.

Tiny and Wynnie were the last to embrace them, and as Lucas filled a plate at the breakfast buffet, Juliette stepped out of Tiny's arms and said, "Thank you. I can't imagine going through any of this without Seeley and all of you. We are so lucky to be loved by you and all these wonderful people."

"We're the lucky ones, darlin'," Tiny said.

"We thank our lucky stars every day that you and Lucas are back where you belong," Wynnie said.

Doc slid his arm around Juliette, hugging her against his side, and said, "They'll never be alone again."

Chapter Thirty-Four

LUCAS HADN'T BEEN too nervous when they first arrived at the hospital, but by the time he had his pre-treatment blood drawn and they finally got to the infusion room, he was trembling. The nurse was wonderfully patient, and she explained everything step by step, which helped. Lucas handled it like a champ, but Juliette couldn't claim the same.

Seeing the son she'd spent her life trying to protect hooked up to an IV in a fight against a disease they'd never seen coming brought a vast range of emotions, from grief to anger and everything in between. But none was stronger than the hope in her heart. It helped that Seeley was there with them, making sure they were comfortable, offering to get them food and drinks, and trying to distract them, and probably himself, from what they were feeling. He kept the conversations light and positive, suggesting they plan another camping trip for the spring and talking about the upcoming holidays.

Lucas was quiet on the way home, and when they pulled up in front of their house, Juliette swore there was a collective sigh of relief.

"One treatment down," she said as they climbed out of

Seeley's truck. She noticed Seeley and Lucas exchanging a glance she couldn't read. "What?"

"What, *what?*" Lucas snapped.

"Never mind," she said, wondering if she was seeing things. "Long morning."

Seeley grabbed the bags they'd brought to his house for the weekend and slung his arm over her shoulder. "Now you can relax."

"We all can," she said as they headed up to the house.

Her thoughts stumbled when they reached the porch. Hanging from the rafters was a gorgeous, and enormous, porch swing, with a blue cushion along the seat and several colorful throw pillows. "What is *that?*"

"It's your new porch swing," Seeley said. "Cowboy and Dare set it up while we were at the hospital."

"It's *gorgeous*, but it's more like a swinging couch," she said with awe. "I've never seen one so big."

"We made it extra-long and deep so we could all fit," Seeley said. "We're going to make one for my place, too."

"You guys *made* it?" She looked at them with disbelief. "This is what you've been working on?"

"It was Doc's idea," Lucas said flatly.

"But it was Lucas's design, and he worked really hard to get it done for you today," Seeley said.

"Lucas…?" she said with utter astonishment.

He pushed his hands into his pockets, his shoulders rising in a shrug, a smile finally curving his lips. "I know how hard all of this is for you. I wanted you to have something to be happy about when we got home."

"Oh, sweetheart." Tears sprang to her eyes. With all he was going through, he was worried about *her* happiness? "I love it, but knowing you're getting the treatment you need to be healthy is the only gift I need to be happy." She hugged him. "I love you so much. Thank you."

"I love you, too. I'm kind of tired. I'm going to lie down for a while."

"You don't want to try out the swing first?" she asked.

He shook his head. "Maybe later. Hey, Doc, would it be too much trouble for you to bring the dogs over?"

"I'll be happy to. I need to check on the horses anyway."

"Thanks."

"Let me know if you need anything, honey," Juliette said as Lucas headed inside. She wrapped her arms around Seeley, smiling up at him. "You guys are sneaky. Thank you for thinking of me."

"I'm always thinking of you, but the swing was also for Lucas. Tiny suggested he might need a purpose. Something to focus on other than treatments, and he was right."

Her heart took another hit. "Well, Dr. Whiskey, he's seemed so depressed lately, the last few weeks have rarely pulled a smile from him, and he just gifted us one. I think it was exactly what he needed today, too."

"And that smile on your face tells me it was what you needed, too."

She went up on her toes and kissed him. "Will you try it out with me?"

"I thought you'd never ask."

They climbed the porch steps, and he put his arm around her as they sank into the cushions. She rested her head on the front of his shoulder and put her hand on his leg with a sigh. "This brings back memories."

"Try to keep your hands to yourself this time," he teased. "I wouldn't want Lucas to catch you feeling me up."

"Fine. How about my lips?" She got up and straddled his

lap, smiling down at him.

Heat flared in his eyes, and he threaded his fingers into her hair, drawing her lips closer to his. "I think you mean *my* lips, darlin'." He nipped at her lower lip, giving it a gentle tug with his teeth, sending desire skittering through her. "And I *never* want you to keep them to yourself."

AFTER SEELEY LEFT to pick up the dogs, Juliette answered the group texts that had come in from his family, updating them on how the treatment had gone and sharing that Lucas was resting. Then she went inside and checked on him.

He'd dozed off, so she brought a blanket outside and snuggled under it with her feet tucked beside her on the swing like she used to. She sat there for a long time, thinking about not only the last few months, but her life and all that she'd been through. It still hurt to think about how all the people she should have been able to trust had deceived her. But she'd made the right decision not going after her father. It would have upended their lives even more, and none of them needed that.

She looked out at the barn, remembering how her grandmother had taught her about horses. Hazel was a tough lady. "*I miss you,*" Juliette whispered. "I wish you were here to see how brave Lucas is and to see me and Seeley back together after all this time. I'm scared for Lucas but hopeful. I'm sad for what he's going through, but I'm happy our family is finally together. You should see him with Seeley, Gram. Seeley is an amazing father, and I think Lucas needed him more than I ever knew."

She drew in a deep breath. "These last several weeks were

harder than everything I ever went through with my parents put together. I don't think I could've gotten through them if you hadn't taught me to be strong. Who am I kidding? I couldn't have gotten through the last sixteen years without you telling me I could do it. I wish I'd visited you more often. I hate that I let my fear of my father keep me away. I hope you know how much I love you and how much I appreciate everything you have ever done for me."

A gust of wind swept over her cheeks like a caress, and she closed her eyes, her grandmother's voice tiptoeing through her mind. *I love you, too, Juliegirl.* She smiled into the breeze, goose bumps rising on her arms. "I love you, Gram."

The sound of a horse galloping brought her eyes open, and she saw Layla riding toward the house from one of the trails. She pushed to her feet, hoping Lucas had reached out to her. She waved to Layla and heard a truck pulling down the driveway. It was Seeley.

Juliette looked up at the sky. "Why do I feel like you had a hand in this?"

Seeley climbed out of the truck, and the dogs bounded toward the house. She loved them up as Seeley strode toward her with a duffel over one shoulder, carrying a deep, covered crock. Layla slowed her horse to a walk, and the dogs ran toward her.

Seeley whistled, commanding, "*Here,*" and the dogs doubled back to him. He gave Juliette a curious look that she knew was about Layla's arrival.

She tried to silently relay that she was just as curious.

He nodded and held up the crock. "Dwight made Lucas chicken and dumplings."

"That was nice of him." She came off the porch as Layla

dismounted. "Hi, Layla."

"Hi, Dr. C. Hi, Doc," she said sweetly, looking cute in jeans, a tan sweater, and a down vest. "How's Lucas?"

"He's doing well, resting," Juliette said.

"Would it be okay if I talked to him for a minute?" she asked.

"He's in his room. Let me make sure he's up to company," Juliette said. "You can come in and wait inside."

They headed inside with the dogs and found Lucas coming out of the hall into the living room. Sadie ran to him, but Seeley kept Mighty and Pickles by his side.

Lucas looked tired, but when he saw Layla, he looked a little guilty, too.

"Hi," Layla said nervously. "I just came by to talk to you for a minute."

"Is that okay, Lucas?" Juliette asked. "If you're not up to it—"

"It's fine," he interrupted, petting Sadie.

"Jule." Seeley nodded toward the kitchen. "Help me find a place for this?"

"Sure." She followed him and the dogs into the kitchen.

Seeley set the crock on the counter, told the dogs to sit and stay, and whispered, "Any idea what's up with them?"

Before she could answer, Lucas's voice cut through the silence. "What are you doing here?"

Juliette put her finger over her lips, shushing Seeley. She knew she shouldn't eavesdrop, but she couldn't help it.

"Checking on you. I'm worried about you. What do you think I'm doing here?" Layla snapped. "You haven't answered my texts in over a week, and you're avoiding me at school. If you don't like me anymore, and you don't want to go to the dance, then tell me to my face." Her voice escalated. "Don't hide behind your stupid phone or pretend you don't see me at the other end of the hall. You told me your heart was mine *forever*. If you didn't mean it, that's *fine*."

Juliette grabbed Seeley's arm, aching for them.

"But *I* meant it when I gave you mine," Layla fumed. "If you're pushing me away because you're sick and you're scared, *don't*. I want to be with you whether you're sick or not. If you only have a week or a month or a year, I want to spend it *with* you. So *please* just be honest. Look me in my eyes and tell me if you're done with me, and I'll give you your mom's necklace back." There was a beat of silence. "Here. Take it."

"Holy shit," Seeley whispered. "He gave her our necklace?"

Juliette shushed him again. She peeked around the corner and saw Layla holding out her hand with the necklace in her palm.

"I don't want it back," Lucas said angrily. "When a Whiskey gives his heart away, it's forever."

Seeley put his arm around Juliette, drawing her back against his chest, and kissed the top of her head.

"Then what *do* you want?" Layla asked a little softer.

"*You*," Lucas snapped. "*Us*. The way we were. Without cancer, or a port in my chest. I just want to be a normal kid and hang out with you without worrying about if I'm going to feel too sick or too tired to hang out. You don't need that shit in your life. You can have any guy you want. It's not fair for you to be with someone like me."

"My cousin was right. Boys are stupid," Layla said exasperatedly. "You're the only someone I want, Lucas. I get that having cancer sucks, but I'm not going anywhere. I read about what you have, and you're going to get better. But if you get sicker along the way, you can rest your head in my lap, and if you're tired, you can sleep and we'll see each other when you're not too tired. I'm made from hearty stock, whether I'm a Braden by blood or not. And if you think I'll get bored or whatever, then know *this*. I'd rather have time to get bored with the boy I love than no time with him at all."

She thrust her palm with the necklace in it toward him. "It's your call. What's it going to be?"

Juliette held her breath as Lucas looked at the necklace.

His brows slanted, his face a mask of pain. "It's not even a question for me." He took the necklace out of her hand, his head bowed, eyes downcast.

Layla's shoulders sank, a pained sound falling from her lips.

Tears welled in Juliette's eyes, and Seeley held her tighter.

"I'm sorry," Lucas said quietly but emphatically, and finally met her gaze. "I never meant to hurt you." He lifted the necklace between his finger and thumb, the charm dangling. He took the chain in both hands, ducking his head a little as he held it open wider, to put it on, but then he slipped it over Layla's head and said, "Fair warning, I might lose my hair."

She half laughed, half cried, and threw her arms around him. "You'll still be the hottest boy in school."

"*Yay!*" Juliette exclaimed, and the kids spun around, wide eyed. She slapped her hand over her mouth. "Ohmygod. I'm sorry. I didn't mean to eavesdrop."

"Yes, she did," Seeley said at the same time Lucas said, "Yes you did."

Layla laughed, and then embarrassment pinked up her cheeks. "I can't believe you heard all of that. I'm sorry for raising my voice."

"I've already forgotten it," Juliette said, wiping her tears.

"I haven't," Seeley said. "It was beautiful, Layla. Lucas is a lucky guy."

"I am lucky." Lucas laced his fingers with Layla's and said,

"But she did call me stupid."

"You were being stupid," Layla insisted.

Seeley laughed. "That's a rite of passage, buddy. All teenagers are stupid sometimes. Girls and boys."

"It's true," Juliette said. "That's why God makes teenagers cute, so when your egos get in the way, there's a *little* something keeping your friends close."

"Now that the romantic crisis is over, is anyone hungry?" Seeley asked.

"I am," Lucas said. "Want to stay for dinner, Layla?"

She nodded. "But I have to be home before dark."

"Am I allowed to ride?" Lucas asked.

"I don't think you should tonight," Juliette said. "In case you get tired or feel bad while you're out."

"It's okay. I can ride by myself," Layla said.

"I'll make sure she gets home safe, buddy," Seeley offered.

As they headed into the kitchen, Lucas said, "Mom, can I talk to you for a sec?"

"Of course," she said.

"Layla, I'll be right in," Lucas said.

"Come on, Layla. I could use your help," Seeley said.

Juliette waited until Layla and Seeley were in the kitchen to ask, "Are you okay?"

"Yeah, but are you mad about the necklace?"

Boy, her heart was taking a beating today. "No, honey. It's your necklace. You can do whatever you want with it. I know how much it means to you, and now I know how much Layla means to you, too."

His lips quirked into a slightly bashful smile, but it only lasted a second before he said, "Do you think Doc is mad?"

"No. I know he's not. If there's one thing you can count on with us, it's that we'll never tell you not to follow your heart."

Chapter Thirty-Five

DOC STARTED UP Tiny's old truck and turned on the heat, so it would be warm when he and Lucas went driving. As he climbed out of the truck, a gust of wind sent a flurry of leaves sweeping across the ground and spiraling into the air. He and Lucas had finished building the second swing, and they'd hung it on his porch two days ago. It swayed on its chains as he climbed the front steps. He could hardly believe it was Thanksgiving already. Doc always enjoyed holidays with his family, but this year he had more to be grateful for than ever before.

As he walked through his front door, one of the people he was most thankful for was coming out of the kitchen, her hair piled on her head in a messy bun, a few sexy tendrils framing her beautiful face. Her burgundy sweater hung off one shoulder, showing a hint of the black tank top she wore beneath it, and her black leggings left nothing to his imagination.

"Aren't you a vision of gorgeousness?" He drew her into his arms and kissed her. The heels on her ankle boots brought her lips that much closer to his. "You got a hot date while Lucas and I are out driving?"

She wound her arms around him. "No. I'm going to Sasha's

to bake pies with the girls."

"Won't you get your pretty sweater dirty?"

"I'll take it off while we're baking. I wanted to be ready in case we're running late. You're meeting us there, right?" They were having dinner with everyone in the main house in a few hours.

"Yeah."

The last few weeks had been a roller coaster of highs and lows. A few days after Lucas's first treatment, he'd been hit with the fatigue they'd been warned about. It had lasted a few days, but even when it lifted, he wasn't his old self. He'd had his second treatment a week and a half ago, and within days he was tired, moody, and uninterested in eating. He complained of a metallic taste in his mouth. He'd begged out of school at the end of last week and had asked if they could stay at Doc's house from now on since he was off school all week for the holiday break. They'd moved the horses and had settled in.

Juliette ran her fingers down the front of Doc's cut. "Why are you wearing this?"

"I'm teaching Lucas about representing the club."

"He has *years* before he prospects."

"It's never too early to learn." He kissed her again.

"I'm excited for his surprise," she said. "I hope it perks him up."

Lucas's hair had started falling out, and he'd been withdrawing again. Without the swing or riding to distract him, they'd decided to surprise him with Doc's old truck. Doc had planned on giving it to him on his sixteenth birthday, but given that he needed a new project and wanted to learn to work on old cars, now seemed the perfect time.

But Doc had another surprise in store for him. One he

hadn't shared with Juliette and that he hoped would help Lucas more than anything material ever could.

"I hope so, too." He kissed her again, then called upstairs, "Almost ready, Rodeo?"

Lucas came out of his bedroom wearing a baseball cap. "I changed my mind. I don't want to go driving today."

Doc and Juliette exchanged a knowing glance. They'd known he might say that. "Come on, bud. It'll be good to get out of the house."

"I'm getting out later for Thanksgiving dinner," he complained.

Earlier he'd tried to get out of going to dinner tonight. Nothing tasted good to him anymore, and he'd lost weight. Doc had a feeling he was self-conscious about that, too.

"A'right. If you don't want to pick out a color for Rebel to paint your truck, I guess I'll let him know." Doc walked away.

"Wait! What?" Lucas ran downstairs. "What truck?"

"It's just my old truck. It's not a big deal."

"Are you kidding?" Lucas asked. "Mom, is he kidding?"

"No, he's not. You're getting your license in the spring, and we know you want to learn to work on cars and trucks. We thought you might enjoy working on your own."

"We're going to set it up in Dare's garage over the winter," Doc explained. "He and I will teach you how to work on it."

"But it was Tiny's," Lucas said incredulously. "You said you'd never get rid of it."

"I'm not getting rid of it. I'm giving it to my son."

His eyes brightened. "Seriously? Like, *for real*?"

"For real," Doc said with a laugh.

"I can't believe this!" He hugged each of them. "Thank you!"

"Before you get too carried away, there're some things you need to know," Doc said. "That truck is not to be driven like a hot rod. It's part of Tiny's legacy, and I hope you'll treat it as such."

"I *will*. I promise. It was yours. That means as much to me as it does that it was Tiny's."

Juliette put her hand over her heart. "That makes me so happy."

"That makes two of us," Doc said, overwhelmed by Lucas's sentiment.

"Can we still go see Rebel?" Lucas asked.

"The truck's already warming up."

LUCAS SPENT AN hour looking through colors with Rebel in the office of his auto shop before finally announcing, "I know what I want."

"Great. What color?" Doc asked.

The rumble and roar of motorcycles sounded outside, drawing Lucas's attention.

"That sounds like a hundred bikes," Lucas said with awe. "Is it always like this around here?"

"No," Rebel said. "Something must be going on."

"Like what?" Lucas's eyes widened. "Turf war?"

Rebel laughed. "You've been watching too much TV, Rodeo."

"We'd've gotten a heads-up if things were going south like that," Doc explained. "We'll check it out in a minute. Let's finish up with Rebel first. What colors did you choose?"

"The same colors it is now," Lucas said proudly.

Doc cocked a brow. "You sure you don't want something different?"

"I thought I might, but black and silver are cool, and I like that it'll be the same as it was for you and Tiny."

"Black and silver it is." Doc heard more motorcycles rolling in.

"Good choice. Keep it classic," Rebel said. "I hear your old man and Dare are going to show you how to fix 'er up."

"They are," Lucas said excitedly.

"Dare knows what he's doing." He hiked a thumb at Doc. "He's better with horses than cars, but he won't steer you wrong."

Doc scoffed, and Lucas smiled.

"I suggest we wait to paint it until you're done with your overhaul," Rebel said. "You don't want to accidentally nick your new paint job."

"Good idea," Lucas said.

"Let me know when you're ready, and I'll get the paint ordered," Rebel suggested.

"Sounds good." Doc put a hand on Lucas's shoulder. "Let's see what's going on next door."

They headed outside and over to the entrance to the clubhouse. As Rebel reached for the door, Lucas said, "I guess I'll wait out here."

"Nah. You're coming in with us," Doc said.

Lucas looked confused. "But you said you don't let kids in the clubhouse, and Kenny said only hangarounds or prospects are allowed inside."

"He's right." Doc put his arm around Lucas's shoulder. "But you're the reason we're here."

"What do you mean?" Lucas asked.

"You'll see," Doc said, and they followed Rebel inside.

Nearly every seat was taken by Dark Knights wearing black leather cuts, and they all turned to look as Doc and Lucas walked in. Tiny, Cowboy, and Dare stood at the front of the room, arms crossed, Tiny's fingers drumming.

As Rebel went to take a seat, Lucas whispered, "Am I in trouble?"

"No. Just be respectful."

Lucas stood a little taller, drawing his shoulders back.

Tiny looked at Doc, giving him a single curt nod.

"Let's go," Doc said quietly, keeping his arm around Lucas's shoulder as they made their way to the front of the room. He could tell by how rigid Lucas was that he was nervous, but that was okay. Learning respect for the club started now.

When they reached the front of the room, he slipped his arm off Lucas, and they both faced Tiny.

"Doc, Rodeo," Tiny said with a nod to each.

Doc nodded. "Tiny."

Lucas mimicked the motion and said, "Sir."

Tiny's beard twitched, and Doc knew he was suppressing a smile, as Doc was. His father set a serious stare on Lucas and said, "Doc tells me you're starting to lose your hair, and you don't like it."

"Yes, sir. I hate it."

"I can't say I'd be happy about it, either. You've got great hair, son. Just like your old man."

"Yes, sir. My girlfriend likes it," he said, earning chuckles from the guys.

"My old lady likes my hair, too," Tiny said. "What bothers you most about losing your hair?"

Lucas shrugged and looked down at his feet. "I don't want to be bald, and look different from everyone else."

Tiny gave a nearly imperceptible nod to Doc.

"Want to know what pisses me off about it?" Doc asked.

Lucas met Doc's gaze. "I didn't know you were pissed off about it."

"Everything about this disease pisses me off," Doc admitted. "You're my son. I would burn down the world for you. I'd give my own life for you, and I can't get my hands on this fucking disease to tear it to shreds. And now it's taking one more thing from you that I can't stop, and it's making you want to hide away, uncomfortable in your own skin. So yeah, I'm pissed."

Lucas's chin trembled, but he set his jaw, once again showing how unbelievably strong he was.

"We would all burn down the world for you, Rodeo," Tiny added. "Your uncles." He glanced at Cowboy and Dare, who nodded in confirmation. "And every brother in this room."

Collective "That's rights" and "Hell yeahs" rang out from the other men.

Lucas swallowed hard.

"You see, Rodeo," Tiny said. "In this family, we have a saying. Nobody rides alone."

Tiny pulled off his bandanna and tossed it on the table as Dare and Cowboy grabbed two chairs from behind the table and placed them in front of Doc and Tiny. Tiny pulled a pair of scissors and an electric clipper from his back pocket and handed them to Lucas.

"What are these for?" Lucas asked.

"If you're losing your hair, we're losing ours," Tiny said, and he and Doc sat down.

Lucas stared at the clipper. "You want me to shave your

heads? You don't have to do this," he said urgently. "Do Wynnie and my mom know you're doing this?"

"We don't need their permission," Tiny said.

"They'll be *pissed*," Lucas said.

"I guess we'll find out if your mom loves me for more than my hair," Doc teased, and more chuckles rang out.

"Wynnie can still run her fingers through my beard," Tiny said, inciting more laughter. "Now get to it, Rodeo."

"*Doc*," Lucas pleaded.

"You're not going to change our minds, bud. This is called solidarity."

Lucas groaned. "What if I mess up?"

"You won't," Dare said as he and Cowboy stepped beside Lucas. "I set the clipper to leave stubble. Just start at the front, and run the clipper over the top of their heads and down the back."

As Lucas stepped behind Doc, Cowboy said, "When you're in the clubhouse, you start with the president of the club out of respect."

"Sorry." Lucas moved behind Tiny.

Ezra got up and started videoing, as Doc had asked him to earlier that morning.

"I don't know about this, Tiny. When's the last time you cut your hair?" Lucas asked.

"I don't remember," Tiny said. "It's been long ever since I was a kid. I just trim the ends."

"Are you *one hundred percent* sure you want me to do this?" Lucas asked.

"I've never been more certain of anything in my life, son," Tiny said. "I'm donating my hair to a company that makes wigs for kids with cancer."

"You *are?*" Lucas asked, his voice cracking.

"That's right. You should feel good doing this," Tiny said.

"You need to cut off his ponytail first," Dare said. "And since he's donating it, we want to get as much as possible, so give me a minute." He took the elastic band that held Tiny's hair in a ponytail off and resituated the ponytail at the center of his head. "Now hold it up with one hand, and cut with the other as close to his skull as you can."

"I hope Wynnie forgives me," Lucas said, and everyone laughed. With nervous hands and his uncles by his side, he cut off Tiny's ponytail and handed it to him.

Tiny's fist shot up in the air, waving his mane.

The room exploded with cheers.

As Lucas shaved Tiny's head, Ezra, Hyde, and Taz started chanting, "*Let's go, Rodeo. Let's go, Rodeo,*" and all the guys joined in, cheering him on as he shaved Doc's head, too.

When he was done, Tiny and Doc pushed to their feet, running their hands over their newly naked heads, and more cheers rang out. Doc pulled Lucas into a hug. "You did good, buddy."

"Holy shit. Tiny has a neck," Dare said.

"Did you guys know his ears were that big?" Cowboy joked, and laughter rang out.

Tiny laughed and said, "You wanna see how big my fist is?"

Cowboy and Dare tossed their cowboy hats on the table and sat in the chairs, and more chants rang out as Lucas shaved their heads. When he was done, Dare brought out a box of clippers and said, "Who's next?"

Every man in the room rose to his feet, offering to go next. Doc had never felt prouder to be a member of the club than right at that moment. As they formed two lines, Lucas's jaw dropped, and he said, "Are you guys making them do this?"

"No. I told them I was doing it, and they all jumped on board," Doc explained. "Dwight wanted to be here to support you, even though he's got nothing to shave off, but he had to cook Thanksgiving dinner."

"So they're all just doing it for *me*?" Lucas asked.

"That's called brotherhood," Tiny added. "Nobody outside of these four walls knows what's going on in here. Not Billie or Sully or Sasha or any of the other guys' families. It's not anyone else's business. They're showing solidarity for a future member."

Lucas beamed. He threw his shoulders back and held the clipper out for Doc. "Will you shave my head?"

"It would be my honor."

ON THE WAY home, Doc said, "I need to check on a new rescue and the rehab horses, but I'll drop you off so you can shower and get ready for dinner." Juliette had texted earlier to say they'd had a rescue come in, but not to worry, she was handling it. "I'll try to be quick so we're not late meeting the guys." They'd all agreed to meet in front of the main house so they could walk into dinner together and surprise everyone with what they'd done.

"Can I go with you?" Lucas asked.

He hadn't joined Doc when he did rounds on rescues or rehab horses since receiving his diagnosis. "Are you sure you want to do that, buddy?"

"Mm-hm. I'm realizing that sick horses need even more love than well horses."

"They sure do. Are you sure it won't make you sad?"

"It *will* make me sad, but it'll make them happy, and the truth is, it made me sad before I knew I had cancer. I stopped because I didn't think I could handle it. But that was selfish."

"No, it wasn't. It was an act of self-care. Everyone has their limits, and I'm glad you know yours. I don't want you to do anything that makes you unhappy."

"I want to see them. I can handle it now."

And he did. Beautifully.

What a joy it was to see Lucas showering the healing horses with love again. He talked about the horses as they drove home to get ready for dinner, and it was easy to see that spending time with them had not only helped the horses but also helped Lucas gain a little freedom from his fears. Doc loved seeing Lucas taking control of the aspects of his life he could control.

The dogs bounded downstairs with Lucas after his shower. He looked handsome in a navy sweater and jeans, and he looked tired, but he also looked so damn happy, Doc knew today was a day neither of them would ever forget.

"Wow, you look great." Doc ran his hand over Lucas's head. "How does it feel?"

"It's gonna take some getting used to, but Layla said I look hot." Lucas had taken dozens of pictures, and selfies with Doc and Tiny and all the guys and had sent a number of them while they were still at the clubhouse.

"Of course. I mean, you look like me and your mom, and there's nothing better than that." He laughed. "Seriously though, hotness has nothing to do with hair or bone structure or eye color. Hotness comes from who you are on the inside resonating to the outside. I just want you to know, I understand all these changes are hard, and your mom and I couldn't be prouder of you for the way you're handling things."

"Thanks. I'd be really messed up without you and Mom and everyone else helping me through it."

"Support helps, but you're stronger than you think, Rodeo. There's nothing you can't handle. We'd better get going. We don't want to keep the guys waiting."

As they grabbed their coats, Lucas said, "I still can't believe Gus showed up and got his head shaved." Ezra's father, Pep, had brought Gus to the clubhouse when they'd almost finished with everyone else. Ezra had gotten both of them on video, while Dare and Tiny shaved their heads. "You weren't kidding when you said your family never leaves anyone out. Pep said he'll be at dinner tonight, too."

"That's right. He and Ezra had a lot of rough years, but things are better now." As they headed out, Doc handed him the keys.

"We're not walking?"

They'd had a big day, and Doc knew Lucas might putter out early, but he wasn't about to say that. "It'll be cold and dark after dinner. I'm pretty sure your mom would rather we drove."

When they got to the main house, Gus ran over to them. "Hurry! I can't wait to see Sugar's face when she sees my hair!"

Doc picked him up and kissed his cheek. "You and Lucas are going to be stealing hearts and taking names."

"I don't want anybody's heart but my Sugar's," Gus exclaimed.

"And I'm good with Layla's," Lucas said.

"I wanna see Layla!" Gus said, wriggling out of Doc's hands as they joined Tiny, Dare, Cowboy, Ezra, Rebel, Taz, and Hyde. "Is she coming to dinner?"

"Not tonight. She's with her family," Lucas said. "But maybe I'll see if she can come over tomorrow."

"Are we ready to do this?" Tiny asked. He had his bandanna tied around his head again.

"Yeah. I hope the girls don't get mad at everyone," Lucas said.

"If they do, we'll tell them to talk to you," Dare joked.

"I'll hide behind Doc," Lucas said, and they all laughed as they filed through the door.

When they entered the dining area, Tiny threw his hands up and said, "Happy Thanksgiving!"

There was a collective gasp. Birdie squealed and ran over, leading the pack, sparking a flurry of commotion as the women all talked at once with surprise and delight.

"*Mom*, look at Dad!" Birdie yanked Tiny down by the front of his shirt and ran her hand over his head. "I love this!" She grabbed Lucas next, tugging him down, too. "You look badass! Layla better watch out. There might be a stampede of girls at your next competition."

As his mother and the girls fawned over Lucas and Gus and the rest of the guys, Doc's attention remained locked on Juliette, standing back with tears in her eyes and a hand covering her mouth. He went to her. "You okay, darlin'?"

"*No*," she said with a laugh, tears streaking her cheeks. "You did this for him, didn't you?"

"There's nothing I wouldn't do for him, but I just announced what I was doing, and the guys made their own decisions. The whole club took part."

"Seeley, look how happy he is." Lucas was taking a selfie with Wynnie, Tiny, and Gus. "I can't even..." She threw her arms around Doc. "I love you so much."

"That's good, because I was a little worried you only liked

me for my hair."

She kissed him, and as she stepped back, Lucas didn't just walk over. He *swaggered*, which was new, and said, "What do you think, Mom?"

She rubbed the top of his head, and then she caressed his cheek and said, "I'm wondering where my baby boy went. You look so grown-up and handsome and so much like Seeley, it takes my breath away."

"Wait until you see me when I'm a Dark Knight wearing my cut. Right, Doc?"

"Heck yeah." He high-fived him.

Juliette covered her face and said, "What have I gotten myself into?"

Doc put his arms around their shoulders as they headed for a table and said, "Don't overthink it, darlin'. There's no getting out now."

Chapter Thirty-Six

JULIETTE AWOKE EARLY Monday morning to Seeley's harsh whispers.

"Jesus. No fucking way. Bring her here." He was sitting on the edge of the bed talking on the phone, his body rigid.

She glanced at the clock, scooching closer to him. It wasn't quite five. She put her hand on his back, rubbing gently. He looked at her, his face a mask of distress as he mouthed, *Sorry.*

She sat up, whispering, "It's okay," and kissed his shoulder.

"Yeah," he said into the phone. "I'll meet her at the clinic. Thanks, man."

As he ended the call, she said, "Did something happen?"

"Some asshole's dogs attacked his horse, and he dumped the horse in a field." He pushed to his feet, pacing angrily as he navigated on his phone. "I've got to call the service and see who's filling in for Hannah while she's away."

Juliette climbed out of bed. "I've got a few hours before Lucas has to be at the hospital for his treatment. I'll help you."

"They said the horse is a fucking mess, darlin'," he said sharply. "You don't need to see that. You should get some sleep."

"*Excuse* me?" She knew he was tired. They all were. They'd had a wonderful, low-key weekend, but they hadn't slept well in weeks. It probably didn't help that they still couldn't keep their hands off each other, and they'd stayed up late last night making love. Although in a broader, more important sense, being intimate helped them both tremendously. They worked hard and worried twenty-four-seven. They were each other's sounding boards *and* comfort zones, and sometimes, like now, as she reminded herself to use a kinder tone, they had to work harder to find that balance. But when they came together, everything else ceased to exist, and there was only the two of them and the love they shared.

"I'm a vet, Seeley. There's nothing I haven't seen."

"I didn't mean it like that. I just...*fuck*. I'm sorry." He scrubbed a hand down his face, looking at her apologetically. "I'm tired and edgy, and I was trying to protect you. But you're right. You don't need that kind of protecting."

"It's hard to turn off those protective instincts, isn't it?"

"Harder than you know. Sorry, darlin'." He pulled her into a hug. "I kept you up late last night, and I figured you'd want to rest."

"And give up a chance to live out my teenage dream of working with you to save horses?" She smiled up at him. "No way, Whiskey."

"No wonder I love you." He kissed her, then smacked her butt. "Now, get your pretty little ass in gear. We've got to go. I'll text Tiny, and we can leave a note for Lucas."

They quickly dressed, and she pulled her hair up in a ponytail as they headed downstairs. They found Lucas standing at the kitchen island eating, with all three dogs sitting at his feet. He hadn't eaten much dinner last night.

"You're up early," she said, eyeing his plate. "Are those *pizza rolls?*"

"Yeah. I was hungry." He held up his plate. "Want one?"

Seeley snagged one and popped it into his mouth. "Ugh."

"More for me." Lucas grinned. "Mom, do you want one?"

"No. Thanks," Juliette said, and turned on the coffee maker. "I'm glad you found something you could eat."

"They taste weird, but I woke up starving. Why are you guys up so early?"

"We've got a rescue coming in," Seeley said.

"Can I help?" Lucas asked with wide-eyed hope.

Seeley looked at Juliette and arched a brow. "What do you think, babe?"

She remembered what he'd said about the horse being a mess.

"Please, Mom? I want to help. I won't get in the way, and I'll do whatever you say."

"The horse is in bad shape," she cautioned. "It was attacked by dogs."

"I can handle it," Lucas said confidently. "You're both vets. It's in my blood. Tell her, Doc. I've been fine with the rehab horses." He'd been joining Seeley every morning and evening when he did rounds since Thanksgiving.

She had to smile at his in-his-blood comment. He'd definitely learned to use that to his advantage. She looked at Seeley, silently asking for his two cents.

He shrugged. "If it's too much for him, he doesn't have to stay."

"Yeah. I can walk home," Lucas said fervently.

Home. This really had become their home. "Okay. But dress warm." It had snowed last night, and several inches blanketed the ground.

"Awesome. Thank you!" He shoved the last two pizza rolls in his mouth and put his plate in the dishwasher before running upstairs.

THE POOR MARE was in heart-wrenching shape. The dogs had viciously attacked her, shredding part of her leg and the flesh at her elbow and leaving multiple bite wounds on her body. She was in shock, but they managed to get her off the trailer and into the hospital, where they worked quickly to check her vitals, hang an IV bag, and give her pain relief and mild sedation, so they could begin the arduous and painful process of cleaning her up.

Tiny had been waiting at the clinic when they'd arrived. He stood by the horse's head, petting her, quietly telling her she was safe and loved. The tortured emotions in his eyes and voice mirrored the ones Juliette was wrestling with.

"It's like she doesn't know we're here," Lucas said as Juliette and Seeley assessed her wounds.

"She's in shock. When a horse is in a lot of pain, they turn everything inward," Seeley explained. "It's taking all her energy to fight through the pain and the fear."

"Is that why she's grinding her teeth so loud?" Lucas asked.

"Yes," Juliette answered. "That's how you know a horse is in severe physical and/or emotional pain."

"Our girl's been fightin' for her life for who knows how long," Tiny said.

"Is she going to make it?" Lucas asked.

"We hope so," Juliette said.

"She's a fighter. She's not giving up," Tiny said.

"Whose dogs were they?" Lucas asked. "How did that guy find her?"

"The dogs belonged to the bastard who owned her," Seeley said. "And she was found by sheer luck. A neighbor had been on his way to pick up a horse for his daughter when he saw the guy's truck and trailer pulling out of a dead-end dirt road that he knew led nowhere. On a hunch, he went down that road and found the horse."

"Did he call the police?" Lucas asked. "They should arrest her owner and do *something* with the dogs so they don't do it again."

Seeley nodded. "He called the police and animal control. They'll get their due."

"The sad thing is, dogs aren't vicious like this by nature," Tiny said. "Whatever he did to those dogs was probably equally cruel as the things this girl's endured."

"I *hate* the guy who did this to her," Lucas said angrily.

"Me too, buddy," Seeley said. "But our girl needs to feel safe. She needs hope and love, so why don't you go walk off that anger."

"Come on, Rodeo," Tiny said. "Let's go check on the other horses." He and Lucas took off the sterile gloves they'd worn to pet the horse and walked out together.

"Do you think this is too much for him?" Juliette asked.

"No. He cares a great deal, and he's really good with the rehab horses. He connects with them, and he wants to know their stories, start to finish. He's trying to understand the process, which is a good thing, and he's connecting with the wounded horses. Falling for them the same way we do. But as the pieces are starting to fall into place, he's realizing some people do horrible things, and he's getting angry about it. That's not a bad thing."

"Like I did when I first came here," she said, remembering the first time she'd seen Romeo, how quickly she'd fallen in love with him and how angry she'd been at the people who had neglected him.

"Exactly. It's a whole different experience when you see a horse suffering and get to be part of its healing."

They were flushing out and debriding the horse's wounds when Lucas returned, and the horse was quaking from the pain.

"Tiny had to go take care of something. Can I pet her?" Lucas asked, reaching for gloves.

"Sure, honey," Juliette said. "But steer clear from the wounds on her jaw."

"You're okay, girl. You're doing great." Lucas gently petted her, his voice soft and loving. "I know it hurts, and you're scared, but you're safe now. Nobody will ever hurt you again."

Juliette and Seeley shared a knowing smile from opposite sides of the horse.

Over the next couple of hours, Lucas was a big help, supplying them with fresh cotton gauze to scrub the horse's wounds with antiseptic, helping to refill the buckets, discarding trash, and whatever else they asked him to do, while telling the horse how brave and strong she was.

While they finished tending her wounds, Lucas went to prepare a clean stall and hang a hay net for her. "He's pretty fucking amazing," Seeley said.

"He is, isn't he?"

"You're amazing too, darlin'. I love working with you."

"Me too. It's even better than my teenage dreams."

He leaned in and kissed her. "What would I have to do to convince you to come work with me instead of Jade?"

Her heart skipped. "Are you joking?"

"No. We make a good team. Our dreams might have been obliterated when we were teenagers. But every day, every minute, every damn second is a chance to restart those dreams, and I want that with you. What I want more than anything in this world is for Lucas to be healthy. Second to that is for the three of us to have the life we'd always hoped for. If you worked here, you'd have flexibility for whatever you and Lucas need, and there's the added bonus of working with me every day."

She laughed. "You're serious?"

"Yes, darlin'. I'm serious."

She got goose bumps.

"You don't have to answer now. I know that beautiful brain of yours will pick it apart with what-ifs. *What if we don't work out? What if it's too much togetherness?*"

"You're not wrong," she admitted.

"We have sixteen years to make up for. I have no qualms about this. We've been talking about bringing in someone permanently, and there's no one I'd rather work with than you. But I don't need an answer now. Take some time and think about it," he said as Lucas walked back into the room.

"She's all set," Lucas said. "Can we stay here again this week, so we can spend time with her?"

Juliette was still processing all that Seeley had said. "*Um.* That's up to Seeley."

"My house is your house," Seeley said. "You never have to ask."

"Awesome." Lucas petted the horse. "What's her name?"

"I don't know that she's ever had one," Seeley said.

Lucas looked thoughtfully at the horse. "Can I name her?"

"Sure," he said.

Juliette looked at the time and realized they had to get going to get ready for his treatment. "I'm really sorry, but Lucas and I need to get showered and get ready to go."

"That's okay. I'll finish up here and bring Sasha and Tiny up to date, so they can watch her while we're gone. I'm going to call the service and get someone in to handle the night shift, and then I'll meet you at the hospital." He looked at Lucas. "You were an incredible help, bud. Thank you. Do you want to think on her name for a while?"

"Nope. I want to name her Brave Heart."

"Like the movie?" Seeley asked.

"No. Two words, because she has a brave heart."

"I love that," Juliette said.

"Me too."

Lucas moved in front of the horse and said, "Welcome to the family, Brave Heart. You'll never be alone again."

Chapter Thirty-Seven

"SEELEY JUST TEXTED. He should be here soon," Juliette said after Lucas had his blood drawn. Now that they both knew what to expect on treatment days, they were less anxious about them.

"Can we get something from the cafeteria before we go to the infusion room?"

"Sure." Before his last treatment, he'd stocked up on snacks, but when he'd gotten his infusion, he hadn't wanted to eat any of them. Instead, he'd shared them with the nurse who was helping him. As they headed to the elevator, she had a feeling this would become his new routine. *Blood draw, cafeteria to stock up, share snacks while getting his treatment, go home and chill.*

"That was intense this morning," he said. "I liked helping you guys."

"You did a great job, and I think the love you showed Brave Heart made a difference." They stopped at the elevator, and she pushed the button.

"I can't understand how anyone could dump an injured animal out in a field like that. That guy's a monster."

"Unfortunately, the world is full of them," she said as they stepped into the elevator.

He pored over the snacks in the cafeteria like his choices had the power to create world peace. He finally chose an array of sweet and salty snacks, along with a couple of bottles of water and two Dr Peppers. She'd bet one of those Dr Peppers had Seeley's name on it.

"Sure you don't want a pizza with all that?" she teased as they headed up to the infusion room.

"*Ha ha*," he said sarcastically. "I found out that Layla's wearing a blue and gray dress to the dance."

She was happy he'd brought it up. He'd been so tired lately, she was wondering if he still wanted to go but didn't want to ask in case it upset him. "Are we getting you a blue suit or tie?"

"Everyone's wearing jeans and a dress shirt and jacket."

"Okay. We'll go shopping and see what you like. You might want to ask Layla for a picture of her dress so we know what shade of blue to match."

"I've already got one."

"Look at you, Mr. Ready to Do It Right," she teased as they pushed through the doors to the infusion room and headed up to the desk.

"Juliette."

The deep voice shot fear through her veins, but in the next second, that fear iced over with prickling vengeance. Hatred coiled around her heart as she swept her arm in front of Lucas, pushing him behind her, and turned to face her father.

"*Mom!* Why'd you—"

"Quiet, Lucas," she said, keeping her voice low to avoid a scene, her eyes never leaving her father. He had the same stoic face he'd had years ago. His hair was thinner and gray, his dark brows making him look as sinister as he was to his core. He was dressed in a business suit and tie. He could pull the wool over other people's eyes like a wolf in sheep's clothing, but not hers. "What are you doing here?"

"I came to see my grandson," he said with the practiced smile of her youth.

"Mom, is that *him*? Is that your father?"

"He was *never* a father. This fraud is a deceitful con man." She stood taller, seething, "How did you know we'd be here?"

"Have you forgotten how well connected I am? Do you think I didn't know you'd moved back?" he said with amusement, further infuriating her. "That you're shacking up with your lowly biker boyfriend?"

Rage tore through her, but she forced herself to remain in control. "Seeley is *ten* times the man you'll ever be," she hissed. "I had a nice chat with Ana, by the way. You two deserve each other. I hope you treat your son with her better than you treated me."

"Ah, yes. Ana. She's a well-behaved one."

"You make me sick," she fumed, shaking with anger. "Get out of here, and don't *ever* come near us again."

"I see you're still overly dramatic." He lifted his chin, speaking around her. "Lucas, how are you feeling, son?"

"Don't you dare speak to him." Juliette moved to block his view, but Lucas stepped around her, getting in her father's face.

"Don't call me *son*," Lucas seethed. "I know what you did to my parents, you lying bastard."

Her father didn't even flinch. "You poor boy. She's poisoned you with lies to cover her own tracks," he said with the lethal calm of a venomous snake.

"Like hell she did." Seeley stepped in front of Juliette and Lucas, towering over her father. "This is going to end in one of two ways," he said through gritted teeth. "You're either going to walk out of here and never come near *my* family again, or they'll wheel you out of here on a stretcher. I suggest you choose wisely."

Her father's eyes narrowed. "This isn't over."

"Watch your back, old man. Because it's about to be." Seeley put his arms around Juliette and Lucas, leading them away from her father. "Are you okay, babe? Lucas?"

"Uh-huh," she said, trying to regain control as Lucas said, "I'm *fine*. What a prick. He called you a lowly biker."

"I've been called worse."

"You're going to let him get away with it?" Lucas snapped.

"He's not getting away with anything. Right now, what I care about is that you and your mom are okay." He led them to a row of chairs far from the other people in the waiting room.

"I'm fine," Juliette reassured him as she and Lucas sat down. Seeley remained standing, like their personal bodyguard. "Just shaken up. I'm sorry you had to see that, Lucas."

"It's *fine*."

"No, it's not," she said. "We didn't go after him because I didn't want to put us back on his radar. But we've been on it the *whole* time. We have to do something."

"I'll handle it," Seeley said firmly. "He'll *never* get near either of you again. I'll make sure of it. But we have more important things to think about right now. Lucas, are you okay to get your treatment? Or are you too upset?"

"I'm not upset. I'm pissed, but I'm not going to miss my treatment because of *him*."

"Juliette? Do you want to stay with us, or are you too shaken up? Do you want me to have Cowboy come take you home?"

"No. I'm fine, and I can drive myself home."

"You're not going anywhere alone." Seeley pulled out his phone and started thumbing out a text.

"Who are you texting?" she asked.

"My old man, to get some of the guys over here to make sure that cretin doesn't get anywhere near this room while Lucas has his treatment and to set up extra security at the ranch, and Lucas's school."

"At my school?" Lucas asked.

"Don't worry, Lucas. This isn't our first rodeo. Nobody's going to notice our guys." He continued thumbing out more texts.

"I'm not worried. I think it's badass."

"We don't need all that," Juliette said.

Seeley looked up from his phone, his dark eyes as serious and commanding as his tone. "*Yes, we do.* Your father thinks he's above the law, and now that he's been shut down, he's got something to prove. I'm not taking any chances."

Chapter Thirty-Eight

AS SOON AS Lucas was settled with his treatment, Doc knew what had to be done and wasted no time putting the gears in motion.

Hours later, under the cover of night, he stared down at the man kneeling before him in the snow, blindfolded and gagged, his hands bound behind his back. Gone were the fancy jacket and tie, his shirt ripped at the collar. He was shaking, from the cold or from fear was anybody's guess, but Doc hoped it was the latter. He wasn't the type to carry hatred in his heart, but he despised this piece of shit with every fiber of his being.

"Take off the blindfold," Doc gritted out. "I want this fucker to see my face."

Cowboy pulled it off, and Marvin Adkin blinked several times, fear rising in his eyes as he took in Doc, Cowboy, Dare, Rebel, Hyde, and Taz.

Doc eyed Adkin. "Not quite the cushy evening you had planned, is it, Marv?"

Adkin bitched, the gag muffling his voice.

"What's that? I can't quite make it out." Doc took out his switchblade and began cleaning his nails with it. "Let me fill in the gaps for you. I would've preferred to do this hours ago, when you egregiously invaded my future wife and our son's personal space." He crouched in front of him and pointed the knife at him. "But you see, *Marv*, some things take time. I had to call the PI, and he had to coordinate with the FBI, and they had to get a search warrant. All that shit takes time."

Letting that sink in, Doc pushed to his feet and began walking slowly around him. "I bet you were excited to get that text from Ana and to meet her at the park." Standing behind Adkin, he bent down, speaking into his ear. "*Surprise.* She's already in protective custody." He stood and continued walking around him. "Your girlfriend made a deal with the Feds, Marv. She sold you out. We know all about your hidden safe, and the money laundering, and a shitload of your other illegal activities. And that text?" He stopped in front of him, staring him down. "That took time, too."

He crouched again, enjoying the anger in the asshole's eyes. "Our computer guy had to hack her phone to send that text asking you to meet her at the park." He pointed the knife at him again. "I admit, I was a *little* worried you might not show up, and my guys would be waiting with that van forever. I mean, it can't be easy to get out at night when you're married. But then I remembered that your wife had her book club meeting tonight."

Doc laughed. "Level with me. Did you *know* there's no book club? Did you know your wife is probably on her hands and knees right now sucking your buddy's cock? Your *lawyer's* cock?" Anger rose in Adkin's eyes anew. "I was surprised to find out that Wilson Chambers, the man you trusted with *all* your wrongdoings, has been fucking your wife for years."

Adkin's face reddened as he spewed muffled words against the gag.

Doc pushed to his feet, looking at the other guys. "Did you guys catch that? I don't think he knew his wife was fucking another man. That's a shame, Marv. You see, we have pictures. Actually, we have a collection of pictures of you, too. Some with Ana, but cheating isn't against the law. Although, having a small dick should be. It's no wonder your wife cheated."

The guys chuckled.

"But my PI's been a busy boy these past few months, Marv. He managed to get some pictures of you and some sketchy guys. He's good, too. He has one of those big-ass cameras that can see a zit on a fly's ass. Now, that wouldn't be so bad, if you and those guys weren't involved with things like extortion and bribery. I sure hope *those* don't get leaked to the press."

"That'd be uncomfortable," Dare said.

"It sure would. I don't like to be uncomfortable, and you know what makes me uncomfortable, Marv?" Doc nodded to Rebel and Hyde.

They grabbed Adkin's arms, hauling him to his feet.

Doc stepped closer, speaking through clenched teeth. "I get uncomfortable when people talk shit about my family." He pointed the knife at him. "You have said some awful shit about both of my families. Maybe you thought I'd forget what you said after all these years, but my memory is as sharp as a fucking tack."

He brought the knife closer, holding it against Adkin's jaw. The blood drained from the fucker's face. "You feel that fear? That's how your sixteen-year-old daughter felt when you lied to her and fucked her over. That's how she felt when you made her marry the wrong man." It took everything Doc had not to finish off the fucker right that second. "What do you have to say for yourself?" He pushed the knife beneath the gag and sliced it, sending it sailing to the ground, and handed the knife to

Cowboy.

"You're going to pay—"

Doc grabbed him by the shirt, hauling him off his feet. "Shut your fucking mouth before I rip off your arm and shove it down your throat." He dropped him, sending him stumbling backward into Cowboy's chest.

"You are one stupid motherfucker. Now you've gone and pissed Doc off," Cowboy said, and with a push of his chest, Adkin stumbled forward.

"You've fucked with the wrong family," Doc warned.

The asshole spit at him.

Doc's fist connected with his jaw with an audible *crack*, knocking him off his feet. "Get him up."

Rebel and Hyde dragged him to his feet.

"Real tough, hitting a guy who's tied up," Adkin said, spitting blood into the snow.

"Kind of like when you sicced two bodyguards on a nineteen-year-old kid," Doc said. "But you're right. I don't need to sink to your level." He nodded to Cowboy, and Cowboy cut the cable ties off his wrists.

Adkin rubbed his wrists. "You have no idea who you're dealing with. You're all going to prison for this."

"I don't think so." Doc lowered his voice chillingly. "You see, right now we're out on a horse rescue. In fact, we met a police officer at the field where the horses were last seen. We're on his bodycam, heading into the fields to search for them."

"And we'll be on it again after leaving the property half an hour from now," Cowboy added.

"That's right. We're your worst nightmare. We're *ghosts*," Doc said.

"You stupid idiots," Adkin said. "There are traffic cameras all over."

"If only they hadn't been hacked and disabled," Dare said. "But we're just lowly bikers. What do we know?"

Fear fell over Adkin's face like a curtain. "My...my phone is tracked. I've been gone too long. My wife will worry. The police will probably show up here any minute."

"That could have worked in your favor," Doc said, glancing at Hyde.

"If we hadn't left your phone in your car at the park after we tossed you in the van," Hyde said.

"Did I forget to mention that your wife will be getting a text from you soon telling her that you got a flat and that she needs to come get you at the park?" Doc asked. "She won't find you, of course. But she'll find pictures of you and Ana in some very precarious positions."

"You son of a bitch," Adkin fumed. "You won't get away with this."

"Here's the thing, Marv. After tonight, nobody's going to give a shit what you say. They're going to be too riveted to their televisions and smartphones as your cushy little life falls apart piece by fucking piece. But in case you get the urge to *try* to bring our names into this, you should know that we're well connected, too. If any of our names are mentioned, you won't last a day in prison. I did mention you're going to prison, didn't I?"

"It was implied," Cowboy said.

"Right." Doc set a dark stare on Adkin. "You do remember the ranch that you threatened to close down helps previously incarcerated individuals, don't you, Marv? The thing is, all of those guys we've helped over the years are still buddies with the lifers they knew in prison. You know about lifers, don't you? They have nothing left to lose, and they're *very* appreciative of the work we've done to help their buddies. They won't take kindly to any of us being bad-mouthed."

"You son of a bit—" Adkin threw a punch, clocking Doc in the jaw.

He never saw the uppercut coming as Doc's fist connected with the underside of his jaw, sending him flying into the snow on his back. Doc was on him in seconds, seeing red, his fists flying, anger roaring out with every lightning-fast punch. "For Juliette and our son." *Crack.* "For the years you stole from us." *Crack.* "For Hazel…"

With every punch, he saw Juliette's blue eyes, dripping with tears after learning the truth of what her father had done. He saw Lucas's tortured face when he found out he'd been lied to, and he saw years of his own emotional torment spent trying to fill the big black hole Adkin's deceit had caused in his own fucking heart.

What he *didn't* see until Rebel and Dare tore him from his rage-induced fury was the blood pouring from the prick's mouth and nose, his head lolling from side to side, crimson seeping through the snow.

"It's over, Doc," Dare gritted out. "He's done."

Doc fought to get free. "Not done *enough.*"

Cowboy stepped in front of him. "You've got a family waiting on you. Pull your shit together, and let the Feds have him."

Doc ground his back teeth, knowing he was right, but fuck if that made it any easier to diffuse his rage and walk away from the fucker who hurt Juliette.

"Let him squirm in prison, mate," Taz said. "Somebody'll make him his bitch."

"He'll be paying for his sins forever," Rebel said.

Cowboy's eyes narrowed, holding Doc's stare. "How about we avoid you paying for yours?"

"Mine's not a sin. It's fucking retribution." He yanked his

arms free.

"One phone call, and you'll have that." Cowboy stepped closer. "You want more blood on your hands, you're gonna have to go through me."

"Think of your family, mate," Taz said.

"You want your boy visiting you in prison?" Dare asked.

Doc stared them all down, wanting nothing more than to take Adkin's last breath, but he wasn't a stupid man. He wanted the motherfucker to suffer. "I'm not doing shit. That fucker's not worth it. Tie him up."

As Cowboy and Dare cable-tied Adkin's wrists and ankles, Doc pulled out his phone and called Reggie. "It's done. Give us ten minutes. Then he's all yours."

DOC TOOK THE long way home, needing to cool down and get his head on straight before going back to the ranch.

When he finally got to the entrance, Tiny was leaning against his truck beneath the Redemption Ranch sign. *Fuck.* They'd told Tiny they'd gotten a rescue call, too. He hoped to hell Cowboy and Dare hadn't crumbled under the pressure and told Tiny the truth when they returned with an empty horse trailer.

Doc pulled up behind Tiny's truck and went to talk to him.

"Heard the rescue went to shit," Tiny said.

Thank you, Cowboy and Dare. "Yeah. Must've been a fake call."

Tiny rubbed his jaw, shaking his head. "Y'all still can't lie for shit."

Fuck. Doc clenched his teeth.

"And you boys wonder why I had so much gray hair. Looks like he got a shot in. Is he still breathing?"

Doc nodded. "Feds have him."

"You put your brothers and other good men at risk. Do I have to worry about you all going to prison?"

"No. We covered our asses, and I didn't make them come with me."

"I have no doubt about that." Tiny's eyes narrowed. "Do you feel better?"

Doc rubbed the back of his neck, weighing his answer. "If I say yes, are you going to think less of me?"

"Nothing could ever make me think less of you."

"In that case, *yes*. With all the evidence the Feds will have against her father, he'll be put away until he's too old to piss by himself. But I won't feel whole again until I see my boy sleeping safe and sound in his bed and I have Juliette in my arms."

"Understood. This was a long time coming. If I hadn't made a promise to your mother not to touch that fucker, I'd've done it myself after he had those two bastards beat the shit out of you years ago."

"You knew about that?" *What the hell?*

"I guess you missed the memo about the unfortunate accident those two bastards got into. Nobody puts their hands on my kids without paying a price."

Holy shit. He'd had no idea. "Why didn't you tell me?"

Ignoring Doc's question, Tiny said, "What are you going to tell your gal about tonight?"

"That it must have been a fake call."

"Why not tell her the truth?"

"Because I love her, and there are certain things she doesn't need to know."

"Sounds about right. Listen, son, if this comes back to haunt your thoughts, you talk to someone. Don't let that shit stew, ya hear me?"

"Loud and clear."

Tiny nodded and pulled him into an embrace. "Love you, son."

"Love you, too."

As Tiny walked back to his truck, Doc couldn't get over what his father had done for him. "Hey, old man."

Tiny turned around.

"Did Mom know what you did to the bodyguards?"

"Not until the night Lucas took off. Juliette let it slip out that the assholes beat you up, and your mother asked if I knew about it. I couldn't lie to her, so I fessed up and said they got their due."

"*Wait.* Juliette knows you did something to them? She never said anything about it."

Tiny cocked a grin. "Guess she didn't think you needed to know. G'night, son."

Doc stewed on that as he drove home.

As he came through the front door, the dogs appeared at the top of the stairs. He quietly closed the door, and they retreated into Lucas's room. He took off his boots and set them aside before making his way upstairs. Lucas was fast asleep with a dog on either side of him and one at his feet. Doc wasn't proud of having beaten that man, but he was proud knowing his boy and Juliette would never have to worry about him coming into their lives again.

They'd have to deal with the media, but he'd already consulted with Reggie's sister, Shea Steele, the owner of a highly regarded public relations firm. She was as well connected as the governor himself, and she'd already been putting the wheels in motion to control how things unfolded. He knew when shit hit the fan, they'd be in good hands.

He made his way downstairs, and when he walked into the bedroom, Juliette closed the book she was reading, her smile like sunshine to his stormy thoughts. "Hi, darlin'."

"How'd the rescue go?" She crawled to the foot of the bed.

He hated lying to her, but it was for the best. "It must've been a false call," he said as she rose onto her knees and put her arms around him. "We couldn't find any sign of horses."

"I'll never understand people who do things like that." Her brows knitted. "What happened to your mouth?"

"Two of the guys got into a scuffle, and I got caught in it."

"What is it with guys? You never see women having scuffles. Does it hurt?"

He shook his head. "No."

"Good." She pressed a tender kiss to the cut.

"Thanks, babe. How was our boy tonight?"

"He was good. We had a quiet night. Layla came over after, and I offered to watch Gus so Ezra and Sasha could have some private time. We all watched *The Sandlot*. The kids were happy, and I got to cuddle Gus. It's been a long time since I got to cuddle a little one."

"I'm glad you had a good night. And Brave Heart?"

She smiled. "She's a fighter. I think she'll pull through. Lucy, the girl from the service, will check on her every four hours tonight."

"Good. I'm going to take a quick shower before I come to bed." He kissed her and took off his cut, tossing it on the dresser as he headed into the bathroom, hoping to wash away the remnants of the shitty night.

He turned on the shower and stripped down while the water heated up. He stepped beneath the warm spray and tipped his face up to it, letting the hot water ease his muscles.

The shower door opened, and Juliette stepped in with him. She wrapped her arms around him and rested her cheek on his chest. "Are you okay?"

"Yeah." He embraced her, wondering how she'd known he needed her. She hadn't just become his everything. She was the blood in his heart, the love in his soul, the very air he breathed. She'd become his fucking life force. He kissed the top of her head. "But I'm even better now. It was a long night. Tell me something good, darlin'."

"I've been thinking about your offer to work together."

"And?"

She gazed up at him. "Well, there's the whole sleeping with my boss thing to consider."

"That's a definite perk," he said arrogantly.

She laughed and kissed his chest. "Does that mean I'll be paid in sexual favors?"

"Those'll be your bonuses."

"This deal is sounding sweeter by the minute. What if you get tired of seeing my face?"

"Darlin', I've seen your face in my mind every day since the first day I met you, and not once have I been sick of it."

Her smile lifted his heart. "In that case, I'll talk to Jade tomorrow."

"Is that a yes?"

"Yes, Dr. Whiskey. If you still want me, I'll happily accept your offer."

He touched his forehead to hers, tangling his fingers in her hair. "There'll never come a day when I won't want you, darlin'." With a gentle tug, he tipped her face up and lowered his lips to hers. As happened so often, their love took over, and the rest of the world fell away.

Chapter Thirty-Nine

JULIETTE STUDIED THE childlike drawing on the wall of Dr. Santowski's office, trying to hold on to the hope she saw in it. It was the end of January, almost seven weeks since Lucas had rung the bell after his last chemotherapy treatment. They'd all breathed a little easier over the holidays. He'd had another PET scan earlier in the week, and they were waiting for the results to see if he needed further treatment. Lucas was feeling good and bouncing back beautifully, and he'd already put on some of the weight he'd lost during his treatments.

That alone should give her hope that today's news would be good.

She was hopeful, but she was also scared. She was having flashbacks to the first time they'd been in that office, sitting just as they were now, with her and Seeley flanking Lucas. As if they could protect him from the invisible disease that had brought them there. Lucas had been vibrant and had seemed healthy then, and they'd clung to hope because of that, only to have their legs kicked out from under them.

Even with the trials and tribulations of Lucas's treatments and the ups and downs of life in general, their lives had been really good the last few months, and she worried they might not have any luck left.

It had been two months since the confrontation with her father at the hospital. They'd gotten lucky, and hadn't had to go after him. The morning after that awful confrontation, she'd learned that Ana had made a deal with the FBI, and her parents and many of her father's cohorts in crime had been arrested. It was all over the news—how they'd stormed her parents' house and the houses and offices of all the others, including Josh's father, which made her wonder how much Josh had known about that situation. She'd been shocked to hear that her mother had been arrested, but according to reports, her mother had known about, and been part of, some of her father's shady business dealings.

She'd learned through the press that her father had been found badly beaten in a field. He claimed not to remember how he'd gotten there or who had beaten him up, but the media had a field day blaming it on a shady business deal gone wrong. The media had exposed a list of things her father had done, including how he'd deceived her and Seeley. Seeley had kept his promise to protect them. He'd hired Shea Steele, a high-powered public relations professional, and she'd done an incredible job of handling things for and with them to minimize the media circus.

But what her father had done to them was nowhere near the worst of his wrongdoings. It appeared the rumors were true, and he had an even more sinister side. He'd actually had people murdered to further his career and businesses. To say Juliette was relieved when the judge had deemed her father a threat to society and had sentenced him to be detained until the trial would be an understatement.

She felt safer than she ever had.

She glanced at Lucas, who was thumbing out a text, and wondered how scared he was today. He hadn't said much other than he couldn't wait to get today's appointment over with. She was in awe of his strength. What her father had done to them and having cancer had forced him to grow up faster than any kid should have to, but he'd stood strong against those storms, showing the world that there was nothing he couldn't survive.

He was so much like Seeley, he even always went the extra mile for his girl.

The Snow Ball had taken place five days after his last chemo treatment, and he'd been completely exhausted. But he was determined not to let Layla down. Seeley had been equally determined to make their night unforgettable. Juliette had planned a low-key pre-dance get-together for the kids with Layla's and Robert's families, so their parents could take pictures of all of the kids together. Seeley had taken it a step further, renting a limousine and giving the kids a Dark Knights escort.

Despite the bitter cold, he and Tiny had led the pack ahead of the shiny black limo, and Cowboy, Dare, Ezra, Rebel, Hyde, and Taz had driven their motorcycles alongside and behind the vehicle, giving the kids an air of royalty when they'd arrived at the dance.

Lucas, Layla, and their friends still hadn't stopped raving about it.

They'd moved in with Seeley a few days later, right before Christmas, and they'd had the best holiday ever. Hazel's house was too special to sell. For now, they were going to fix it up, and possibly rent it out. Juliette had started working with Seeley right after the New Year, and Lucas often joined them on rounds. Brave Heart had spent three weeks in the hospital before moving to the rehab barn, and she was doing great. She and Lucas had bonded deeply. Three days after her arrival, she was whinnying when she saw them and had tried to groom Lucas's head. Queenie and Contessa were also well on their way to living a long, healthy life, and they'd both found a place in Lucas's heart. He and the horses had been healing together.

They all had.

Lucas was back to school with his friends in Weston, and he was spending more time with them outside of school. He was enjoying working on his truck with Seeley and Dare, and he and Layla were still incredibly happy. She'd become part of their family, joining them for dinners and bonfires and hanging out at the ranch with Lucas and Kenny. They even let Gus tag along sometimes, which Gus loved.

"What?" Lucas asked, eyeing her as he thumbed out another text.

"Nothing." Thinking fast, she said, "I was just thinking about how much you look like Seeley." He'd never completely lost his hair. The stubble had grown to something akin to a crew cut. Some areas were sparser than before, but like Seeley, the short hair made his sharp, handsome features stand out that much more.

He glanced at Seeley, who cocked a grin and said, "You're a lucky dude."

Lucas scoffed, a smile playing at the corners of his mouth as he went back to texting.

Dr. Santowski walked into the room and said, "Good afternoon."

"Hi," Juliette said, motioning for Lucas to put his phone away.

"Doctor." Seeley stood and shook his hand.

"It's nice to see you again," Dr. Santowski said as he went around his desk and sat down. "Lucas, how are you feeling?"

"Fine. *Good*," he said. "Do I still have cancer?"

"Honey, give him a second," Juliette said, although she was anxious to know, too.

Dr. Santowski smiled. "That's okay. I'm sure you're all anxious to hear the results. Lucas, I'm happy to tell you that there was no evidence of active cancer on your scans, and you are officially in remission."

"Yes!" Lucas jumped to his feet, doing a fist pump.

With tears of joy, Juliette and Seeley hugged him, and each other, nervous laughter bubbling out, along with thanking God and the doctor, and embracing their son again and again. Dr. Santowski patiently waited, allowing them to revel in their relief and excitement.

When they finally took their seats, grinning like they'd won the lottery, which they *definitely* had, Lucas said, "Can I get the port taken out now?"

"Absolutely," Dr. Santowski said. "Your parents can make an appointment. It's an outpatient procedure."

"Does this mean I'm cured?" Lucas asked. "Can I start bull riding again?"

"We don't use the term *cured* until you've been cancer free for five years, but this is the first step to getting there, and as far as bull riding goes, once your incision has healed from the port, you can return to your normal activities."

"No more scans?" Lucas asked.

Dr. Santowski explained that Lucas would need to have follow-up visits every three months for the next year, and then they would move to every four months the following year, and every six months for the third through fifth years. "We'll do exams and blood work, but unless we see something concerning in your blood work, or you experience symptoms of the cancer returning, like swollen lymph nodes, night sweats, itching, and the other symptoms we've gone over, there's no need for scans..."

Most of what he said after that was a blur, but when they left the doctor's office, hugging and so very grateful for their good fortune, Juliette was pretty sure anyone within a ten-mile radius could feel their joy. Seeley sent a group text to his family and Lucas texted Layla and his friends. In the parking lot, Lucas yelled, "I'm cancer free!" at the top of his lungs, and there were more elated hugs and *I love you*s.

As they climbed into Seeley's truck, Seeley asked, "Are we dropping you at Layla's, or are we picking her up to celebrate?"

"Neither," Lucas said with blatant disappointment. "She had to go someplace with her mom, and she won't be back until late."

"Oh, honey. I'm sorry," Juliette said.

"Maybe you can celebrate with her tomorrow," Seeley suggested. "It's Saturday. You'll have all day."

"Whatever," he said sadly.

"Lucky for us, that means you're all ours tonight," Seeley said as he drove away from the hospital. "What do you want to do?"

"I don't know. Maybe get pizza and *not* think about cancer."

"Sounds like a plan," he said.

The dogs greeted them in the driveway, lifting Lucas's spirits. As he loved them up, he said, "Guess what, guys. I don't have cancer anymore!" The dogs fed off his excitement, jumping up and barking. "I think they're happy for me."

"We all are, buddy." Seeley draped an arm around Juliette. "Our boy is in remission."

Her heart was bubbling over with joy. "I don't think I'm ever going to stop smiling."

"Just the way I like it." Seeley kissed her.

Lucas barreled past them with the dogs, sprinting up the porch steps. "Can you unlock the door?"

"I forgot to lock it. It's open," she said.

Lucas threw the door open, and as they followed the dogs inside, "*Surprise!*" rang out from their living room, where Layla, Robert, and a handful of Lucas's other friends from school and bull riding were cheering and clapping, along with Seeley's family and their friends, Buck Waller, and Layla's and Robert's parents. Colorful balloons floated around the room, and a CONGRATULATIONS, RODEO! banner hung across the patio doors with sparkly streamers dangling all the way to the floor.

Lucas looked at Juliette and Seeley. "Are you kidding me? I can't believe you did this! Thank you so much!"

"Thank your girlfriend," Seeley said. "This was her idea."

Lucas's jaw dropped, and his gaze found Layla, who looked like she was going to climb out of her skin if she didn't hug him soon. "I thought you were out with your mom."

"I *am* out with my mom. She's over there." Layla pointed across the room to Brianna, and then she threw her arms around him and said, "I'd never miss such an important day."

"Thank you." Lucas sounded choked up, and he leaned back but didn't let her go and said, "What if I'd gotten bad news?"

"Then we'd take down the banner and be less excited," Layla said. "But we'd all still be here to support you because we love you."

Lucas's eyes teared up, and right there in front of everyone, he gave her a sweet peck on the lips that made her cheeks pink up. As she stepped out of his arms, he looked at her father and said, "Sorry, Mr. Braden."

Hugh laughed. "It's all right, Lucas. Congratulations. We couldn't be happier for you."

Lucas beamed, his gaze returning to Layla, who looked extra cute in a gray shirt with MY BOYFRIEND KICKED CANCER'S BUTT emblazoned across the front in '70s-style pastel colors, a black miniskirt, gray tights, and black boots. His eyes lit up, and he said, "That's a great shirt."

"I'm glad you like it," she exclaimed. "I got you a cool shirt, too."

Her little brother, Christian, shouted, "*Now*, Layla?"

"Yes, Christian." As Christian ran over waving a black T-shirt, she said, "He's been asking all day when he could give it to you."

Christian shoved it into his hands. "Look at it, Lucas!"

"Thanks, buddy." Lucas held up the shirt, pride shining in his eyes as he turned it for everyone else to see. REMISSION was written across the chest in white, and ACCOMPLISHED was angled across it, printed like a stamp, in red.

As cheers rang out, he pulled the T-shirt on over his long-sleeve shirt and held his arms out, showing it off, earning whistles and catcalls from Dare and Cowboy. He hugged Layla again, and everyone converged on him.

Juliette and Seeley made their way around the room, their hearts overflowing as Lucas was showered with love and hugs and happiness, and they were, too.

As the night wore on and everyone ate and mingled, celebrating Lucas's good fortune, Juliette got swept away by the girls. They were gathered around her, chatting about everything from Lucas and the party to Sully's upcoming wedding and Sasha's lack of a wedding date. Six months ago, Juliette never imagined their lives would look like this.

She glanced across the room at Lucas, huddled together with Layla and their friends, with smiles on their faces and snacks in hand. A few feet away, Seeley was laughing about something with the guys. These people had become her and Lucas's family.

She was still so overcome with emotion, she didn't think as she picked up a fork and tapped her wineglass, drawing everyone's attention.

"*Um...Hi*," she said with a little laugh.

Seeley lifted his chin, silently asking if everything was okay.

She held his gaze, answering all the questions in his and everyone else's curious expressions. "Sorry to interrupt. I'll only be a minute. These last few months have been a little crazy, and I feel like we've barely had time to breathe. Lucas and I were alone for a very long time, and we went through some really difficult situations. But we got through them, and I know there's *nothing* the two of us can't get through. I mean, look at my incredible son. He is so freaking brave and smart and strong. I got really lucky to be his mom."

She looked at Lucas and said, "I couldn't love you more, Lukey boo."

"*Mom!*"

Laughter rang out. "You're never living that down, Lukey boo," Dare shouted, and more laughter rang out.

"Okay, okay. I'm sorry...*Rodeo*." Juliette looked at the faces of the people who had been there for them every day since she and Seeley had come together and said, "As I was saying, while we *can* get through anything, we couldn't have gotten through these last few months as well or as loved as we have without all of your support. There are no words big enough to express how much that means to me. Thank you for welcoming us into your family and loving us enough to be our soft place to land. We truly appreciate each and every one of you."

"Yeah," Lucas said. "Thank you *all* so much."

Juliette lifted her wineglass and said, "Here's to all of you, for helping us stay strong and sane during what I hope was the hardest thing we'll ever have to go through."

"Here! Here!" Tiny called out, sparking another round of cheers.

As everyone clinked glasses and drank, Seeley's dark eyes held hers, and he strode toward her, mouthing, *I love you.*

It was hard to believe they'd been together for five months already. What a roller coaster it had been. But their love was stronger than their battles, and she knew that no matter what life threw their way—illnesses, disagreements, Lucas playing one of them against the other—nothing could ever tear them apart again.

Chapter Forty

EVERYONE HAD BEEN on such a high, the party ran late into the night. They'd cleaned up but had left all the happy decorations in place. Lucas was too tired to check on the horses with them, and when Doc and Juliette got back to the house, he was nowhere in sight.

"He's probably asleep," Doc said.

"I hope so. It's midnight."

"Why don't you relax. I'll check on him." He gave her butt a pat and kissed her.

"I'll go with you."

They headed upstairs and peeked into Lucas's bedroom. Doc warmed at the familiar sight of him sprawled across the bed surrounded by the dogs. He put his arms around Juliette from behind and whispered, "Our boy is in remission. I'm so fucking grateful."

"Me too," she whispered. She turned and hugged him. "I'm still going to worry every time he gets a cough or doesn't feel well."

"We all will, darlin'. Including Lucas," he said gently. "That illness might test our faith, but it won't test our love. I know in my heart he's going to be fine, and he'll live a long, happy life. I can feel it in my bones."

He kissed her again and took her hand. "Come on, darlin'. I have a surprise for you."

"For me?" she asked as he led her downstairs and through the living room.

He grinned. "No, for my other darlin'. Of course for you." He reached between the streamers and opened the patio door, leading her out to the deck.

"It's freezing out—" Her jaw dropped, and those beautiful baby blues took in the new hot tub, the twinkling lights strung above it, and the dozens of pictures of them from the summer they'd first met dangling on ribbons from the strings of lights. Between the pictures, also hanging from ribbons, were handfuls of wildflowers. There were pictures of them on horseback and lying in the grass at night, on sleeping bags on the floor of the old cabin, and at the lake. There were selfies of them making faces and kissing, photos of Juliette scowling, and some of his favorites of her wearing his cowboy hat.

"Where did that hot tub come from? And where did you get all those pictures? Ohmygod, look how young we were."

He put his arms around her. "Young, beautiful, and so damn happy, everyone could feel it."

"*Seeley.* How did you do this without me knowing?"

"I had the hot tub put in while we were at the doctor's office. Why do you think there were so many streamers on the windows and patio doors?"

She cocked her head. "Everyone knew about this?"

"Yup. Even Lucas."

"What?" She swatted his arm. "You guys can't keep secrets from me with everyone."

He laughed. "Too late, darlin'."

"*Seeley!* You're a crazy man."

"Crazy about you." He kissed her.

"I can't believe you did all of this. Are these the pictures we took on your phone? I thought for sure you got rid of them."

"I couldn't get rid of them. I kept them on a thumb drive. How about we try out our new hot tub?"

"What if Lucas wakes up?"

"Trust me, babe. He won't come out here. He told me he won't even get in the hot tub after us until we disinfect it."

"*What?*" They both laughed. "That's awful!"

"At least we know he's not coming out here." He started taking off his boots, spurring her into action.

As they stripped, she said, "*So cold, so cold, so cold.*" They climbed into the hot tub and sank into the hot water up to their necks. "*Ah.* This feels so good." She put her arms on the sides of the hot tub and rested her head back, looking up at the stars. "This is *amazing.*"

Doc was across the hot tub, arms out in the same position, but instead of looking at the stars, he was admiring her. "You sure are, darlin'."

She looked at him and *swished* through the water toward him. "Get over here, Whiskey." She grabbed his necklace, pulling him closer, and as his arms circled her, she said, "When did you start wearing a necklace?" She lifted the silver chain up, and for the second time tonight, her jaw dropped. Dangling from the end of the necklace was the engagement ring he'd had made for her. A pink diamond surrounded by a halo of white diamonds, which were surrounded by white baguette diamonds, like flower petals. Her eyes flicked to his.

"I wanted to re-create the night when I gave you our necklace," he said as he took the necklace off and freed the ring from it. "But it was too damn cold to take you out to the lake."

She laughed and covered her mouth, her eyes tearing up.

"With everything we've been through, living for the moment has taken on a new meaning. None of us knows how long we have on this earth, but I know I want to spend whatever time we're gifted with you and Lucas. We're going to have worries and challenges, baby, and we'll deal with them together. I look forward to watching our son grow up to be the incredible man he was always meant to be and to seeing you get old and gray and more beautiful by the day. What do you say, Peaches? Will you do me the honor of being my wife and changing your name to Whiskey, like it was always meant to be?"

She laughed, tears flooding her cheeks. "It's you and me forever, Seeley Whiskey. I told you I was never letting you go, and I meant it."

As he slipped the ring on her finger, he said, "You and me forever, darlin'," and sealed their vows with a kiss.

Epilogue

"I'M SORRY, DID you say *pregnant*?" Juliette asked her doctor over the phone.

She'd been feeling sick for the last few weeks, and after everything that happened with Lucas, she'd gotten scared. But Lucas just had his three-month checkup, and thankfully he was still cancer free. He was bull riding again, and their lives were finally back to normal. She hadn't wanted to worry Seeley, so she hadn't said anything and had asked their family doctor to order blood work.

"Yes. You're pregnant."

"Are you sure you have the right person? This is Juliette Chambers."

"Yes, I'm sure these are your results, Juliette."

"But...Something's not right. You're sure I'm not sick? There's not anything else off in my blood work? Because I can't get pregnant."

"Did a doctor tell you you're infertile? Have you had fertility tests done?"

"No, but I tried to get pregnant with my first husband many years ago, and it never happened."

"That could have been an issue on his side. Did *he* have fertility testing done?"

"No. We were really young and didn't even think about it, to be honest. But my fiancé and I have been together since last summer, and we've never used contraception."

"Well, you're definitely pregnant, and not using contraception probably has something to do with it."

"You're positive? Should I have another test done, in case it's a false pregnancy?"

"I don't think that's necessary. Do you have an ob-gyn? I can refer you to one if you don't."

"Yes, I have one, thank you. But I'm definitely *pregnant?* You're certain?" The shock was slowly wearing off, turning to hope.

"Yes, Juliette. You are about nine or ten weeks along."

"Nine or ten weeks." She sounded as awestruck as she felt. "I can't believe it." Her eyes teared up. "Thank you."

"Are there any other questions I can answer for you?"

"*Um.* No. Thank you again." She ended the call, nervous and excited about telling Seeley. "I'm pregnant," she whispered excitedly. "*We're* pregnant." She had to tell Seeley! She turned to go find him, and he was standing in the doorway, looking as shocked as she was.

"Did I just hear you say we're—"

"Pregnant? Yes!"

"Baby!" He swept her into his arms and kissed her. "We're pregnant?"

"Yes!" Tears streamed down her cheeks. "I can't believe it."

"I can. I've got super sperm." He kissed her again, both of them laughing. "How far along are you?"

"Nine or ten weeks. I guess that Valentine's Day lovefest

paid off."

He laughed, but he had tears in his eyes, too. He put his hand on her belly and said, "I get to see you pregnant and rub your feet and buy you pickles and ice cream at midnight."

"*Ew.* How about whipped cream and ice cream?"

"I'll get you anything you want, darlin'. Why didn't you tell me you thought you might be pregnant?" he asked.

"I didn't think I was. Being pregnant wasn't even on my radar. I haven't been feeling well, and after what happened with Lucas, I got scared. I didn't want to worry you, so I called Dr. Winsom and asked him to do lab work."

"Baby, please don't hide things like that from me. If you're ever scared, *lean* on me. That's what I'm here for."

"I will from now on. I'm sorry."

"It's okay." He hugged her, and then he crouched in front of her and put both hands on her belly. "Hi, baby. It's your daddy."

Tears flooded her cheeks. This was what Juliette had wanted all those years ago. This was how Lucas should have been welcomed into the world. With his daddy showing him what it meant to be loved from the moment they discovered he existed.

"Your Mommy and I love you very much, and you have the greatest big brother..."

Oh God. Lucas. How is he going to feel about this?

"Be good to Mama, tiny one." Seeley kissed her belly and pushed to his feet.

"Seeley, how are we going to tell Lucas?"

Lucas walked into their bedroom. "Tell me what?"

She and Seeley exchanged glances, and she quickly wiped her tears.

"Oh no. Is my cancer back?" Lucas asked frantically.

"*No*, honey. No," she said.

"Is one of you sick?" he asked, his expression pained.

"No, Lucas. It's nothing bad," Seeley said. "We just found out your mom is pregnant."

"*Pregnant?*" he asked incredulously.

"Yes," she said. "I know this is a shock. It was a shock for us, too."

"Wait. Let me get this straight," Lucas said with a smirk. "This is your second child together, and you've never been married. I think you should've had that safe sex talk with each other instead of me."

They both laughed.

"You're both doctors," Lucas said emphatically, but also teasingly. "You know how this works."

They laughed again, but Juliette was worried.

"Lucas, can you be serious for a second?" she asked. "How do you really feel about this?"

He shrugged. "I don't know much about babies, but I love Gus, and I think it's cool that Doc has a big family, so…"

"You're not upset?" Seeley asked.

"No. I think it'll be fun to have brothers and sisters."

Relieved, she said, "Well, hopefully this is just *one* baby."

"Whatever," Lucas said. "Since the wedding is at midnight, can I miss school tomorrow?"

"No," Juliette said.

"Come on, Mom. You're pregnant. Don't you want to sleep late in the morning?"

"Dude, it's way too early for you to be pulling that crap," Seeley said.

"*Whatever.* I'm going to see the horses."

"If you want to help decorate, we're starting in an hour,"

Juliette said. He and Seeley had built a beautiful arched altar for Cowboy and Sully, and everyone was getting together to help decorate the big house for dinner and the yard for the wedding.

"I know," Lucas said as he headed out.

Seeley put his arm around Juliette and said, "That went better than expected."

"Thank goodness. I'm so excited, but let's not mention our news to anyone until tomorrow. I don't want to steal any attention from Cowboy and Sully on their big day."

"Okay." He put his hand on her belly again. "So, it turns out we *can* get pregnant."

"Sure looks that way."

"And our boy wants a big family. The way I see it, we've got three years before he goes to college. We could probably have two babies in that time."

God, this man. "How about we get through one baby and a few more uneventful doctor visits for Lucas first?"

AT THE STROKE of midnight, beneath the light of the moon, serenaded by the soft sounds of Sasha's guitar, on the land that had brought them together, Doc sat between Juliette and Lucas as Cowboy and Sully exchanged their vows. Cowboy and Sully stood inside a heart of lanterns, in front of the wooden arch Doc and Lucas had built. The white silk draped around it billowed in the breeze, constrained by tethers of greenery, roses, and other colorful flowers and, in homage to the ranch and their roots, rope.

Doc watched his younger brother, who had always known

exactly who he was—a natural-born protector, a Dark Knights biker, and one hell of a rancher—standing tall and proud in his jeans and cut, cowboy hat perched on his head, ready to take on his most important role yet. *Husband.* Sully stood beside him, a picture of simple elegance in a scoop-necked lace gown and white fur shrug, her golden-brown hair hanging loose and wavy, her loving eyes on her soon-to-be husband.

Doc remembered when Sully had first arrived at the ranch, a scared little bird who hadn't had a clue who she really was. But she'd saved herself from that cult, proving she wasn't a little bird at all. With the help of many, but mostly Cowboy, she'd broken free from the cages of her past and had found who she was always meant to be. A beautiful, fierce Friesian and the only woman on earth to complete Callahan "Cowboy" Whiskey.

As Cowboy said his vows with tears in his eyes and love in his heart, Doc looked at *his* loves. Lucas was taking a picture of Cowboy and Sully. He showed it to Layla, who had joined them for the ceremony. Doc's heart squeezed. Lucas and Layla reminded him so much of himself and Juliette. He prayed their young hearts would never endure the heartache he and Juliette had, but he knew first loves usually came with heartache. *A rite of passage*, his mother had once said. It hadn't made it any easier for him back then, and the thought of his son having his heart broken slayed him. But he and Juliette would be there to help him through, just like his parents had been there for him.

Juliette was dabbing her tears with a tissue. He was in awe of everything about her. She was a loving mother and partner, a caring friend, and a compassionate veterinarian. He knew their baby, like Lucas, would be as strong and loving as she was.

She looked so beautiful in the moonlight. He and the other Dark Knights were wearing jeans and their cuts, but the girls had gone shopping together for outfits. She was positively glowing in a long-sleeved peach sweaterdress that clung to her curves and had what she called a scarf collar that crisscrossed around her neck and a sexy, but not too revealing, cutout just beneath. She'd paired it with tights, knee-high leather boots, and a pretty shawl. He couldn't wait to see her round with their baby and to pamper her the way he wished he could have years ago.

She glanced at him, smiling a little bashfully as she wiped her tears, and said, "That's going to be us one day."

He leaned in and kissed her. They hadn't set a wedding date yet. He hadn't wanted to wait long before he found out she was pregnant. Now he *really* didn't want to wait. He'd been thinking about it all afternoon. He wanted it all, and he wanted it now. His girl, his son, their baby, a ring on her finger, and his last name as hers. What were they waiting for, anyway? *Fuck it.* "Let's get married."

"Isn't that what this ring is for?" She held up her left hand, wiggling her fingers, her engagement ring twinkling in the moonlight.

"I mean now," he said, vaguely aware of Cowboy and Sully being pronounced man and wife. Applause rang out, and everyone rose to their feet, clapping and cheering. They pushed to their feet, too, and Doc took her hand, speaking loudly, so she could hear him over the celebration going on around them. "I don't want to wait! Marry me *tonight*. *Now*. Let's bring our baby into the world the right way. With rings on our fingers, my last name as yours, and our son by our side!"

"Baby?" Birdie exclaimed. "Did he say baby? Is Juliette pregnant?"

There was a collective gasp, and as the din of the celebration quieted, Gus said, "What's pregnant?"

Juliette's eyes widened, crimson spreading over her cheeks as she whispered, "What happened to not stealing their thunder?"

"Holy shit," Dare said. "Doc's done it again!"

As laughter rang out, Doc felt guilty. He looked at Cowboy and Sully, holding hands, still beaming with joy, and said, "I'm sorry. Forget I said anything. That was rude. I just got carried away."

"Hell no, bro," Cowboy said. "If Juliette is in, we are, too."

"We don't want to steal your thunder," Juliette said.

"You're not stealing our thunder," Sully said cheerily. "You're adding the lightning, making it an even more unforgettable night. We would be honored to share a wedding anniversary with you guys."

Doc squeezed Juliette's hand. "What do you say, darlin'?"

"Say *yes*, Mom!" Lucas said. "Do it! We're all here. Even my baby brother or sister."

She laughed and shook her head. "I guess we're getting married!"

Doc pulled her into his arms and kissed her, and cheers rang out. There was a flurry of activity as everyone took their seats again. Doc and Juliette stood inside the lantern heart, in front of the altar he and their son had built, and with Lucas by their side, they pledged their everlasting love and were pronounced husband and wife.

As he kissed his bride, the celebration began anew. They were showered in hugs and peppered with questions about their due date and how Juliette was feeling. Lucas was cheered on for how great of a big brother he'd be, and he ate up the praise. Champagne bottles were popped, and toasts were made by just about everyone.

"I'm really happy for you all," Birdie said. "But while you've been busy getting engaged, and married, and having babies, and finding love on this ranch, I'm still single. *Me.*" She motioned to herself, planting a hand on the hip of the one-piece wide-legged paisley pantsuit dwarfing her petite frame. "I mean, *really.*" She pointed at their parents. "This is your fault. I expect you to find a good-looking single man and have him walk onto this ranch and *only* have eyes for me. I'm giving you six months to get that done. Got it?"

Tiny burst into laughter.

"Sweetheart, that's not how love works," their mother said.

"My butt it doesn't," Birdie said. "Billie and Dare's first kiss was in that barn." She pointed to the barn. "Cowboy and Sully met here. Doc took one look at Juliette right here on this ranch and fell so hard, it lasted all these years. And Ezra? He kissed the flipping life out of Sasha as a teenager, and she was never the same again. Then he came to *live* on the ranch, and now look at them."

Everyone glanced at them. Ezra was holding Gus and had one arm around Sasha. "Love you, Bo Peep," he said, and kissed her.

"See?" Birdie crossed her arms, staring at her mother. "Dad took one look at you and came to the ranch and never left." She lifted her chin triumphantly. "Tell her, Dad."

Rebel cleared his throat and said, "It's going to take a mighty strong man to take on that one."

"You're not wrong, son," Tiny said, before turning a softer gaze on Birdie. "I love you, darlin', but we didn't pick your brothers' and sister's partners."

"That was the magic of the ranch, honey," her mother said. "We might've nudged things here and there, but we don't choose our children's forever loves."

Birdie groaned. "You guys suck. I need cake! Can we cut the cake? Or is *that* controlled by the magic of the freaking ranch, too?"

As laughter and jokes ensued, Lucas nudged Doc and said, "I love it here...*Dad*," and hurried off to get cake with Layla, as if he hadn't left Doc slack-jawed.

"Did he just call you Dad?" Juliette asked.

"Uh-huh" was all he could manage. As they made their way toward the happy mayhem that was his family, he looked at his beautiful pregnant wife and at their adventurous, healthy boy, and he was sure his heart was going to pound right out of his chest. These were the moments he lived for. They'd shared hundreds of them over the last eight months, and he looked forward to a lifetime filled with them.

Are you ready for Birdie Whiskey?

Birdie Whiskey is ready for love, but the man who knocks her off her feet is the last man her family would ever accept. Come along for the emotional ride as the Whiskeys' belief in second chances is put to the test, and Birdie faces her toughest decision yet—stay loyal to her family or fight for the man she loves.

Meet the Silvers at Silver Island

Secrets are made on the sandy shores and in the sweet small towns of Silver Island, where friendships run deep, passions run hot, and the sexy Silvers are considered island royalty. Being born into the Silver empire comes with certain expectations, but these strong-willed siblings are breaking all the rules.

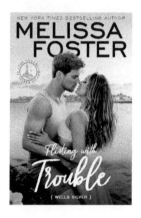

Victoria Braden never expected to become a widow at thirty-two, much less still be trying to figure out how to move on five years later. She'd planned to drown her sorrows in alcohol on what would have been the anniversary of the date she'd met her late husband, not flirt with trouble and lose herself in a night of passion with Silver Island royalty, playboy Wells Silver. Forgetting Wells was supposed to be easy. But apparently the pushy player didn't get the memo.

Meet the Whiskeys' cousins, the Wickeds!

Set on the sandy shores of Cape Cod, the Wickeds feature fiercely protective heroes, strong heroines, and unbreakable family bonds. When the woman who helps save his life needs a little saving herself, Zander takes on a role he never saw coming.

Meet the hot, wealthy, and wickedly naughty Bradens at Ridgeport, and join these fiercely loyal dirty-talking billionaires as they fall head over heels with their forever loves.

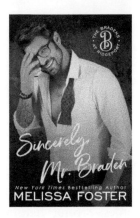

Come along for the fun, sexy ride as this business-savvy, pleasure-oriented billionaire gets the shock of his lifetime and finds out his ever-efficient virtual assistant is not the man he thinks he is but a beautiful businesswoman who knows many of his secrets and has some of her own in *Sincerely, Mr. Braden.*

New to the Love in Bloom series?

If this is your first Love in Bloom book, there are many more love stories featuring loyal, sassy, and sexy heroes and heroines waiting for you. The Whiskeys is just one of the series in the Love in Bloom big-family romance collection. Each Love in Bloom book is written to be enjoyed as a stand-alone novel or as part of the larger series. There are no cliffhangers and no unresolved issues. Characters from each series make appearances in future books, so you never miss an engagement, wedding, or birth. Check out the collection below, download series checklists and other reader goodies, and dive in.

Check out Melissa's online bookstore to enjoy early releases, discounted pre-orders, exclusive savings on bundles in all formats, special edition ebooks, and other special offerings. Ebooks can be read on any e-reader, and audiobooks can be listened to on the free and easy-to-use BookFunnel app.

See the Love in Bloom Collection
MelissaFoster.com

Shop Melissa's Store
shop.MelissaFoster.com

Download Series Checklists, Family Trees, Maps, and More
MelissaFoster.com/RG

More Books By Melissa Foster

LOVE IN BLOOM BIG-FAMILY ROMANCE COLLECTION

SNOW SISTERS
Sisters in Love
Sisters in Bloom
Sisters in White

THE BRADENS at Weston
Lovers at Heart, Reimagined
Destined for Love
Friendship on Fire
Sea of Love
Bursting with Love
Hearts at Play

THE BRADENS at Trusty
Taken by Love
Fated for Love
Romancing My Love
Flirting with Love
Dreaming of Love
Crashing into Love

THE BRADENS at Peaceful Harbor
Healed by Love
Surrender My Love
River of Love
Crushing on Love
Whisper of Love
Thrill of Love

THE BRADENS & MONTGOMERYS at Pleasant Hill – Oak Falls
Embracing Her Heart

Anything for Love
Trails of Love
Wild Crazy Hearts
Making You Mine
Searching for Love
Hot for Love
Sweet Sexy Heart
Then Came Love
Rocked by Love
Falling for Mr. Bad

THE BRADENS at Ridgeport
Playing Mr. Perfect
Sincerely, Mr. Braden

THE BRADEN NOVELLAS
Promise My Love
Our New Love
Daring Her Love
Story of Love
Love at Last
A Very Braden Christmas

THE REMINGTONS
Game of Love
Stroke of Love
Flames of Love
Slope of Love
Read, Write, Love
Touched by Love

THE RYDERS
Seized by Love
Claimed by Love
Chased by Love
Rescued by Love
Swept Into Love

The Gritty Truth
In for a Penny
Running on Diesel

THE WHISKEYS: DARK KNIGHTS AT REDEMPTION RANCH

The Trouble with Whiskey
Freeing Sully (Prequel to For the Love of Whiskey)
For the Love of Whiskey
A Taste of Whiskey
Love, Lies, and Whiskey
My Whiskey Redemption

THE WICKEDS: DARK KNIGHTS AT BAYSIDE

A Little Bit Wicked
The Wicked Aftermath
Crazy, Wicked Love
The Wicked Truth
His Wicked Ways
Talk Wicked to Me
Irresistibly Wicked

WILD BOYS AFTER DARK

Logan
Heath
Jackson
Cooper

BAD BOYS AFTER DARK

Mick
Dylan
Carson
Brett

SUGAR LAKE

The Real Thing
Only for You
Love Like Ours

Finding My Girl (Graphic Companion Booklet)

HARMONY POINTE
Call Her Mine
This is Love
She Loves Me

SILVER HARBOR
Maybe We Will
Maybe We Should
Maybe We Won't

STANDALONE ROMANTIC COMEDIES
Hot Mess Summer
The Mr. Right Checklist

HARBORSIDE NIGHTS SERIES
Includes characters from the Love in Bloom series
Catching Cassidy
Discovering Delilah (F/F)
Tempting Tristan (M/M)

More Books by Melissa
Chasing Amanda (mystery/suspense)
Come Back to Me (mystery/suspense)
Have No Shame (historical fiction/romance)
Love, Lies & Mystery (3-book bundle)
Megan's Way (literary fiction)
Traces of Kara (psychological thriller)
Where Petals Fall (suspense)

Acknowledgments

Although everyone's experience may differ, I hope by sharing this story I have shed some light on emotional abuse and cancer and some of the ways in which they affect not just the victims and patients but those around them. If you or someone you know is suffering from abuse and in need of help, the following is just one of many resources available online: https://www.apa.org/topics/crisis-hotlines. For help and information regarding cancer, the American Cancer Society offers a wealth of information at cancer.org.

While writing a novel is mostly a solo adventure, I have several people to thank for their help and encouragement along the way. Heaps of gratitude go to Mark Yoffe, retired medical oncologist/hematologist, for his guidance and endless patience with regard to Hodgkin's lymphoma. Any and all errors, and the fictional liberties I have taken for the benefit of the story, are my own and not a reflection of Mark's expertise.

Many thanks to one of my loyal readers, ER nurse Jennifer Babin, whom I had the pleasure of chatting with several times while researching and writing this story. Jennifer, thank you for sharing your emergency medicine experience with me and for answering all of my questions.

I am also grateful for the help of my friend, Registered Cardiac Invasive Specialist Erin Pettazzoni, who accepted my calls and texts without hesitation and offered invaluable information.

I had the pleasure of speaking once again with Susan Pierce, the owner of Red Bucket Horse Rescue, about several of her rescue stories. Brave Heart portrays a modified version of Susan's rescue Milah. Thank you for sharing her story with me. I hope I have done her justice.

I'd like to thank outstanding artist Andrey "Anund" Kuznetsov for allowing me to use the image of his necklace on this book cover. The beautiful piece was part of my inspiration for the necklace Seeley made with his grandfather. If you'd like to purchase that, or something similar, please visit artifactoria.com.

A special thank-you goes out to Avery Filipe for shouting "Brave!" when I was brainstorming names for Brave Heart with her mother, my close friend and one of my trusted assistants, Lisa. Speaking of assistants, Lisa and Sharon, as always, I appreciate everything you do for me, your ability to change directions on a dime, your sense of humor, and your friendship. I have no idea how you keep up, but I'm truly grateful that you do. Terren Hoeksema, thank you for all the things you do to help as you are able.

I am indebted to editors Kristen Weber and Penina Lopez for making my books shine and going above and beyond in trying to meet this deadline, and to my team of eagle-eyed proofreaders: Lynn Mullan, Elaini Caruso, Juliette Hill, and Justinn Harrison.

Last but never least, a hearty thank-you to my sanity savers and close friends Amy, Tasha, and Sue. I couldn't love you more, but then I do, every single day.

Meet Melissa

www.MelissaFoster.com

Melissa Foster is a *New York Times, Wall Street Journal,* and *USA Today* bestselling and award-winning author of more than one hundred novels. When she's not writing, she's hanging out with her four-legged copilot in the sweet small towns of Cape Cod. Melissa also enjoys discussing her books with book clubs and reader groups and welcomes an invitation to your event.

You can find Melissa's books at most retailers and in her online bookstore, where she offers exclusive discounts, bundles, and special editions. http://shop.melissafoster.com